About the Author

Nadya Dukhina was born in a small province of Russia and began writing as soon as she learned the alphabet. She was four years old. At the age of 22, she received her master's in journalism and moved to the United States, where she earned her second master's — in marketing. She barely spoke English and had no funds for living. Back then, it seemed she would never be able to write in English as well as she wrote in Russian. Back then, so many things seemed impossible.

Most of her struggle is in the book; the rest was left for later to intrigue and inspire readers.

The Illegal

Nadya Dukhina

The Illegal

Vanguard Press

A CIP catalogue record for this title is
available from the British Library.

ISBN 978-1-80016-436-9

Vanguard Press is an imprint of
Pegasus Elliot Mackenzie Publishers Ltd.
www.pegasuspublishers.com

First Published in 2023

Vanguard Press
Sheraton House Castle Park
Cambridge England

Printed & Bound in Great Britain

To my mother, all alone in Russia.

I would like to thank Albert Podell for inspiring me to start this book and I would like to thank dr. Sevil Gamer for inspiring me to live, love my life, and finish this book.

CHAPTER 1

Back then, I didn't know that I would recall that bus ride many-many times in the future. I didn't know that sharp and snowy American night on the screen of a cold, shaking window would get burned into my mind as a permanent tattoo and become a personal shelter for my distant subsequent feelings and regrets.

Back then, everything was alien, even the forest of blue-purple seats and the dark and clear aisle. Random words echoed from the front of the vehicle and a non-stop slamming toilet door a couple of rows behind. The only familiar subject was Vera, my childhood friend. Her head rested peacefully on my bony shoulder. Her Russian goodbye tears had already dried up into American adventure excitement, while my cocktail of cognitive dissonance was a mixture of anticipation with apprehension, and complimentary white wine the airline generously provided us with. It was very yellow and very sour. Vera drank twice as much as I did. She passed out shortly after we boarded the bus. I wondered what she was dreaming about.

We were sliding away from New York into a sparkling northern blizzard. Snowflakes were dancing in the air without any order, lit by random road lights; as if they were escorting us into the uncertainty on our first night in the USA. Neither Vera nor I had ever been outside of Russia. My sleeping friend had always desired to move abroad. She was following all news about foreign scholarships and affordable colleges; she wanted to study "somewhere in Massachusetts" and write and speak in English most of the time; she had excellent knowledge of degrees and their requirements, and it was she, who woke me up at five o'clock in the morning on Saturday to say that Clark University from somewhere in Massachusetts had just opened Master's programs in our hometown, and we were qualified to apply, and we could come to America for the last two semesters and graduate there. That's how we ended up on that bus.

It was taking us to Worcester. Somewhere cold and snowy. It was January 2009.

Two medium-sized orange suitcases of ours were stored in the baggage cabin. They were brand new. We had bought them together a couple of weeks before leaving our motherland. We loved doing things together. We grew up in the same building, went to the same school, then to the same university, and then slid into the white world of unknown — together. We were both 22 years old, and back then, we thought it was a lot.

Vera and I met in a kindergarten and became inseparable right away. We played all the same games and shared similar dreams and family concepts, life views, and denial of death. She was the sister I always wanted but was never given. Both of us were the only children in our families with only mothers. Her father died when she was a child, and mine simply left. It was very common for men in Russia to leave their families. Most of my friends were raised by single mothers. I never understood why men didn't care about their children. One of a few persons I knew who had both parents was Dmitry, my former athletic blue-eyed boyfriend. I missed him terribly. We met very banally on a dating website I was looking for a soulmate; he was looking for fun, so we got something in between. He was a goalkeeper in a Russian soccer team. Soccer was his biggest passion and my biggest passion was him. I loved everything about him, but he kept disappearing from my life for days and weeks over and over again. Then he was seen with another girl. I cried, and cried, and cried until the early morning phone call woke me up, and Vera's voice gratefully announced the opening of Clark University in our hometown. After that, I didn't have much time for crying. I was studying and getting ready for my biggest trip abroad. I still don't know whether I truly wanted to come here, or if it was the desire influenced by Vera, or my way of forgetting Dmitry. He reappeared in my life once more shortly before I departed, but the month of another waiting game broke my heart into smaller pieces. My mom surrounded me with all the love and care she could give. She cooked my favorite dishes, spoiled me with desserts, and became the best listener at nights. She was trying hard not to look devastated at the airport. She even managed to smile, but tears wouldn't stop flowing out of her kind, beautiful eyes. She was now all alone in Russia, and in the whole world.

My eyes became watery as I thought of her. I wanted to get enclosed in her warm arms. There are no arms like hers anywhere else but there, where I left her, in Astrakhan, my hometown. I was eight hours and thousands of miles away from it, going further into the depths of the new world, where I was all of a sudden, an adult person responsible for all judgments and decisions. I felt like, the bus was driving me away from my childhood and I would get off of it a completely different person. It was my welcome and goodbye at the same time. I didn't want it to ever arrive and let me out into the brand-new adulthood, and yet I couldn't wait to inhale that fresh winter air.

Without fully waking up, Vera pushed up the armrest and laid her head in my lap. Free airline alcohol made her overly excited and verbose, and she kept listing the facts she knew about New England, Worcester, and Clark in particular all the way from the airport to Port Authority. During that hour, I learned that Sigmund Freud taught in Clark University, that Valentines' cards originated in Worcester, and that Elizabeth Bishop, her favorite poet was born there as well. She fell asleep shortly after we boarded the bus. I rested my head on the rubber below the trembling glass. It felt so warm and cozy. I closed my eyes and began enjoying that temporary comfort.

"Wake up! We have arrived," Vera shook my shoulder.

I shivered away my bitter-sweet Russian dream. Lights on the ceiling above my head were on. Vera's face looked tired, but happy. Her dark wavy hair needed a brush, her big green eyes were sparkling, and thick pinkish lips froze in a shy smile. I quickly stretched and put on my coat.

The coordinator of our program waited for us at the empty bus station. The outdoor air felt so fresh and alive. We pulled our heavy suitcases from the bus and walked towards that short, thick, smiley man in a snow-white hat with wide brim. His face was kind and welcoming.

"Ms Ivanova and Ms Kulikova?" he enquired semi-loudly in a pleasant manner, without letting his smile go.

"Yes, it's us!" we answered, smiling.

"I'm Ted!" he stated, taking Vera's suitcase and riding it to his van. She instantly took over my bag. "How was your trip?"

"It was long," she mumbled, giggling, embarrassed by her imperfect English, "but we good! Nice here!"

Ted nodded and packed our suitcases in his van.

Night-time Worcester didn't look too foreign. Quiet, cozy streets were switching between green and red lights, short old buildings, stores and other businesses, that would open their doors after removing layers of snow in the morning. Ted kept talking in his mild, friendly voice, without pausing between words, making it sound as a chain of random syllabuses. I didn't understand a single word but nodded every time we made eye-contact through the front mirror and giggled every time he laughed. My exhausted friend took another nap in the car. It was 3 o'clock in the morning.

Vera truly believed in her good fortune, she always said that everything happens for a reason, that the world is on your side and you can achieve anything you want. She was admitted to Clark, got her visa and came here — that was a true sign that she picked the right way. She saw beauty in everything, opportunity in every misfortune, happy-ending in each circumstance, and a hope — everywhere. I didn't want to confess I had fears, and felt insecure, and wasn't sure if I had made the right decision. I didn't share her excitement nor did life, she had to head back to Russia the same night we arrived in Worcester. She zipped back her suitcase right after she opened an email in the lobby of a student dormitory. She had gotten a terrible note from a relative, her mother was hit by a car and fell in coma the day we landed in New York.

It was like a thunderstorm in the middle of a clear day. All the words, fears, exhaustion were gone that very moment. Only one thought kept knocking in my mind, it couldn't be true.

She didn't cry. She became all pale and asked me to call a cab. I didn't know what to say or whether there was anything to say. I didn't know what to do. If only I could do anything. I hugged her tightly, repeating that she's going to be all right, she's going to be just fine.

Vera nodded silently. The cab arrived.

Ted was nowhere to be seen. He left as soon as he introduced us to our room in a hollow dormitory hall and arranged to meet downstairs the next morning.

The cab quickly got us to the Union Station, which looked even more abandoned than an hour ago.

"Where are you guys actually going? There might be no busses until morning," the cab-driver uttered.

"We're going to New York," I answered.

"If it's an emergency, you should go to Boston, and take a bus there."

"It is an emergency," Vera murmured. "Can you drive me to Boston?"

"I could," he said, touching the meter. "It's going to cost you much more, though…"

"No problem," Vera stated.

The driver dropped me off at the campus. Pale and silent Vera refused my offers to escort her to New York. She didn't want me to go to Boston with her either. Every word, every eye movement seemed to be a great effort for her to make. She gave me a brief hug. I could feel the weakness in her arms. I wanted to comfort her, but nothing came to my mind. I only repeated that everything was going to be all right. She nodded, and the cab quickly disappeared behind the curtain of falling snow.

I returned to the campus empty and disoriented. I threw my bag on top of the suitcase and sat on the edge of the bed. It felt odd to see this big orange suitcase all alone. It was standing right between two beds, one of which was supposed to be Vera's. The room was terribly hollow — it felt like nothing in the world could ever bring life to it. I didn't want to unpack, I wanted to wake up and realize it was only a bad dream. Fear and hopelessness filled my lungs. I wished I could just go back to Russia and give up on everything that was planned. I didn't want any Clark university, I didn't want any master's program, I didn't want any America any more, I just wanted to go home. Vera's sad eyes were in the space right in front of me, all frozen, with no hope for solace. Her mother's voice was ringing in my ears. I drifted down the memory lane, to recall the first time I saw her. Was it at one of the kindergarten parties? Was it snowy New Year's Eve when she took us both to a hill to slide down with a bunch of other kids? I remembered her watching every movement of ours as we were sliding and showing signs with her hands. Neither Vera nor I understood any of these signs. I couldn't recall how I met her mother.

Eventually, I wrapped myself up in a thick American blanket and passed out. I had no strength to change my outfit, only enough to remove my boots. I immediately went to familiar Astrakhan. Everyone was fine and healthy; the sky was clear and blue. Vera, with other friends and my mom, were welcoming me back. My mother gave me the warmest hug. Her smile was kind and loving. The alarm rang loudly and unexpectedly. Why on Earth did I come here, was my first thought.

Ted met me by the dormitory entrance door and walked me over to the main building of the university, which took us about 10 minutes. It was a delightful bright day — half-yellow and half-white with a clear blue sky above lively streets, with welcoming libraries, coffee and souvenir shops, students, professors, other people, and fresh winter air. Ted was continuously saying something I didn't understand. I kept nodding. This time I could clearly see his face — it looked very kind. There was a semi-permanent smile on it, right below an old-fashioned mustache, and small mischievously-happy eyes. He wore a wide cowboy hat.

Clark University was made out of brown brick. Old and historical, the main tower with a big clock on top of it kept the spirit of 19th century, when it was found. A monument of Sigmund Freud was proudly sitting in the middle of the square — the Red Square — just like the one in Moscow, but much smaller. Dr Freud taught in Clark right before he turned widely famous and made the university unique among the rest of Massachusetts' institutes. Clark University became number 81 on the list of best national universities.

Ted presented me to the dean, a chubby elderly man with a smiley face and small serious eyes. We walked through the maze of hallways, where Ted introduced me to one auditorium after another, however, I hadn't memorized any. Our final destination was Clark's library, which was located on the first floor of the main tower. After a brief explanation on how computers and printers worked, we landed on a couch. Ted asked me whether I wanted a cup of coffee. I refused, although I craved it. I then realized how hungry I was. As he joined a short line to the coffee booth, I made myself comfortable on the couch and started scanning the new unknown environment, busy students, smiley faces, books, computer monitors — there was so much to get used to.

I suddenly felt lonely. I was so anxious to get in touch with Vera and find out what was happening. I was anxious to get back to my room and digest everything that had occurred in the past 24 hours, and at the same time, I was scared by the thought of being left alone. I thought of how familiar Clark University was to the students in that library, how familiar they were with the country they lived in, and the language they spoke. I recalled Astrakhan State University, its hallways, auditoriums, and parks, where we often rested after long classes. I smiled, recalling my friends' faces, our jokes, our traditions, our lifestyle. It felt like I hadn't seen them in ages.

My future seemed uncertain. Initially, I had a clear plan of relocating to the capital of Russia and becoming a writer. I had high expectations, which were fed by the praise of many professors. I was constantly inspired, and proudly demonstrated my high level of knowledge of my native language with charm and beauty. I had the gift of putting words together. Yet, I was sitting all alone in the middle of an unknown world, experiencing my first morning abroad, and I could barely express the simplest thought.

In order to encourage me to learn English, my mom used to say that it's the language aliens speak, since I was interested in the cosmos and planned to become a cosmonaut during all my kindergarten and elementary school years. I read a lot of books and magazines about space, planets, galaxies — anything related to the unresearched endless void. I spent long hours planning my trips across the Universe; while learning about spaceships and stations, until my dad told me it wasn't serious, and I should consider a career in medicine or law. He said that and left us a few months later, just a few weeks after my seventh birthday. He just packed his suitcase and left, wresting one-third of our small family away from my heart. I didn't know what had happened and why he had gone. I was crying and looking in a window for months. It became my secret dream that one day he would return back home, and we all would be happy together like in good old days. But it never happened.

My mom, a beautiful tall blond blue-eyed woman, hoped for years to hear his sweet proposal, before and after my birth, but as time passed, she lost her strength, faith and confidence. And when the economy went down after USSR disappeared along with my father, her girly dreams were wiped out forever. She faced a difficult period of raising a child alone in a newly reborn Russia with an alcoholic leader and no jobs on the market. She had to work hard to provide us with the necessary stuff. By the end of every week, my mother would suffer from a terrible back pain that would paralyze her, and I often called the ambulance to come over and give her an injection of a strong painkiller. She had incurable spine damage.

Later, at the end of my first day in Clark, I returned to the same library. It was empty and quiet. I signed in to my email and the first message, with the subject typed in capital letters silently screamed, "VERA'S MOTHER HAS JUST DIED". There was nothing in the body of the message. It was sent by a very good friend of ours. I turned off the computer and walked away. The almost irresistible desire to go back in time to the bus that brought us here was ripping my heart into small pieces. If I only knew, it was the last time I would see Vera's smile and hear her melodious voice — full of life and excitement — I would never let her stop talking, I would never allow her to sleep, I would hold her tight, memorizing every word she says, every sound of her beautiful laugh, every little thing about her. I would freeze ourselves in that ride — as I knew she would never be the same again.

Later, I learned that Vera had arrived at the hospital exactly one hour before she lost her closest soul in the entire universe.

Ms Kulikova was always kind and supportive. She had an open mind, a kind heart, and a very gentle composition. She cried day and night when Russian Submarine Kursk sank along with 118 young men on board, she prayed for victims and their families of the 9/11 tragedy. She always donated money to help homeless, sick, abandoned kids; she supported freedom for all living creatures by being a vegetarian and not attending zoos, circuses and other institutions of cruelty. She cheered me up every time kids bullied me in school. She kept saying my scarred arm was beautiful and it made me very special.

"Forgive them for not seeing your beauty. They are too young and too blind." she kept repeating. And I learned to forgive. Now she's dead. And nothing's really left of her.

Ms Kulikova was Vera's best friend. She would never judge her she would always understand and support her. She was there for her all the time. She convinced my mom to let me come to America and give me this wonderful opportunity to see the world. She was so happily sad, letting her only daughter out of the nest of love and comfort, waving from the other side of the customs in the airport, holding back tears and keeping a comforting smile, "Everything is going to be all right." It was the last time I saw her. Yet, I couldn't recall how I met her, no matter how hard I tried.

CHAPTER 2

I am tall, slim, and blond. I have grey-blue eyes, small ears, and long hair. I look like a typical Russian, although I don't feel like one. People would describe me as beautiful, and some would call me gorgeous, but I myself don't measure my appearance with compliments, and I don't have any opinion about the person I see in the mirror. I am what I am.

I do, however, have an opinion about Worcester. I didn't fall in love with it. Its Main Street which stretched from South-West to North-East of the town with DMV, City Hall, a couple of museums, coffeeshops, restaurants, groceries, liquor stores, prostitutes, and drug dealers on it did not fascinate me. It was not a pleasant street to walk on, unless you enjoy hearing offensive comments and unsolicited compliments of men in worn-out dirty clothes and plastic flasks in their hands. Ill-looking prostitutes in their 50^s and 60^s didn't seem to mind them. Perhaps, they had no choice. Drug dealers were probably the most considerate people on the street — they stood quietly, ready for any action. Luckily for me, I've never seen them in action.

And yes, there were many other streets and avenues in Worcester. Some were beautiful and quiet; others were noisy and alive. There were lovely parks with lakes, ducks, and mothers with strollers. There were a lot of students and professors. There were different neighborhoods, many of which I hadn't even visited. I missed most of the Worcester in order to remain a good student.

My major was marketing.

Weeks were all the same. They started at 8 in the morning and ended on a Friday night. The long-empty weekends were nearly killing me with endless loneliness, reminding me over and over that I was a stranger in the new world. I was homesick. I missed my mom, my friends, I missed Vera. I tried to call her several times, but she never picked up the phone. I felt an enormous pain in my chest when I thought of her. My soulmate was going through the worst thing that could happen to her on the other continent, and I could do nothing to help. Sudden thoughts of Dmitry would interrupt the grief and bring the smell of his cologne into my abandoned room. I would do my best to shake it off my mind. I often lay in the campus bed, thinking about the world I had left behind, and the world I had entered with hopes and expectations. I would always come to the conclusion that it would be highly illogical to practice homesickness and in the worst-case scenario I could always return home, in the best-case scenario, America would become my home. The latter seemed very hard to imagine.

My campus room was painted orange and green, it fitted 2 twin-sized beds, 2-bed stands, one spacious walk-in closet, and one window with no view. It was neat and newly renovated. I lived there alone for the first ten days, with Vera's bed all empty. I often imagined her there; and how great it would be to have my best friend by my side and to discover, learn, and understand another reality together. Sometimes, falling asleep, I dreamed that all the recent past was just a nightmare, and I would wake up to a new sunny day with Vera next to me, still sleeping like a baby. I would walk out quietly not to wake her up and return with two cups of fresh-brewed coffee. In ten days, a skinny Chinese girl took the second bed.

For the very first month, I went strictly to classes and back home without stopping anywhere, besides a grocery store to buy the cheapest yogurt for breakfast. I watched other students, how they behaved, how they dressed, spoke, and walked. I tried to appear as laid-back and carefree as they were. It felt like I didn't have much luck. I was constantly tense.

I didn't understand professors, yet I was afraid to ask to repeat. I didn't want them to see how bad my English was, especially for someone getting a master's degree. I often pretended to understand. I nodded when it was necessary. I smiled. I looked down at my notebook to avoid questions at a time of any awkward pauses. I had no idea what most of them were talking about. I felt very shy and rather silly to pretend, sometimes I thought it was so obvious, and a random question would ruin the whole illusion I had created. The first one was asked unexpectedly in the international marketing class.

"Is it the same in Russia, Ekaterina?"

Ekaterina is my full name. It's very Slavic. It is as well Greek. My father named me after his grandmother, who was the love and honor of his big family, whom he adored more than anyone else I'd heard of. And yet, he never called me by my name. My mother called me Katen'ka or Katyusha. She would often scream "Ka-tyu-sha!" from the balcony of the eighth floor of the old soviet building. It would mean it was time to go home. There could be different occasions and tones of that scream, but their meaning would be always the same — go home.

That's exactly how my seventh birthday was starting, "Katen'ka! Hurry up! Guests are waiting!"

She was wearing my favorite dress and I was running towards the entrance of the building. I nodded happily, squeezing a few rubble bills in my fist, which I had just won in a chess game with local intellectual alcoholics. Unfortunately, I couldn't share this pride with my mom as I would get punished for hanging out with bums, and the only way to conceal it, was to hide the money somewhere no one would access. The dark and stinky basement next to my building's entrance door was the only idea that came to my mind. I slipped inside without giving it much thought. After my eyes had adjusted to the gloom, I proceeded further into that space.

"Katyusha!" I heard again and rushed ahead to find some spot to store my reward in. I discovered a fence of pipes up to my waist, and praising myself for a quick solution, bent over to put the money on the other side of it. I forgot about the money as soon as I touched the fence. I forgot about my mom, my guests, my party, and my birthday. The forceful power of electricity took hold of my right hand and froze my entire body in frightening helplessness.

The echo of "Katyusha" reflected in my head. The smell of burning flesh along with my loudest scream filled up the air. I got completely paralyzed. The time had stopped. Enormous fear conquered my mind and I started using all my strength to detach the hand from the pipe. I was fighting a mortal battle with an unseen enemy, which was stronger than me, stronger to the point, that it held me entirely without a chance for movement, to the point that it took away my last hope for survival. I didn't want to believe that disastrous energy was killing me, a life-loving child, who appreciated everything she was given and never asked for better, who didn't want to die, who just turned seven and was running home to celebrate this happy occasion.

It felt like my lungs were packed with endless supply of oxygen; I screamed non-stop as loud as I could, as hard as I was able to. I was frightened to the point that I didn't feel any pain. I kept trying, and trying, and trying to break free, as it was so unfair and undeserved, so sad, so tragic to leave this world so early. I didn't know why it was happening, why then, why to me, why didn't it have any mercy on me, what had I done? I gave up straggling and allowed this cruel force to take over. I shut my eyes and began waiting for my small broken heart to stop beating. My mom's crying face flashed in my exhausted mind. I hoped it wouldn't to be too painful to die. It was my last desire before I passed out.

I woke up to my mother's warm smile. People in white coats surrounded us. They were talking neither loud nor too quietly, I couldn't understand anything they were saying. A big tear was crawling down mom's cheek. I could barely endure the pain in my right arm. Everything seemed like a bad dream.

"Am I going to die, mommy?" I mumbled quietly.

"Am I going to die?" I repeated.

She couldn't say a word. She was crying soundlessly, covering her face with both palms. Her shoulders were shaking. She almost lost everything she had in the whole world.

It was the first time I saw her crying. It was the first surgery in my life. It lasted five hours. They said no one survives 420 volts. It was the first chance to live a second life.

My father happened to be an electrician. He came to see me in the hospital once, days after my first surgery. He smiled and said everything was going to be all right. Then he packed the rest of his stuff and left. Just like he never existed. I didn't know why he left and for how long. The house instantly became so empty without him, I had been waiting for him for months, looking in the window. Yet, I never saw him again. He used to call me "Kid". It was a shortcut between us, a small and narrow lane. Later, the lane became a road, then an endless highway, which separated me, being no longer a kid, from him, being no longer a father.

Why did he leave us? I often asked myself.

My damaged arm became the witness of his last smile and silent "goodbye". I always wore long sleeves, hiding its ugliness from other cruel kids. I could only leave it bare being all alone in my room, I was ashamed of this dark-purple, soft wrinkled skin, that covered the entire arm, from fingers to the shoulder.

"It's exactly the same in Russia," I answered the international marketing professor as I had no idea what he asked me. He said he would assume it was different, but since I was Russian, he believed me. He also asked if he could call me Kate, and since then, it became my permanent American short name.

Studying in the U.S. was very different from studying in Russia. Professors were friendlier, students were respected. It did hurt my patriotic feelings to admit that the American system of education was much more convenient than the Russian. The way I could organize my schedule and pick classes, submit my homework electronically, message professors with questions and get immediate answers, was quite impressive. All possible options were available in the United States, for those who failed a class, there were options to go over it again for extra payment, there were a number of collected credits for those who wanted to transfer to another school. It was convenient. Russian education was far from convenient, although, it was stronger, it didn't leave students much of a second chance, sometimes you only have a choice of studying through sleepless nights or the freedom of being thrown out of your school. Russian system was crueler and more demanding, which didn't necessarily mean it produced good and self-confident specialists, but strong and intellectual people — for sure.

My classes were long, but not tiring. I missed home. I sent an endless number of emails to my mother and Vera. I waited for news from Vera but never received any. I wrote to my other friends. I described every day, every new adventure, every new thought. Every single night lured me into dreams about Astrakhan, I saw my favorite streets, parkways, cheap neighborhood bars, and faces of people I loved. I was terribly homesick. I felt homeless in the middle of that beautiful winter.

The student visa I was on, only allowed me to work 20 hours a week and only on campus. I was lucky enough to be accepted for a catering position in Clark, to serve the same students I was studying with, the same professors, the president of the university, the alumnus, international and national visitors. It gave me just enough money to pay for my room and food.

The time I would be left with after my job and classes would only be enough for homework and sleep. Later on, I learned to use my time wisely and started socializing at drunken students' parties, getting accustomed to beers and shots in dive bars, staying till the last call, and not having any recollection of how I got home the next day. Gradually, I got to know more students. I developed some acquaintances to go for coffee, for a drink, for a walk and started to feel less lonely. I tried hard to adjust to a new culture. I started to watch American movies one by one, go out to events in Clark, and read local papers. I wanted to get as familiar as I could with the country and stop my useless cravings for Russia. By the end of the second month of living there, I started making progress.

When spring finally arrived, I started going out with a charming Polish guy from the International Marketing class. First, he began seating himself next to me during classes, then he started escorting me to my campus room day after day, and eventually, he asked me out with adorable courageous shyness.

Gentle and caring, he surrounded me with so much love, which made me forget about Dmitry and homesickness. The time we spent together flew with enormous speed. I had something to look forward to, I had feelings, I had desires, and I finally had a life. Classes became longer. My English got better. I didn't hesitate to speak up my mind any more.

Bartek was a handsome tall blond guy, full of ambitions and expectations from life. He had a child-like face and a very kind smile, that kind of smile would make you forget about all your worries. He would bring a bouquet of beautiful flowers to almost every date and kiss my hands before leaving. He would focus on my right arm, attention to which would instantly make me feel uncomfortable, and kiss it all the way from the wrist to the shoulder. He kept repeating it's beautiful and he was in love with it as much as he was in love with me. I never told him about all the torture this very arm caused. I was always ashamed to share my sad stories of abuse and humiliation. I never knew why most of the kids in school made me a subject of ridicule for years. I never knew why I had to pay such a high price for staying alive. Almost everyone in the whole school found my soft wrinkled purple-skinned arm extremely funny, and I often ended up surrounded by cruel kids in the school's bathroom. They forcefully rolled up my sleeve and held me tightly, looking at my injured limb with disgust. They would touch it with pencils as if it was diseased, they would try to stab the thin wrinkled skin to see what was under. I held my tears, and I bit my lips not to scream from pain. They would spit on it one by one. Eventually, they would go away, leaving me all alone on a cold floor, on which I often wanted to die.

My new boyfriend always managed to make me laugh and feel needed. After a couple of weeks of dating, we started meeting every day, and after a few more dates he gave me the key to his apartment. He proposed to apply for a working visa together to have a legal 1-year permission to work, so we could eventually file for green cards.

Bartek adored Atlanta. His uncle immigrated there when Bartek was a little kid, they didn't remember much of each other, however, they spoke on the phone every once in a while, and the uncle sounded very eager to have us there. He promised to help us with jobs and a place to live. He called Atlanta heaven on Earth, the weather couldn't be better, people are the nicest in the country, night-life and day-life are perfectly arranged for youngsters like us. Neither Bartek nor I had ever been there, yet, both of us couldn't wait to see it.

Bartek became the most important person in my life very fast. In no time at all, I couldn't imagine myself without him. We planned everything together, we studied together, we spent all nights and mornings together. Together we skipped unimportant classes and socialized with other students. We even invented new words of Polish-Russian-English origins, that only we understood.

Once classes were over, we decided not to wait until the graduation party and leave Worcester at our earliest convenience. I had almost moved into Bartek's little apartment by Elm Park. During my free time, I was searching for affordable apartments in Atlanta on Craigslist. I was overly excited to get there and see this heaven on Earth with my naked eyes. Every night Bartek brought delicious desserts from the bakery he worked in, along with a bottle of wine; we looked at the dwellings I picked for us while enjoying the food and wine. It was the happiest time since I had left Russia. I loved the way he treated me, the way he talked to me, the way he looked at me; there was nobody I knew of, kinder and tenderer than him. I couldn't wait for his shifts to end, to get enclosed in his warm arms and talk about our future and everything that would come to our minds. Until I received an email.

"I can't forget you. I miss you terribly. Dmitry."

I read it about 10 times as if I was trying to make sure it was real. My heart started pounding anxiously, giving me bitter-sweet dizziness with every beat. I couldn't determine, whether this news elated or frightened me. I got up and walked back and forth in my small campus room for a few seconds, then I sat back by the computer, not knowing what to do. Dull hopelessness filled up my mind. I had to admit — I missed him, too.

I thought about Bartek. I recalled his childlike smile, his eyes full of love and care, his strong and tender arms, the smell of his perfume, sound of his calming voice. I thought about Atlanta — the heaven I had never seen before. It became so difficult to breath.

I tried thinking about all the negative sides of Dmitry. He always mistreated me. He never truly cared for me. He let me down, he cheated on me. I never felt happy with him. "Sorry, it's too late. I'm engaged to the man I love," I typed with my hands shaking. I got up and walked back and forth for a few minutes again without sending it, then I sat down and rewrote the sentence, "I have a boyfriend, so please, don't contact me again." "I don't love you any more." "I miss you, too."

I took a deep breath and sent the last message.

I hated myself terribly for being so weak. Many times, I dreamed about finding a man, who would truly care about me, a man, that would give all his love without demanding anything back, the one, who would appreciate me the way I am. And now that I had found him, I was ready to part our ways forever. I threw him away from my life and my mind in a blink of an eye and felt zero regrets, as if he had never existed. My heart was warm. My chest got filled with love and lust I hadn't experienced in a long time. Everything else became unimportant.

That afternoon Dmitry and I exchanged a lot of messages full of beautiful words, confessions, regrets, and his possibility of relocation to the U.S. I imagined showing him Worcester and Boston, learning English and exploring American culture together. I thought of where we could live. Boston? New York? New York! How could I forget about it! It was Vera's dream to relocate there after graduation. I had heard so much about the glory of it back in Astrakhan, on the old bench by our building. Yes, it had to be New York.

I kept savoring the scene of meeting Dmitry at JFK airport in my mind. I couldn't hide the excitement. I wanted to scream. I wanted to dance. I couldn't believe I survived for so long without him. I fell asleep with sunrise, barely getting an hour of rest that long happy night. I saw colorful dreams of him lifting me up with his strong hands and kissing me passionately, non-stop, until we ran out of breath. I saw us living in a high-end apartment with a gorgeous view. I wasn't familiar with the shapes of skylines in big cities, but I knew for sure it was New York.

A heavy door knock woke me up in the morning. Tired and sleepy, I slowly opened the door and saw Bartek in the bright light of a hallway.

He looked sad and exhausted. Even his childlike face seemed to grow old overnight.

"What happened, baby? I was waiting for you all night," he murmured, not daring to enter the room.

I caught myself thinking, that in my brand-new reality I totally forgot about our romantic involvement, our nights and mornings together, and our plan to cook chicken and mashed potato the previous evening. I totally forgot I wasn't single. I forgot about his existence.

"Come over… I need to tell you something…" I didn't know how to start. Yet, I was determined not to delay the unpleasant confession.

He walked in. He didn't look like the main person in my life any more. I didn't feel anything towards him, besides pain. I hated myself for doing this to such a good person, to someone who hadn't done anything to deserve it, to the man, who treated me better than anyone else did.

"Dmitry is coming to the U.S." was all I could say.

He sat on the edge of the sofa and stared into nowhere. He knew about Dmitry.

"I know… I know… It's not easy for me either. I do care for you a lot, Bartek, but it's just stronger than me…"

He didn't say a word. Instead, a big tear started to form in his eye. He blinked it away, stood up and turned towards the window.

I didn't dare to move.

"Bartek," I uttered, almost crying. "Please, forgive me! I am trapped in love just as you are… I'm totally powerless here!"

He looked in the window for a few more seconds, then took a deep breath, turned back and kissed me on my forehead. Then he gave me a very sad smile and promptly walked away.

It was the last thing I ever wanted — to hurt him. And now, when everything had happened, I couldn't hold my tears any more — I was crying like a child for all the unfairness in life, for all the broken hopes and hearts, for loved and abandoned ones. The world seemed so imperfect and cruel. And yet, I felt partially relieved.

I started working on Dmitry's papers for a tourist visa, and in the meanwhile, I looked for colleges with sports scholarships. I didn't have the funds to apply for my own work permit and pay $400 for a plastic card that would allow me a year of work. I had a bit over a month till my student visa expiration and I was confident enough I'd find a well-paid position in New York and would be able to extend my stay.

I only had $500 in cash to carry to the Big Apple. I already knew I'd sleep at the airport for the first couple of nights. I didn't mind anything.

I was leaving Worcester on a very rainy day. An empty bus drove me to the Union Station. It passed by Clark University and its monument of Sigmund Fraud, a lonely and wet Main Street, banks and groceries, City Hall, and finally reached Union Station from which I took a Greyhound bus to New York.

I felt a bit sad to leave. So many things happened to me there, so much I learned, so many faces I had memorized. I thought about Bartek, I truly hoped he would find someone he really deserved, and soon enough, he would teach her to drive in Atlanta, buy her flowers, and kiss her hands. I secretly wished he would contact me once he would be over this feeling; I thought we could make good friends.

My Greyhound was leaving right on time. Rain became so strong, that I could barely see through the window. We made a small circle around the bus terminal and got off towards the City of Dreams.

CHAPTER 3

Random trees and raindrops didn't interact with my flow of thoughts. I lay my head on a cold shaking window and sank into a deep thinking — deeper and deeper with every mile. Heavier and heavier; thoughts were switching one another, leading me to endless sadness and fear. Strange bus philosophy, all my existence I dreamed to change life's decorations outside of windows, first it was the space between school and home, then university and people, then countries and challenging decisions, and the final trip seemed to have neither decoration nor a destination. I recalled that cozy bus ride from New York to Worcester and instantly sensed Vera's head resting on my shoulder. It made me feel even lonelier than I had already felt. I was going completely in the opposite direction, all alone this time, just like a leaf fallen out of a tree — with no home and no past.

The realization of making a mistake in the moment of making this mistake is probably one of the most unpleasant realizations. However, it doesn't always save us, moreover, it adds a feeling of insecurity and self-disappointment to that mistake. I was overwhelmed by thoughts about Dmitry and my irrational decision to give him another chance. There were so many chances given already, so many betrayals forgiven. How many more should I deal with? Why should this time be different? I thought. Then I told myself, it could be different. Maintaining a relationship is hard work, but this work will work for you if you work for it first. We will make it work, I smiled.

"New Yoooooork!" announced the bus driver, as we entered the jungle of towers, lights, and people.

My heart shivered inside — both fear and excitement filled it. I pulled my backpack out from underneath my seat and got back to watching big city's life through the screen of the window. Besides crowds of people, there was a beautiful picture of New York's fall with all its yellow-orange leaves and grey skyscrapers on the other side of the bus. Fall always reminded me of an old lonely lady who had only memories left to her own. New York's old lady was different, she was much lonelier, but she would never admit it.

We arrived at the dirty and crowded Port Authority. After eight months in a quiet, deserted Worcester, it seemed like an endless unpassable mart. I barely made it outside of the terminal.

The street was full of homeless and unhealthy-looking people, mean police officers, and garbage. Plastic bags were flying in the air just like birds. All possible urban sounds were combined into an endless unpleasant orchestra of emergency cars' sirens, jail songs, street fights, cursing and screaming, and conversations in different accents, which I could hardly distinguish. I had never felt so exposed to the world as then, standing in the middle of New York City, excited, but scared like a child, having no place to go to and not knowing anyone there. It was getting dark.

I entered the subway.

An hour later, the Air Train delivered me to JFK airport. My plan was to check heavy luggage for a couple of days and sleepover until I'd find a room. The first endless night I spent was in an Internet café, torturing computers one after another in order to get better service. I had sent about twenty emails and wrote down the same amount of phone numbers. I was terribly exhausted, but the three hours that I had left myself to rest in the morning didn't comfort me enough to fall asleep. After a few trials to pass out on a bench, I returned to computers and began killing time by playing chess online. I didn't win a single game.

New day was sunny and promising. I set myself in a good mood, and as soon as the sun got up to 9 am I started calling regarding rooms for rent.

My first NYC phone experience was pretty painful, I didn't understand half of the accents, destinations, and renting requirements. I kept asking and re-asking. I was cursed twice, or I thought I was. I only had $500 for a room, and some change for transportation, food, and other expenses until I'd find a job.

My English didn't let me express myself as much as I wanted, nor allowed to understand others as clearly as I wished. I was fighting for every room I called about, explaining to people that I will find a job right away and pay the rest of the month and the deposit. Using my broken

English, I was advertising how goal-oriented and intelligent I was. Whoever wouldn't hang up the phone, would learn about my master's degree from Clark University and my journalism and catering experience. However, my master's didn't help me with a room, nor with a job. Although, I did make some appointments that day.

My first stop was Euclid Ave, the heart of Brooklyn's East New York. At that time, I had no idea why the area was so gloomy and dismal. An endless chain of fried chicken places and liquor stores decorated the street I walked. People didn't seem too friendly. All the way to the "room", I was thinking about whether I should keep going or turn back, but decided that, being homeless myself, I didn't have much choice.

There was a big family in a two-bedroom apartment. Mother, father, and an infant slept in the bedroom, and grandma and two older kids were in the living room. They offered me a decent-sized bedroom for $500 a month and agreed to charge weekly. I said I had to think about it. I had never come back. After all, JFK airport didn't seem that bad of a place.

All the way back to the subway stop I was thinking about this miserable living. I was always afraid of poor existence at the bottom of life, just like those people in that apartment or the ones on the street, just like millions of others on this beautiful and cruel planet. I could forgive myself for having only $500 at the age of twenty-two, but I couldn't imagine fighting for food at the age of fifty. It scared me because I understood how easy it was to slide down, and how hard it was to get up. Even harder was each additional decade. I had to hurry.

I got into the subway and rushed toward my next appointment.

The other one happened to be in Manhattan. The same train brought me from the dark East New York to a fancy looking Chelsea. I had much more pleasure walking those streets, they were clean and cozy. I was gazing at small restaurants, funky stores and supermarkets, while figuring the way to my appointment. With every step I liked it more and more, with every "help needed" sign, I got more and more determined to rent the room regardless of its size or condition. I thought it would be nice to find a job within walking distance from home. I already saw myself returning from work every night, tired, but happy. I smiled as I walked. I couldn't wait to get there. Unfortunately, the price was a bit higher — twice of what I could afford. The landlord was asking for

$1000. Due to my poor English, I only understood that I could pay weekly but didn't realize that $500 was only a security deposit. Goodbye beautiful townhouse and a sunny room! I left very disappointedly.

My next stop was in Astoria, it involved a broker who wanted his part; then I went to Washington Heights and waited for half an hour by the building door. Nobody ever showed up.

The next sleepless night, I spent in the same Internet café. I was exhausted but couldn't afford to sleep. I needed a place; I needed a job. I had to start moving forward. I missed Dmitry. I wanted to do my best to get established in the City of Dreams — at least somehow — before he arrived.

The next day I checked out Flatbush in Brooklyn and Maspeth in Queens. The first one was against my boyfriend coming there, the second place' the landlord requested a sexual encounter once a week. I turned both offers down right away. The last appointment that day took me to Jamaica, Queens.

It appeared to be so different from what I had already seen. It looked like little India, which was also Caribbean and Mexican friendly. An infinite number of stores with cheap jewelry and clothing stretched throughout wide Jamaica Avenue. Music of all possible cultures was playing from all possible stores. People were chatting, bargaining, and singing. It reminded me of bazaars. There were a couple of them in Astrakhan, but neither was as big or had a distinguished character.

Sherry was the landlady, who gladly agreed to rent me a room, knowing about my very limited funds. She allowed me to delay the deposit until I'd found a job, and even suggested checking out a few Indian restaurants in the area. I liked her. And decided to stop my search.

"I'd rather rent the room to an educated young girl who has problems with money, than someone who doesn't, but will bring me a bigger deal of troubles later on," she said to me, half-smiling and slowly nodding as if agreeing with her own thoughts.

The room was a little bigger than a typical apartment's bathroom, it fitted one twin bed and a small dresser. It was part of the two-floor house with a backyard. Sherry told me I was allowed to use the backyard as well.

She was a beautiful, self-confident, slim woman around her mid-forties, but didn't look older than thirty-five. She appeared to me as a strict, but friendly, knowing-exactly-what-she's-doing woman. I liked the way she treated me. Yet I barely understood her Trinidadian accent, and I don't think I started to understand it better after a while.

I began my job-hunt the very next day I moved in. Without resumes or any proper skills, I walked through every door of restaurants, bars, burger places, jewelry stores, and hair salons I saw, asking for vacancies and telling them that I could do literally anything, lying about selling jewelry, shampooing, serving burgers and bartending experience in Worcester. The first and the last place that accepted me without asking for any experience. It was a Spanish bar. All the manager said was to wear something sexy and be there on time. When I asked, for which position she was hiring me, she responded, "Bartender."

I felt happy and secure for the first time in the past week. I had a home and a job. The offer was thirty dollars per shift plus tips. I congratulated myself on finding a job on the first day of hunting. Bartending didn't seem too bad compared to cleaning or housekeeping. Happy about my first steps towards big goals, I bought a couple of packs of beers and returned to my new home, to share my luck with whoever was present there.

There was Sherry and two more tenants in the backyard, a man and a woman. Each of them already had a drink and seemed to enjoy the night. It was around 9 p.m.; I walked into the outdoor space with two boxes of beer and caught Sherry's smile right away.

"Bring a container with ice, you, lazy man," she softly commanded the man, then winked at me.

"Sit down, honey," she pointed at the empty chair next to her.

The man stood up lazily, and then introduced himself and the other woman. I nodded but memorized neither name. I only remembered, that they were both flight attendants from Egypt and stayed in the house every time they stopped in New York.

"What on earth can't a man in love do?" Sherry joked. "He's hitting on me ever since he moved in."

I smiled and sat down.

"How was your job hunting, honey?" she asked right away, not giving me a chance to comment on the previous phrase.

She had big brown eyes and dark short hair. Her eyes sparkled every time she smiled. She had a thin neck and she always wore massive earrings.

"I got a job as a bartender," I answered.

"My goodness! Good job, hun!" she exclaimed. "Where is it?"

"In the bar on Hillside Ave."

The steward brought a big container with ice and quickly filled it with the beers I bought.

"Kate got her master's in Massachusetts," Sherry explained to everyone.

"Congrats!" I heard from other tenants.

I smiled again and thanked them.

"Which school did you attend?" asked the woman.

She looked fresh and rested.

"Clark University," I stated, confident she had never heard of it.

"How did you like it there?"

"I loved it." I pronounced emotionlessly.

The Egyptian man had already moved closer to Sherry and had bravely survived a couple of failed trials of hugging her. He seemed to take it as a joke, as much as Sherry did.

"Should I go on a date with him?" she asked mischievously.

At that moment I accidentally made eye contact with the man and felt awkward not giving a positive answer.

"Why not!"

"He wouldn't leave me alone if I wouldn't go," she laughed and slightly hit his cheek.

She was definitely enjoying his attention, yet I didn't like him so much and thought she could find a better-looking guy.

I didn't want to get involved in their romantic conversation and moved closer to the woman. We exchanged a few phrases till Sherry's cell phone rang. She answered quite agitated, repeating, "I'm all right, dad! Leave me alone, everything is good!"

I felt relieved when the woman started talking to her colleague, I finally could sink into myself. All of a sudden, memories about my own father recalled themselves and started to drill a hole in my heart. I remembered the day he took me out to the country. It was around five in the afternoon, and I was around six. He walked me along the river, telling stories about foreign lands and islands, about ships and pirates, about creatures in the very depths of oceans. Then we found a spot right by that river and I helped him make a fire. He wrapped all the potatoes he brought in a foil and put them inside the pile of burning woods. I remembered his tender voice, curly brownish hair and the taste of potatoes which was the best of what I ever tried. I couldn't recall anything else about that day. Only a savory taste and a mild voice that stayed in my childhood forever, so distant, yet, so dear. Even though so many years had passed, I could feel that day so close that it seemed possible to strengthen my arm and touch his curly hair. He would probably smile at me. We never went back to that river again, the place where I felt endlessly happy, calm and loved. I wondered if he did the same.

Sherry hung up the phone and cursed loudly. Then she joined the conversation of stewards.

Beers had slowly multiplied my sadness and I apologized for leaving the party. I had to get a good night's sleep, I had to rest before my first shift, but more than anything I felt the need to cry. I broke into tears as I entered my room. I kept asking myself, why did he leave us?

I was tossing and turning for most of that night before I managed to let those memories go, at least for a while. I needed some sleep. I focused on the pleasure of not having to come back to the hostile airport. I finally had a bed in a warm room.

And a job.

The next morning my mind was fresh and clear. I woke up around 8. It was quiet in the house. I made myself a bowl of cereal and a cup of coffee and continued unpacking my suitcase. I didn't find anything sexy in there. The only dress I had barely showed my cleavage and ended just a bit above my knees. It was the best I could do.

I showed up right at 8 p.m. as we agreed. The manager wasn't there. Two masculine Spanish guys greeted me by the bar.

"New bartender?" one of them asked.

"Yes…" I shyly responded.

"Follow me, I'll show you how to clean the tables," he commanded, getting off the bar stool.

Then the second guy told him something in Spanish.

"Never mind," the first uttered, "Just chill for now!"

I sat down next to him by the bar and put my little purse on my knees. I was looking around that place. Old wooden tables with missing chairs, probably thirty years ago painted walls, wires hanging in corners, and an old pool table in the back of the bar. I thought that I hadn't been to a spot like that. Yet.

I didn't know much about mixing drinks. Technically I didn't know anything about it.

"Excuse me," I interrupted the conversation of the two masculine guys.

They both instantly looked at me.

"… should I maybe practice making drinks…? The manager probably didn't tell you that I don't have much experience in it…"

"Doing what?" the second one asked with obvious annoyance in his voice. He had small brown eyes and a big bold head with an old thick scar on it. I assumed he got it in a fight.

"Hmm… drinks…" I answered obediently, "I thought I will be a bartender…"

"Just chill, fifteen more bartenders are coming tonight!" said the first guy.

The one with the scar slowly got up from his stool, walked closer to me and elaborated.

"Look! They buy you drinks; you make money on it! One beer is five dollars to your pocket. You gotta make them buy you beers!"

"Flirt with them, dance with them, it's your problem how you do it. They will buy. Not the regular beers though, but small ones, you know. They cost ten dollar — five go to the bar, the other five go to your pocket. You get one ticket for one beer. At the end of the shift, you get five dollars per ticket. Got it?"

I didn't get it but nodded in response.

My worst expectations started coming true after I saw a curvy Spanish woman in a tight short dress leisurely walking in. She gave a sweet kiss to each of the guys, allowed one of them to touch her butt, and waved to somebody in the back and sat between me and the pair. She didn't pay any attention to me, she was speaking Spanish with guys and seemed to enjoy herself. Then two or three more similar females walked in. By 9 p.m. there were ten or fifteen prostitute-looking women.

For a moment I thought about leaving that place, but my insecure financial situation made me stay. At least to watch what was going to happen.

"Regular" bartenders took their positions by the other side of the bar when the first bunch of drunk-ish men arrived. Scantily dressed girls at the age of forty and fifty began flirting with customers right away. I saw one of them put ten dollars on the counter to get her a small beer, then she immediately got a bonus ticket she tucked into her bra. She made a sip and got up to dance with the man. Extremely loud, Mexican music filled every corner of the place with its bachata and meringue. More men were coming.

"You gotta talk to them and flirt with them. Don't just sit!" yelled one of the girls behind the bar, trying to over-scream the loud music, while opening beers and pouring shots of tequila, "What are we paying you for?"

I nodded, faking a smile and got up from the stool.

"Wait," she stopped me. I looked back at her.

"You gotta hide this. It's not gonna work," she said firmly, pointing at my right arm.

I felt both embarrassed and hurt. Dull heaviness filled my chest. I wanted to leave that place immediately and never come back there again.

"Sorry. I'll wear long sleeves tomorrow."

I forced myself not to think about it. Money was my first and ultimate reason for being there. My eye caught a man who sat alone with a bucket of beers. I approached him and felt relieved as the bartender let me out of her loop. The man wasn't paying attention to me.

"Nice jacket!" was all I could say to start.

"What?" he yelled.

"Jacket. I like your jacket!" I repeated louder, trying to hide my nervousness.

"Habla Espanol?"

"No…" I sighed, getting disappointed.

"Baila!" he offered in a demanding manner. Then he got up and squeezed my arm, looking straight into my eyes and keeping his mouth open. He smelled like sweat and vomit.

I felt disgusted, but the need for money was stronger.

"Cerveza!" I claimed, looking back into his eyes, with growing anger.

He picked one Corona from his bucket and handed it to me.

"I don't like these ones," I uttered impatiently, "I like small ones!"

After the bartender behind the bar told him something in Spanish, the customer unwillingly bought me a small $10 bottle of beer.

I got my first ticket and went to dance.

I had no idea how to dance the bachata or meringue, neither I could distinguish one from another. All songs played there were absolutely indistinguishable to me.

I danced a few more times, having collected a few more tickets. I truly hoped nobody would ever find out about this experience of mine. I was so ashamed of having to do that with a master's from one of the best universities. I wanted to get very drunk.

It seemed impossible with those little beers they gave me. So, I started smuggling regular ones into the bathroom. I needed the buzz to deal with the situation. I was never a good dancer, not even at parties I truly enjoyed; I would dance on special occasions, drunk enough not to care about my movements and other people's opinion. And now, with these wasted stinky strangers, it took me a lot of strength to overcome my own principles. I needed more buzz.

I lost my shame in a few hours of dancing and drinking. I started demanding small ticket bottles from wasted customers, one after another. They all looked the same to me. I forgot who I had already danced with, they refused to buy me beers, I lost the count of everything. I barely stood on my feet and hated their endless love for dancing. I hadn't danced that much in my entire life.

At the end of the shift, around four in the morning, I got my fifty dollars for tickets and thirty for the shift. That meant I had ten dances. Just ten? It seemed like fifty. I thought I might have danced with some people for free.

My feet were hurting like never before. I could barely walk home. I craved my soft bed throughout the entire night; however, it didn't seem soft as I lay down. I was tossing and turning for hours in order to find a better position — my body was aching. I continued dancing and drinking in my dreams. I woke up very tired.

Welcome to New York, I told myself.

I returned there the next day. And the third day, which happened to be the last. I made about the same amount of money. I felt about the same pain in my feet and saw the same dreams all night long. The only difference was — I kept getting drunk, and on the third day, incapable of walking for five minutes, I had to take a cab home. I knew I would never go back there.

Meanwhile, I made acquaintances with one of the girls, who repeatedly praised the job, saying, "What could be better? You chill, dance, drink, and get paid for this!" Exactly. She was in the right place with the right people. There was probably nothing better for her and at the end of the day, it's all that matters, whether you're happy or not.

I was walking down the street the very next night, pitying myself and hating myself for this weakness. I thought about my nearest future and it instantly made me feel insecure. I tried to fight those gloomy thoughts and decided to rest and do nothing that night. I was too tired from all my recent activities, moving from Worcester, living at the airport, looking for a room and a job — it felt as if all these events got mashed into one never-ending day, which took all my strength away. I was looking for a bar.

I ordered a margarita from a teenage female bartender in a more-or-less okay-looking bar. It seemed big and abandoned. I counted how much I was allowed to spend and agreed with myself not to get wasted. I missed Dmitry. I needed his hug. I always felt calm and secure in his strong arms, even though I never knew how long those hugs would last.

All the papers for his tourist visa were sent to the American Embassy in Moscow. We were only waiting for the date of the interview. I was so impatient to finally see him, and at the same time, I didn't want him to see this misery of my living. Deep inside, I was scared to sink into this misery and start taking it as normal. I owed myself a better future. I promised myself to start sending resumes, beginning the very next morning and continue until I would find a job, I wouldn't be embarrassed to tell people about.

"Hi beauty!" the harsh voice interrupted my thoughts and I assumed it was addressed to me.

I looked to the right and saw a big-boned Indian-looking guy a couple of chairs away. He was smiling. There was nobody else on that side.

"Hey…" I mumbled.

"What are you thinking about?" he tried to flirt, moving slightly closer. It made me quite agitated.

"I need a job," got out of my mouth, "Do you know if anybody is hiring?"

"Yes," he smiled, without taking his time to think, "my uncle."

"Rooooon!" he shouted at the door behind the bar, at the very end of it, "Rooooon, we need you!"

I fell in stupor, watching that door slowly, as unwillingly, moving open and an old chubby guy with long black hair and a mustache appearing in it.

"I'm Shawn, by the way." the Indian fellow extended his hand, while the chubby guy walked towards us.

"I'm Kate," I smiled, shaking it. I felt rather shocked by the way things were happening as I didn't expect to be offered a job, I only wanted to give some attitude to the one who was trying to flirt with me.

Shawn cleared his throat and grinned at Ron, shaking his leg under the bar counter. He seemed very excited.

Ron slowly approached us and took a deep look at me, then at Shawn, then at me again. He looked like a comic actor.

"Who is this man? Do you know him?" he asked me with his face overly serious, pointing at Shawn with caution.

I started laughing.

"He is looking for a job, I think." I answered, not knowing what else to say in order to keep up the joke.

"No ugly man I accept here," he looked at Shawn, then pointed at me, "What's she name?"

"Kate." he smiled.

"She want work?" he asked.

"She is looking for a job."

"Tell she, she got a job!"

Then he turned to me. He looked like a typical Native American aged man from a picture in a school history book. Yet, without feathers.

He moved closer to me and bent down, resting his elbows at the bar counter, "Let me aks you something... Did you ever serve drinks?"

"Well... I did," I lied, "I did catering in Massachusetts, Clark University... Sometimes we had occasions, where..."

"Shhhhhh," he interrupted, putting his index finger to his lips, "If I tell you come work the day after tomorrow, will you come?"

I found his accent hilarious, similar to Sherry's, but still more understandable.

"Absolutely!" I admitted.

"What is the day after tomorrow?"

"Saturday!" I stated.

"Which day is Saturday?"

"The day after tomorrow," I laughed.

"Okay. She hired!" he uttered and smiled for the first time.

"Thank you, Ron!" I was so shocked and excited that I could barely put words together, "How should I be dressed?"

"Just casual," he said, "wear whatever comforts you."

I couldn't believe such luck. An attempt of pitying myself in a local bar got me a job. And that job seemed more or less suitable for the beginning. It was hard to hide the excitement. My new fellow and I had a couple more drinks on a house and left the bar to relocate to another one. I felt like continuing the party but didn't want Ron to see me drunk.

"Oh, I forgot to ask," a thought struck me all of a sudden as we walked towards the other place, we could land on Jamaica ave. "There is no dancing in Ron's place, is there?"

"Dancing?" he, cleared his throat. "What kind of dancing?"

"Never mind," I breathed, "just thought of something."

As I learned later, Shawn happened to be a very positive, open-minded, and caring person. He was a tall, massive, dark-skinned man in his early thirties. His eyes looked kind and seemed to be laughing on their own, yet there was a hint of sadness in them. He had a harsh voice and often cleared his throat while talking as if something was bothering him. Perhaps it was due to those mint cigarettes he smoked every twenty minutes. He listened carefully to each word of my half-broken English, and never interrupted me. I instantly felt comfortable in his company.

After a few drinks, Shawn revealed some of his past. He told me he used to be illegal in this country. He came here from Trinidad as a visitor with the intention to stay. He turned illegal six months after he arrived. Years later, he married a woman precisely for a Green Card which cost him $10,000. It was one of the most important events in his life — to become a legal permanent resident, just like everybody else, to stop being afraid of getting deported and begin enjoying life. Shawn was always dreaming about becoming a police officer. He was volunteering for a local precinct during the day and working for long after-hours as a security guy at a few nightclubs.

"One day I will become a police officer, I'm telling you!" he declared several times that night.

He appeared to like helping people, just as easy as he got me, a stranger, the job. It seemed like he had a big heart, although, I didn't know whether it was a good thing for New York's police.

He was the first person in The Big Apple, I spoke to about my dream of becoming a writer. It was a very sensitive topic. I constantly expected people to make fun of me, an immigrant, who could barely express her thoughts.

Who? You? Writer? Give me a break! Write letters to your mother!

"It's all up to you, how you'll be able to master your English," Shawn stated. "You may stay in the Russian community and forget everything you had learned, or you may put all the efforts you can to make it excellent!"

The job at Ron's bar was much better than the previous one. I only had to serve drinks and chat with people. I learned how to make all the famous cocktails, even though the crowd was not too picky about what they drank. Mixing whiskey with soda was pretty much the top of my daily routine. The bar had never really got busy, about fifteen to twenty customers would stop in a span of my seven to eight-hour shift. Some of them would leave after a drink or two, others would binge till closing. The busiest nights would make me $120, the slowest — around $70.

"It used to be mad busy years ago!" Ron would often repeat. "Maaaad busy! I had 5 bartenders, even that was not enough."

"My wife," he showed me a faded picture of a Trinidadian woman in her mid-forties.

She played the main role in maintaining that place. They opened the bar together a few decades ago and took excellent care of it. Advertising, promoting, making it a perfect spot for any day or night of the week, hosting birthday parties, baby showers, concerts of Caribbean celebrities, and anything that a bar could host.

"It was aaaaaalways packed with people," he'd say, "even on Mondays!"

His wife died from terminal cancer ten years ago. Since then, everything changed. Ron started to drink heavily, he stopped caring about people and the bar gave up on promotions and DJs. It turned into an abandoned and sad place. Most of the customers were returning from years ago only to support old Ron and the memory of past days.

Ron had recently turned 60, but he looked much older.

He left Trinidad when he was 18. A young man went through all immigrants' difficulties, he lived on New York's streets, slept on benches, subway stations, in Central Park. He struggled with the alien country until he joined U.S. forces. Then he got naturalized, acquired a wife and a steady future.

Ron's job was giving me enough money to pay bills and put a little bit on a side. I sent out my resume every night after long shifts and attended interviews almost every morning. My English was too poor, and my confidence was down to zero. Every time, sitting in a waiting room, I observed the rest of interviewees, they looked so relaxed, so cheerful, so American. I thought of myself as somewhat totally opposite. I felt like a strained gloomy foreigner. It made me sink deeper and deeper into a swamp of hopelessness with each failed interview, one by one, getting ready to remove my rose-color spectacles and start looking at things the way they really were, nobody needed me.

Will I ever call this alien country my home? I kept screaming within my head. I didn't know. All I knew was I missed Dmitry and wanted to fall asleep in his arms to forget about all worries and troubles.

Most of the customers at work were not completely indifferent towards me. Every night I would leave with a new phone number in my pocket, which I would get rid of as soon as I would pass a trashcan. Ron helped me to stay away from wrong people, arguments, sudden misunderstandings, angry or overly intoxicated customers. He would replace me at the bar during drunken fights and send somebody to drive me home if we would finish late. He became more of a caring uncle, than a boss. He shared a lot of stories from his youth on slow nights; he told me about the beauty of Trinidad and warmth of the ocean, friendly local people and endless summers. He taught me to cook shark and to make signature Caribbean cocktails, he would often let me grab a few beers for home, he liked to teach me how to flirt safely to get more tips, and one rainy night he called me to the back room and offered to become his lover.

My naïve worldviews broke into small pieces.

"You are a great person, Ron, but I have a boyfriend" I vocalized, "and I love him more than anything in the world!"

"But he in Russia!" Ron looked at me as I was insane.

"But he is coming here!" I cried.

It felt unreal. I didn't know where the major misunderstanding had happened. I kept asking myself what I had done wrong to make him think this way about me. I went back in time to the first recollection of him and step by step analyzed each of our conversations. I couldn't figure out what exactly had sent him the wrong message. Was I too friendly or too polite?

My next shift in the bar wasn't so pleasant. Ron began mocking me by copying my body movements, accent, and even my voice. He was overemphasizing my politeness, my disability to understand all the words properly and a constant need of re-asking what was said. Most of the people were laughing at his performance, some of them looked at me pitifully, and I had only one way of dealing with it — to pretend that everything was all right.

"Look," he started saying to entertain customers. "She said she will be a writer. What sort of writer, she don't speak English?"

My job hunting became more intense. I was ready to accept any position that wouldn't involve alcohol, food, cleaning, and working at night. The jobs I was offered involved selling vacuum cleaners, unknown insurances, services I understood nothing about, and lots of other things I wasn't good at.

The situation with Ron was getting worse and worse. I had no more tolerance for the harassment I was going through, nor I had another job that would pay my rent and expenses. I felt entrapped.

One of these days at work he called me to the kitchen and tried to kiss me.

"Stop it!" I shouted, pushing him away.

"What's the matter?" he murmured with lust in his voice. "Am I not nice to you? Didn't I help you when you needed job?"

"But you needed a bartender as well!" I cried anxiously out of unfairness.

He squeezed me tighter, trying to reach my lips with his.

"I am good to you, you good to me… Don't hesitate, baby… kiss me, you will like it… I promise we'll make it our little secret… I am a great lover." he was breathing right into my face, getting closer and closer.

Awfully disgusted, I turned angry and pushed him away as strongly as I could, using all my strength enhanced from disappointment, sadness, hatred and readiness to give up on all my materialistic needs. He fell down on the cobbled floor and hit his head on a radiator. Time had stopped. I froze watching him lying on a side with his huge hairy belly pumping out of his tight dirty shirt. He didn't move. I killed him, I thought.

I bent towards him and cried, "Ron!"

He didn't move.

"Ron, are you okay?" I shouted louder, shaking his shoulder.

There was no answer.

I tried to find a pulse on his neck but was too nervous to feel anything. My throat grew dry. I was shivering.

"Oh my God." I said loudly, feeling my brain turning into a powerful machine of producing solutions. I thought about the police, jail, court, his relatives, and my nightmares. I thought about all possible circumstances, I recalled all I knew about accidental murders. I rushed out of the kitchen to the bar in panic. It was all empty. I was thinking between calling 911 and running away.

"God… My God…" I kept repeating to myself, holding my head as if it was going to split into two parts.

I hated that bar, Ron, New York, Trinidad. Scared and confused, I pulled my purse from the shelf under the counter. All plastic containers, pan-sharpeners, erasers, and a bunch of other little useless things that were there fell down in a second. I started looking for my jacket, trying to remember where I had stored it hours earlier, and only after I made a mess in all cabinets, a sudden glimpse in a mirror revealed that it was already on me. I took a deep breath, trying to put my thoughts in order.

"What's up, Bonita?" I heard a loud masculine voice coming from the entrance.

It was one of the permanent customers. He looked relaxed and smiley.

"Ron!" I yelled, "He lost... he fell down... He passed out in the kitchen... And doesn't stand up..."

His smile was gone. He ran to the kitchen, breaking a half-broken door that separated it from the bar, went down on his knees and started checking the pulse on my boss's wrists.

"Call 911!" he screamed.

The very next moment medical workers were carrying Ron to the ambulance car. A few strangers stopped by to see what was happening.

"I know this guy!" a random drunk noted, "Robert? Roger? What he name?"

It was getting dark outside. Ambulance lights were coloring up the block and curious people's faces. A following emergency sound carried away my employer and abuser; I could still hear it a couple of minutes later. Then it disappeared.

"So, what happened?" asked the customer.

It was chilling and fresh outside. One of the nicest evenings of the past few weeks.

"I don't know," I breathed, feeling exhausted, "I walked into the kitchen — he was on the floor..."

CHAPTER 4

It had been raining heavily for a few days in a row.

I ate non-stop, slept a lot, and spent hours on the phone with Dmitry. I would let him speak most of the time and learn about his soccer success, English classes, and preparations for the visa interview. We would talk during my very late nights and his early mornings, lunches and dinners; I spent about ten dollars a day on calling cards. I didn't say a word about what had happened in the bar.

I constantly felt homeless. I had a roof above my head and four walls supporting it, yet I had no home. I felt like I never had one. I felt like I was pointlessly flying around the world, like a yellow leaf, that's not alive any more, but not yet dead.

I was waiting for news. Good or bad news. Every new day of silence scared me, and at the same time — comforted. It was not my fault. I was only protecting myself, I kept repeating. Yet, nobody had to know about it.

After the fourth day passed noon, I decided to call Shawn.

"I don't know anything about this!" he yelled. "Which hospital did they take him to?"

I was embarrassed to admit, that I didn't even know where he was. I was not even quite sure he was alive. I felt the urge to finish the conversation with Shawn as soon as I could. However, the same night he called me back with an offer to grab a drink. He said he had good news.

I walked into another uninhabited bar a couple of blocks away from my house. Spanish music was playing all over the place, but the clock was showing only 7 pm and dance party hadn't started yet. Shawn sat alone by the bar, wrapped in a leather jacket a couple of sizes bigger than himself. He grew a little beard that made him seem older, other than that he looked happy and cheerful. At that very moment, I noticed how warm and kind his smile was. I realized how glad I was to see him.

"I ordered you a margarita," he cleared his throat and moved a big glass towards me, giving me a hug with his other arm.

"Thank you. I'm so disorganized these days…" I tried to excuse my behavior, seating myself down and removing my black cardigan, "I didn't even ask them where they were taking your uncle."

"It's okay," he smiled, "he is fine. I went to visit him today."

My heart shivered inside. I thought of what he might know about that night.

"Sooo… what happened to him?" I asked promptly.

"He had blood in his brain," Shawn answered, "but now he seems to be all right."

"Wow…" was all I could say.

"So, what happened to him?" he asked me the same question.

I found it pretty hard to lie, looking into his big brown eyes. I looked away and breathed.

"I don't know… He was already on the floor when I came to the kitchen…"

"I see," he murmured.

"Didn't he tell you how…?" I mumbled.

"He didn't."

"Well… I hope he'll feel better soon."

"I'm sure he will," Shawn smiled joyfully, "Ron is a strong guy. He is a fighter! They'll keep him inside for a couple more days just to monitor. I'm sure he'll open the bar the same hour he'll arrive home!"

Shawn laughed. I forced myself to laugh, too.

"How is your job hunting, by the way?" he asked.

"Well, nobody wants to hire an alien with no proper papers, so I sent a few resumes to Brooklyn's Russian companies. Most of them are looking for Russian-speaking secretaries… Not what I would want to do, but I have no choice. Plus, I have limited time to find a job on books to be able to open a working visa, before I'd turn illegal. I have a couple of weeks."

"What if you won't find anything within this time?"

"I guess I'll stay for a few months just to earn some money and show New York to Dmitry. Then we'll have to go home…"

"To Russia?"

"Yes, Shawn, to Russia. That's the only place I can always come back and live and work legally…" I breathed, "I wish I were a citizen of the world!"

"I thought, your home is here!" he exclaimed, "I thought you love it so much and want to stay here!"

"I do, but it's not easy… I don't want to live a life of an illegal immigrant and freak out every time police pass by, or any bad accident happens. I want to live in peace."

"But nothing is easy! You are young and healthy and have to fight for your dreams! You have done so much to be here as you are. You've got a Master's! Not every American has Masters! You can't give up so easily… And would you be able to live in peace in Russia?"

"Listen!" Shawn moved closer and started whispering, "So many immigrants come here illegally and live miserable lives. They have almost zero chance to live legally in this country, because they entered illegally in the first place. You have everything you need. You have chances. You're smart, educated, and beautiful. You can achieve anything you want. Think about, how many people want to be here, in your shoes. Wouldn't your friends from Russia use the first opportunity to come here? Of course, they would. Wouldn't a Mexican guy, who crossed the border and now has to work for years to pay for the service, which took him over this very border… wouldn't he rather come here on a student visa with chances of having a real future? Of course, he would!"

He took a deep breath and continued, "It's a country of immigrants. If not us, who is going to build it?"

"You are right, Shawn, I'd love to make this country a better place, but I need to think about myself first. I want to build a good career. I don't want to work as a waitress for the rest of my life and worry about staying away from troubles!" I uttered.

"You just have to work on yourself!" Shawn stated, "I was illegal in this country for five years. I worked three jobs to save money for the fake marriage! I was sick and tired of everything but never lost hope. Now I'm a citizen of this country, and I'm about to become a police officer. All dreams come true. You just need to know for sure what you want."

I nodded and sank deeper into my thoughts. I knew I had to come up with a plan and stick to it. I started drawing beautiful pictures of my successful career as a writer, imagining myself sitting by a huge window of my writing room, looking at the sunset and thanking the Universe for this gift of life. I knew those tipsy fantasies would be erased from my memory by the morning and the enormous need for water would quickly replace them.

"Anyway," Shawn tapped my upper back and smiled, "our dreams will come true! Cheers to that!"

"Cheers," I responded. "For the bright future!"

The nearest future didn't appear too bright. An early phone call woke up my exhausted mind and I realized how hungover I was. The voice on the other end of the wire said I was invited to the interview for a secretary position in Brooklyn. They also said it had to happen within the next three hours. I had no choice.

A cold shower and iced tea gave me a slight relief, but an annoying, almost two-hour train ride to Coney Island brought everything back. I even thought to return home in the middle of the trip, but the need for a job was stronger.

There was a ground-level wholesale storage full of stoves, refrigerators, heavy dusty boxes, and two little offices at the end of it. I walked straight to one of them as soon as I saw a short and chubby man waving at me. It was Steve, the owner.

"You are too good for me," he said, sucking a lollypop while reading my resume, "I need somebody simpler, without a master's degree."

"Well… I don't think I'll do a worse job than anybody without a master's…"

He gave me a smiley gaze. Then he chewed up the lollypop and rode the computer chair to the trashcan to throw the stick. He grabbed a new candy.

"Would you like one?" he asked.

"I'm fine, thanks," I murmured.

"Too bad, these are really good," he pointed out.

He moved back to the table. It was full of papers and files, different invoices and sticky notes — everything looked disorganized and messy. I wondered how he managed to do his work… and what happened to the previous secretary.

Steve was wearing worn-out baggy jeans, sneakers, and a size less colorful t-shirt, which didn't help hide his extra pounds. He was in his late forties, as short as, probably 5'2", and seemed to have a bit of a complex next to tall women.

He continued looking at my resume, sucking another lollypop.

"Have you ever worked as a secretary?" he asked without taking out the candy from his mouth.

"I haven't, but I…"

"Okay." he interrupted. "Bookkeeping?"

I didn't know what it meant and assumed it was a fancy word for a librarian.

"No." I smiled.

"Why do you think I should hire you then?" was another frustrating question I got.

"Well… I'm extremely organized, neat, goal and detail-oriented, a fast learner, love to work and very enthusiastic about this position!" I answered confidently, even though half of it was a lie.

"And I love literature!" I added regarding bookkeeping.

"Sounds good… Where do you live?" asked Steve, signing some forms on his messy table.

"Brighton Beach," I answered, as I recently read on the Internet, that a potential employer would rather hire someone who lives nearby.

Steve looked at me. Then back at my resume.

"Where in Jamaica?" he wondered, removing the lollypop from his mouth.

"Last stop of the F train…" I mumbled getting red. I completely forgot to fix the address on my resume.

"But I was thinking to move to Brighton Beach soon." I lied out of my embarrassment.

I thought that I had lied. But a week later I was unpacking my orange suitcase in the very same Russian neighborhood, Brighton Beach. Steve hired me after that long and annoying interview.

This company was not qualified to provide me with a working visa; however, I had no other options. My legal status was about to expire, and I decided to do my best to conceal this fact.

"Are you leaving me?" Ron asked, making a really sad face when Shawn took me to the hospital where my ex-boss was successfully recovering.

"Give me a hug," he murmured, making his eyes look smaller and sadder, "where have you been all these days?"

"I didn't want to bother you. Shawn told me you were fine…" I said giving him a light hug, just because he asked for it.

I didn't feel sorry for him. He seemed so miserable in that washed out gown and bruises on his arms. Nasty old man with a taste for young women. How many of them did he harass in that kitchen before I appeared? He will recover and come back to that trashy bar, will hire another girl or two, and will start everything over again. And maybe one of these Trinidadian girls will go for it out of fear of losing the job. Natural selection. Almost natural.

"How are you feeling?" I asked out of politeness.

"Oh… I had such a headache last night, the nurse had to give me a pill, then my blood pressure went up, I called the nurse again… But otherwise, it's okay… it's okay…" he cried quietly. And added, "but listen, you gotta come to the bar sometimes!"

There was no awkwardness in the air. We left after the meaningless chat as smoothly as we came. Shawn drove me home in silence. I had to pack my belongings.

"I hope we'll still hang out sometime… after you move over there," he sighed sadly, turning off the car's engine.

"Of course, we will!" I gave him a warm hug.

It felt like he was a brother I had never had but always wanted.

"I'm sorry for Ron," he murmured, "I feel guilty for what happened that night."

I shivered.

"Did he tell you?"

"Not really…I guessed." Shawn looked down. "I knew he likes young girls; I should have never suggested you to work there. But I didn't know you at that moment. We had just met."

"It's okay," I was touched by his sincerity. "This job gave me good support for a while, I was able to finally buy a warm winter coat and winter boots for the upcoming cold winter, and the second suitcase. I hope I'll soon have more things to fit in my two suitcases — my mobile closets. But the biggest happiness is that I met you in that bar! I'm so glad I walked in that night!"

"Really?" he asked with a sad guilty smile, after giggling at my suitcases.

"Absolutely!" I exclaimed. "I just feel bad for damaging your uncle..."

"He is not my uncle," Shawn responded.

I was all packed by the next noon. I sat in the backyard with Sherry and a couple of other tenants while waiting for a cab. Stewards were gone to another flight. My former landlady knew someone in a taxi service who owned a mini-van and agreed to drive me to Brooklyn for half the price.

We spoke about nothing. Sherry gave me a couple of suggestions like not to trust people and not to let them use my kindness. It was a pretty short stay in her lovely house. I will miss it, I thought.

She smiled sadly when the cab signalled outside. I felt like the same vulnerable leaf, which flew there from Worcester, and now, again, was going towards the unknown.

"If you'll ever need anything, if you ever have problems or difficulties, or if you need a place to stay, you are more than welcome!" Sherry declared, giving me a warm squeezing hug.

"Thank you so much for everything, Sherry," I said, squeezing her tighter. "And you too! If you need anything, don't hesitate to call me."

I nodded to other tenants that happened to be there before the driver helped me carry two suitcases to the cab. It was all I had.

"I'll stop by to see you! I'll be coming to visit you sometimes!" I screamed from the window of the cab once it started moving.

Sherry smiled and waved.

I was sad and happy, leaving the warm house. I truly planned to stop by in a while, but it didn't happen.

My cab passed all possible neighborhoods and landscapes, driving through narrow and wide streets of lonely people right in the middle of the universe, the greatest but saddest city in the world. I thought about life, decorations, thought about my recent moves and hopes. What had changed since I came to New York? Did my hopes become stronger or weaker? Am I more determined to stay in the United States? I thought of all those people I had met, or haven't met, all immigrants who came here to achieve their goals and build a happy life in an imaginary land — did they get what they wanted? All these grocery store salespeople, housekeepers, waiters, street cleaners over fifty years old, were these their dream jobs?

I felt like New York could turn my life into the sweetest dream as much as it could turn it into the worst nightmare. Only thoughts of Dmitry would stop my anxious overthinking. Very soon, I'd be in his arms.

Brighton beach appeared to be sunny and alive, even too crowded, more like a big bazaar under a noisy railroad. People, their dresses and manners, the names of stores and restaurants reminded me of old USSR. I hadn't really lived in USSR, before I moved to Brighton.

The apartment I inhabited was small and cold. It had three tiny rooms and an eat-in kitchen. The new landlord, an athletic Russian guy in his late thirties, greeted me indoors, thanked me for coming on time and explained the house rules. There was a special shelf for me in the refrigerator, one special hanger for a towel in the bathroom and ten square inches on the shoe rack. My room was as tiny as the previous one, besides it had a twin bed, a small computer table, and a stand with a TV that transmitted Russian channels. One of the other tiny rooms was occupied by an elderly couple, and the third one had a guy of my age and his mother in it. I was only wondering how both of them managed to fit in that space.

I called Shawn to report that I had moved, then I did some grocery shopping, had a housewarming beer in my room, and passed out. Then a real boring life began.

My every new day started with waiting in a line for the bathroom, then catching the train to get to work, then sitting in the office surrounded by men in their forties and fifties from nine to six, and then catching the train to get home. Eating and talking with neighbors after work became my biggest entertainment. They were babysitters, housekeepers, and waitresses that didn't speak English at all and seemed to be fine with everything. Every morning they would go to work as they have been doing forever, every night they would come back home to watch Russian shows and fill every conversation with local complaints. Nobody seemed to want to change anything.

"I'm glad. I've been doing babysitting for ten years already," the mother of a young guy told me. "I like it, and it pays well. I make $500 a week."

"Sometimes $550," she added whispering. "Not everybody makes this much in Brighton!"

"I came here fifteen years ago. Two years after, I brought my wife," was the story of the elderly man from the couple's room. "I do constructions, she is a waitress in a coffee shop around the corner. Not that we like it so much, but what else can we do? We are illegal here."

"Legalizing," they said, "is too much work. And who would care whether you are legal or not in Brighton? Some Russian companies are purposely looking to hire somebody for cash, so there are no taxes involved."

They seemed to enjoy the local life. Food, society, restaurants, bars, ocean, Russian movie theatre — everything was available there, all in Russian language and for Russian-speaking people.

The mystery to me was not why they didn't mind living the rest of their lives in Russian area of a foreign country with no language, ability to travel, express themselves, reach career goals, and explore the world of unknown. The question was, why did they leave Russia in the first place?

Steve's job granted me the most boring duties, I was scanning, typing, printing, answering the phone, and running around the block to get coffee when other employees needed it. There were three people in the whole company, Steve in his private office, Russian-speaking man from Uzbekistan shared the same space with me, and another Russian-speaking man occupied the last little office. They both spoke perfect Russian but preferred to communicate in English. Even though neither one was really communicative.

There was not a lot of work, which turned most of my time into counting. I counted hours from the beginning till the end of each day. I would set up a goal to survive until lunch, then I would rest for a few minutes eating at my desk, then I would wait passionately till six, and my most favorite moment would be the first second outside.

The job didn't pay a lot. After taxes, I had only $330 of my weekly check to deposit into my poor account. It was about half of what I was making at Ron's bar. There were a few moments when I considered finding another bartending job but gave up on that idea as I recalled my experience at Ron's. The only thing I liked about this position was the clean office without any drunk people harassing me, regular hours — nine to six, Monday through Friday.

Fridays were my favorite. I would often call Shawn and we would meet in Manhattan. It was a long way on a train to get there, and much longer to get back. But I loved those Fridays. We would meet on Time's Square, walk northwest in search of a less crowded place, and then start drinking and sharing the newest news. Shawn would tell the latest gossip from Jamaica, its bars, stores, people we both knew, and Ron's place as a highlight of each night out. I had nothing to share since I moved to Brooklyn. My life stopped and froze in one long, almost endless, day. Shawn's stories cheered me up and made me feel alive. For a few hours spent with him, I would forget about my boring life, days of counting and waiting, nights of listening to depressing conversations in the roaches-infused kitchen. I would laugh till I felt pain in my upper abdominals and wish that night could last forever. Yet, as forever would come to the end, we would have to hug each other and part ways going in absolutely opposite directions.

Sometimes we met on Saturdays and spent out nights drinking the same way.

Every Sunday was rather sad. I would wake up after partying with Shawn and realise how much I missed him, and how empty my life had become since I stopped seeing him that often. He was so independent and self-sufficient, even with bills he had to pay, people he had to deal with, and jobs that occupied most of his time. His positive thinking always inspired me. I never wanted to let him go, it felt like my last piece of freedom would go away with him, my true excitement would leave me, and I would have to come back to the prison of my everyday life. Shawn seemed to be my only real friend in a country of aliens, in which the main alien happened to be me.

I didn't try to make any new acquaintances in Brooklyn. In a span of three weeks, the only people known to me were my roommates. My goal was to make more money before Dmitry's arrival. The date of his interview was approaching, and I had to look for a bigger room in a better area. I started to search for an additional job and found catering in evenings for three days a week, from 7 p.m. to 12 a.m. I managed to increase my income to $600 weekly. I thought I would get used to the new tiring schedule soon, but I never did. Catering's location wasn't too convenient and changing two trains from downtown Brooklyn to Brighton Beach sometimes would take me longer than an hour. I would often fall asleep on the train, on the way back home, and wake up at the last station, Coney Island. I would sigh, cover myself with the scarf from the first chilling nights of the year, and wait until the train would turn back.

On one of those days, I went out of legal status. Simply the expiration date on my student visa passed and a hollow fear filled up my mind. Nothing major had happened, every morning arrived to turn into night as usual, trains and busses ran on schedule, Steve sucked his favorite lollypops, and even cops looked at me with the same facial expressions. Everything remained the way it was. Except I turned illegal. And thoughts of it started to drill a hole inside of me, a big and wide hole.

Time was crawling slower and slower between my endless jobs and Dmitry's date of the interview. He already bought a train ticket, which would take him from Astrakhan to Moscow to find out whether his USA trip was happening.

We practiced all possible questions and answers he could be asked at the American Embassy. He was only coming here for a month to see a friend, he did not intend to study or work here, he did not plan to change his tourist visa to any other kind, and of course, he wasn't going to stay longer than he stated in the paperwork. Very easy. Yet so complicated.

One of the weekends, recovering from a busy work schedule, I opened my old Russian email, which I hadn't checked for weeks and found a fresh note from Vera. It was very tragic. She was taking strong antidepressants along with alcohol, she was crying and crying and crying. Her mother was the only close person she ever had, the only parent after her father died from lung cancer long ago. Her mother was her best friend, her babysitter, her adviser, her life coach and sometimes, it seemed to me, the entire meaning of her being. I had never met anybody that close to their parents. Now, Vera was all that was left of her family.

At the very end of the email, there was her new phone number.

I took a deep breath before dialing. It had been almost a year since she had disappeared from my horizon, the Internet, and probably life itself.

"Hi, my angel!" I whispered once I heard her worn-out voice.

I barely recognized it. There was always something melodically sweet, naïve and playful in that voice. It lost all of it.

"Who is this?" Vera asked with such hoarseness as if she had been smoking all day long.

"It's me, Katya," I said a bit anxiously. "How are you, my baby? I miss you so badly here…"

"Heeey…" she seemed to smile. "I'm… ah… I'm a little better with these pills. They turn my brain off; I just don't think about anything."

"It's better than crying every day."

"It is. I just don't want anything. You know… Just nothing"

"I know," I murmured, not quite knowing how it feels. "You need to get stronger and let the time pass. I wish I could do something for you. Is there anything I could do?"

"No, honey," she sighed, "thank you, but it's my battle."

"Is anybody supporting you? Are you still friends with Nina?"

"Well… Nina has found a boyfriend, a very poor guy, who is focused mostly on sex and alcohol. She is busy satisfying his needs…" Vera whispered hopelessly. "How are you doing?"

"Oh, dear… I thought she wanted to find a tycoon; she had always been dreaming about being a wealthy housewife. But hey, she has to support you nowadays. That's what friends are for."

"It's okay, I'm used to being alone," she laughed. "And I guess, you don't always find what you look for. He cheats on her while she prays for him. So simple and banal."

"I feel bad for her then." I sighed and changed the topic, "What else do you do, my dear? How do your days pass?"

She laughed in a sad manner.

"I wish I did something. Or I don't wish to do anything… I'm just not doing anything. I go from one therapist to another, then to my mom's grave. I go there three-four times a week, every week. Life is so unfair. Who would think?"

"I know…" I breathed, not knowing what else to add.

"How are you?" Vera inquired after a short wave of silence, which felt a bit awkward to me.

"I'm okay… working in a small office in Brooklyn as a secretary, answering and transferring phone calls, creating and printing invoices, but I don't really like it, it's just okay for now," I laughed. "You have to start somewhere…"

"Oh my god! So, you are in New York? You finally made it there?" she seemed to smile again.

"I am… You were right; it's a magic city. I'm still hoping you will come back one day."

"Well, let's skip it for now…" she let out. "How is your personal life? Any cute loving American boy?"

For a second of silence, I thought about Bartek. I knew Vera would love him. He would surely make a great husband and a father. I smiled for a moment, thinking of him. I hoped he forgave me. Then I took a big gulp of air and said, "Well… Dmitry is coming soon…"

"Which Dmitry? That one?"

"Yeah, we got back together."

"No way… you must be really silly to do that. I'm sorry, but he is a bastard. Don't you remember how he treated you?"

"I remember… I do… But I do love him, and I'm sure it will be different this time." I mumbled, believing or rather forcing myself to believe in what I truly wanted.

"Well… You are sorry for Nina, but you are not better. I think he is using you to come to the U.S. Who is buying his airplane ticket, may I ask?"

"He is," I lied to defend my sanity.

"Well, at least there is something he is capable of…" she muttered angrily.

Vera's hatred towards Dmitry was mutual. From the very first time he saw Vera, he decided she was "too close to me". It was partly true. She was always a better friend to me than anybody else, a better friend to me than I was to her. She would often neglect her personal life or study for the sake of me, even though I wouldn't necessarily do the same for her. She loved me in spite of everything.

"Well, regardless of all the unfairness of life, I hope you'll choose the right door towards your peace and happiness. With or without him." she pronounced tiredly.

"Thank you," I said, feeling relieved from the disturbing topic. "I miss you so much."

"I miss you too," she breathed. "Sometimes I think how would it be if Katyusha would be here? I think I'd be happier. I'm absolutely sure."

We agreed I would call her once in a while, and I promised to forgive her if she would choose not to pick up the phone.

"My poor little friend," I started repeating to myself, "my poor little friend." No matter how old we are, we always learn how to live, how to deal with losses, how to handle failures, how to forgive, and how to forget. Nobody taught us this in school. Nobody taught us how to continue living without searching for solace in alcohol, drugs, or any other substances. We graduate from the best schools with our best degrees ready to get on top of the world, yet we crawl throughout life, acquiring bandages — one after another, learning to get up after every fall, knowing basically everything, but substantially — nothing.

It was the beginning of November. My first year in the United States was coming to an end. I successfully managed to get along with two jobs and make some extra cash to rent a bigger room in a better area and buy Dmitry an airplane ticket to come here. His interview date was approaching.

So many times, wasted Shawn listened to my drunken stories about Dmitry and endless love, about how easily one person can replace the entire world for you.

"I wish you to find it out yourself one day!" I kept telling him.

"I so wish I don't." he normally replied. "I Don't even think I'm capable of it."

In a free from two jobs time, I started looking for a bigger room, a room that wouldn't mind a couple. Unlike my other searches, this one went fast and smooth, the very first place I saw suited me perfectly. It was a huge room in a two-bedroom apartment for only $400 a month. The apartment was located on Kings Highway, which happened to be a few stops closer to Manhattan. The "landlord" was a Turkish man close to his forties, chunky and tall, with shiny baldness in the middle of his head. He spoke pretty bad English after three years of living in America, but it didn't make him any hesitant, he took his time to verbalize every thought, using difficult words, often of wrong meaning. He was a diplomat with a four-year mission in New York, who decided to rent a room to make some extra cash. His name was Adil.

Shawn moved me from Brighton Beach to Kings Highway. He came early afternoon, right after Adil had managed to call me twice to offer help with carrying bags, which I had to refuse politely. All my stuff still fitted in two medium-sized suitcases. The second one was plain black. We placed them into Shawn's car. I quickly returned to the apartment to check my room and the bathroom and left the key on the kitchen table. There was nobody at home that sunny but chilling day. I didn't feel any sadness.

Adil met us happily and friendly, welcoming us through the wide-opened door. He wore blue jeans and a white T-shirt with an "I love NYC" sign. His bald spot was shining as if he had polished it for that special occasion. I wondered if Shawn noticed it as well.

He helped us carry my suitcases into the room. It was bright, and it smelled like spring, every inch was clean and refreshed, my new roommate had definitely spent a lot of time preparing it. After a short introduction to the apartment's amenities, Adil invited Shawn to the kitchen for a coffee while I was unpacking.

I quickly pulled out the blouse and the skirt I had planned to wear to work the next day, some of the make-up, and my big tall mug with the "Clark University" sign on it. While looking for my purse and shoes, I could hear Adil constructing his heavy sentences and questioning Shawn as if he were the head of a police department. I didn't know where his friendly-bossy tone came from, whether it was the result of him serving an "important mission" in New York or the way his broken English sounded in his Turkish accent.

"I would now apologize and question you with what career you do?" I heard my roommate's loud and well-separated words.

"Well…" Shawn answered, "I volunteer for police in queens."

"Queens is a bad area," Adil asserted. "Very-very bad."

"It's not that bad." Shawn laughed. "It's the largest borough in New York, there are different neighborhoods, just like in Brooklyn."

"I have been there," Adil stated, pronouncing every word as clearly and slowly as he could. "Be careful over there. You may…might get in trouble."

"Okay," my friend agreed.

I felt awkward to keep unpacking. After the most important items were removed, I went to the coffee party to take Shawn out for dinner and thank him for moving me.

"Let's go to a Turkish restaurant. It offers a variety of delicious food. I will treat you with treasure... Pleasure." Adil exclaimed as he saw me in door with a small purse hanging over my shoulder.

I wanted to find an excuse to avoid his company, but Shawn already answered "Sure," and we went towards the place.

It was a small cheap Turkish kebab eatery, filled mostly with Turkish people. A folk Turkish song was playing in the background. As soon as the waiter arrived, Adil told him something in their language, without letting him communicate with us. The server nodded and left.

"I told him to bring the most delicious Turkish dish. Veal, meat veal, a kebab," he explained.

Shawn and I thanked him.

"So, what exactly do you do?" Shawn asked and cleared his throat immediately.

Adil smiled, then laughed. Then he laughed more — until two little tears appeared in his eyes. He took a napkin and wiped both out.

I looked at Shawn.

"I am accomplishing a mission here. I am a diplomat. I work in Turkish consulate." he finally verbalized with pride.

"Wow," stated Shawn. "That's really great! How do you like the US?"

The diplomat laughed again.

"It's okay," he answered. "I like Turkey better."

"So, when exactly is your boyfriend coming, Ekaterina?" Adil changed the topic that caused him so much laughter.

"He has an interview in three days... and if he passes it, he is coming right away. In five or so days," I answered, watching his reaction.

"I very hope he will pass," he said, smiling. Then he coughed loudly and apologized.

We started eating in silence as soon as food appeared on the table. I sneakily kept exchanging eye contact with Shawn in order for him to see the reflection of my concerns. He met all my looks with a slight smile.

I felt relieved when the bill finally arrived. The diplomat didn't let us pay for anything, not even leave a tip.

"When we go to Russian place — you pay. Turkish place — I pay." he uttered. "I am a diplomat. I don't pay tax... Taxes in this country!"

Then he gave Shawn a prolonged look as if he wanted to add something but returned to the bill without making a sound.

I started searching my mind for a possible decent reason not to come back home and not to have Adil with us, as he had already shown his concern regarding where we were going and when I was expected to be at home. The best possible excuse I could come up with in a span of seconds, was to visit Shawn's pregnant sister, who happened to live nearby.

"If you will need any help, don't be hesitate, call me," the diplomat said in an official manner before he gave Shawn a semi-judging look and started to walk toward home.

Speechless, we watched him walk away for a few seconds. I couldn't believe we were finally free.

"Wow! This guy is something else!" Shawn concluded, mocking Adil's heavy accent. "I am accomplishing a mission here... I am a diplomat!"

I couldn't stop laughing. I laughed to the point of not being able to walk properly, constantly hitting Shawn with my shoulder, trying to find support for my weakened body. He did such a great job, copying Adil, that one would easily confuse the original with the duplicate.

Although the situation was very funny, the awareness of the downside of it started drilling into my mind. I had to live with that guy. I had to share the space, the kitchen, the bathroom, the hallway, the entrance door — everything besides my bedroom. This night would pass by, and Shawn would go back to Jamaica, but I'd be the one who'd have to come back to the funny diplomat and live under the same roof with him. This thought frightened me. Yet, I decided not to verbalize it and enjoy the night.

"Anyway," Shawn smiled, getting out of Adil's heavy accent, "let's find a place to drink to Dmitry to get his visa!"

Shortly after, we found ourselves in an Albanian bar a few blocks away from the building I would soon start calling home. It was so crowded, that we could barely move around. They served us French fries, chicken wings, and free tequila shots, which kept us full and happy for the good part of the night.

After we laughed out all our tears, Shawn told me that Ron found a new girl to work in his bar. He said she was Trinidadian, seventeen years old. She sneaked through the Mexican-American border a few days ago. Now she is a bartender.

"If you could only see Ron's sparkling eyes when he found out there is a newcomer in the Trinidadian community!" Shawn said. "He hired her right away."

"Oh my God," I cried, feeling sorry for the girl. "If he hasn't started harassing her yet, he will get there very soon."

Shawn took a deep breath and grabbed a piece of chicken, "It's really hard to be an immigrant. Especially for a girl. Especially if you just came here. The danger is everywhere."

"Right," I sadly agreed. "You don't have many rights, so everybody can take advantage of you."

Shawn coughed loudly. Then he looked straight into nowhere and murmured thoughtfully, "You know, maybe some girls won't mind doing it for Ron. He probably gives them some extra money or something they're in need of. Trinidad is such a poor country, who knows what kind of life this girl had there — maybe she is thankful for what she's got now."

"If she had such a bad life there, she would be thankful for the cash she'd make bartending. And if she'd decide to find a sugar daddy, she can look for him on her own, and find a better deal! Ron is just manipulating poor hopeless people!" I almost yelled. "If he is so horny, he should hire a prostitute! I'm sure they will gladly serve him!"

"Or not so gladly." Shawn laughed, looking at me and putting a chicken bone on a side of the plate.

Then he added, "I don't mean to insult you, but you are so naïve sometimes! First of all, you can't understand the entire situation, because you came from a different background. You never had to do any kinds of dirty jobs in Russia, you don't know how real poverty tastes. And that's great! I'm truly happy for you. Some people fight for every piece of bread since they are born. I'm not defending Ron, but we don't know what hell is and what heaven is for these girls. Second of all," he cleared his throat, "I don't think prostitutes love their job and really enjoy doing it. I'm sure, there is a sad story behind every prostitute."

I didn't know whether I agreed with him about prostitution or not. I didn't want to give it much thought. All I knew was that my anger towards Ron was growing.

"Nasty pedophile!" I managed to add. I had no more words.

The night passed by fast. In no time Shawn and I were walking toward my new home, both tired of laughing and drinking. I wasn't very excited about my first night in my new clean room. Shawn's car was parked by the entrance. He promised to drive carefully, and I promised to keep him updated on Dmitry's situation and my new life in general. It was 2 a.m. when I gave him a warm goodbye hug and went inside the building.

I heard the click from the inner side of the lock before I realized I tried to insert the wrong key. I pushed the door to open and walked in. Lights went on right away and I saw the sleepy face of my new roommate. I jumped from an unexpected surprise.

"Oh… I'm sorry. Did I wake you up?" I asked him in a stupor.

"No," he muttered angrily, "I need to tell you something."

"Okay," I agreed.

"Come in," he said, walking into the kitchen. He wore white boxers and a white sleeveless shirt, neglecting any type of shoes.

I took off my coat and followed him. He sat down and offered me a cup of tea, but I politely refused.

"You know," he uttered, taking his time and thinking to find proper words, "it's not good what you do."

"What do you mean?"

"It is wrong. Very wrong. The girl your age shouldn't go out with guys that late and drink."

"He is my friend…" I stated.

"It is very bad. Your boyfriend is coming soon but your behavior is so unacceptable. It is very bad, Ekaterina." Adil noticed angrily. "You should not be out with strange mans this late. You must be home after dinner. Only bad behavior woman's act like this."

"My boyfriend and I are contemporary people," I remarked nicely even though I found these comments absolutely unacceptable. "So, it's okay."

"Listen to me," he started. "This Shawn is a bad guy, I got it right away he walked in…"

"I'm so sorry, but I have to wake up in five hours from now," I got up. "I really have to sleep. I didn't sleep well the previous night. I'm sorry. Good night."

"Ekaterina," he started following me to my room, "woman's should not go to bars. Especially with mans."

"Okay." I uttered, closing my room's door, "Good night!"

I tried to think why he cared so much about what I did, especially, since it didn't cause him any trouble or inconvenience, but couldn't come up with a decent explanation. I felt that it was absolutely unfair to me, furthermore, unjust and rude, yet, as his roommate, I decided to remain calm and not to raise arguments. I only hoped he wouldn't bother us once Dmitry would arrive.

The next day at work started later than usual. I didn't hear my alarm and arrived at Steve's one and a half hour late with a terrible hangover and a huge bottle of water in my hands. I rushed to my desk as if nobody had noticed my absence, turned on the computer and picked up the first phone call.

"SteveCo, how can I help you?" I answered hoarsely.

"Come into my office," said Steve, and for the first time in the month of work, I could say he was mad.

His office was right next door, so I appeared there in a second.

"Sit down," he commanded.

I sat on the edge of a chair. And put my arms on the knees.

"I don't care what you did last night, I don't know what you did this morning, but I do care to see you here exactly the time we open the warehouse!" he yelled the last word so loudly, that a bit of an echo reflected in the air.

"I'm so sorry," I murmured, looking down. "It won't happen again."

"It's been two hours." he exaggerated, and I didn't feel like correcting him.

"I'm so sorry. I promise it won't happen again." I repeated.

"I don't care if you broke up with your boyfriend, moved to a new place, or found a new friend or anything else on Earth had happened to you. Just be responsible!" he yelled the entire sentence and moved closer to me to look into my eyes.

I looked back at him and saw so much anger in his eyes. I wouldn't think being late could get someone so upset. At the same time, I knew it was my fault and I should have at least found a way to inform him that I couldn't make it on time.

"It will never happen again, I guarantee." I pronounced.

"Go do your work now." Steve uttered, and turned back to his messy pile of papers.

I came back to my desk empty and exhausted. I felt like the entire day was going to be bad. It was only Monday.

After that incident, I started hating Steve's job even more. It was boring, low paid, and now, rude. It was my main torture of the day; every day. Things started to happen the way I didn't expect them to be, every morning I woke up to go to the job I hated, and every night I finished work to return to the place I didn't like. I would get into the apartment before the diplomat and quickly sneak into my room. Staying there with lights off, I would hear his footsteps approaching my door and freezing by it, as he was trying to find out whether I was inside. He would call my cell phone and touch the door's handle. Thankfully, he never tried to open it. He would go to his room eventually, leaving me with gloomy thoughts of what was going on.

Once something bad starts and grabs all your attention, it makes all the things go wrong, everything turns upside down and the more you focus on it, the more damage it causes. After all these unpleasant incidents, I lost my job at catering "because it got slow", and all my hopes to find inner peace disappeared.

Three days of losses got squeezed into a long emotional day that never seemed to end or change and was bothering and worrying me deep inside, until the judgment morning arrived, and I called across the ocean to find out what my future was going to be like.

And the answer was "Yes". He got the visa.

CHAPTER 5

I couldn't remember myself feeling elated after a sleepless night on a rainy morning. I was trying to recall the last time I had so much excitement and love for life. Was it the day I got admitted to Clark University? Was it the moment my mom approved my desire to travel abroad? Was it when I met Dmitry for the first time? Or when I realized I was in love with him? I couldn't recall what was the last occasion that made me feel so happy. Everything that happened in past seemed unimportant.

I was trying hard to suppress my emotions at work. I loved everything I did. I loved every piece of paper I scanned, every invoice I printed, and every phone call I answered. I could barely hide my smile. I wanted to dance.

After negotiating the time, I could leave the office, Steve and I agreed on 4 p.m. Yet, I left at 3, as I saw his car driving away from the office gate. I didn't care whether the rest of the employees noticed my absence or not. I didn't care about anything in the world at that moment. I was going to JFK airport to meet the love of my life.

I arrived almost one hour prior to the landing. It equaled an eternity to me. Not being able to focus on reading the book I carried all the way in my purse, I was walking back and forth from wall to wall of the 2nd terminal. My hands were shaking just as on the first innocent date. I tried to calm down, practising breathing exercises, but my rapid heartbeat kept disturbing the process, so I quickly gave up.

I thought, my worn-out heart wouldn't handle the moment I would meet Dmitry. It became almost impossible to breathe as passengers from his flight started showing up. I froze in an uncomfortable position, standing on my tip-toes to have a better view.

Then he appeared.

"Dima!" I screamed, getting through the crowd towards the line, which was forbidden to cross. "I'm here!"

Dmitry was the most handsome guy in the terminal, about six feet tall, slim, blond, with bright blue eyes and a charming smile. He wore a snow-white sweat suit and sneakers that instantly brought back memories from the recent, but almost forgotten past, in which I waited for him outside of the stadium after classes, very tired, but extremely happy. After his soccer games were over, we walked towards our homes together. The way was quite long, but it was never enough. At least for me.

"Dima!" I screamed louder.

He looked across the waiting faces of people as he had forgotten what I looked like. Then our eyes met.

"Katyusha!" he shouted, smiling and walking towards me. "I can't believe this!"

He threw his bag and a suitcase on the floor and squeezed me in his strong arms. I squeezed him back, feeling his heartbeat, the one, I thought, I might never feel again. We stood like that for decades or seconds, hugging each other tighter as we were trying to get into one another.

"I so missed you. I soooo missed you!" Dmitry finally exclaimed, placing his face in front of mine. There was so much love in that face.

I was looking at his sky-blue eyes, charming smile, and perfectly white teeth and couldn't believe it was happening. It felt like forever without him, and at the same time, now, in his arms, it felt like there was no distance in the past, there was no past.

I wanted to say many words but was afraid to break into tears.

"No more separations." I breathed, barely holding up.

"No more!" Dmitry repeated.

"I love you," I said.

"I love you too, Katyusha, I love you more than anything in the world!" he stated with the sweet and melodic voice I wanted to get dissolved in. I smiled and hugged him again, I couldn't get enough of it. I couldn't wait to get to our room together. I didn't believe I managed to survive so many months without him.

"So how was your flight?" I finally asked on the air train on the way home.

"Very exhausting. Very long." he smiled tiredly. "Food wasn't great, but service was good."

"Never saw so many classic Jewish people, you know, in black hats and with curls," he added. "It felt like we were going to Israel."

"You'll see even more in Brooklyn." I laughed.

The apartment's door magically opened itself before I managed to insert a key into the lock. Adil was at home. I cursed him in my mind.

"Heeeey. Welcome. Welcome, my friend," he greeted Dmitry.

"Thank you," Dmitry said with an innocent Russian accent, shaking Adil's hand.

"How was your flight?"

"Okay. Good." Dmitry answered.

"I know. I know," my roommate laughed, keeping us indoors. "You know I used to like to fly before, but lately too much trouble for me."

Dmitry laughed and nodded without understanding what his new Turkish friend said.

Adil stood by the entrance in his fancy business suit and smiled widely as if it was his happy day and his loved one arrived. I felt annoyed.

"He doesn't speak much English," I started to speed up the greeting. "He is very tired."

I forced a smile and dragged Dmitry's suitcase into the room.

"Oh… how is he going to look for job if he don't speak much English?" I heard Adil's concern while we were entering the room.

Dmitry didn't feel comfortable turning his back on his new roommate. I hadn't told him about bothersome Adil yet. I had to tell him so many things.

"We'll figure," I uttered.

"You know…" he continued, taking his time remembering words and walking towards us, "I think he might… may register for a professional language school. He must try."

"We'll figure," I repeated angrily, hiding my boyfriend in the depth of our room and shutting the door. "See you later."

As soon as we locked the bedroom door from the inside, we started kissing like never before, hungry for the taste of each other, for the reimbursement of what we missed, for the happiness, for love. We were removing each other's clothes impatiently, madly, ripping off buttons and threads out of stitches. We were kissing and biting, whispering non-verbal moans, and tasting, tasting, tasting. Our restless breath filled the room, and as it seemed, the space outside of it, it filled the entire world outside. I couldn't hold it any more and started to moan, savoring every moment of that magic trip. I didn't care whether Adil could hear us. I didn't care about anything. None of us was able to control the situation, as we became one inseparable creature in the middle of the universe.

It seemed like a dream from which I didn't want to wake up. It seemed like a fairy tale. How could I survive all these long months without him? How could I even doubt the decision to reunite? How could I think I was happy before that very moment? I didn't know.

Exhausted and joyful we spend an hour just holding each other. Then Dmitry passed out. I was watching his gorgeous and calm face in a state of deep sleep for hours. I couldn't believe it was him, real him, there, with me. Nothing seemed important any more, neither the immigration issues, nor annoying job hunting, there was just that one moment — beautiful and endless.

The very next day, our biggest adventure began, the adventure of exploring harmony, insanity, connections and reactions of love. I was overly ambitious, he was shyly curious, and together we were almost a family.

His professional camera instantly got filled with panoramas of Central Park, Rockefeller Building, Statue of Liberty, Brooklyn Bridge, Times Square, MoMA inside out, Metropolitan Museum, random people and restaurant dishes. Every minute carried endless supplies of joy, we were high on views, high on the 'new to Dmitry' climate, high on New York, high on each other. Just like two kids, we started to learn about the world from the beginning, all lost in its capital and each other's passion we were making the best of it.

Avoiding Adil became more of an amusing game. We moved as soundless as we could within the apartment on weekends and late at night, we threw coins to decide who was going to the kitchen for water or snacks, yet we agreed that if one of us gets into his trap of conversation, another one would have to come up and join the torture.

Everything we did, turned into a funny and engaging activity, seeing places, seeking places, being on time for events, escaping boring occasions, tasting free wine and snacks in museums or liquor stores. I was spending money I had saved as there was no tomorrow, as I had won a lottery. With all days off I begged out of Steve, I felt like I went on a little vacation, the sweet and beautiful vacation in New York with the man that meant the whole world to me.

I loved everything about Dmitry, the way he ate, the way he walked, the way he brushed his hair, even the way he sneezed. The biggest pleasure was seeing him happy.

"Marry me," he proposed once, standing on the red stairs of Times Square in black pants and dressy shoes, stretching out his right hand to me.

"Okay," I responded flirty, using his hand to get up the stair. "When?"

"I would marry you tomorrow if I were a citizen. I would marry you right now!" he smiled, squeezing me in his arms. I squeezed him back. Sudden chilling rain scared people off of the stairs. Everyone ran, covering their heads with plastic bags, newspapers, anything they had handy that wet cold evening. Only we remained there. We held each other as if nothing was happening, laughing loudly at people, at the weather, at noting in particular, all soaking wet, without money and real home, but with love for life and for each other, incredibly happy and high.

"Let's not delay with legalization in this country!" Dmitry kept saying. "Sooner we'll do, sooner we can marry and live like normal people."

We dreamed a lot. Sometimes we would take a train and go to Brighton Beach at night, smuggling a cheap bottle of wine. We would climb up a lifeguard's seat, wide enough for two people and gaze at ocean, talking about eternity, the Universe, and everything that would come to our minds. It would be cold, so we would cuddle, wrap up in each other and sip the wine right from the bottle.

"You are my universe," he once shouted, raising the bottle of wine up as to cheer with the ocean. "You are my universe! I'm living inside of you! I want to marry you, to buy a house somewhere in suburbs of New York and raise... let's say... two more little universes together."

We often fell asleep right on the lifeguard seat. We would wake up to the chilling breath of dawn, in each other's arms, and go home exhausted but happy.

I acquired a habit of arriving to work late and tired. Steve got in a habit of screaming at me. Theoretically, we were both wrong, but practically he was always right. I had nothing left to do, but to apologize and silently look at the stains on his glasses with a secret desire to wipe them off, while he was breaking his throat getting overly vocal. I knew that at the end of a day he could find someone like me any time, but would I be able to quickly find a similar position? I had jobless Dmitry to support. Steve started giving me more tasks and made me stay at work longer, while my boyfriend was waiting outside, on the cold winterish street, under the noisy F train passing by every five minutes.

"Don't worry," Dmitry comforted me, "you won't stay there forever. Once you'll become a successful writer, this idiot will regret everything."

I only hugged him stronger. He was my biggest support.

"Just think about it, he will always be there, under this annoying train, doing his annoying work, which obviously doesn't make him happy. And you — you will become a famous writer. This is just a stage for you, and it's a lifelong mission for him."

With Dmitry I didn't feel homeless at all. I felt I was at home. He was my home, comfortable and cozy little mobile home. I would feel great anywhere, if he would be beside me.

We took a look at a few jobs on Craigslist, offered by Russian-speaking people. They were mostly hiring movers, busboys, dishwashers, cleaners, and construction workers. We agreed that this would be his first step. Not a dream job, but something to get going.

I spent $100 to buy him a suit from the discount store around the corner, a few more dollars to get him a cell phone and connect it to a provider. We created his resume rather full of exaggerations and lies, pretty much like any other resume. I was sure Dmitry would get accepted to the first position he'd be interviewed for. There was no way anyone would stay indifferent towards him.

However, he had steady bad luck. I kept getting his text messages, which informed me of how badly he was treated at interviews, managers were rude, owners were mean and demanding. I only suggested not to get discouraged. It is not easy to find a job as a foreigner, especially without any knowledge of English and a work permit. Employers, that didn't necessarily care about their business being legally organized, often manipulated illegal residents or newcomers, knowing they didn't have any choice.

I didn't mind supporting both of us for a while. We had no extra funds, only money for food, transportation and bills. At the same time, we didn't need anything else, enjoying each other was all we could ask for those days. Every night I returned from work to get wrapped in his cozy arms, and it would make me forget about everything that bothered me.

Probably for the first time in my life, I was so strong and confident, nothing could discourage or disappoint me. Even when I lost the job at Steve's due to being late and "being stupid", even when I realized Dmitry wasn't looking for jobs and learning English while I was struggling to support us. He just never made it to any of the interviews for unknown to me reasons. I let it go. He wasn't supporting me, but he was my biggest support.

He helped me choose clothing for new interviews, he polished my shoes, and even ironed my blouses.

"Who is this?" Dmitry asked all of a sudden, once he saw a message from Shawn that said, "Missing you, Kate. How is Dmitry liking it here?"

"Oh, I wanted to introduce you guys, long time ago, but he was busy working." I exclaimed, brushing my hair in front of a mirror built in the wall of the room. "Shawn, I told you about him. My friend, I met him in the bar I worked in Queens!"

Dmitry squinted his eyes on me in suspicion. After a few seconds of silent questions, he looked back at my cell phone and began digging in it with aggressive strength, as he was trying to find proof of his suspicion. It was the first time I saw him so angry. My memory took me back in time to one of the Astrakhan evenings, when he found "I love you" from Vera and didn't believe it was her. I asked myself whether he actually started disliking her after that.

"What's the matter?" I sat next to him on the edge of the bed. He seemed more like a stranger than my Dmitry.

"Nothing," he snapped, "tell this son of a bitch you are done with him."

"What?" I asked helplessly.

"And then delete this idiot. You are mine, but he acts like he can contact you anytime anywhere. He is nobody to miss you!"

"Hey!" I muttered. "Are you jealous?"

"I don't trust anybody," he said, giving me an irritated look, "It's me or him"

"Please, stop it, Dima! He is my friend, he did help me so much with finding jobs, and moving. And he was so excited when he learned you got a visa!" I explained helplessly. "You don't understand how his friendship is important to me."

"I see," he let out, "even more than me."

He hit the button to dial Shawn's number and passed the phone to me.

"Stop it!" I yelled, trying to hang up.

"Me or him." he asserted.

I gave Dmitry a frustrated look and met his eyes full of madness and hatred. Then Shawn picked up.

"Hey girl!" he answered happily "It's been a long while!"

"I know," I agreed sadly.

"Is everything all right?" he asked.

That voice was so warm and positive, it felt like a breath of spring entered my heart in the middle of a cold winter. That very moment related me to him even more, it felt like he was my close relative, I had never thought about him this way before.

"Tell him!" Dmitry shouted in English.

"Shawn," I started, barely holding up from breaking into tears, "you are a great guy…"

"No great guy." Dmitry managed to yell in English.

"What's going on there?" Shawn murmured politely, and seconds of awkward clean silence passed between us.

"My boyfriend doesn't want us to continue our friendship." I finally said it.

"Oh…"

"I'm so sorry, I'm so very sorry…." I was almost crying.

"No sorry," Dmitry shouted, then grabbed my phone and snapped "bye" before he aggressively hung up.

"See, it was easy!" he giggled sarcastically.

"It was." I sighed, thinking about Shawn's kind eyes.

I felt so miserable at that moment. I thought I would rather not have a friend like Shawn than have him and lose him in such an offensive-betraying manner. I felt helpless.

"It's okay," Dmitry smiled and hugged me warmly. "You'll find new friends, just let them be girls, all right?"

I found new friends and a new job right away. It was a men's clothing store at Flatbush Avenue, ruled by Russian-speaking Jews, packed with illegal immigrants taught to fool customers. I had never seen anything similar before, Russian jail songs were playing all day long, gangster-looking shoppers were overpaying for cheap poor-quality suits and fake brand-name shoes of the wrong sizes. Salespeople had no rest or money, but lots of respect for the boss. My wage started and ended at $7 per hour.

"It's okay!" Dmitry kept saying. "It's a temporary job until you'll find a better one."

Yet it took me more than a month to realize, that he got comfortable doing nothing. He didn't go to any interviews since he came to the country, he didn't earn a penny. He played computer games, drank beer and ate chips. He stopped fetching me from work as he did before. He would open the apartment's door with a wide smile and ask one question, "what's for dinner." He would kiss me on my forehead, my eyes, my nose, and say how much he loved me and how great it was to live together, and I would melt. He was new to the country. He probably still had a cultural shock. He was not that kind of person. He would never let me down.

I couldn't live without him. That was something I knew for sure.

Dmitry was the only child in the family, the same as me. Yet, unlike me, he had both loving parents who gave him warmth and support, and taught him to feel special and needed. He called them almost every day. I never got to meet them.

The job at the Flatbush Avenue store was extremely exhausting. Every day started at 9 am and finished 12 hours later. I and a bunch of other illegal immigrants had to sell clothing to local men twice or trice the price than they really were. We were taught to lie about prices, quality, brand names, sizes, and countries of origin of suits, shirts, jeans, and shoes to thankful prospects. "That's my store, man! That's my store!" they would often claim.

You wouldn't see any prices there, each item had a small tag with a triangle, square, star, or a circle, which specified the lowest amount it could be sold for. Prices we voiced were much higher than the lowest range, so if a customer bargained, we had a room for negotiation. If someone still wanted a better deal, we had to ask the boss "for a special discount". The boss would stand by the counter with a cigarette between his lips and an attitude of a God and give a customer a prolonged thoughtful look. Then he would say in a heavy Russian accent, "Okay, my friend. Only for you, because you always shop here. Don't tell anybody else I gave you such price!"

After getting a "good deal" a customer would leave the store happy and grateful, not knowing that he paid at least twice of what it really cost. None of us got any commission for overcharging, only a wide employer's smile. We worked for pure enthusiasm. We were girls and guys in our early twenties; friendly, talented, and full of hopes for the future. Ready to change the world, we all had only one common problem — we were illegal.

I was surprised by how friendly all the salespersons were. Always willing to help one another, cover up for each other, lend money, switch days off, and go out after tiring and busy weekends. I got along with everyone right as I started working. I made friends and acquaintances, and got really close with a smiley positive girl, Natasha. She was about 5.2, slightly chubby and clumsy. She liked wearing tunics; she had plenty of them, all of different colors and structures, lengths, and styles. Her unnaturally-bright green eyes, in combination with orange curly hair, made her face look like a painting, a painter of which was a happy life-loving person. She came here on a "Work and Travel" program for one summer but stayed for a few years. She kept thinking she would make more money and go back home, graduate from the university and start working in an oil company just like her uncle. Yet, as time passed by, she began liking the U.S. more and more, comparing it to Russia and its Russian mentality. Then Natasha met Kostya, a member of Brooklyn's Russian mafia, and decided to stay here. Her mother didn't approve of it and stopped talking to her. Natasha called her, messaged her, and used all other methods to get in touch and explain everything, but nothing worked. Eventually, she gave up and started sending her one email a month just to let her know that Natasha was alive and okay. The mother never replied. Only from a younger sister, my new friend would learn that everything was all right at home; that her mother was perfectly fine, and that nothing seemed to bother her from the outside.

She was raised by her only parent as well. Her father left after her sister was born. He went straight to another woman who was younger and wealthier than her mother. Both daughters were prohibited to talk to their father, who refused to pay aliments and faked proof of income to make it legal. They grew up not knowing dad's love, same as me, same as many other children in Russia.

Natasha missed her mother. She slightly envied me having my mom on my side and suggested taking good care of her. I wished I could. I missed my mother, too. And a few times I was about to give up my American struggle, but she happened to be the only one to encourage me to move ahead. She was the only one who was always sure I would get what I want. She suffered a lonely life without me, struggling with the terrible back pain on the eighth floor of an old soviet residential building. She needed me. But for my own sake, she didn't want me to return to the country of lies and corruption.

Natasha introduced me to Kostya right after a few days of working together. Regardless of all my fears, he turned out to be a very sweet and friendly person. He performed so many roles in her life, he was her partner, he was her father, he was her caring brother, a good friend, and of course, a powerful defence.

Dmitry didn't like hanging out with strangers, no matter how much I wanted him to meet my new acquaintances. Disproportionally with me getting social, he was turning more and more uncommunicative. He claimed he was antisocial. He said he had always been antisocial and never really liked people. I started discovering a new side of him, the side I had never known before.

"Is he okay?" Adil would ask from time to time. "He never talk me word."

I didn't know how to respond.

"Does he have job?" seemed to be the most important question for our roommate.

"He does," I lied.

Since Adil was barely home, I thought it was fine to lie. I felt it was a rule of the house, not to accept any jobless people.

About twice a week at night, as I would crawl to the kitchen to have a glass of water, Adil would immediately jump out of his room, all sleepy and tired, in his white underwear, turning on the light and staring at me dazed. The brightness would make me squint and hide my unadjusted eyes.

"Is everything all right?" he would ask me, coming closer

"Yes," I would answer annoyed, thinking that the commitment with Dmitry to help the one who gets into Adil's trap seemed to be expired.

"You sure? You look tired." he would examine my eyes like a doctor at an appointment.

"I'm just sleepy…" I'd say, showing my irritation and stepping back.

He would grab my shoulders and squeeze them.

"Ekaterina! You can say me! I am the officer, I know. I can read people. You don't look okay."

"Because of this bright light, Adil! I'm sleepy!"

He would stand semi-mad in the middle of the kitchen, taking his time on finding proper words.

"Is he upset you? Humiliate you?"

His eyes would also be red from the light. I wondered why it was so important to him to get up in the middle of the night and talk to me.

"No, Adil, everything is perfectly fine!" I would tell him.

He would think about more words and sentences, but not being able to find them he would ask, "Why don't you sleep then?"

"I was sleeping. I got up to have a glass of water."

"I have to wake up in a couple of hours, good night." I would tell him and turn around to walk back to my room.

"Ekaterina!" he tried to grab my attention one of these nights.

I looked back at him with anger and impatience.

"I grew up in poor family," he giggled nervously. "In poor village. I have three more siblings. I am only one who success. Succeeded. Nobody helped me. I made money for college and studied for life. Good life. Honest life."

He smiled and stepped closer to me.

"That's why I became successful. I developed my own strength during hard times. I moved to the capital and became honest police officer and diplomat. None siblings is working. Why? Because they comfortable living on my money with my old — very old — mother."

"What I want to say, Ekaterina," he concluded, "help is no always good. Sometimes it is better to throw people into life and let them explore themselves."

I had no idea, what exactly he knew about Dmitry. I developed sympathy for him from the story I learned. I felt sorry for all his efforts left unappreciated by his family. I thought he was a great person until the next night, he met me in the kitchen and continued annoying me.

Dmitry changed a lot since he arrived. With days and weeks that passed, he stopped being ashamed of living on my salary and not trying to change the situation. His attitude affected his personality as well, and from the caring and tender gentleman he was, he grew into a moody teenager. There were a few times I talked to him about getting at least a part-time job, but he turned all my offers down.

"Am I too stupid to clean apartments or do construction? I'm a smart handsome guy and I want to do normal work." he would get really mad.

"It's not about that!" I would argue. "I don't think I'm too stupid and ugly to work where I work. But no normal position has been offered to me so far. It's all temporary until something better will come up."

"But you are illegal!" he would scream. "And I'm not."

"But you are on a tourist visa, you can't be officially employed as well." I would respond.

"I won't do any crappy jobs," he would finally say, "I'll wait until I get the one that's worth my potential."

Okay… I thought I would wait a little longer.

These conversations would always upset me. I could have chosen to sit home and wait until a better job would come along, but who would pay our bills then?

He would smile afterwards and give me one of his warmest hugs, telling me that everything would be fine, and the day would come when we would turn into rich American citizens. He would kiss my eyes, forehead, and lips, and disclose how much he loves me. I would forget about everything on earth. At the end of the day, what's more important than love?

Sometimes I thought I was too pushy with him. I also thought I was too unprepared to invite him to a foreign country. I blamed myself as he did. Natasha kept saying I was wrong and as a gentleman, he was supposed to work and help me, instead of being dependent on me. She heard all my possible excuses for him and didn't find any of them substantial.

"He has to work, damn ass!" she uttered. "Your roommate is so right, he has to!"

"Kostya offered me to take care of me," she shared with a smile, "but I don't want to depend on anybody."

I agreed with that. I wouldn't want to be supported by anybody either.

"I love him, but I prefer to spend my own money," she said. "You know unless I'm pregnant or something."

Natasha met Kostya simply in a bar, where he was often relaxing with his mafia partners. She came there with her girlfriend and was about to leave when the crowd of "not too sober guys" flew into the spot. She paid for drinks and sat quietly, waiting for a girlfriend to use the bathroom. All of a sudden, she heard, "Don't go."

The voice was coming from behind her back. It was like music. Don't go.

She turned around and saw a face that was cute and drunk at the same time. It was tender and masculine, happy and serious, and very brave. She couldn't stop herself from smiling, even though she tried.

"Don't go," he repeated.

And she said, "Okay."

On one of the days of that endless tiring routine, I left work much earlier. As I quietly entered the apartment, right before I wanted to announce my arrival, I accidentally heard Dmitry's Skype conversation with his parents. They were offering to send money. How great was my disappointment when he refused the offer! He said, "I'm fine. I'm a big boy."

"I'm so proud of you, son!" his father responded, barely holding up from crying.

"I always knew you'd do it! Your mother and I are admiring you moving to the foreign country and living on your own, supporting yourself without speaking the language," he added emotionally.

I lost my balance for a few seconds, standing by the entrance door and trying to calm my breath. Through the thin line between the door and the wall, I could see him enjoying himself and sipping a beer. A couple of empty potato chip bags were sitting on the floor next to the plate of food.

"Proud of you?" I asked, walking inside the room, once he finished the conversation. I was full of anger and sadness. I was disappointed. I remembered Vera saying he was only using me to come to the U.S. For the first time I thought, she might be right.

"Were you listening? Such a bad manner," Dmitry threw at me.

"Proud of what exactly? That your girlfriend works 12 hours a day to make sure you have a place to live in and food to eat?" I yelled.

"Stop it!" he snapped, turning away from me and walking towards the kitchen. He looked tipsy.

I walked after him and grabbed his shoulder from the back.

"No, honey, it won't work like this," I stated angrily, "It is unfair that I have to work hard to support you. I can't look for a better job, because I have nothing saved, I can't save because I spend so much money on you. And it's been almost two months!"

"What do you want from me?" he laughed, filling the kettle with water from the sink.

"I'm not paying the rent for the next month. Whatever will happen, I'm not paying."

"Fine," Dmitry said playfully, still not looking at me. "This Turk likes you, he'll just let you suck his dick — and the problem is solved."

I couldn't believe what I heard. It was out of my imagination.

"What did you say?" I asked.

"Listen, just leave me alone," he threw, very annoyed, putting the cattle on the stove and looking for the bag of his favorite tea in a cabinet.

I tried to stay sane. I quickly analyzed whether it was me, the inadequate one. I must have done something wrong to turn him against me. For a second, I thought he was jealous of Shawn, yet, it had nothing to do with the money.

"What I wanted to say is that it's unfair I have to work so much and neglect my sleep and rest to support two people. Why don't you let your parents send you some money since they offered?"

"I want them to be proud of me!" he snapped, walking back to the bedroom. "Don't worry, I'll get a job and will pay you back every penny you spent on me! Now leave me alone, I'm too tired."

"Tired from what?" I followed him to the bedroom.

He didn't answer. I waited a bit longer, watching him get comfortable on the bed with my laptop.

"You know," I sighed, "I'm moving out. I don't care. I'm not paying for you any more. Enough is enough."

He shut the laptop, got up, grabbed my shoulders and looked into my eyes so deeply.

"If you dare to do something like this, I'll call immigration right away. And you will go to prison and then to Russia for good. You are illegal! I-LLE-GAL"

Then he released me and walked back to the kitchen, holding my laptop under his arm.

I sat down on the edge of the bed. I was looking at the wall. I didn't think about what he had said and whether he really meant it. I was hurt by the thought, that he didn't love me. He didn't care about me. He used me to come to this country, and now, when I started demanding appreciation, he showed he had none.

I went over our history and his behavior before and after arriving here, his words and promises which never came true, circumstances that made us break up in Russia, circumstances that made us fight in the U.S. I thought that I was such a fool to get involved in this again and acquire a burden to carry through my already not so easy immigrant life. I turned frustrated and confused, and the awareness of the mistake I made came way too late. It struck me with powerful strength, just like in thrillers, when a character is looking for a mysterious creature, investigating throughout the plot, not perceiving until the end that the mysterious creature is the character himself.

How far could he get with this? How far could I get? I needed to remain calm, at least, till I figured out what to do. I told myself, I would find a solution once I managed to get my clear mind back.

We hadn't been talking much for a week after that. Dmitry apologized for the recent scene indifferently, making it sound as if he was stressed out himself, not having any money or a job. I didn't raise that subject again. I didn't ask for anything and didn't discuss anything with him. I just stopped buying groceries for home and leaving cash on the table every morning. I started to enjoy being at work, among bright and happy people. We would grab a drink a couple of times a week after work. We would talk about Russia, about what was missed the most, and what we loved America for, the country we all hoped to remain in. We would discuss immigration news and share hopes for certain laws to pass and make legalization easier. We were young and full of strength, and after we left everything we knew behind, we didn't have much to fear. Only a long way to go.

I didn't rush home after work any more. On the days we didn't go for drinks, I bought shots of vodka or gin and sipped them on the way home. I would listen to my favorite music in headphones and enjoy an hour of slow walking — it was the only joy I could afford. I started saving money secretly.

"Come on, baby," Dmitry said one of those days, "you don't want me to die from hunger."

"I'm not supporting you any more," I stated.

"You brought me to this country, you are the one who is responsible for me," he murmured playfully, trying to kiss me.

I quickly removed myself from his arms.

"I didn't force you to come," I declared. "You were the one who wanted."

"Yes, because you didn't want to come back to Russia." he smiled.

"This conversation makes no sense." I noticed. "We speak different languages."

He hugged me and pulled me to the bed, starting to kiss my neck and unbuttoning my shirt.

"If I'd say I don't want to be responsible for you, would you go back to Russia?" I asked.

"No," he looked at me playfully.

"I'm very serious right now," I uttered.

He began kissing my ear and whispering, "Come on, baby, who cares about stupid money. You are making just enough to support both of us. The time will come, and I'll find a good job to support both of us, so you'll be able to work on your English and write. At the end of the day, what's more important than love?"

"I don't trust you!" I yelled. "It's just unbelievable!"

"Yes, I am unbelievable and unpredictable. Stop talking, let's make love. You have been avoiding me lately." he moaned.

I pushed him away and sat on the bed.

"You are not going to get a penny from me any more!" I yelled. "We didn't agree on that, I want to be able to save and find a different job, I don't want to carry a burden with my already complicated life."

He got up and laughed.

"Fine! Then I'm calling the immigration department. They will be here in a minute! In case you move, I know where you work and how to find you!"

"What are you going to do then?" I asked sarcastically.

"I'll figure something out," he winked at me.

I was thinking how impossible the entire situation was. I became illegal precisely because of him. If only I could turn back the time, I would never help him to move here, I would never reply to his first email, I would apply for work authorization in Clark, and by now, I'd probably have a better job with possibilities of extending the work visa. My entire present would be so different. Yet I couldn't go back in time.

I wanted to smash his face.

"What are you trying to achieve, Dmitry?" I inquired. "What is the point of it? What's next?"

"I'm only asking you to support me while I don't have a proper job."

"What is a proper job for you?"

"Something related to soccer or computers. You know, I was always good with computers."

"How long do you think it will take you to find one?"

"How am I supposed to know?"

"Listen," I asserted, trying to keep myself calm, "you are not doing anything to find a job, and it's been two months."

"You know what?" he smirked, "You should be happy I'm willing to be with you, regardless of your ugly arm. Who else will put up with this disgust?"

All of a sudden, everything I had been living for vanished at once. It felt like the sun wasn't shining outside any more, and no more was the wind blowing. I was all alone in the whole world. Pain and tears got stuck in my throat. I had nothing to say.

Nothing was holding me to Dmitry any longer. Dull pain inhabited my heart and drilled a hole in it. I forced myself not to think about my hurt feelings, no matter how hard it was, and began constructing my escape plan. I needed a new place to live and a new job.

I told the boss that I had to leave because my ex-boyfriend might be chasing me there, and unexpectedly for me, he turned very empathetically.

"Anytime, Katya," he said. "Take care of your needs first and just let me know when you'll find a new job. You're always welcome to come back here."

I was truly touched and impressed, as I prepared myself for a fight rather than support.

Sooner than later, I got hired as a waitress at a Brighton Beach restaurant. I didn't know whether it was better or worse than working in the store, but I was grateful to take the first step away from Dmitry.

It was a bit sad to leave Flatbush Avenue. Knowing of my last day there, Natasha baked a cake and the guys brought some champagne. Right after the last customer left, we locked the door and organized a little party. The place I worked for barely a month, treated me as part of a family. I was very thankful and emotional, more than that, I promised to stop by sometime some time in future. I knew I was not going to come back there to work.

The new job didn't have much to offer, minimum wage, and minimum tips. This small restaurant right under the railroad of everlasting Brighton Beach Avenue was a second home to loads of illegals, mostly girls from Kazakhstan and Uzbekistan. They didn't speak any English, nor did they need it there.

A bunch of bald-headed Russian guys in their late twenties and elderly soviet men and women dressed in fur would stop by for cheap, partially prepared food and a few shots of vodka. Some would stay there endlessly, getting drunk and eventually falling asleep on tables. The restroom would be out of service quite often.

I celebrated my first New Year in the U.S. working in a restaurant. It was a strange and new 2010 to me. I had put a lot of hope in it, right at the beginning of the year, by drinking champagne with strangers and wishing everybody all the best. In Russia, we say, "the new year is going to be the way you celebrate it". That was a sad one, meaning the entire year I would spend with strangers. A year of solitude.

At least I'll always have myself, I laughed at this thought.

I was allowed to work a double shift, which perfectly fit into my Flatbush store's hours, so Dmitry wouldn't guess I changed the job. Little by little, with my new boss's permission, I started bringing personal items to work — whatever could fit in the backpack. Dmitry was always at home, which made it complicated. The only way to move out was to go to work one random day and never come back.

Finding a room became a new problem since I had spent all my money and didn't earn enough yet to pay a deposit and one-month rent. I was ready to sleep in the restaurant, on the mattress in the kitchen, but was too embarrassed to ask the boss about it.

After a long week of search, I finally found a room that didn't require any deposit at all; furthermore, the owner took weekly payments of $100. The room was furnished, pretty big and sunny. Everything seemed to be fine, except the safety of the neighborhood. It wasn't a good-looking area, and a young girl like me attracted way too much unsolicited attention. However, I had no other choice.

The following day I brought some of my belongings to my "new home" in a black garbage bag. I walked around the new room, sat on the sofa, and wished myself a smooth run. A mild excitement of breaking free was tickling my stomach.

The next day, I had a short shift at the restaurant due to moving. I needed to pick up the rest of my stuff from the apartment along with my two, now half-empty suitcases, and I had no idea how I was going to do that, Dmitry was always at home. I went through all possible scenarios and outcomes, but all of them crushed badly with him calling immigration. A light hope entered my mind along with a new idea. I didn't know whether it was going to work, however, I didn't have the luxury of choice, nor I had any time to think.

Dmitry was playing video games on my laptop. He faked a smile when he saw me walking in.

"Thank God it's you!" he giggled. "I thought the Turk was entering our room."

"Oh…" I mumbled.

"Why are you so early? It's not even 6!" he asked, continuing looking at the laptop screen.

"I don't feel well," I said tiredly, "my boss let me go home."

"Oh… I'm sorry," he let out without looking at me.

I took my coat off and sat on the edge of the bed, next to him.

"I passed out at work. I got some bad flu, I think." I murmured.

"No way!" he looked at me for the first time. "You do look tired, lie down here."

He moved towards the other end of the bed and closed the laptop. I tried to look as miserable as I could. He put the laptop away and touched my forehead, then my hair, then whispered, "I'm sorry."

"May I ask you for a favor?" I moaned.

"Sure!" he uttered.

"Would you go to the pharmacy to get me some flu medicine?" I asked quietly.

He thought for a few seconds, then responded, "Okay".

The closest pharmacy was about ten minutes away. I as well counted in a minimum of five minutes of buying the variety of medications I wrote down for him to get. I could barely hide my excitement and calm down my heartbeat. I couldn't believe that my plan was working, and that he was really getting outside of the apartment.

I gave him the list with names of drugs and vitamins, and $50 cash after he got dressed and was ready to go.

"I really appreciate it, thank you," I whispered, trying to look as sick as I could.

He sat on the bed, held my hand and kissed me on my forehead. Then he looked at me with so much warmth and love.

"It's nothing. All I want is for you to be happy and healthy, my love."

A wave of regret went through my body.

Then he left.

I jumped out of bed right after the door sounded locked. Forcing myself not to think about what he said, I pulled suitcases out of the closet and started throwing whatever I had hanging. I emptied the room, then the bathroom; I threw the laptop on top of the mess I had in one of my bags. For a moment I felt as I was betraying Dmitry leaving him like that. I thought of his last warm look full of love and care. Then I reminded myself of him threatening me with calling the immigration police and hurting my feelings by commenting on my weakest spot. It helped me to pack faster.

I got ready in less than ten minutes. And in half of the time I gave myself to escape, I was already pulling my two almost empty suitcases towards the door. My heart was jumping and screaming out of the excitement and seemingly unrealistic accomplishment.

Then the entrance door lock clicked.

I froze in the position I was standing. The air turned greyish and my knees suddenly felt weak. The seconds between the first and the final click of the door seemed like long minutes. So many thoughts passed through my mind in a span of this short eternity, so many ideas, which failed before being fully considered. In my mind, I buried myself alive.

Right after the door got wide open, big Adil's head appeared in the light of the ceiling lamp. He closed the door from the inside and jerked as he turned to me. I felt both relieved and frightened.

"Ah!" he exclaimed. "You scare me, Ekaterina!"

Then he looked at my suitcases.

"What is going on? Are you leaving?" he asked in confusion.

My brain turned into a powerful computer which processed so many different operations in seconds, I thought of half a dozen of lies and excuses, that would help me to leave the apartment promptly. And then I decided to tell the truth. Adil might be a nagging fellow, but he didn't deserve such treatment.

"I'm leaving, Adil," I stated bravely. "I know I should have told you before, but I'm literally escaping from Dmitry. We broke up and I need to leave. Don't you worry, please, about the rent. His parents will send him money every month."

"So he don't have a job?" he looked shocked.

"Not yet." I speeded up, "Adil, please, I gotta go now, I'll explain everything later, but now I need to go. He'll be back in five-ten minutes, he won't let me leave."

"Okay." Adil agreed surprisingly. "I'll help you!"

He took my black suitcase and carried it outside of the apartment, then to the exit of the building. I walked right behind him dragging my orange suitcase and a bag, hoping that Dmitry was not returning yet. We went outside and Adil automatically turned right to get further from Kings Highway. I kept walking behind him, not able to believe he got so understanding and supportive. Since the day I moved in, I was thinking of him as a close-minded, and annoying person, who only likes to judge others and teach them how to live, and now, following him towards a safer place, I was regretting everything I thought of him to the point of remorse. I silently wished I were nicer and friendlier.

"So where are you going to live?" he asked me once we reached a quiet street four blocks down.

"Ah… It's east-ish…" I said.

"East-ish!" he laughed. "Okay, Ekaterina! Let's request a taxi."

I called a car service and turned off my phone to replace the sim card with the new one I recently got. I threw the old one in a trash can in a corner.

"Now you have a new number?" Adil asked shyly.

"I do. I don't remember it by heart, but I'll call you once I'll organize myself in a new place, okay?"

"Okay," he smiled, "call me, don't forget. I'm leaving the US in three months; I want to keep in touch with you."

"Oh, are you going back to Turkey?" I completely forgot he was here only on a temporary mission.

"Yes. I was thinking a lot about staying… But what will I do here? Work on the gas station?" he laughed louder. "America is not for everybody. New York is not for everybody."

I nodded.

"I'll miss you, Adil," I murmured sadly.

Then the cab arrived. Adil fitted both of my suitcases in the trunk and gave me a big, warm, prolonged hug. I also squeezed him in my arms, repeating "thank you, thank you so much for everything."

"You're welcome, Ekaterina!" he kissed me on my forehead. "You are a very good girl! Call me, don't forget me. Let me know if you need anything. I very… really mean it."

"Okay!" I smiled.

"Bye!" he said, shutting the car's door as I sat myself in the backseat.

"Bye," I repeated.

I could still see him seconds away. He was waving from the corner of Ocean Ave and Avenue R. Then we disappeared from each other's horizons. I felt like I had betrayed him by avoiding him and making fun of him behind his back. Only that day, did I realise how understanding and caring he could be. I would definitely call him as soon as I would get a chance. I would invite him to a Russian restaurant and would pay for it as I promised. I thanked him again in my mind.

My thoughts returned to Dmitry. A dull void filled my chest. How would he feel back in the empty room? The cruel memory threw me to the rainy gloomy Astrakhan day when a handsome guy approached me and playfully jumped under my umbrella. He smiled and straightened his hand to shake, saying, "Dmitry. You must be Ekaterina?" It was our first date.

My eyes started getting wet. I forced myself to stop thinking about it. I double-checked with my memory, that I suspended my Facebook page temporarily, and permanently got rid of my old Russian email. He wouldn't have any ways to contact me.

I thought about calling Shawn one of these days, now since I was free from my burden. I turned my cell phone on to check whether I had copied his number to a new sim card. I gladly noticed that I did. I checked for the numbers of Natasha, my new employer, some salespersons from Flatbush, and girls from my new job. Every number I needed was saved, even Dmitry's. Then something hit me like a thunderstorm — there was no Adil's number. I couldn't figure out how it was possible. I continued checking over and over again, I restarted my phone twice or thrice — it was unbelievable — no number. I tried to think about other ways of contacting him before he would go back to Turkey. I couldn't come back to that apartment, it was too risky to write him a letter, and I didn't even know where exactly he worked. He didn't have any profiles on social networks, nothing that could give me a way to get in touch. It was clear, I had lost him.

CHAPTER 6

It felt like another chapter of my life was over. I left Dmitry, and unfortunately, Adil in the past, moving towards a new, balanced and happy life. At least, I thought so.

I didn't like my new room. I delayed unpacking for a week. I had no wish to adapt to the apartment or the neighborhood, and my only happiness was being far from Dmitry, who I missed and hated at the same time. I took it as a temporary step till I would figure out something better. It was the beginning of January, a year since I arrived in the U.S.

The main Avenue that crossed my street was Nostrand. It was mostly full of liquor stores, cheap fried chicken places, and Chinese restaurants. People didn't seem too friendly, some of them looked like drug dealers, most of them — like drug addicts. The neighborhood reminded me of Worcester.

My room was a part of a two-bedroom apartment, where the living area was occupied by a pregnant Afro-American woman, and another room belonged to a young Spanish couple that smoked pot every night after work. The pregnant woman would often join them.

A chubby gangster-looking Afro-American landlord would come to collect $100 weekly rent every Thursday night. He always appeared serious and straightforward. Tenants seemed to respect him, or were afraid of him, which was the same in that circumstance. He called himself "Dad".

My daily route went from home to work, and the other way around. I tried to avoid coming home late at night as I didn't trust the neighborhood, and once I would arrive in my room, I would stay inside for the rest of the night, watching movies or reading books. I didn't try to make friends with anybody in the apartment, although I was friendly and nice to everyone.

I was lucky to have the same day off with Natasha. Instead of staying at home and socializing with locals, I would leave as soon as I'd wake up and meet her for breakfast in the diner in Sheepshead Bay, the area she lived in. She would always be a little late and apologetic. It didn't bother me at all. I loved spending time with her. I loved her positive vibes and loud contagious laugh. It was exactly what I needed during that period of my life.

We would eat, play Ping-Pong, walk around the area, go for drinks, and meet Kostya, who eventually would give me a ride home and say, "Jeez! Even I wouldn't want to live here!"

Kostya's vocabulary was great, but his accent sounded as if he was speaking Russian, just using English words. He had a mild, pleasant voice. Gentle and thoughtful, he never used a single inappropriate word with us. Tall, skinny, bold and a bit shy, he didn't look like a typical Mafia person, even though I hadn't really met any gangsters before. His facial expression was clear and honest, he didn't smile too often, but when he did, it was sincere. He was into fast driving and loud Russian rap in a car until Natasha would tell him to shut it down. He would always do what she would tell him to do. He loved her, as I thought, more than she loved him.

I didn't get to learn much about his life, because Natasha was always his priority. With her job at Flatbush, her family in Russia, and her mother's situation, Kostya tried hard to surround her with love and attention she wasn't getting from her family, however, Natasha didn't seem to appreciate it. At least, it was the impression I got.

She constantly called her mother. She called her once in two weeks, or, perhaps, sometimes once a week and not getting any result, she would only sigh sadly, hoping the next time would be more productive. I witnessed a couple of failed trials on our days off. She would walk a few steps away from Kostya and me but stay close enough for us to see movements of her lips, and far enough to hear the conversation. Then she would cover her face with her palms and start shaking, holding the phone and a calling card in the same hand. Kostya would give her the warmest hug and take away her phone along with the card and whisper something to her ear.

"It'll get better," Natasha would fake a smile. "Maybe next time it will work."

"Even I tried to talk to her," Kostya stated once. "Impossible!"

My heart was breaking into little pieces for that poor little human being, who only wanted some love and support from the closest person in the world. I kept looking at her sad face, not knowing what would be the right word to say to cheer her up. I never knew what to tell people in these situations. It's always easy to give suggestions but it's hard to follow them. Other people's burdens seem lighter than our own. Their problems seem easily solvable. It's us, being constantly stuck either in the past or in a gloomy present, not knowing what to do with our lives, where to go on this planet, and how to find solace.

I haven't called my mom for so long, I thought.

It was the third week's Thursday when Dad came over to collect money for rent. He looked high and a bit mad. Slowly he walked around the apartment, as he was making sure everything was in its place. He wore dirty jeans, that seemed two sizes bigger, construction boots, a worn-out t-shirt, and a thick gold chain hanging over it. In the silence of tenants, his boots were making dull heavy sounds with the following echo. I stood at my door, holding two times folded $100 bill. Dad stretched his big back and stopped by the couple's room, staring at the guy.

"Maaaan, be careful with that shit, I told you!" he snapped angrily.

"Whoa? What happened?" yelled the tenant.

"Damn! I told you don't sell this shit around here. Imma kill you if I find out you keep doing it!"

The Spanish man got up; came closer to the landlord. He looked a little nervous. The landlord also made a step toward his opponent. There was a huge, obvious difference between the two gangsters, short and skinny Latinos with curly hair made into a ponytail and a fat baldhead black man, about two feet tall and probably three times bigger.

"Yo, I'm not selling white any more, okay?" my neighbor hissed. "I'm done."

"I told you, I don't want to see cops here," Dad pronounced clearly.

"Did I ever give you any trouble, man?" the tenant raised his voice, helping the communication with his hands as if he was singing a rap song, but the landlord didn't pay attention. He turned around and walked through the kitchen, taking his time, looking at supplies and dishes in a sink. For a moment he focused his attention on the pregnant woman, as

94

if he wanted to tell her something, but then changed his mind and looked at me.

The tenants promptly went to their places, and the Spanish one made sure his door slammed as loud as it could. Dad didn't show any sign of irritation.

"How are you doing, young lady?" he asked me.

"Good, thank you," I said, as friendly as possible, handing him money for rent.

"Everything is all right here? You like everything?" he kept questioning me, grabbing the $100 bill and squeezing it in his fist.

"Yes… yes, I do." I responded, quite nervously.

He stepped closer to me and bent down to reach the level of my head.

"You know my cousin? The big boy I came with last week?" he murmured.

"I… I didn't pay attention." I smiled politely, trying not to show my nervousness.

"Listen," he asserted, "He saw you, he liked you, he wanna take you out, you know, dinner, drinks."

I suddenly felt cold sweat on my spine.

"Ah… I'm sorry, I already have a boyfriend." I pronounced, looking away.

"Boyfriend, not husband," Dad stated, keeping staring at me. "Ralfy really likes you."

His look was so heavy and demanding. The cold sweat multiplied and moved up to my head; I couldn't wait to finish that conversation.

"It's nice of him to offer, but I love my boyfriend and my boyfriend loves me. We are planning to get married in a few months." I explained as nicely as I could.

"Okay." Dad nodded in approval.

"Okay."

"Good night." he finished and turned towards the entrance door. "Let me know if anything changes."

"Okay," I said, taking a deep breath in. "Good night."

I breathed a sigh of relief when Dad shut the entrance door from the outside. For the next few seconds of silence, I stood in a stupor, not knowing what to do and what to make of that unwanted attention. I locked my room, and trying to calm down, decided to give myself a month to find another room in a better area. One month, or possibly less. I couldn't think straight at that moment.

I called Natasha to tell her the news.

"Jeez," she laughed, speaking in Kastya's manner. "I told you, nobody normal would live in that area. Even Kostya wouldn't want to end up there. You know? We have to find you a better place."

I began living overly conscious and careful life, staying aware of possible dangers related to the apartment I couldn't call home. Every night, locking the door, I would make sure to put a chair next to it. Every strange sound in the kitchen would wake me up immediately and make me listen to the rest of the silence for minutes, sometimes for hours.

On my very first day off, I went to view a few rooms. The two rooms I liked required pay stubs, which I didn't have. That day, I started realizing how hard the life of illegals was. You can never rent an apartment you like; you can't get a job you want; you are trapped in a frame of doing things you hate and struggling with society and your own self.

A few days passed with no results.

The dwelling remained quiet. I started thinking I overreacted and gave up the idea with the chair by the door. Nothing odd was going on. The Spanish couple kept smoking weed every night, the pregnant woman kept keeping them company from time to time; once she asked me for a quarter for the laundry machine and we engaged in a conversation, in which I learned that she wanted to become a lawyer and she loved playing chess. We agreed to compete one day.

It was Tuesday night, the end of the workday when I changed in the empty kitchen of the restaurant and left. I was tired of the small room I had to come back and sit in every night; I wasn't in a rush to return there. The weather happened to be warm for January and I decided to walk for a few blocks toward the next train stop.

My phone died. I turned to the parkway, enjoying winter freshness and silence, watching cars passing by. I thought of Natasha's family in sorrow, I couldn't imagine what she felt not being able to talk to somebody who raised her, gave her the love and support she needed, and then acted as someone who had nothing to do with her. I missed my mother. Her eyes. Her smile. Her voice. I slowly sank into memories and the warmth of the past. I suddenly remembered crying on my mom's lap as a little child, helplessly and bitterly, not being able to stop.

"Just smile." mom said. "Just smile and all your sadness will go away."

I didn't believe it but smiled anyway. And found out that she was right. It was gone. Shortly after, I was laughing cheerfully.

It made me smile as I thought of it as if I sent that smile back to her and to my child self from an adult, almost 23-year-old woman. Yet, there was a lot of sadness in that recent smile. I felt so lonely and hollow as I was thrown from cozy mom's arms to unknown unwelcoming streets of a big world, where everything was a danger. I felt homeless.

It was almost 10 p.m. when I got off the train. After an enjoyable walk, in silence, the crowd on Nostrand Ave. annoyed me even more. I hurried towards my building. Drunk and mad, people were screaming and yelling, fighting and singing. Little kids were playing by a myriad of liquor stores, which seemed to be open for 24 hours.

It became quieter after I went off Nostrand, there were no people, children, or noises.

The warm day had already turned into a cold night and the young shiny moon appeared in the sky. I slightly smiled at the beauty of late January, continuing walking towards the building I lived in. There was something magical in the air.

Halfway to the destination, I started getting a weird sensation that someone was following me. Through the sound of my own steps, I heard a pair of heavy boots hitting the ground right behind me. Hoping that it was my imagination, I started walking a bit faster and realized the owner of those boots did the same. There were entire two empty blocks to my building, so I decided to change the trajectory, and without looking back, I ran towards the small grocery store across the street. Heavy boots also began to run my way, and before I managed to screech, a huge sweaty palm blocked my mouth from the back.

I wanted to scream. I made an attempt to remove myself from these arms, but after they roughly pulled my head back and my neck cracked, I lost most of my senses. I had no time to guess who it was and why he was doing it, I thought my life was over.

The stranger started dragging me away from the store, breathing heavily, behind my head, with abnormal whistling, coming from his throat.

"Don't do anything stupid here," he commanded with a scary voice.

The cloud of processed alcohol-filled up the air; I suddenly realized who the stranger was. I knew what he needed from me.

After a few seconds of harsh dragging, my senses returned with the sharp pain in the spine. It was a staircase. I shut my eyes, preparing to get hurt, and the next moment my tailbone hit each of the steps leading down. I suddenly felt dizzy and thirsty. Leaning on the cold cement, I was trying to get a big gulp of air, but the pain wouldn't let me. My entire back was hurting as if I had fallen from a three-story building. I thought my tailbone was broken.

I sensed the sharpness of a knife on my neck before I got to face the stranger.

"Don't do anything stupid," he repeated, looking at me.

I nodded.

The huge black man in a hood moved me a little further from the stair, and a pile of dust and dirt went up into the air. We were in a basement. He removed my coat and started pulling down my pants along with the shoes. Instinctively, I held it up until he grabbed my hands and pinned them behind my head.

"Please," I cried. "Don't do this to me."

"Shut the fuck up!" he hissed, putting the knife back to my throat. "I'll kill you if you won't fucking shut up."

I couldn't believe it was happening. I still had a little hope that someone might pass by and save me, or salespeople would see me from the grocery store and call the police, or an enemy was chasing him tonight and would soon come over. Anything, fire, flood, earthquake — something had to happen. I was afraid of what would happen if nothing happened.

But nothing happened. I got a shot of terrible pain in my lower belly and groaned helplessly.

"I told you to shut your fucking mouth up, bitch!" the rapist screamed and smacked my face so hard that I felt the taste of the iron in my mouth. Then he put his knife back to my throat and said, "I swear the God, I'll kill you. I don't give a shit!"

The pain was getting stronger and stronger, and for a second it felt like my mind was about to shut down to save me from the enormous torture. I thought it could have been a bad dream, and I would wake up, loving and thanking life even more. Yet, unfortunately, I was as awake as possible.

I closed my eyes and started crying silently. I was no longer sure if I wanted to live. There was no meaning in anything. Rivers of tears were crawling down my cheeks, and a terrible pain felt in my entire lower belly and all over my face. I kept thinking where would I go once it's over? To the hateful apartment and then to the hateful job in the morning, as if nothing happened? An illegal, with no rights for a normal living, only for a poor existence, I already fell on the bottom of that very existence. I was not afraid to lose my life, because I didn't have a life.

"Kill me, I don't care," I murmured, crying, and trying to remove my arms from his huge palm behind my head, but I was so weak, that all my efforts were nothing to him.

He smacked me again in response. It was much harder than the first time, but I didn't feel pain any more, that half of my face was already numb, and only light tickling went through my cheek.

The rapist bent down towards my lips and began kissing me, pushing his tongue into my closed mouth. I tried to turn my head away, but he hit me with his forehead, and I saw an explosion of all possible colors in the air. The very next moment I was choked by his tongue almost in my throat, the instant odor of something rotten made me feel so sick, that I barely held myself from vomiting.

He started to jerk faster, giving me more sharp pain. I was only silently hoping that the end was close. His breathing became more rapid and harsh. He was looking into my eyes and releasing new scary sounds from his throat along with the disgusting smell. A few seconds later he ejaculated.

An enormous weight squeezed me for a couple of moments. Then he quickly got up, staring at me and breathing heavily.

I didn't move. Time froze. I wished it was a bad dream again, I thought it couldn't be real, it just couldn't be. However, it was.

"If it's a boy, name him Tom. If it's a girl, call her Jessica." he laughed, zipping up his pants. "It's a free gift from me, babe! I'd rather do that on a date, but you didn't choose to."

I remained on the ground, watching him shaking off the dirt from his clothes and walking up the stairs. He looked back at me, lit his cigarette, and disappeared into the darkness of the street. I lay powerless, not being able to get up. The entire body was hurting. I felt miserable. I hated the whole world including myself. At that moment I wished he had killed me.

The memory of another basement instantly entered my mind. The basement that was burning my right hand without any apparent chance for survival, the basement that almost killed me with its voltages at the age of seven. The basement eventually let me go. Just like this one. I still remembered it clearly, perfectly, as if it was yesterday. There was a similar staircase and a heavy door that I thought I had closed behind myself forever. I didn't.

Why didn't it kill me in the first place? I shouted inside of my head.

This time, there were no relatives waiting for me at home, there was no mom to comfort me in the hospital like almost 15 years ago, to cry over my disaster and nurse me physically and mentally. There was nothing besides the hostile room on the third floor.

I finally pulled all my strength together to walk a few feet and pick up my pants and boots. Each step was hurting enormously, each move was an effort. It felt like a sharp knife was still operating inside of me, and it was the worst kind of pain, the pain of stolen self.

My sore tailbone kept me dizzy, so I had to sit down on the stairs for a while. I didn't know what to do. I didn't know where to go. My cell phone was dead, but even if it was on, who would I call? Who would really care about me in this country?

Somehow, I got dressed and slowly climbed up the stairs. I had to sit on the ground again in order not to faint. I did the same in half of a block, then in another half. I had no other choice besides returning to the room I hated. It took me almost half an hour to make it there with all the rest breaks from walking. I put my phone to charge and went to wash away all interactions with that man. I was looking at my body in the mirror for long sad minutes after the shower, cuts and bruises were everywhere — one after another, my face was swollen… and the pain of every single move completed the memory of something I would never forget.

I wanted to cry but couldn't. I felt destroyed and humiliated. I was endlessly tired. Enormous weight put me to bed and blurred my exhausted mind, which began to look for shelter in memories. I recalled the bus to Worcester and Vera, so cozy she was sleeping on my lap. How excited and childlike we were, and horizons seemed so bright and beautiful. It felt so distant as if a decade had passed. Then I recalled one long winter day, the end of it when every child was picked up from the kindergarten by their parents and was taken home to a warm meal and cartoons on TV. I watched them all leave the changing room, waving goodbye and smiling. As I realized it was only me alone waiting for my mom, dull fear struck my mind — what if she never came? What if she had left me? I wanted to cry. I was holding my small backpack on my knees and looking at the entrance door with a silent scream, please, come for me. Suddenly the door opened widely, and my mom ran into the room with apologies and hugs. She smelled like winter. The freshness of the outside got mixed with her semi-sweet perfume, in which all my fears were deluded. I felt so safe and cozy in her arms. Then we promptly left the kindergarten. I felt this warmth and love again, laying on the bed of the hostile apartment, all alone in the whole world. The freshness of that winter and her perfume seemed to fill up the air of my room as well. I fell asleep as I inhaled the imaginary smell.

The cruel morning came unexpectedly. The alarm clock ended a sweet dream of me being in Astrakhan, sipping beers with friends in the café next to my university. I told them about my weird semi-nightmare in which I came to America, moved to New York, met Ron and Adil, and parted with Dmitry again. I told them about my jobs, including dancing in the Spanish bar and fooling customers on Flatbush. I told them about the crooked neighborhood I lived in, and about the rape at the very end of the dream. I felt so happy to be with them again, so calm and relieved. Then I woke up and saw the scary wall of the room with a half-broken mirror on it. There was a swollen red-blue face. And it was not a dream.

I called my boss to let him know I was sick. I felt so weak and absent-minded, that I didn't even remember his response. Not able to focus on anything, I went to a Russian online portal to look for a cheap room, similar to the one I lived in Brighton Beach. I started to appreciate that apartment, full of illegal people, and that neighborhood, where I could walk around days and nights without any fear.

After I made a couple of calls, I got one from Natasha.

"What?" I heard. "Are you serious? You are not joking, right? Are you?"

It took me a while to remember that I did leave her a voicemail that night, right before I went to bed.

"Yes…" I said, gaining the pain back after artificial indifference.

"Oh My God! Do you know who was it? How?" she shouted loudly and anxiously. "How are you?"

My eyes started getting wet, and all of a sudden, I wasn't able to breathe a word, holding myself from crying.

"Katya! Are you there? Are you okay?" she kept yelling.

"Yeah…" I heard myself saying with a voice I couldn't recognize. "I just want to die…"

"Wait!" she shouted. "Are you at home? Kostya and I will pick you up in a half an hour, okay? You'll stay at my place, okay?"

I started crying out of that kindness and support, this time I was sobbing on the phone, biting my already damaged finger. People's kindness always touched me.

They arrived twenty minutes after I hung up the phone. Natasha ran into the apartment and gave me the warmest hug I haven't had since I last saw Shawn. I didn't know I had any friends in this country until that moment. I didn't know I could trust anybody or rely on anyone. I thought I was homeless and absolutely lonely. I started crying again.

"I'm sorry," I kept saying, "I'm sorry… I can't hold myself…"

"Are you stupid? Oh my God!" she murmured, looking at me in a daze. "What did he do to you… What did he do to you"

Kostya came closer and sat on his knees, grabbing my hand. He looked away after we made eye contact.

"Gosh," he said.

"How many of them were there?" he asked, looking back at me.

"One…" I answered.

"How did it happen?" Natasha asked.

"Last night… on the street… He dragged me…" I could barely speak.

Kostya got up his knees and sat next to me on the bed. Natasha gave me a few valerian pills to calm down.

We packed all my stuff in Kostya's car and went towards Natasha's apartment. I was so thankful for the care they surrounded me with but couldn't open my mouth to say anything in order not to start sobbing again.

Natasha sat on a back seat with me, holding my head on her knees. We drove in silence for a few minutes, and then Kostya asked, "Did you go to the police?"

"How would she go?" Natasha yelled. "She is illegal!"

"So what?" he noted. "They are not immigration!"

"But once they will figure you're an illegal, they have a full right to report you," she remarked.

"Maybe you're right." Kostya concluded and asked me, "Do you know who that guy was?"

Pain attacked my jaw and it became hard to talk.

"I know." I breathed.

"Wait!" Natasha exclaimed. "You know?"

"I know who that guy is," I pronounced, feeling that calming pills had started to work.

"So, who is it?" they asked in the rhythm of each other.

"Ralf. The cousin of the landlord." I mumbled.

"Is it the guy…" started Natasha.

"That's him," I interrupted her.

"Mother fucker." Kostya uttered with anger.

"It's over now… It's over… You are in a safe place." Natasha repeated calmly, gently touching my hair.

She let me stay in her room and share the full-size bed until something would come up. Kostya left after he carried my suitcases upstairs. Natasha organized ice packs for my face and other bruised parts of the body, even though it seemed too late to take care of them. She made a hot cup of chamomile tea and gave me an emergency contraception pill, "the morning-after".

"I'll give you another one tonight, then you should be good," she explained before she went to work.

I nodded.

My heart and mind went back to Russia to my aunt. We used to be soulmates. She was a little younger than my mom, but I always felt as if she was my elder sister. She would share so many things and thoughts with me that she probably wouldn't share with anybody else. I don't know how we got that close, that I would tell her most of the stuff I would never tell my mother. I tried the first cigarette with her, I had my first glass of champagne on her birthday, and from her, I first learned about things you wouldn't read in books. And now, sitting on the edge of my life, I wanted to call her and cry about what had happened to me. I knew she would console me if she were alive.

She was raped in her teenage in somebody's garage. It took her a lot of courage and strength to return to a normal life. She saw that rape in every single dream, as she told me, for many weeks. Later on, in a month and a half, she found out she was pregnant. Without much money, without telling anybody about what had happened, she went to some student-practitioner and got an abortion. It was as painful as it could be, just a terrible reminder of the rape, of the life, which wasn't welcoming her. She couldn't build a decent relationship with men, she was afraid of them, and she avoided them. It took her many years to find a great person, who loved her more than himself, and who she fell in love with. It was the biggest gift in her life. They wanted a continuation of their feelings, the product of their love. That's when the result of the abortion showed up, she couldn't have kids.

I slept all day long.

My rescuers came back in the evening to check on me. They brought lots of sweets and chocolate along with a couple of DVDs with comedy movies.

"I don't know if it's a good compliment," Kostya said, "but you look better than this morning."

Tall and skinny, he looked funny in his baggy blue jeans.

I smiled. The first time in the day.

We ate and watched movies all together while in Natasha's bed. I realized we had never been so close to one another before. Certain predicaments shorten the distance between people. I wished there were different circumstances that would bring us together. We hung out until I fell asleep again. Throughout the dream, I heard the two of them talking in the kitchen. I felt calm, knowing I was not alone.

"I hope I'm not going to start hating men." I told Natasha in the morning.

"This is not a man, but a piece of shit," she remarked.

"I know…" I said. "But all men crave sex most of the time, and want to get it, doesn't matter what price they have to pay."

My friend went to work. I locked myself up in the room and stayed there until very late at night, watching movies and stupid TV shows. I couldn't imagine doing anything else.

"Think about Beethoven, Tchaikovsky, and Vivaldi next time you think of men that way," she texted me from work. "At least these dudes created beautiful stuff. You know."

The message made me laugh.

Little by little I told Natasha the whole story, finishing with his final phrase, "If it's a boy, call him Tom, and if it's a girl, call her Jessica." Too odd that I memorized names.

Natasha said that people like him should be electrocuted. I would wish for another punishment for rapists and murderers. I always thought they should die with some use for society as organ donors or as material for cancer research and medical experiments. If you took one life, then save another. If you damaged somebody, help somebody else to recover. Only like this, it could be fair. Only like this, we could find a balance.

The next day I started my room hunting and called my boss to inform that I was getting better. He didn't sound understanding. He said that it was my duty to return to work tomorrow.

"I have no duties," I told him calmly. My face was blue and terribly swollen, and my body remained sore, I didn't want to leave Natasha's room, not to mention go to work and serving tables of strangers. I hung up the phone and decided to look for a new job as well.

Finally, I was able to tell Natasha how thankful I was for all the support and help they provided. I was so lucky to have a friend like her, who became so dear to me in such a short period of time. I couldn't wish for a better one. I thought of how amazing people's connections are, a little while ago we were total strangers, and now I considered her my best friend in the United States.

"I'm sure you would do the same," she said, squeezing me in her arms.

"I definitely would," I stated and squeezed her harder.

I looked at her kind face and noticed that her bright green eyes got watery. I made an effort not to start crying.

"Thank you, thank you so much," I repeated.

I lay in bed in my pajamas when Kostya rang the bell. He walked in smiling, looking fresh and happy, lightly dressed and smelling like spring in the middle of the endless winter.

"What's up girls?" he rejoiced. "Wanna go see a movie?"

Natasha looked at me.

"Ah… I'm sleepy. But you guys go." I murmured.

"I don't want to go without Katya!" she told her beloved.

"Let's go!" Kostya insisted gaily. "You need some fresh air! Can't stay home all day long."

"I just want to sleep," I smiled softly, wrapping myself in the blanket.

Kostya came closer and sat on the edge of the bed. His face was perfectly shaved, and his brown eyes looked as caring as they could.

"Don't worry, nobody will see your face. It's dark out. Plus, you need some getaway. You're not going to lay in this bed forever, are you?"

My mind quickly played the scene of staying in that bed forever and it scared me.

"You are probably right," I laughed, "Okay."

Natasha kept me busy all the way to the movie theatre in the back seat of Kostya's Jeep. One after another, she told me their funniest stories from recent parties, dinners, and other hangouts in Brooklyn. Kostya only giggled and inserted comments such as "not true", or "hey, it's too much".

"Don't listen to him," she would laugh, "that's exactly how it was! You know!"

Time passed unexpectedly fast and I didn't have a chance to go back inside of my mind or drag any thought out of it, because I was constantly entertained. I laughed and inhaled the chilling air mixed with Kostya's cigarette's smoke.

"All right!" he exclaimed when the car stopped. "Ladies first!"

I opened the door and my smile got off my face in a second, it was the hateful neighborhood of Nostrand Avenue. My throat got dry and new fear filled my stomach. I looked back at my friends, but before I got to say anything, I saw two more cars nearby with Russian-looking bold guys next to them. It was a quiet and dark block, similar to the one where I wanted to die a few days ago.

Kostya put his arm on my shoulder and pointed at the space between two cars.

"Is it him?" he asked clearly and loudly, with no signs of recent laughing.

I looked into the group of people, there were about three guys with huge clubs, standing between their wrongly parked cars, and one of them was holding a big black man. It was my rapist.

"It's him," I said, and looked away.

Natasha stepped closer to me and touched my hand with hers behind my hip. I squeezed her palm in fear. Did you know where we were going? I wanted to ask her. She rested her temple on my shoulder and I got "yes".

"Do you recognize her?" Kostya asked Ralf with a load of a horrifying Russian accent. Now he did sound like the mafia.

"No." the rapist snapped and got hit in his stomach with the club.

He bent down and started releasing familiar scary sounds from his throat.

"You sure?" Kostya inquired, once the gangster got back in the straight position.

"I don't know her, man!" he yelled.

Another guy hit his stomach with the club, but did it so strongly, that the rapist started throwing up blood.

"I don't understand what's the point of saying 'I don't know' when everybody else knows that you know," Kostya stated, looking at him.

"What do you want to do with him, sweetheart? Should we just kill him?" he asked me, and then added, turning to the rapist, "Not a big deal."

I didn't know what to say and squeezed Natasha's palm stronger.

"She is too nice…" he laughed. "She is too nice to wish bad things to people, even bastards like you."

Kostya stretched his shoulders and looked up at the sky. Most of us subconsciously repeated it.

"You see, how unfair the life is… Doing harm to someone nice and innocuous like her, you don't get any harm back. So, someone like her always has to pay double the price for someone like you. And someone like you has a fun and easy life." he remarked. "But it's not right. Everything in this world has to be balanced."

"You know," he continued, "she didn't even know where she was going tonight until she got off the car. You know why?"

No reaction occurred.

"You know, fucking bastard!" Kostya screamed and threw his fist into a man's face.

The impact was so strong, that Ralf started to fall down, but the person behind held him up.

"Because she would pity you! She is too nice to hurt you!" he yelled at the gangster's face.

"But you know what?" he added, looking right into his eyes. "I'm not that nice. And I believe everybody should get their punishments."

The very next second he hit Ralf's stomach with a club and the rapist bent down coughing and spitting. Another guy behind hit his back and Ralf straightened it up in pain, screaming like an injured dog. He started to fall, but the men behind caught him and kept him standing by holding his armpits.

"One thing I want you to do, before I'll break your knees," said Kostya. "Can you guess what it is?"

"I'm sorry. I'm so sorry, man! Imma not do that again…" the rapist stammered. "Imma not, I got my lesson, man. I'm sorry lady. Imma not…"

He was quaking and mumbling something I couldn't understand. He looked sick and scared. All of a sudden, from a brutal gangster he grew into a defenseless child.

"Kostya… It's enough." I breathed quietly, getting worried. My voice was shaking.

But Kostya didn't look at me, he was in the middle of his anger.

"Is it enough, you think?" he asked, staring at Ralf. "I think there is no such 'enough' to cover what you have done!"

"Let them handle it," Natasha whispered in my ear.

One of the guys opened the car's trunk and took something heavy from there. It looked like a big hammer to me. I closed my eyes.

A dull, quick sound finished with cracking exploded into the silence. The wildest scream I had ever heard went through all my nerves and muscles, it continued with sobs and gulps. I felt nauseous.

"Shut up, son of the bitch!" Kostya snapped.

Another strong hit gave birth to the next scream; the kind of scream I only heard in movies, but so close and so realistic. I squeezed Natasha's palm stronger, and she squeezed me back.

I opened my eyes and saw two men holding the rapist's underarms, he was helplessly hanging with his bloody face crooked from pain. He didn't seem to be scared any more; he didn't seem very much alive. Just like me, a few days ago.

"And the last thing for today, Ralfy," Kostya rejoiced, playing with the hammer, "I know, that you probably won't be able to have kids any more…"

With all his madness and strength, he smashed the hammer right between the gangster's legs. The rapist started to howl like a wolf with breaks for sobs and other impossible sounds. And it was not a natural human voice.

"But if it'll happen somehow, call them Tom and Jessica," Kostya pronounced loudly and clearly, standing next to the gangster. Then he nodded at his companions.

Russian guys rested their arms and Ralf fell down on the ground. He just collapsed as if he was made of bricks. He was crying and mumbling something not understandable, quaking in the mess of his vomit and blood.

"Thanks, guys!" Kostya shook hands of each of the Russian men.

"No problem." replied one of them. "See ya."

The slight police siren sound blew from somewhere.

"Get in the car! Faster." Kostya commanded.

I don't remember how we managed to jump on the back seat within a second, and pass a decent number of blocks towards Midwood, non-stop, with a favorable green light at every street, make a U-turn at Ocean Parkway and park in the dark available spot by a residential building.

The night was silent. There were no people on the street. Kostya rolled down the window and lit a cigarette.

"Maybe no movies tonight." he smiled as soon as we all breathed a sigh of relief. "I know one nice bar around here."

CHAPTER 7

That winter happened to be cold and long. Every day seemed endless on its own, with no sign of the warm weather approaching. I had a feeling it would be the everlasting end of January.

I found a new room in Kensington, Brooklyn. Natasha and Kostya helped me with moving. I felt so close and related to them. They became my American family, which was not really American.

I had never gotten to know what happened to Ralf. I didn't even know whether he was alive. I tried to ask Kostya, but he only laughed at how curious I was.

"There are times in life when you better not know about certain things," he explained. "Remember, the lesser you know, the safer you are."

My new room was huge and orange. It had plenty of walk-in closets and furniture, and a tremendous red clock on the wall. My new roommate was a girl around my age, Slavic-looking Kazakhstan citizen, who slept, but mostly had insomnias, in the other room of that two-bedroom apartment. She bartended in a local bar and attended English language school just to remain in the country legally.

Her name was Rita. She looked a bit absent-minded as if she was constantly solving a difficult puzzle in her mind. She was big-boned and tall with sand- colored hair, interested in art, and brands, and spending everything she had at all these sales around.

Rita's room was packed with finished and unfinished paintings of different sizes — all in bright colors, but very sad-themed. She was a painter and a member of AA.

"I relapse sometimes," she mentioned, laughing, "but then I get back on the wagon for about a month, I paint and deal with these horrible insomnias. Then I relapse again and party hard."

"Or drink alone at home..." she added with a shy smile. "I sleep like a baby after a good buzz."

My new roommate spoke loudly and clearly, turning her lips on the right side while talking. Her small brown eyes were constantly running around the apartment, as they were checking whether everything was in its right place.

She didn't think of AA meetings as something productive and really helpful. She said she attended them purely for fun. She also said it was a miserable way of living. Drinking is a prison of slavery to the burden, that controls your life, and AA meetings are a prison of slavery to the desire to get that burden back. Two sides of the same coin, and this coin constantly flips, which makes you change sides and fling from one prison to another. She couldn't figure a way to walk away from that coin and lock the prison's door behind her, so she decided to enjoy meetings and have fun, listening to embarrassing drunken stories of strangers. She always had a bottle of booze by the bed. She said she had a soul hole she was trying to fill up with art, but sometimes the hole would get bigger, and then she would have to fill it up with whiskey, vodka, tequila, or whatever would be available at the moment.

"Have you ever been to an AA meeting?" she asked all of a sudden while getting ready for work.

"I don't think I need it… yet," I tried to make a joke of it, wondering whether I looked like anyone who had drinking problems.

"You should!" she smiled friendly. "It's so much fun. If you are ashamed of something, you'll listen to their fucked-up stories and will realize, that you are innocent next to them! I'll take you one day if you wouldn't tell them I keep the booze at home."

"Okay," I laughed, "sure."

I found her a bit odd. She seemed to be so close and so available, yet so far away, in a different dimension, out of reach. Once, when she was at work, I sneaked inside her room to take a look at her piled up by the wall art and realized, I had never seen anything like that. There were paintings of dead animals and people with vital organs exposed — all in bright colors of a rainbow. There were colorful scenes of funerals, happy in sad, sad in happy, the meaningless existence of the creatures on this planet. It was not a celebration of life, but of death.

After the recent incident, I became more sensitive to the outside world. I started appreciating good things more and listening to my inner self. I was happy to live in a safe area with a harmless person, even though a strange one.

I kept rewriting my resume. I needed some source of income. My roommate suggested looking for a babysitting position.

"It's not much fun, but not bad either. You cook, play with the baby, then you put the kid to sleep and do whatever you want, as long as you don't set the house on fire." she laughed.

"It sucks to be illegal," she added. "How did you manage to end up like this with all these possibilities of switching visas?"

She was partly right. There are often ways to keep yourself on track, however, not in my case. After an international student gets master's, he/she may acquire one-year work authorization, through which they may get a three-year work permit if they find a sponsoring company. It would also mean they have to stick with that company for these three years, not everyone would find such a perfect place so fast, and not everyone would find a qualified job at all. Good positions are usually waiting for specialists who speak perfect English and don't require additional effort and a bunch of immigration paperwork.

So, what to do after your permit ends, if you haven't found "the job of your dreams"? Language schools simply wouldn't accept you with American master, so the legal way is to switch to a tourist visa, which is six months long. Then you may extend it for six more months. Then it's over unless you saved money for another master's, bachelor's, or PhD with daytime attendance. And you don't have a credit history to qualify for loans.

I admitted I was pretty careless with not knowing what I wanted to do. First, I planned to stay and apply for a year's work permit, then Dmitry broke into my life and I missed the deadline, or, to be honest, gave up on it in order to save money and be able to rent a room in New York for the first time. I didn't know what would happen if I would do everything differently. I, honestly, didn't even want to know.

At the moment, the difference between Rita and me was not too big, we both couldn't work legally, the only huge benefit she had over me, was she could apply for any work or student visa, and I couldn't.

I found a nanny's job soon enough. The online newspaper "Russian Reklama" was a bible for all Russian immigrants in Brooklyn, offering all low-end jobs as housekeeping, babysitting, waiting on tables, and escort services. The very first number I dialled from that "Bible," friendly invited me to the interview.

I got the job right away. The Ukrainian-Jewish couple asked me whether I knew how to cook and if I liked kids. My both "yesses" made their tired faces smile.

The man in his sixties and his wife in her forties had a late child, a three-year-old boy. The father was working as a salesperson in a local bookstore and the mother was a travel agent. I assumed none of them made a lot of money, but none of them knew anybody to leave the child with either. We agreed on $70 a day, a full day until one of them shows up.

I wasn't too happy with the salary, but I didn't have much of a choice. The very next day I was cooking, playing, reading, storytelling, and trying to put the kid to sleep. The boy wasn't active at all, he looked half-alive as if he had just woken up after a long and difficult surgery.

The couple returned late at night with a $70 cash trice folded and fixed with a paper clip, and brief apologies. They never asked how the child behaved or whether there was enough food in the fridge. They didn't care about their kid's health. Neither did I. I only aimed to save some money and move on. I kept coming back every morning and leaving late at night. The job was getting more and more tedious, and every day seemed so much longer than previous. Yet, there was nothing I could do at this point — I needed money.

In the meanwhile, Rita gave me contact of the man who was helping immigrants to become refugees. It was cheap, she said, and very reliable. The man was not a lawyer; however, it didn't stop him from giving lectures to fifty people at a time during each appointment, and working with hundreds of immigrants every month, guiding them through all legal procedures and complicated paperwork. He didn't advertise his service, illegals and almost illegals were passing his phone number from one to another with the last hope to be able to call themselves residents one beautiful sunny day.

I scheduled an appointment for the earliest available date. It gave me a splash of aspiration and ambitions to live through the boring poorly paid work.

Everybody was complaining, there were no jobs at the time. Natasha went to several interviews for catering positions, but all they could offer was a day or two a week. She couldn't wait to leave the job on Flatbush Ave. None of the girls wanted to stay there, but none of them could find anything better.

I was missing Dmitry. More and more. No matter, how hard I tried to switch my attention to something else, I found myself constantly being with him in my thoughts. There was an endless dialogue in a form of a silent monologue about everything and nothing. I was wondering how he was doing alone, whether he had found a job or not, whether Adil treated him good, and vice-versa. He never came to the store to look for me — it was the only way I could figure all his threats were empty. Sometimes I blamed myself for leaving him as I did. I thought of that chaos I created by running away from the one I loved, getting myself in a horrible predicament, instead of spending time with someone so dear, instead of learning to understand each other better. I kept asking myself whether I was ever going to see Dmitry again. Deep in my heart I wished I were.

Boring days at work came together into one long week that seemed longer than a month. I got to learn a lot about immigration process online, people's cases and consequences. I already knew the best way for me to stay in the country, but there was no man to marry and no money to pay for that.

One of these days, I started wondering how my Clark University acquaintances were doing. My only touch with them was happening through Facebook. I deleted my profile a while ago, running away from Dmitry, and the same while later, I realized I missed it. I went on the website and recovered my page.

One day the father-boss returned home around noon. The old, quiet man walked into the room where I was sitting by the kid's bed with my laptop. He looked tired. I thought, he must have a difficult life, he looked much older in his sixties, both his hair and beard were pale grey, and even his eyes seemed to lose their color.

"You are early today," I greeted him, mostly in order to say something.

He stopped in the middle of the room and smiled, looking into nowhere. At that moment, even his clothing seemed so pale and tired.

"Want some tea?" he asked quietly, making brief eye contact with me.

"I… don't," I responded, hoping he would let me go earlier.

He pulled out the chair and sat next to me, staring at the window, that faced nowhere.

"I have a business offer for you," he stated, staring at the same spot.

"Okay…" I nodded, looking at him.

The man started to observe the room and the ceiling, squeezing one palm with another.

"I know, what we pay you is not enough to make a proper living. Therefore," he stopped for a second, glancing at me and getting back to the ceiling, "therefore I'll pay you $150 a day if we'll get a little closer."

I couldn't believe what I heard. I wanted to scream out of disappointment.

"I'm sorry," I answered, "but I'm not that kind of girl."

"How are you planning to make money then?" he looked straight into my eyes with strong disapproval. "You know, there are plenty of girls out there, younger and prettier than you, who would take your position without thinking."

He pointed at my right arm as he said "prettier", and I instinctively pulled a sleeve to cover it.

"Good for you." I smiled, getting up.

"What do you think, you are a fancy American? So noble and untouchable? You have no papers! Sit quietly and accept any help God sends you."

In silence, I walked to a hallway to get the coat and purse. My hands were slightly shaking.

"Okay! okay!" he followed me. "I just wanted to help you out. But if you don't want — you don't want. You don't have to put things so radically. Come back to the kid."

I grabbed all my winter accessories and made sure I didn't forget anything. I was dressing on the way out, walking outside of the apartment, where I could still hear the old man's growls.

"What am I going to tell my wife? Where is our nanny?" he yelled, once I left his line of sight.

"Tell her your nanny left, because your nanny is not a prostitute! And she couldn't accept the help that God sent her, even though she is not a fancy American!" I shouted back as loud as I could. I wanted all his neighbors to hear it.

My body was shaking from anger and disappointment, from hatred towards men, from all the misery I had to go through during the past month. I tried to wind away from the recent emotion and started to think about Beethoven and Vivaldi, as Natasha had suggested, carrying myself away from the disgust of understanding the animal instincts of males.

I was tired.

The next step was as familiar as it could be. I needed a new job, something that would feed me and pay my bills. I was walking home slowly, looking for job advertisements in grocery and clothing stores, bars and restaurant windows. I was not in rush. I was trying to extend the time before I would reach home and open up "Russian Reklama" and craigslist to go through all the junk again.

Rita happened to be at home. I wasn't too happy about it; I didn't feel like talking to anyone or explaining anything. I just wanted to be alone to analyze my life and check the job market.

Luckily for me, Rita didn't ask anything. She was so delighted when I arrived, she couldn't wait to show off her new dresses and sunglasses she had recently bought at the sale in a local store. She entered my room with all the merchandise she got, as soon as I walked in. Item by item, she started displaying her new goods.

"Very nice," I murmured emotionlessly, but it didn't seem to bother her.

"Guess, how much does this coast?" she asked playfully and flirtily, holding a disco-style golden dress.

"Hm… Fifty bucks?"

She laughed gaily and exclaimed, "Don't you want thirty?"

"Nice," I smiled, thinking about the old man and trying to calm myself down.

"Hold on!" she uttered and disappeared for good ten minutes.

I pulled out my laptop from the bag and let myself lie down, stretching my back on the bed. It was warm and cozy. I didn't feel like looking for a job yet and went to Facebook again. All was the same, people's statuses, photos, videos, nothing significant I missed there. I went to my page and all of a sudden, my throat got dry, among all the junk I saw a friend request and a message from Bartek. I couldn't believe my eyes. It had been half a year since I last saw him holding up from crying in the empty Clark's campus room. I hadn't heard from him; I hadn't thought of him. I delayed for about a minute before reading his message, thinking about what would make him contact me.

Then I opened it nervously.

"Hi, Katen'ka!

How are you doing? How is everything with your career and personal life?

I recently joined Facebook (am I too old-fashioned?) and added quite a few friends from Clark. I'm glad you are on Facebook too.

I'm also very glad to know that you stayed in the U.S. I see you live in New York. I hope it treats you well, and more than that loves and adores you. It is so hard not to adore you, sweet little angel!

Amazingly, we are going to visit your wonderful city next week for a couple of days, and it would be great if you could give us a little tour around, or just have a glass of wine or a cup of coffee with us.

Looking forward to hearing from you, Ekaterina."

It made saliva in my mouth taste sweet. I smiled, happy, that he wasn't mad at me. I wondered how much he had changed, how he looked, how he sounded — a kind positive person, the one who actually made my life happy and carefree. I thought of his sunny smile and lovely attitude. He was a perfect boyfriend, perhaps, the best one I ever had.

Bartek, Bartek… I even started to forget there was such a sweet character in my life.

I read it over and over again, wondering who were "we" in that message. Was he coming with his uncle? Or a friend? Or a group of people?

"Ta-ta-tam!" my roommate jumped back into the room in a new dress and heels, and with tones of make-up on her face.

"Hold on," I uttered, rereading Bartek's message for the fifth time.

"I just wanted to invite you for drinks to my bar. My friend is working tonight, lots of discounts!" she stated gaily, but I wasn't really listening.

"Hey girl!" she yelled, coming closer to me.

"I'm going, I'm going!" I said promptly, not moving my gaze from the monitor, "Just let me write a message to my friend."

I got so deep into thinking of how to respond that I didn't hear whether she said she would wait outside, in the bar, or in her room. Or whatever options were available.

I sent him my greetings back with the message of my eagerness to meet. I told him, I could barely wait to see him, finally, after half a year of not knowing anything about him. I didn't tell him that this city didn't treat me as good as he thought, and nothing had really worked out. There was literally nothing to tell him about my life. I took a deep breath; everything will be just fine.

No matter how hard my life was pushing me down and showing no light at the end of my tunnel, Rita and drinks were waiting for me, an appointment with the immigration refuge specialist was scheduled for tomorrow evening, and Bartek was about to brighten up my life in a week. Things were going forward somehow.

I put a pair of cheap warm sneakers on, and neglecting make-up, went out to look for Rita.

It happened to be the same bar I went to with Kostya and Natasha after I last saw Ralf. That night I was too frightened from a recent scene of revenge and didn't look around at all. We took a table in the corner to share a bottle of Tequila. Then Kostya drove us home. This time I noticed it was a typical dive bar by the F train stop, dark and old, with older men flirting with young bartenders and a couple of Orthodox Jews watching baseball on soundless TV screens. The space was pretty big, and it smelled like alcohol and fried chicken. It was called "GD." Rita waved at me happily from the back, sitting by the bar with drinks prepared, inviting me to start the party. I thought the place was a mess. At that very moment, I had no idea that soon enough it would become my second home.

"Why did you dress up so much just to come here?" I smirked, sitting down next to her.

"My boyfriend may stop by later," she explained, "Let's drink for us!"

She raised one of the two glasses with some liquid of orange-red color.

"I didn't know you have a boyfriend," I stated, picking up my glass, not knowing what was inside.

She put her palm on my shoulder and said, "Hold on! Toast! I want us to be not what we think we should be, but who we really are. Never afraid to be yourself."

Then we clinked the glasses. Rita drank half of it in one gulp.

"It's good. Isn't it?" she asked.

"A toast or a drink?" I winked, thinking about her words.

I automatically questioned myself about what I thought I should be, who I wanted to be and who I really was. There was no straight answer to this, only blank space in the air.

"So, who is your boyfriend? It's been about ten days since I know you, but never heard about a guy in your life."

"Lina!" she screamed to a bartender, "Give me another drink, the same."

I looked at my cocktail — it was almost full.

"My boyfriend is very busy," she murmured. "He owns a few grocery stores and he's mostly in Philly… Do you have one?"

I assumed it wasn't her favorite topic.

"I don't…" I said and thought of Dmitry.

"Some sad story behind it?" she smiled sympathetically.

"Not really…" I slowed down. "We broke up about a month ago."

Then I asked myself, was it really a month? Didn't we break up in December, when he pointed out that I had to support him, or even earlier, a little after he had arrived? Were we really together at all? Were all my feelings mutual? I didn't know any of the answers. All I knew was that I missed him. Still missed him a lot.

I didn't mention any of it to Rita.

"That's my girl! Lina!" she exclaimed once the bartender approached.

"Kate." I nodded.

Lina was a blond, short, and skinny girl with heavy make-up and a vulgar tongue. She leaned on the bar counter and whispered in inappropriate slang how annoyed she was by the guy next to the gambling machine making a move on her, corners of her lips were always looking down, making an impression that she was constantly disgusted with something. Heavy alcohol odor and cigarette smoke flew from her mouth with every word she said, her breasts were jumping out of her almost see-through blouse, and according to Rita, she was a very positive and modest person.

"Why are you drinking so slow?" Rita asked, ordering her third drink. "I was on the wagon for more than a month and I got pretty thirsty!"

I now understood why she went to AA meetings and ordered my second drink, finishing up the first.

"I was expelled from my language school today," she told me once she got pretty boozed. "Please don't tell anybody."

"What's going to happen to your visa now?" I asked.

"It's gone. I assume they reported to the immigration already. Soooo…" Rita looked down.

"Oh, I'm so sorry. Why did they expel you?"

"I skipped a lot. Do you know what is the worst part? I was attending classes in that stinky damn school for two years, paying for it to be here legally, to be able to switch to a working visa after I would save some money and find a better job… And now what? All these efforts were for nothing! I could have just sneaked through the border illegally; it all would be the same."

"Maybe it was not for nothing. You must have at least learned something there." I tried to cheer her up.

"Learned?" she gave me the sharp and judging look as if I didn't know what I was saying. And I really didn't.

"Gimme a break! These schools only exist for people like us. They provide us with visas and we provide them with money. To make it all legal they teach us English a certain number of hours a week."

"Fuck them," she yelled. "Lina! Another round!"

"By the way, the fact that you came here legally gives you an opportunity to legalize in the country, so it's not the same. For the ones who sneaked here, it's much more difficult even through marriage. They would have to go back to their countries and wait for a few years before coming back here. For some, it would be totally impossible." I informed Rita.

Rita shrugged her shoulders, "Anyway, it's not much fun, being expelled. If only my grandma knew about it…. She was working hard to save money for me to come here. I don't want her to pity me, I want her to be proud of me."

When it turned twelve, Lina put plastic cups filled with water on the bar counter — it meant, that all possible inspections stopped working and everybody could smoke inside. The very next minute the place turned into a big smoky mess. I didn't mind anything any more.

"Who do you want to be?" Rita asked me, lighting up a cigarette.

"A writer," I said shyly. "But I don't write."

"What kind of writer, that doesn't write?" she laughed loudly.

I shrugged my shoulders, "I mean to write sometime in the future. I need to improve my English first."

Rita's eyes brightened up instantly and her lips got organized in a hazy smile, "Will you write about me?"

I giggled.

"No, I'm serious," she exhaled cigarette smoke. "Do you think I'm an interesting character to write about?"

I gave it a thought and nodded, "You definitely are."

"I always wanted somebody to write about me," she smiled.

Then she gazed into nowhere straight ahead of her and remained in this position for a while. I got a feeling she was thinking about something dear and valuable, but rather impossible.

"And what about you? A painter?" I interrupted her thoughts.

She smiled and looked somewhere in the air behind my back.

"I want to be a good wife and a mother. More than anything in the world."

I could see the sadness in her eyes through the smile. There was something deep and innocent, full of love, hope, and sorrow; it was past twelve already and her boyfriend didn't even call her.

"I'm twenty-six years old," she sighed, "Katya, I want to have a husband, a kid, or better two. I want to wash clothes and decorate home, do homework with kids and cook dinner, waiting for a husband to come from work."

"Are you going to get married to your boyfriend?" I dared to ask.

"Ah… he is very busy now. Maybe."

"Do you love him?"

"I do." she breathed.

"Does he love you?"

She took her time to light a cigarette.

"I smoke only when I drink," she giggled. "I don't smoke on daily bases, but when I'm drunk, I can kill for a cigarette. Do you want one?"

That night had turned into a global drinking event, toasts, cigarettes, fried chicken, and working-class guys were all over the place. We laughed, danced, smoked and drank, enjoying ourselves. It became absolutely unimportant, what kind of place it was, what kind of people, food, and alcohol was there. I had a feeling I had tried all possible drinks, and before I started losing memory, I memorized that my bill was only twenty dollars, that Rita wanted to turn vegan, a fat guy was annoying me with his attention, and an older grey-haired man announced specials for upcoming Valentine's Day. Lina said he was the owner.

The final part of that night got mixed up with my nightmares. I saw my mother, burying me, crying and asking God "Why?" She was down on her knees on the dirty ground with no make-up and messy hair, sobbing so hopelessly and bitterly, with the facial expression I had never seen before. She kept repeating "my baby, my little baby…"

I got up, shaking off the nightmare. It was a dream, just a dream. I needed to call my mother. In that dark routine of recent happenings, I forgot to remind her of my existence. I forgot to remind her, that I love her.

"What's up?" Rita jumped into my room, as she was still drunk, and lay on the bed next to me. "How are you feeling?"

"Terrible," I laughed. "Can't believe we drank so much."

"It's not even so much," she stretched. "Sometimes I can't stop shaking and want to call 911. That is so much!"

We both laughed.

"So, did the skinny guy hire you?" she asked me with curiosity.

"Which skinny guy?" I mumbled. "I only remember the fat one who was annoying me all night, asking for my number."

"No, the fat guy left early. The skinny guy in a suit I'm talking about."

I tried hard to recall someone in a suit, but instead got a new wave of headache.

"God damn it, I don't remember any guy in suit," I told her. "What about him?"

"Oh, I see, you need to practice more drinking," my roommate laughed. "He came after twelve. A real estate agent. He said he could bring you to his company to try you out. Something, you can make a lot of money of. You wanted to try last night."

"Don't remember any of these…" I muttered.

"Still wanna try?" she giggled.

"Well, I can't think of anything right now," I said, holding my head as if it would stop the headache.

"He gave us his business cards before we parted… I think. He even escorted us home once everybody left the bar with the sunrise."

"Why the bill was so low?" I remembered about twenty dollars check. "I thought it was going to be at least eighty."

"We don't charge people, especially friends, a lot, so we can get good tips. Good for us, not much fun the owner though. But as long as he doesn't know, it's all fine."

Half of that day was spent in a shower, mixing cold and warm water, I was trying to get rid of toxins and cool down my hot-burning body. I felt a bit better before leaving for the refugee consultation. Only after I exited my building, I remembered that I forgot to call my mother. Just like the day before and the day before that day.

Barely alive, I entered the office on the 17th floor of Manhattan's downtown skyscraper. Young girls quickly registered me at the entrance and sent me to the auditorium, where I saw about twenty people like myself. They were mostly my age, all Russian speakers. I was surprised to find out most of them were legal in the country; unlike me, they started to look for proper ways of staying here in advance.

Once everybody had arrived, a man in his sixties came up to a small stage. He accepted skype calls, turned on transmitters and receivers, and introduced himself, making clear he was not a lawyer. I was surprised how many people knew about him, even though he wasn't advertised anywhere.

His specialty, was refugees. He consulted every lost soul, creating a peculiar case for each one, that was supposed to prove he or she was in danger in their own country and came here with the only purpose to save their lives. Reasons for abandoning homelands varied from discrimination based on race or nationality, political or religious views to the danger of being homosexual, or any type of sexual, but traditional. To prove the threat to life back home, victims and "victims" had to have evidence as papers from doctors, concluding that they had indeed been beaten up, or undergone attempts of assassination, or anything else that might show the impossibility of existing in the country of origin.

After his speech was over, the lecturer, asked everybody to leave the room and organize a line, he gave each of us up to ten minutes for a free private consultation.

"You see," he said, after I described my situation, "you've been in the country for almost fourteen months, six of these fourteen months you remained illegal. It's not very good for the case."

His eyes were strictly fixed on mine and his voice remained calm.

"I always tell people, it's best to start this right after arrival," he continued, "but, however, there is a way to make it happen for you. To be honest, I can't guarantee it will be successful. I'd say fifty percent, or less."

"I couldn't make it earlier," I interrupted him to earn more sanity in his eyes. "I didn't plan to stay here."

"That's why most of the people become illegal. Some of us can't make the choice till the rest of our lives, going back and force with decisions," he stated calmly, not raising or lowering his voice.

"My price isn't too high, nor too low. Your case will vary between five to six thousand dollars. What we can do is to send you to a psychologist, you will have to attend sessions every week for a couple of months, saying how desperate you were in Russia and how scared and emotionally exhausted you were here to start the process of refuge. It will explain to judges why you didn't do it earlier. Although, the fact that you managed to go to Clark University isn't too good.

In addition, it may take a few years to get an interview scheduled. You must be prepared to not be able to travel outside of the country for the next... Let's say five years."

He looked deeply into my eyes.

"Even once you'll have a travel document, you won't be allowed to visit Russia. What you can do is fly through a third country with an American travel permit, and then you can go to Russia with your Russian passport. It seems complicated, but people get used to it."

"You don't have to answer right now," he said at the end. "As I said, I can't guarantee success, and I would probably give it even less than fifty percent, but if you decide to go for it, call the office and we will start working on it right away. We do also split payments if our clients are not able to pay everything at once."

He handed me a business card, the same one I got from Rita, and ordered, "Tell the next one to come in."

I felt drained when I got out of the office. It was cold and fresh outside. Russian-speaking guys were smoking cigarettes and discussing something loudly.

The procedure was too complicated, and the lack of guarantees bothered me a lot. I couldn't afford to pay for less than 50% chances and wait for an interview for years. I put his business card in my wallet next to the one I already had.

I thought about my mom with pain. Poor ageing woman, how lonely she must be there, surrounded by my portraits in the empty apartment on the 8th floor, waiting for me patiently, going to church every single Sunday to light a candle for my health and luck. She had never admitted how distant her life had become without me, how pointless and gloomy it was. She would always cheer me up, cure all my wounds with her eternal love, without having a single complaint about her reality, I was everything she had. How many more years she would have to age in solitude? Would I ever enclose her in my arms, as there was no separation at all?

"I love you, mommy." I sent an email as soon as I got off the train in Brooklyn.

It was late evening when I got home from the frosty winter. I walked into my room in a heavy coat and snowy boots, shook upside down my last night's purse, and among all the mess, I saw the business card of a real estate agent Ryan Shagon.

I dialled his number the same minute.

Unlike me, he perfectly remembered who I was and how we met.

"I want to try," I said. "Can I start tomorrow?"

I started off with a couple of successful deals. My manager didn't care about me not having a license, not to mention, being illegal in the country. As long as I brought clients, he was fine with everything. I advertised the company's exclusive listings and showed the apartments I was contacted regarding.

I came to the office every single morning — on weekends and weekdays. I didn't care about days off, because I didn't mind the job, furthermore, I considered it the best job since I had arrived in the U.S. I didn't make any friends, as all agents were constantly on the phone or out at showings. I was getting 50% of the monthly rent right after a contract would be signed. Ryan was getting 10% of my deals and didn't mind driving me around and help taking pictures of apartments. Sometimes he would drive me to showings, but mostly he was teaching me how to talk and act in order to manipulate clients. I found this part very annoying.

Ryan had a talent for pushing people to apply for apartments by convincing them it was the best deal on market. He told them, there was no way they could find anything better-cheaper-bigger-closer-to-the-subway. The expression on his face along with the semi-professional and semi-casual friendly look attracted people and made them trust him. However, none of those apartments was worth looking at, and Ryan would often make fun of people for not doing enough research and renting trashy overpriced Brooklyn apartments instead of decent Manhattan dwellings.

I could never push people to do things. Especially if I myself didn't believe in what I was saying. I was very shy. I was shy of my English, my accent, and my poor knowledge of real estate. However, I enjoyed being on my terms. I chose apartments I wanted to work on, I built my schedule, I created my ads, and I developed my strategy. Ryan taught me to advertise for free on craigslist. It was illegal as brokers had to pay fees for placing ads, but owners themselves didn't have to pay anything. So many times, potential renters were accusing us, agents, of posting on behalf of landlords, threatening with calling New York State Department which would revoke our licenses. I, personally, had nothing to lose, so I consistently ignored these threats and continued doing the same.

I was trained to lie about neighborhoods as well, turning the ones with bad reputation into prestigious ones. Crown Heights was called Prospect Heights, Bedstuy grew into Clinton Hill, and Bushwick became Williamsburg. Official borders of fancy neighborhoods were constantly and magically expanding for my clients, as borders of bad ones were proportionally getting altered. Tiny studios were advertised as "spacious one-bedrooms", one-bedrooms were two-bedrooms, and three-bedrooms were mansions.

I often thought of Dmitry. I hated myself for that. I tried to imagine those thoughts as shapeless nuggets, just like a few jellyfish gathered in one spot, but dry and flammable ones. I imagined them multiplying as I was thinking more and more about him, and once this thinking became unbearable, I would light them with a lighter and watch them burn, saying goodbye with the hope of never dealing with that gang of dry jellyfish again. The gang would return and get burned over and over again, yet, every time it would happen less and less frequent. I congratulated myself on doing a good job, and sometimes days would pass without me thinking about him at all. Although, a random smell, word, sound would collapse all my pride as a house of cards. I hated him for loving him.

It seemed like it was safe enough to contact Adil. I thought of writing him a letter. Time-to-time, I recalled his body getting smaller and smaller on the screen of a cab window, waving on the corner by the grocery store. My heart would fill itself up with endless warmth and pain at the same time. I felt awful to admit, the reason I wanted to write him was to find out what was going on with Dmitry.

On one of the nights of tiresome and result less showings, I stopped by GD for a quick drink or two and found Rita by the bar counter. She was saying something to sober-looking Lina, who this time didn't seem talkative at all. The place was empty. It was around eight and my roommate was quite tipsy. I saw signs of crying on her face, even though she was wearing a smile.

Surprisingly, she was not surprised to see me.

"What happened?" I asked without greetings, seating myself next to her.

"He was supposed to come, but he didn't…" she giggled. "So, I'm celebrating…"

I hugged her, feeling bad for a poor girl, thinking about Dmitry and those occasions back in Russia when he would disappear for days and then come back as if nothing happened. I would wait. Wait and forgive everything.

"Do you really love him?" I asked, still hugging her.

She nodded. She was wearing a pink dress of an unknown to me fabric and high heels. I looked at the dress and thought, it could as well pass for a sleeping gown, but didn't mention it to her.

"He is not married, is he?"

"He is not, he is just very busy with work," she cried.

"Is he American?"

"Albanian," she answered, "but he is an American citizen."

I didn't know what to say to support her. I thought of Dmitry again and murmured as I was as well giving this suggestion to myself, "You will find the right man. You're worth dozens of caring and loving men. Don't waste your time, waiting for the one, who isn't going to come."

She nodded. I realised that I was waiting for something that would never happen as well. I had already forgotten about the pain Dmitry caused me. Time changes our memories and perception of happiness. Every current love is always the strongest, but after everything is gone and you become completely free, there are barely records of feelings, only matters of facts.

"Did you always want to come to the U.S?" I asked to switch her attention.

It didn't take her a second to respond, as she had this answer ready, "No. My mother abandoned me as I was a child. She fled from us with some man. I almost don't remember anything about her. My grandma raised me. She adores me."

She smiled a very sad smile, "I really want her to be proud of me, I really want her to be happy, you know? Now I have nothing to be proud of, so I don't call her, even if I'm dying to hear her voice."

She stopped talking and ordered another drink. I didn't find any connection between the question and the answer but nodded. In any case, I felt her pain.

"So how did you decide to come here?"

"Oh! Right!" Rita exclaimed. "My grandma saved some money for me. She said I could achieve so much here. She always believed in my intellectual capacity. She lived her life in poverty, you know, she didn't want me to repeat her misfortune. So, she sent me here. Imagine, how badly she loves me? She sent her only child, all right, grandchild, you know what I mean, away from her."

I wanted to ask her, whether she ever tried to reconnect with her mother, whether she knew anything about her, and what happened to her father, but her eyes suddenly turned shiny and a big smile occurred — I knew, something else came to her mind.

"You know, I always had a plot for a novel in my mind! I was even trying to paint it, but I couldn't. All I know is it's writeable. Listen.

The guy, right? Or a girl! Let it be a girl. You know, the adult one. So, she goes through a lot of shit. She lives a hard life. Literally hard, you know. Her boyfriend abandons her, and her bosses harass her, so she has to go from one job to another; all men she meets mistreat her, and nothing works out. She gets fired time-to-time too, because… I don't know, she just gets fired. She's trying to live as normal people do. I don't want to say she isn't normal. Not that she's abnormal. I mean, nobody is very normal, so she is as normal as everybody!"

Rita laughed loudly.

"Who's normal, right?"

I nodded with a smile.

"So, life doesn't treat her well. She has nobody. She's very lonely. You're getting the picture, right? Everyone abandons her. People she trusts betray her. So, she… Oh, yeah, I forgot to say, she drinks a lot! She has to deal with her hard life somehow, right? She… knows she needs to change something."

She stopped and gazed into nowhere.

"And what happens then?" I wondered.

"I haven't come up with it yet," she scratched the cheek of her now serious face. "That's what I have for the moment. I'll let you know the continuation some other time!"

"Okay." I vocalized in a stupor.

"Oh, yeah, and she suffers from insomnias!" Rita added.

I giggled not understanding what it was all about as this part of the plot wasn't even worth telling.

Rita laughed loudly, then grew serious, "It's not much fun, you know. Especially when you want to die in sleep but can't fall asleep. Has it ever happened to you?"

"I don't think so," I answered.

"You see?" she winked.

Looking elated and satisfied, she fell deep into thinking. I didn't know where her mind went. One would easily get lost in the kingdom of her thoughts.

That night I had to carry Rita home. Somehow, I managed to get her to bed and take off her shoes. She kept repeating, "I need to join the U.S Army, they would issue me citizenship right away. They would also give me a lot of benefits," she said. She would do it as well, but she was happy in love and her "sweetheart" would never let her go there. She also told me she didn't want to die in her sleep. She said she would soon decide, whether her character should die or stay alive. She asked me to wait and not to write about it quite yet. She would come up with something. I was too exhausted to think about it.

A heavy girl didn't remember anything in the morning. She drank pickle juice right from the jar of pickles and complained about a horrible headache and shortness of breath. She genuinely smiled, and it appeared to me, that physical suffering was more bearable to her, than mental, and in fact, it did a good job suppressing the latter one.

"I gotta go back on the wagon. Damn it, I just can't stop once I start. It's unbelievable, no matter how hard I try to stop — I keep drinking till I'm off."

I took a day off the day Bartek arrived. I was plucking my eyebrows, doing refreshing masks, and exercising all morning. I carefully chose my outfit, combining dressy black pants with a grey blouse and a light-blue cotton scarf. I was so happy to finally be able to see his smiley face and kind eyes again. His sweet voice kept repeating a distant, yet a very familiar word in my head. Katen'ka.

Does he have a Valentine? I smiled, thinking about it.

We agreed to meet in Time Square by the red stairs. As soon as I got there, I realized how bad of an idea it was, I hadn't seen so many people for a long time. I looked around but hadn't noticed anyone Bartek-looking. I double-checked my appearance in the small handy mirror and accidentally dropped it on the ground. I bent to pick it up. As I made sure it wasn't broken, I put it back in my purse. Nervousness wouldn't go away.

"Katen'ka?" I heard a Polish accent from behind.

I turned around and saw his smile. I almost cried, so childlike and innocent, he looked like an angel in the middle of crowded snowy Times

Square full of worn-out tourists. Preparing myself to fall in love with him, I ran towards him and gave him a warm hug. He squeezed me in his arms even stronger; I barely held myself from overwhelming emotions.

"Let me look at you," he said, stepping back. "Katen'ka, you are even more beautiful than you were six months ago."

"Come on!" I smiled, blushing. "I'm so happy to see you."

I did think he became more handsome, as well. His eyes were full of life and love, his blond hair got messy from wind and snow, and he looked so natural and present. He kept his sporty grey winter jacket unzipped, so I could see the dark-green vest with a white collar pumping out from it.

"Me too," he grinned warmly. "By the way, let me introduce you to someone!"

He looked back and shouted, "Molly!"

There was a young woman in a long orange coat. She was talking to a "Spiderman" but rushed towards us as soon as she heard Bartek.

She walked easily and freely, smiling cheerfully, demonstrating her perfectly white teeth.

"These guys are crazy," she giggled, and pointed at the Spiderman. "He said he can get naked for $100."

We laughed, and then Bartek introduced us. And literally, the second before he did it, I played that sentence in my mind, exactly the way it was, besides the names. And annoying dull irritation filled my stomach.

"Kate, this is my wife, Molly. Molly, this is Kate," he stated gratefully.

"What's our plan for today?" he asked after we exchanged our "nice to meet you".

I felt like my heart was stubbed in the rudest manner, unexpectedly. I wasn't happy or excited any more, I just wanted to go home. At the same time, I knew it was all my fault, I built that different reality and lived in it for a while, so why was I so hurt? It was not a date. I didn't even think of Bartek at all before I saw his message. I was never in love with him. Why was I so disappointed?

"You guys want to walk in Central Park?" I asked in order to say something.

"We are up to anything here," Bartek agreed, and kissed Molly on her lips.

I faked a smile.

We started walking towards Central Park. The couple held their hands.

I had to admit Molly was cute, a little shorter than me, with pale skin and curly orange hair. Her voice was somewhat high pitched, which sounded funny, but charming. I was sure Bartek adored her. Maybe even more than then he adored me.

"How did you guys meet?" I asked.

Bartek laughed.

"It's such a story, actually!" Molly started. "His uncle asked me if I wanted to marry a nice cute guy for $20 K. He said I won't have to do much, besides filing taxes together, signing a few papers, taking a few pictures together, and appearing at the interview. So, I thought, why not!"

"Why not, she thought," Bartek giggled, wrapping his arm around her shoulder.

"So, we decided to go for drinks and get to know each other better," she disclosed. "And we did! I fell in love with him right away!"

"Is it possible not to fall in love with this cutie?" she asked me joyfully.

I faked a smile again, thinking whether she knew about our affair.

"And after some amount of alcohol he kissed me…" she continued.

"No, you kissed me," he said playfully.

"And after half an hour of making out we decided to forget about the money thing and everything. Bartek said he was taking me home for the continuation. I didn't mind," she smiled flirtily.

"Wow," I exclaimed, trying to look amazed, yet deep inside I got carried away to Worcester, to our romantic evenings with wine and tasty dinners. I remembered the flowers he gave me every time he saw me. I recalled the way he kissed my hands and fingers, and never stopped repeating how gorgeous I was. Then Dmitry appeared. He was a total antipode, and I still chose him over a really great person.

I realized how frustrated I was, while Molly spoke about their growing love.

"Did you get your papers?" Bartek asked me after his wife finished the story.

"I'm working on it," I lied.

"I just got a green card! We had an interview two weeks ago. So, we are traveling now, the day after tomorrow we are flying from JFK to Poland to visit my parents, then going on a road trip to Germany and Netherlands. That's why we are in New York, basically."

"It's very exciting," I murmured, not able to sound excited.

"It is," Molly confirmed. "Atlanta is great, but it's nice to get out sometimes."

"What do you guys do there for living?" I asked by the way.

"Molly is an accountant and I am an assistant of the marketer." Bartek explained, fixing his hair.

"And you?" he inquired shyly.

"Real estate." I uttered it with pride. So far it was my first job in the U.S. I wasn't ashamed to mention.

"That's nice," Molly shouted. "If we decide to move here one day you can help us find a place!"

She looked at Bartek playfully, grabbing and squeezing his entire arm with her hands.

We reached the park. I felt exhausted. I wasn't jealous or mad. I got very tired and upset with myself. I didn't love Bartek, and that day, looking at him and his wife, I finally understood why. He was an open book. Nice, short, and easily readable book. I had a way more complicated taste in literature.

We spent a couple of hours in the park, making pictures of Molly and Bartek in snow, by trees, on bridges, by monuments, and anywhere else they would want. I kept the smile on, getting madder and colder. Right after Molly had told us she got hungry and would like to get into a warm restaurant for some food and wine, my phone rang. It was Natasha. I lost the last wish to spend time with the couple.

"Oh my god!" I yelled in the receiver. "I'll be there soon."

"What do you mean?" I heard before I hung up the phone. With enormous relief, I apologized, giving each of them a hug and wishing them a nice trip in case I was unable to see them before they departed.

I rushed back to Brooklyn, all disappointed and exhausted, but happy to finally be alone. All I wanted was to get in a hot shower and wash off the day. That was exactly what I did. I fell into a deep sleep as soon as my head touched the pillow, forgetting to return Natasha's call and renew all my real estate ads.

A new day came sooner than I had expected, dragging the chain of more days without any productive results. The money I earned at the very beginning of my short real estate career was spent faster than I had expected. I started to work harder. I posted ads on craigslist all night, and got up at 7 a.m., no matter how tired I was, answered all emails and text messages, and continued posting till the time to go to the office would come.

The only exemption I made was on St. Valentine's Day. I went to GD somewhat dressed up with Natasha and Rita. That's how they met each other. Not able to handle the absence of her beloved, Rita got very tipsy within the first half-an-hour of the party. Natasha turned off her phone with a flirty smile.

"I deserve some fun, don't I?" she giggled, and a bit later three of us clinked our glasses with semi-real smiles, but genuinely true thirst.

I noticed a while ago, that Kostya's existence hadn't become as important for Natasha, as Natasha's became for Kostya. He adored her. His face brightened up with one of the most loving and sincere smiles I had ever known, as soon as he would see her, or even hear about her. Nothing criminally brutal would remain in him in her presence, and he would turn into a defenseless child in need of love and care.

I didn't comment on Natasha's decision. I sighed and turned off my cell phone as well, I assumed he would start calling me in order to find out where she was. I had nothing to tell him.

As drinks were flowing, nothing seemed to matter any more. People were coming in. Three of us turned into five-six-seven or eight of us. I lost the count. Rita kept telling Natasha I was going to write a book about her. She also told me she thought of the development of that plot, she said it was brilliant, and maybe I could write a book about it, but only after I would write about her. We all were laughing. I could barely stand, so I sat on a barstool, while half of us danced, sang, or laughed. After a while, I found myself talking to a stranger about the meaning of life. A while later, loud whistling followed by applause interrupted our conversation, and I witnessed a prolonged kiss between Natasha and Rita. This kiss repeated itself a few more times that night. I pretended it didn't shock me at all, and I was glad that two of my friends really liked each other.

"Don't write about it though," Rita kept uttering.

I remembered feeling sick towards the end of the night. Somebody cared me to a restroom. I fell asleep embracing the toilet and slept till the owner of the bar woke me up and told me that my friends were looking for me. Then Rita woke me up at home.

"You gotta have some pickle juice," she said. "What great fun we had last night, didn't we?"

"We did," I answered, looking at the clock through a horrible headache, wondering how I could manage to work in such a bad condition.

"Now I'll have good stories to tell at AA meetings," she laughed, gulping pickle juice right from the jar and handing it to me.

After a deal I was counting on fell through, dull fear filled my chest. I began realizing I had no more money for existence. Constant nausea started escorting me from one pointless appointment to another. I ended up not having money, neither for rent nor for food. As embarrassed as I could be, I asked Rita to lend me two hundred dollars for a couple of weeks. Of course, she had no money with all the sales and drinks around. She lived one day at a time, as they suggested in AA. A couple of hundreds, I had managed to borrow from Natasha, were added to another few hundred I managed to fetch by selling my aunt's golden ring, to pay rent. I tried not to think about the wrongness of my actions, I tried to focus on one agenda — survival, however thoughts about her were drilling into my mind with incredible strength. I hated myself. I kept recalling my aunt's face, her kind eyes and her calming voice. I remembered the day she gave me that ring, it was my 18th birthday. She said I was adult enough to start wearing beautiful expensive things. It fitted me perfectly. She smiled and kissed me. A few months later, she died.

The more desperate I was turning, the harder it was becoming to handle showings. It seemed like clients felt my urge and disappeared one by one, without explaining anything. At the end of the day, no one owed me any explanation.

I tried borrowing another couple of hundred from my realty but received a kind rejection. I was a new and illegal agent, who rather failed than succeeded.

It was the beginning of March. Cold and snowy March. Just like the day I arrived in the United States, the day greyhound bus was delivering Vera and me to Worcester, to a new and unknown life. To the life that brought me back to New York, back to financial troubles, and this time it was more frightening than before.

I went to GD and asked the boss to give me some hours to work, at least one day a week. He only sighed deeply; the place was way too slow. I stopped by several bars, checking if they needed bartenders, but there was no luck. I went to a few restaurants on Brighton beach and surrounding areas, and left my resumes in a couple of stores. As time was passing, I was getting shorter and shorter on money, which, this time, I borrowed from Kostya. I stopped coming to the office in order to devote all my attention to job hunting. My pride didn't allow me to bother Rita with food matters and I kept cutting more and more ingredients out of my already poor diet till I ended up eating one Snickers a day.

I had no time to waste, as the sharp fear of becoming homeless had already started squeezing my mind, making me dizzy and hopeless. I needed a job, any job, I was ready to work 24 hours a day, every single day, saving myself from one of the worst things that could possibly happen to a human being. As fear was pushing me to stretch borders of acceptable, I started browsing colorful ads with attractive blond girls and numbers as high as $1000 per day of fast cash.

Butterflies would start tickling my empty stomach out of the thought of making $1000 a day. I would be able to quickly pay off my debts and save money for the marriage that will earn me a green card, which will allow me to visit my homeland, which became my most precious dream. I would close my eyes and inhale dry Astrakhan air with the smell of mom's favorite perfume. Tickling would get more intense, making my heart beat faster and faster, as I couldn't believe the possibility of seeing my friends and family, as it seemed unreal. Then the thought of what I would have to do for this money would enter my mind and crash my imaginary visit as a house of cards. I couldn't go for it.

I remembered drunk Rita mentioned joining the U.S army. No matter, how badly I didn't want to do that, I did some research, which showed that only people with legal status are allowed to apply for army jobs. I, honestly, felt relieved.

My Snickers diet was giving me a stomach ache. Every morning I would wake up with an immediate desire to consume a brown-navy wrapped bar right away, then struggle with myself to save it for lunch, while keeping my body hydrated, refilling a water bottle in parks and public bathrooms in between being either rejected or stood up at my hypothetical jobs and congratulated myself if I managed to keep it for dinner — those were my favorite days.

It happened to be one of those favorite evenings with a "full-course dinner" when I was looking at my subway card, which had 2 last days of unlimited rides and exactly 2 more Snickers sitting on the shelf right next to Dostoevsky's "Crime and punishment". I couldn't rest my mind going back and forth from the immorality of selling my body to strangers to fear of living on the cold and dirty streets of New York. I bit my lower lip hard enough not to cry, and hating myself, sent a few recent pictures to a couple of emails provided at the end of colorful escort service ads. I received a phone call in less than half an hour.

"Experience?" asked a harsh Russian man's voice.

"No," I answered honestly.

"Age?"

"23"

"Cup size?"

"34 C," I said.

"What is it in Russian, third?" he yelled at me nervously.

"I really don't know if C is third, must be…" I responded unsurely.

"And how am I supposed to know? Your boobs are not my boobs, helloo!"

I wanted to hang up but thought of the last two Snickers I had left.

"Third."

"Listen," he uttered. "I can try you out tomorrow night. Bring all your make-up and sexy underwear, okay? High heels, you know."

"Okay," I murmured.

"It's just bad you don't have any experience, so I'm risking, letting you in, understand? I'm afraid you'll scare all my customers out. I hope you're not a fragile coed and I won't have to guide you here and there."

"No one will force me to do anything if I won't want to, right?" I asked hopelessly with half-alive childlike voice.

"Listen," he snapped sarcastically. "There is no such thing as if you want or don't want to do. You don't choose, got it? I have no time to waste to teach you. You'll do whatever the hell a client will demand, otherwise I'll lose all the clientele due to your fucking preferences!"

Tears were coming down my cheeks. I could not believe I was treated like this and going for it regardless. It seemed like a nightmare, and the absurdity of it would wake me up in a few seconds, and a sweet relief would stop my rapid heartbeat.

"I want to try," I said firmly, blocking my mind from all possible thoughts.

"Your name?" the rude voice asked.

"Katya," I said, and immediately regretted giving my real name.

"I'm Mike." he sort of greeted me and gave the address on Madison Avenue.

"Don't forget the sexy underwear, so your boobs are exposed, okay? And shave your pussy, customers don't like it hairy." he added, demandingly, before hanging up the phone.

It left me in a horrible emptiness, as everything I went through before in my life was not more than a dream.

I altered my old silken purple lingerie into a vulgar dress, by increasing cleavage area and cutting it as short as possible. My favorite aunt bought it for me in Moscow at an expensive designer's boutique a few weeks before she was diagnosed with cancer. She winked, saying I had to have some luxury underwear.

She always wanted to have kids. Her husband said it didn't matter to him, when they learned she was infertile, he said he would always love her, he said they would find another way. And he found it. With another woman. My aunt mourned him for months, then she decided to start living for herself. Those were the best couple of years of her life. She and I went out quite often, we drank wine and I smoked cigarettes with her kind permission and promise not to tell my mom. One of these happy days of living for herself, she learned about her brain cancer. A cruel doctor reported that she literally had no time left. She said she would rather lose her hearing, yet, literally in no time, she lost her life. Now she's dead, and the last material memory of her got vandalized.

There was the entire night, the day, and a little bit of the evening of hope for something good to happen and stop me from going there. I couldn't even imagine, what.

The last innocent and anxious night kept me awake. I prohibited myself to from thinking about my values, my aunt, or my mom. Hunger, my new friend and enemy, was squeezing and hurting my stomach, releasing a variety of different sounds. I tried to distract myself from focusing on it, I started to think of Worcester, Clark University, Vera, Jamaica, Ron's bar and Sherry's house. Then I thought about Shawn and realized how much I missed him. I blamed myself for breaking up our friendship. Just a thought of his wonderful personality made me smile. I dialled his number, it was half passed ten.

CHAPTER 8

It was already dark when I mistakenly got off the train at Union Square instead of Times Square. I exited the subway by Wholefoods and walked north through rows of tables with hats, scarfs, jewelry; crowds of passing tourists, locals, homeless, chess players. I breathed a sigh of sadness, watching people playing chess. In my mind, I went back to my middle-school years and recalled hours of playing chess behind the shopping mall, while skipping the swimming classes. I suddenly realized it was one of the happiest times of my life. How obvious it becomes after years of struggle, and how unnoticeable it is in present. I felt I was at the very bottom of my existence. Almost through tears, I looked at people rushing somewhere, cars, fireflies and traffic lights switching in between. I listened to the evening, it sounded like a holiday. It smelled like a holiday. Life was blossoming. Yet I wasn't a part of it, I was inside a mobile prison, sentenced to learn to live.

I had one more hour to put myself in one piece. Just one more hour, that seemed so distant and unreal. I was walking slowly towards Midtown, holding a little sticky note with the address. My hands were shaking. My brain was rambling. I couldn't believe I was going for it, even though I gave myself permission to change my mind, there was nothing to change it for better. No miracles were foreseen.

Shawn's kind voice from the previous night kept sounding in my head, calming me down. He wasn't mad at me. He understood everything. He fell in love himself, no matter how badly he didn't want it. She was a police officer in the precinct he volunteered for. She was a mysterious woman no one knew anything about. She had never answered Shawn's questions regarding where she lived, whether she was married or dated anybody, what was her sexual orientation. She only smiled with a gorgeous fascinating smile, Shawn said, was the most beautiful smile he had ever seen. Sometimes it seemed as if she flirted with him, sometimes she totally ignored him. He couldn't figure whether there was anything going on. He took many extra shifts, neglecting his security jobs, and began spending his savings just to see her more often. He wanted to confess, but didn't have courage, he felt so fragile and defenseless around her. He dreamed about her smile, that broke his heart a hundred times a day, and at the same time, gave him a reason to live.

I rang the bell exactly as was told, at 7 pm. It was an old walk-up building. Someone buzzed me in without asking anything. The apartment was on the first floor. I walked in. No one welcomed me. Not knowing what to do, I went to the living room. There were two Russian women dressed in vulgar lingerie, both in their mid-thirties. They were fighting over something, not paying any attention to me. One was slim and blond and had quite a rude face. Another one was brunette and a bit chubby, she looked friendlier. That living room seemed to be a waiting area for clients; it was pretty spacious and had two more doors in it, which led to two more rooms. One of them was closed. It smelled like cigarette smoke. A huge screen on the wall was broadcasting porn soundlessly. "My heart will go on" was flowing from behind the closed door.

"Hi," I shyly greeted the girls who didn't seem to notice me.

"Did Mike tell you whether you are working today, or he only wants to interview you?" asked the brunette one in clear Russian, looking annoyed by my presence.

"Me? I, honestly, don't…" I started murmuring.

The phone rang, and she immediately picked it up with the sweetest "Hello…" I had ever heard.

"…Yes sweetie… yes… any time for you… yeas… see you soon…"

I couldn't get enough air.

"So, you wanna take him or not?" the blond one asked the brunette, pointing at the closed door. "He came for an hour".

"I'm picking up my daughter from a kindergarten now," the brunette stated, brushing her curly dark hair. "I gotta go!"

Blonde looked at me. I had nothing at all to say. I felt like a scared child who lost her mom and couldn't find the right path to get out of the maze of strangers. I only gave her a frustrated look.

"Okay," she snapped, spraying heavy perfume all over her body, and disappearing into the occupied room. I could still hear her super nice "heeey sweetie" while she was closing the door from the inside.

The brunette had counted money and started to pack her electronic gadgets in the little purse. I sat down next to her on the edge of the sofa, holding my heavy coat on my knees, ready to run away any minute. There was no logical reason why I suddenly felt so related to her at that moment; I felt like she was the only person on the planet who could understand me.

"I'm so nervous," I told her.

She stopped packing and looked at me with a sad smile. There was so much warmth and depth in those eyes, so much understanding. That instantly made me want to cry, but I held it.

"Everything will be all right," she breathed.

There was nothing else to say and nothing more to expect. She gazed at my frightened face, and I felt like the lost child had found her mother.

"You'll get used to it... Once you'll start making a thousand a day, you will look at it differently". Then she winked happily and smiled again.

The intercom rang loudly. The brunette switched the porn channel on the TV to the camera by the building entrance and we saw a short, old Indian man. She told me to press "open" for him, he was an old customer and a good guy. I sneaked to the bathroom, before the good guy entered the apartment. He acted as a prospect there, asking how the girls where doing, and who was going to satisfy him. Joking and laughing, the brunette escorted him to the empty room, turned on a slow music, and left, saying "...not me... the new girl will take care of you!"

"Very nice guy," she repeated, approaching me. "He owns a perfume store, if he likes you, he'll bring you a new perfume every week! He also gives good tips!"

"So, what do I do?" The anxiety made my body shake.

"First, change here, in the bathroom, there are different sizes of pumps by the TV." She evaluated me from head to toe and pointed at my right arm, "Make sure you hide this. Greet him nicely as you walk in... start with the touching... then ask how he would like to do it... you know... he usually likes to be on top and he comes really fast!"

She winked.

"Everything will be all right," she murmured, looking at the shiny watch on her left wrist, "Shit! I'm late!"

I was fixing my makeup in the bathroom when she left and locked the door. It became frustratingly quiet and odd in a way, that I could still hear noises and voices from outside as they flew from New York's crowded streets to that very bathroom to show how miserable and lonely I was. Lucky, lucky strangers, I thought. I looked at the lingerie I had to wear and felt so bonded to my problems. I was in a prison of my despair. I automatically thought of Fantine from Les Misérables. Poor thing, I repeated several times in my mind. Now I had a clear idea of what she had to go through, and how unfairly life treated her, and why she ended up so badly.

I didn't want to end up there. I couldn't imagine engaging in it, I didn't know how I would be able to look into people's eyes, whether I'd be able to distract myself from those thoughts outside of those walls. Would I be able to talk to my mother? How many times a day would I have to die while selling my body to strangers?

There was nothing encouraging in those thoughts. I lost the courage to my inner monologue. All the debts that I had didn't seem that important any more. Everything will be all right, I told myself, leaving the apartment. I was walking out slowly, but surely, putting back my scarf, and zipping up my coat on the way. I quietly locked the apartment door and left the building, conscious and anxious, as if I was a burglar, carrying out stolen valuables. I ran towards the subway as I left the building. It started to rain. Tiny drops were flying down to the ground. It felt fresh. I could finally breathe. I took a big gulp of oxygen before I went under the ground. F train promptly delivered me to 18th ave, and I went straight to GD. It was the safest place on Earth. I asked Lina to make a tab for me, which I would pay in a couple of days. I needed endless supplies of alcohol.

Mike called me a few times that night. I dared to talk only after the second Long Island Iced tea when the world became lighter and brighter again. The pimp screamed and cursed in old fashioned Russian language, saying that I scared out all of his customers, that it's not how we do business, and that I will be responsible for that messy evening. Deep in my heart, I admitted that I had done something bad and unfair to him, but at that very moment of a pleasant drunken state, I didn't care about anything any more. I had no clue what was going to happen the next morning, whether I would regret it or not. I only knew I was in a safe place… getting drunk with strangers… and it was all I wanted to know. I didn't remember how I got home that night.

An early phone call woke me up in the morning. Thinking about an angry Russian pimp, I decided not to pick it up, and let it go to voicemail. In the meantime, I consumed two headache pills. I could barely move around, so I decided to go back to bed. Only after a short nap, I remembered the voicemail. A pleasant female Russian voice said she liked my photos and would love to talk to me about the job. I didn't know which ad it was and couldn't recall where exactly I had sent my pictures in that insane despair, yet I called back immediately. She briefly described the sexual massage duties and mentioned up to $500 and more daily salary. She also assured me there was no sex. We arranged an appointment for the same day.

I ran into an empty Starbucks about fifteen minutes late, blaming myself for this unpunctuality. I was hoping my horrible hangover wasn't obvious. After a long glance around, I realized the businesswoman by the window was Snezhana. She gave me the look of a guy, estimating a girl on the first date. I instantly felt shy. She nodded and pointed at the seat next to her.

Snezhana seemed to take excellent care of herself. I noticed her perfectly shaped red nails, well-done make-up, straight and accurately trimmed dark hair down to her chin and sensed a semi-sweet smell of her perfume. Instinctively, I hid my undyed nails in a shadow of a counter-table and moved a little further from her, so she couldn't smell my last night's partying.

"How long are you planning to do this for?" she asked strictly, but friendly as soon as I sat down.

"Well…" I heard myself speaking, "I really don't know. I have big financial problems right now… So as long as possible…"

She smiled warmly. My answer didn't really give any information.

She fixed the pinkish blouse under the grey jacket that perfectly fitted her skinny body and began to introduce her business to me, speaking friendly, but carefully thinking about each word she pronounced. She sat as she posed for an invisible photographer, so glamorous and elegant; I wondered if she learned it from the job. As I noticed later, she was a bit taller than me, which was rare and therefore felt pleasant. She had shiny brown eyes that always stayed focused and looked thoughtful. She seemed to be in her mid-forties. I didn't know how to look at her, how to talk to her, how to treat her in this business encounter of the type I had never had in my life before and never thought I would have.

Snezhana got into this business about 4 years ago, when her husband left her with a little son in a small apartment on Coney Island. She had no funds, no documents, and spoke very poor English. She needed to survive. She borrowed money to rent a one-bedroom apartment in the Grand Central area and send the child to day-care. She advertised a newly-created business online and started accepting "visitors" in the new home during daytime and do outcalls at night. It paid back all the expenses very fast. She finally was able to settle accounts with everybody, acquire a green card through a fake marriage, and soon enough, afford to live the life she never knew before. A loving mother got a chance to invest in her child's future by hiring music, painting, sport, and English teachers; she was finally able to spoil him with better clothing and new gadgets. They got a habit of going to Hawaii or Florida two-three times a year. Everything seemed to be great, except her personal life. Snezhana parted away from friends and avoided making new connections and getting into any affairs with men. A drunk customer broke in to her place once, and she had no choice, but to move out in order to protect her son. She rented an apartment in a quiet Upper East and quickly moved their life to a new neighborhood. Shortly after, she hired a younger girl to work at the Grand Central and share daily revenue. Less money, but less troubles, too. Girls were replacing one another right after they made some "fast money"; a few of them went back to Russia, some got deeper in the escort service, others — built careers in socially accepted fields.

"It's a temporary step to fix your problems," Snezhana explained. "Then it's your choice whether you want to have a good life or to turn it into misery."

I sympathized with her right away. I listened to that story and felt as if it was mine, as I went through it, yet, not only sympathetically, but also absolutely logically, agreeing with every decision of hers, with every thought. I admired her bravery. It does take a lot of strength to get into this. So many people fight with debts all their lives, and extend their existence from penny to penny, accepting all possible help from the outside. It's not easy to step over your values, but once you've done it — everything becomes possible.

Snezhana took me to the "place" right after she made sure I was real and honest. We walked into a small one-bedroom apartment located on the second floor of an old building. The living space looked fresh and clean. It had a big leather couch and a magazine table, which automatically reminded me of a waiting area at a dentist's office. Two slide doors by the couch were leading into a cozy, intimate atmosphere with a massage table in the middle. Each corner of the room was decorated with erotic red and purple lights, and lace burgundy curtains covered the window.

"Don't worry, there is nothing difficult," Snezhana told me in the end. "I'll show you everything step by step. I'll teach you simple massage techniques tomorrow."

I was leaving full of hopes and expectations. I thanked her a few times, she was my survivor. She kept smiling, standing by the door, gazing at me leaving. Don't thank me, I assumed her thoughts, nobody knows what the next day brings.

That night I ate the last Snickers I had and drank a cup of hot jasmine tea. My stomach was hurting terribly, and the hangover leftovers were still giving me discomfort. I was looking forward to making money that would set me free. All my thoughts were about counting how much I should earn a day to have $6,000 by the end of the month… to have $10,000…? Ready to work 24/7, I was too excited to fall asleep, lying in the darkness and pretending not to hear Rita knocking on my door in presence of someone else, who whispered something in Russian, which, I assumed, was Natasha. I waited till they left the apartment, hoping to pass out right after. However, full of thoughts and fears, I couldn't rest all night, searching for a proper position and constantly turning the pillow a cold side up. My heavy gaze registered the beginning of each hour on the electronic clock, up to five in the morning. Then I sank into a deep and short sleep.

I came over to Grand Central's place at 10 in the morning. Snezhana looked fresh and rested as the day before. She wore another tight suit and seemed like she was about to go to a business meeting. Yet she was to stay with me all day. My new Madam explained how to meet and treat customers and promised to be in the apartment for my first week. Her duty was to post ads online and answer all phone calls, screening clients. However, it was not easy to recognize a detective, so she warned me they usually ask many questions regarding the "place" and never take their underwear off. The best strategy for that case was to pretend there was nothing erotic, just a regular massage, although without a license.

"The job is not hard," she said. "You just have to remember that it's a business and you will need to keep the balance between keeping good customers and making money from having a lot of people a day. You want to finish a client faster and take as much as possible to make more money, at the same time you want people to come back — and trust me, permanent customers are more valuable than new ones. They are safe!

It's all up to you how to maintain this issue.

For their better satisfaction, listen to their feelings, and their moans, and try to understand what they like. Most of the guys really enjoy having their scrotum stroked…"

"What is scrotum? I only had a couple of long-term relationships in my life, but we just made love, nothing like this massage!" I asked without enthusiasm. "I also don't want any kissing or cuddling there."

"Don't worry, honey," she laughed, "Scrotum is a soft part under their balls. Just run your fingers down, as if it's by accident. Then go up, leaving it alone, and come back in a few seconds. I swear to God, they will lose their mind!

Most of them understand there is no kissing in the massage business, and if they don't know that, then you make it clear to them. They can stroke you and run their hands all over you, but not in your genital area. The complication comes because a lot of guys would like you to finger their ass holes, and the deeper you go the more they like it, because their wives won't do that for them. You have to play this by ear. And definitely ask for an extra tip.

Remember, you don't have to do anything you don't want! Don't let anybody go crazy. If they want to touch you, they gotta tip you. If they want to undress you, they gotta tip you. If they want to have sex — there are plenty of prostitutes out there! It's clear in the ad that there is no sex!"

I learned so much in one hour. I was a bit nervous, but her kind, sane voice, kept calming me down. The most important part that fought all my fears was the income. Snezhana said the fee was $120 for a half an hour of work and $200 for an hour. She would keep the half of the fee from each client, but all tips would be entirely mine. She also mentioned outcalls once I would get better with massages. They cost $250 plus tips, from which she would only get a hundred. The thought of going somewhere outside of the place frightened me even more.

"Hi sweetie," I eventually heard Snezhana's working speech, transferred from firm and sane to sweet and playful, just like in the other place I escaped from, "Yes... right... no, sweetie, no sex, It's a sensual body work with stress relief... My donation is $200 for an hour. It's Lexington and 40th. Call me when you'll get to that corner. I'll tell you where to come. okay sweetie, I'll see you soon. My name is Sofia."

"You got 15 minutes!" she shouted with her real voice and ran into the room to turn on the lights and the music, "You are Sofia, if they ask!"

With shaking hands, I quickly put the gift from my aunt on and sprayed some of Snezhana's perfume on it. I tried calm down before applying shadows and mascara. My madam covered the massage table with a paper sheet and put some slow erotic music on. She adjusted lights to give the dark room only a little hint of red, pink, and purple. It was pretty cold in the apartment.

Everything will be all right, I assured myself when the makeup was on. I stepped into high heels right after the client confirmed he was at the corner near the building. Snezhana gave him the exact address and the apartment number, smiled to me, and hid inside of a big walk-in closet in the living area. I took a deep breath.

In a few seconds I opened the door with the warmest, "Hi sweetie". Just like Snezhana did.

"Hello," a tall and skinny man walked in. "Brrr, it's so cold outside!"

He looked like an office clerk who took a couple of hours break from work. His shoes were so shiny, that I could see them even in the darkness.

"I know! You must need a nice warm up," I tried to flirt with him, ignoring my wild heartbeat.

"Oh yeah," he smiled. "I can't wait"

"How long would you like to stay, sweetie?"

"Hmmm..." he looked at me from toes to head, "One hour!"

"Good," was all I could say, escorting him to the private room with erotic music and lights on, "Take off your clothes and lay down... You can leave my donation on this stand... I'll be right back in a minute..."

I closed the doors and sat down on the couch, trying to relax, yet my heart was about to jump out of my chest. At that very moment, I wished I could have a drink, a shot of something strong that would burn my throat and tranquilize my mind. Snezhana quietly opened the closet and whispered, "Make sure he left money on the stand, don't be shy to ask if you won't see it! And don't let him stay longer than an hour... actually try to finish him within 45 minutes or so!"

"Ok!" I mumbled.

"Now go!"

I slid the doors open and went into calming atmosphere of slow music and dim pinkish lights. The customer was lying face down naked on the massage table. He didn't even move when I walked in, and I assumed he visited places like this pretty often.

Pieces of his suit were perfectly folded and put near the table. I made sure money was on the stand. Then I grabbed aroma oil and started spreading it over his back.

"How is your day going?" I asked with the sweetest and innocent voice, just in order to ask something.

"It's not bad," he giggled. "Better now."

"What do you do?" I almost whispered, not able to hold my nervousness and sound sexy at the same time.

"Real estate," he said. "How old are you?"

"I'm 21," I lied.

"So, you like giving massages?"

"I love it!" I lied again with a calm and flirty voice.

"Good," he laughed.

We didn't talk more. I was focusing on the massage and listening to the erotic and relaxing music. I started with his spine, massaging it from the lower to the upper side, slightly touching his neck. Once I had rubbed most of the muscles on his back, I switched to the butt. I felt that he liked it and started to work on that area more. I couldn't wait to finish and let him go, but it seemed that time had stopped. I didn't know what to do for the whole hour. As Snezhana told me, I moved my attention to the area between his legs and started touching gently with tips of my fingers. The man started to moan.

"Would you mind turning over, sweetie?" I asked playfully.

"Sure," he said, turning on the other side.

I felt a lot more awkward now, seeing his face and even being able to make eye contact. He stared at me with his big brown eyes that partially reflected the dim lights of the room. I was awfully ashamed, and not knowing what to do, started massaging his hips. He was totally ready for the happy end.

"Aren't you getting undressed?" he asked gently.

"Well... I do... for some extra tips..." I answered shyly, hoping not to get him mad.

"So, go ahead," he murmured.

I slowly took off my dress and panties and watched the changes of his facial expression, it suddenly became more relaxed and pleased.

"Much better now!" he noticed.

I smiled. I forbade myself to think about shame or any other nerve-wracking feelings, all I wanted at that moment was to finish him as fast as possible. I touched his organ and felt that he liked it. Accepting this unspoken permission, I started to work on it. Slowly, I was sliding my hand up and down. He put his palm on my leg and then transferred it closely to the inner side of my thighs. I tried to move back, but he held me. His penis became very firm while his fingers were trying to get inside of me. He started to scream and the very next moment I felt hot smelly liquid all over my hand.

Terribly relieved, I wiped him with a wet napkin and went to dress up and wait in the living room. I sprayed alcohol all over my hand right after washing it with the soap, but it still felt as it smelled like him. I kept wiping it compulsively with aroma tissues which I found on the magazine table. The client appeared in doors, back in his suit and a tie.

"I left money and tips over there" he uttered officially as if it was a business meeting. "Thank you, Sofia. Enjoy the rest of your day."

"Thank you, Sir," I tried to say it, as friendly as I could, hiding all the misery and hatred I had in my heart.

Snezhana got out of the closet the second he left.

"How was it?" she exclaimed.

"Hmm… Not as bad as I thought."

I was shocked by what I had just done for money.

"Ok, let's clean after him, another client may come in 20 minutes!"

She counted money right after we walked into the room. There was $300.

"As I said, I only take $100, $200 is yours," she smiled.

"Oh… wow," I didn't know what else to say.

I made $200 in a spare of 45 minutes. It was my fastest money ever. I forgot about that unpleasant experience. I thought about two more clients like that one… and I'd leave with $500-600 in my pocket… I told Snezhana that I was willing to work twelve hours a day, seven days a week. She laughed.

"Little money gets earned over years of hard work, but big money comes fast and easy," Snezhana shared wisdom unknown to me.

That day I "massaged" two more people and returned home with $500 cash. I was starving. No more Snickers were left, nor I was in need of them. I wanted to have a very special dinner, I thought I would eat everything on the menu, I would order a few dishes and would be savoring them until I was unable to get up. My hands were shaking out of anticipation. I couldn't wait.

Besides hunger, there was a battle of feelings inside of me. On one hand, I was excited about my high income, on the other — disgusted with my new duties. I felt like everyone who looked at me, knew what I was doing. I couldn't erase pictures of recent actions from my head, I tried not to make any eye contact with strangers, and of course, not being able to handle my conflict of feelings, I ended up in GD.

It was Rita's shift. I ordered a big salad, a portion of stir-fried fish with mashed potato, and side orders of mushrooms and vegetables. I hadn't had a meal in a long while, and still couldn't believe I didn't have to starve any more.

"You must be very hungry," Rita remarked loudly.

I complemented my meal with a bottle of beer and suggested Rita to have something as well, but unfortunately to me, she went back on the wagon.

"In a month, or a month and a half, girl," she promised, not looking very happy.

"Is real estate getting any better?" she asked, watching me eating.

My heart bumped nervously a few times before I answered, "Yes, I rented a nice studio today."

"Good!" she exclaimed and smiled. "Lately you were not yourself."

I nodded, not looking at her.

"Have you seen your boyfriend?" I asked to switch the topic.

"Not really," she sighed.

"You never call him by name. Does he have a name?" I tried to make her smile.

"Besnik," she pronounced sadly and then smiled in excitement as something marvelous had entered her mind. "It means faithful in his language. Isn't it cool?"

I nodded unsurely. Every bite of food gave my stomach a horrible cramp as if a sharp knife was operating in there. I barely ate a quarter of what I had ordered.

A new day started with a hangover and an early client, who appeared ten minutes after I walked into the apartment. There was a young-looking well-fit guy, dressed in a suit, probably in his late thirties. He seemed very serious and somewhat disappointed.

"Is that you on the picture?" he asked as soon as he entered.

"Yes, sweetie," I lied.

"You don't look like her!"

"Well... pictures could get a bit of Photoshop sometimes," I murmured flirtily, "but the real pleasure is always real."

I had no clue what I was talking about. The hangover was squeezing my head and shortening my breath. I didn't even know what kind of picture Snezhana uploaded on the website.

"Okay," he said doubtfully, "I'll stay for half an hour!"

He appeared to be in a rush and started undressing as soon as he walked into the room. Nothing seemed to change his mood. He put the money on the stand and lay down on his stomach once he got naked.

Afraid to talk to him, I was working in silence. It wasn't a full ten minutes in when he turned over. I smiled.

"Can you remove this dress?" he asked firmly.

"Sure." I agreed, not asking for tips.

His face looked mean even after I took off my clothes.

Bastard, I thought.

He started touching my breasts and giving me commands on how to deal with the "stress relief", "Slow… Faster… Lower… Faster." It took a couple of minutes to finish, and he finally changed his facial expression to a happier one.

"The girl on the picture had much bigger boobs," he remarked right after it was over. "And bigger lips!"

"Sweetie, didn't you get what you wanted now?" I asked playfully, hiding my irritation.

"I wanted exactly the same girl from that picture," he informed me. "It's not nice to post false pictures, because people come for what they see!"

"I'm sorry if anything was not good, sweetie," I said leaving the room. "I'll see you outside."

He got dressed as fast as he got naked. Without saying anything, he quickly passed the living area — straight to the door. Right before leaving he stopped by the door for a second and smiled at me. I thought he was a pretty handsome man, and perhaps not as mean as he looked. I smiled back, letting him out.

"That was a fast one," Snezhana laughed, getting out of the closet once I had locked the door.

"A weird one," I complained, walking back to the private room. "Different picture, smaller boobs, smaller lips"

I froze in a stupor when I got into the room, there was no money on the stand. Snezhana walked there after me.

"Mother fucker!" she snapped.

I felt used. All the terrible work was for nothing. I realized why he smiled.

"It's okay. Don't take it personally. There are a lot of idiots in our business…" Madame said sympathetically. "At least it took less than half an hour. Can you imagine if he didn't pay for an hour?"

We both laughed. It definitely could be worse.

153

I thanked her, touched by her understanding. It surprised me that she didn't get mad, furthermore, she turned out to be supportive. I was sure the pimp from the first place would scream at me and demand his part of the money.

"But for future, always collect the donations in advance! Don't start if you don't see the money. Nicely mention to pay you upfront if they forget. And take the money out of the room before you start the massage."

"There are a lot of motherfuckers who don't know what they want. The most important thing is not to lose good clients due to them," she explained.

I got back to my normal pretty fast. We were chatting and laughing, Snezhana shared some unpleasant and funny stories from her experience, then looked at my arm and asked, all of a sudden, "I never noticed that before. What is it?"

I instinctively hid it behind my back, "Ah, it is electric. I was 7… I'll be hiding it from clients."

"Poor thing," she said compassionately. "Does it hurt?"

"No," I smiled shyly.

"Don't worry about the business, these suckers only care about your other body parts, not about your arm."

We both laughed. She took off the top of her suit and remained in a white blouse.

"Why are you wearing suits all the time?" I asked her.

"To look presentable if the police came," she laughed.

Seriously? I wanted to ask, but another client called.

It was a very old man with a cane. He looked like he was in his early 100s with two or three hair on his entire head and a couple more on his chin. I escorted him to the private room, and as soon as he made sure there was nobody else in the room, he started touching me everywhere he could.

"Excuse me, Sir," I yelled, taking out his hands, "Would you please be respectful?"

"I'll pay you baby, don't worry," he was murmuring and moving closer to kiss me.

"How long would you like to stay, Sir?" I asked pushing him away.

"How long can I stay? Can I stay all day?" he breathed out heavily.

I got scared and was about to call Snezhana, but calmed down in a second, thinking about money, the end of the day, and a few drinks in my favorite bar.

"Sure sweetie" I answered nicely, "But I need my donation first…"

"Of course!" he smiled. "Here, beautiful"

He pulled out $350 from his pocket. I knew he wouldn't stay for the entire day, however, I was worried he wouldn't, as well, stay alive. To be completely honest, I didn't care a bit if he died on that massage table, what really worried me was how would we handle such a situation, and what we would tell the police and his family if he had any.

"What's your name, gorgeous?" asked the old man, taking off his pants.

"Sofia."

He lay down on his back and refused to have a massage.

"Sofiiiia" he repeated. "Very beautiful name!"

"Thank you" I responded, "What would you like me to do?"

"Just touch me gently… right there"

He looked even older illuminated by all these purple-red lights. "This Is Not Ordinary Love" was sounding in the air… and its atmosphere did not go along with the action in the room.

The old guy kept talking to me and asking questions while I was touching below his waist. His hands were also travelling under my dress. A few times he closed his eyes and opened his mouth for a couple of seconds, without any movements, which frightened me and made me talk to him to make sure he was fine. Then he would come back to life and continue asking questions such as "Do you enjoy doing this?" or "Do you like my little friend?" I kept saying "Yes, sweetie". Finally, he squeezed my hand over his gadget and stared right into my eyes for a few seconds, then he released it. I barely kept myself from laughing.

I waited outside of that room impatiently, craving to wash my hands, and my body, and tell Snezhana how disgusting it was. The old man gave me another $50 leaving and mentioned that he will stop by again. I smiled, cursing him in my head.

"That was fast," Snezhana noticed, getting out of the closet. "Old fart?"

"Yeah," I laughed with disgust. "Very old and very nasty!"

She insisted on giving her only $60 since he stayed just for half an hour. I felt bad to collect all the money, but my Madame assured me I didn't owe her any more. I never thought that people in this business could be as honest and supportive as she was.

Snezhana often shared her emotions, feelings and fears from the beginning of this "career". They resembled mine a lot, which made me feel very close to her. She told me, that no one outside of this business would understand us. And it was true, that she very soon became the only person I could be open up to and share almost everything.

A few days passed as one endless and restless hour of massage. I stopped by GD almost every night, chatting with Rita or Lina, lying about the real estate business getting better, making up stories of funny clients, and giving them appearances of my true visitors.

"I got two extra days off a week," Rita told me once. "Do you think I could do good in real estate? While I'm still on the wagon."

I almost choked, looking at her deep brown eyes that gazed somewhere into the emptiness near me.

"Surely you could…" I said, thinking about how to handle this situation.

"Good!" she exclaimed, leaning over the bar counter towards me. Then whispered, "I'm so sick and tired of this job, you know. Want to do something nice. Like you."

I nodded, swallowing a gulp of my margarita.

"Can I come to your office with you tomorrow?" she asked and stepped out to serve an annoying drunk guy.

It gave me a few seconds to think. I hated lying to her.

Rita returned to me as soon as she made a drink for the customer.

"You know…" I pronounced slowly and quietly, leaning towards her. "I wouldn't recommend going to our office, because it has very bad reviews. Nobody wants to work with us. I'm only waiting for my pay check to arrive to leave the company and go to another one. Then I'll take you with me!"

"I see, not much fun," she winked. "Hurry up while I'm still on the wagon!"

I laughed with relief.

Rita bent towards me and murmured, "Listen, is Natasha gay or something?"

"I don't think so…" I answered. "At least, she never told me. Why?"

"Nothing really," she looked deeply concerned. "We drunk-kissed one more time, you know, nothing special… but a few days later she tried to kiss me again, but I told her I was too sober for that. I got a feeling it hurt her. So, I don't know."

Another customer called her, and she walked away. I started connecting dots between loss of interest in Kostya, kissing Rita, and acting suspicious lately, but stopped analyzing as soon as, Lina approached me to chat.

The 100-year-old man kept coming back, leaving good tips and compliments. He offered to become my sugar daddy and take me to Jamaica, Dominica, Hawaii, France and Spain. I had never heard this expression before, Sugar Daddy. It didn't sound very sweet to me, nor did I want to get trapped in dependence on someone.

I got to know other clients with unusual demands, such as being choked, being tied, being raped with a dildo, being hurt, being humiliated or being seduced "against" their will. They would tell me their dirty fantasies. They would moan, scream, cry, play all possible roles, then put their suits back on and leave as if it was a business meeting they had just attended.

Soon enough, I started doing outcalls, travelling to hotels and apartments with fear of seeing a familiar face, getting raped and hurt, getting videotaped, or entrapped and used in a way I couldn't even imagine. Snezhana told me it was safer, as I wouldn't encounter an undercover cop, since their agenda was mostly to discover whole places with bosses and workers, not a single girl. For some reason, it didn't ease my tension. Again, it felt like everyone around knew exactly why I entered a hotel or a building, especially a hotel. I tried hard to appear as familiar with it as I could, going strictly to an elevator, just like I had been there many times before. Outcalls cost $250. Only $100 went to Snezhana, the rest, including tips, was mine. I would feel a tremendous relief on my way back. Fresh air outside would make all my fears vanish and the thought of an entire night of drinking would brighten up my mood.

A month of torture and a tough schedule made me ten thousand dollars. That was totally enough to pay all my debts, rent, and bills, and put around five thousand in my savings account. It was the beginning of April of 2010, my second cold spring in the U.S. Snezhana became the closest person to me. We would often stop by a local bar for a drink, talking about life, love, money, and immigration. She was the only one I could be myself with, nobody else would understand me.

"You will become an American citizen one day and will get what you want," she told me once at the bar, sipping white wine after a long shift. "You are in the right state and right city for that. Most of the states don't like immigrants. Most Americans think immigrants steal jobs from them."

"Do you believe in it?" I asked.

"Nobody can steal something that you don't have, right?" she smiled at me.

"Right," I smiled back. "But on the other hand, illegals have to work somewhere."

"Well, if an American girl would come to me in search of a job, I would hire her. It would make no difference to me. Yet, it was you who came." Snezhana looked at me.

I nodded.

"There are eleven million immigrants who deliver pizzas and wash dishes, clean houses at a minimum wage, or even less than that. So where are the Americans that can't wait to occupy these positions with no benefits, no overtime pays, and no development? I think it's just an excuse not to work."

Customers were replacing one another. I got a few permanent ones, but even these were getting more and more demanding, asking to make "love" on the fifth or sixth appointment. After I would reject their offers, some of them would leave for good, some would come back in a while, checking whether I had changed my mind.

One of my regular semi-busy days brought me two new random bodies in the morning and a phone call from a third one, who spoke with a terrible accent, as Snezhana said, and got lost, looking for the building. Soon after half-hour lateness, he called up to announce his arrival. I put the music on, dimmed the light and sprayed the perfume. Snezhana went to the closet, and the man ran upstairs unusually fast. I opened the door to let him in. As I locked it after him, I turned around with prepared sweet and happy greetings but went mute once we made eye contact. It was Adil.

I got paralyzed for a few seconds. He looked at me from top to bottom, focusing his attention on my short dress and huge heels, then on my cleavage. Then back on my eyes. His mouth was open.

My knees got weak and my throat dried up, it was the last thing I had expected to happen. I took a deep breath in and waited till he would say something.

"Oh my God," he voiced with almost no accent, continuing to look at my dress.

I made one step back.

"Why, Ekaterina?" his face froze somewhere between horror and sad sympathy.

"I was broke," I replied quietly, avoiding eye contact.

He made a step toward me. He wore a suit with a striped purple tie and looked the same as I remembered him.

I took another step back.

"Didn't I tell you to let me know if you had ... have any financial difficulties?" he asked in a daze. His eyes were shining-wet.

"I lost your phone number," I shot, making excuses as a little child. "Please, don't tell anyone, please... let's forget about what happened today, okay?"

I felt miserable.

"How many money you need, Ekaterina?" he inquired loudly, searching for his wallet in a hidden pocket of the jacket and biting his upper lip.

"Please, don't," I tried to stop him, "I'm done... It's basically the last day... It was only for a few days... I needed to pay for rent. Now I'm good."

I was murmuring other things that I couldn't recall, in a stupor, refusing his money and continuing stepping back. He grabbed me by wrists all of a sudden.

"Let's go from here," he commanded. "Change your cloth and let's go! Right now!"

"Adil," I cried. "Please, leave me now here. You are a good person and I know you want only the best for me, but I'll be fine, trust me."

He squeezed my wrists even harder and muttered, "Marry me."

I took another deep breath and felt an instant pain in my lungs.

"I go back to Turkey tomorrow, let's go together. We marry, have kids, you can teach Russian in local school. My mother will love you and I take good care about you." he said it abnormally fast, not taking his usual time to think; with the hoarseness in his voice. He looked into my eyes, begging for an answer.

"I can't," I cried, removing my hands from his. "I want to live in this country."

He laughed and looked away.

"That's how you want to live? Very good, Ekaterina. Good life!"

"It's temporary," I noted. "And almost over."

"Does your mother know about it?" he wondered.

"No," I answered. "How is Dmitry? Do you know?"

"I don't know," he said, looking down, at the floor.

"Does he still live in that room or has he left?" I cried.

He looked up, then closed his eyes and murmured slowly, "He was waiting you, then he packed his stuff and left too. I don't know where."

I wanted to ask so many questions, but my mind was wimbling; all of a sudden, I needed to find out whether he was missing me, whether he was sorry for his behavior and attitude. Whether he was still in love with me.

"Ekaterina," Adil pronounced slowly, taking his time and searching for right words. "You can't love such man as Dmitry. He is jerk."

Then he took a little more time and held my shoulders with his wide palms.

"Marry me. I know I will make you happy. I am real man with real job, and I know how to take care of woman's."

"Sorry, Adil, but I can't," I breathed. "I really appreciate it though."

I looked at his face. He was still holding my shoulders. His eyes were shiny. His perfume reminded me of Kings Highway, of the layout of that apartment we lived in, a boring office job at Steve's, and late-night conversations about moral issues and life values, Flatbush Avenue store, and of course, of Dmitry.

He rested his arms and said, "Take care." Then he walked out of the apartment, but stuck by the exit, searching for something in his jacket's pockets. I waited. He turned around and stretched out his arm, holding a $500-dollar bill.

"Adil," I snapped, angrily. "Please don't…"

"It's all I can do, Ekaterina. It's all I can do. You must accept it. Just accept it." he stated and put it in my hand.

I was watching his half-bald head disappearing in the maze of the stairs. I never saw him again.

My thoughts of Dmitry came back with new strength and pain. I hated myself for being so weak but couldn't help it. I thought of the last time I saw him leaving for a pharmacy and asked myself again, was it really the last time?

It was May. Over two horrible months of my massage practice. I decided to work as much and as long as I would be able to tolerate, reminding myself of my need to earn about $20,000 for the green card. I told Snezhana I would leave as soon as I'd have enough funds and she met it with huge understanding, furthermore, she wished me not to get stuck in this business. I didn't know what my next job would be. I had no plan. I only knew I had to work on my English in order to make my dream come true.

One of these days, when I was alone in Grand Central, police knocked on the door.

I froze as I sat on the couch.

"Police! Open the door!" they screamed, almost breaking the handle.

I started to shake; all possible thoughts went through my mind. Did anyone inform them? Was any of the recent clients a cop? What would happen if they'd break in here?

They wouldn't catch me doing anything illegal, but they'd see the massage table and this entire romantic atmosphere. I got very scared, I imagined going to prison and then — back to Russia.

All I knew was I had to get rid of the massage table as soon as possible. I rushed to the bedroom to fold it and throw it on the fire escape staircase from the window. As I crept to the private room, the old wooden floor became especially noisy. In order to make it quiet, I had to fold the table in the air, which turned out to be very heavy and difficult. In the meanwhile, police broke the peephole, which wasn't perfectly fixed in the door, and started to illuminate the space with a flashlight. I moved out of the light and stopped breathing. I froze and started repeating to myself, everything will be all right... everything will be all right. In the worst case, I'll go back to Russia.

I waited until they stopped illuminating and continued folding the table. I could still hear their loud voices behind the door. It was hard to figure out how to fold the table, especially in the darkness. My shoulders and my back started to hurt terribly. I pushed it into the case and sneaked as fast and as quiet as I could to the living room to throw the table on the fire escape stair. Suddenly, all the noises stopped, and I didn't know whether I should be happy about it or not.

I opened the window and pushed the heavy table onto the iron staircase. I pushed it as far as I could with my shaking hands, and at the same time I did it as carefully as possible, so it wouldn't fall down. Very nervous, I closed the window back and covered it with curtains. In a second, I took a few books from the shelf and put them on the same windowsill. The very next moment I heard police screaming right down that window. I was not sure what they did, but I felt the motion of the staircase.

They probably saw me pushing that table, I thought, all shaking. But there was nothing I could change.

I ran back to the private room to remove all the seductive lights and hide them in the closet. Then I heard, "We know you are inside. Open the door, otherwise, we'll break it!"

I swallowed something big and painful that got stuck in my throat. My thoughts turned into a complete confusing mess, one after another, after another. They pointlessly circled around, just like a carousel. I tried to catch the proper one to make a plan of what to do. I couldn't. I took a deep breath and ran towards the fire escape. I removed all the books from the windowsill and opened the window. There were two cops downstairs right by the end of the stair. I closed the window.

"Open the door!" they yelled louder, banging on the door. It felt as if the entire apartment was shaking. I lost my last hope and sat down on the sofa, waiting for a miracle, but knowing the police would finally break-in. And it happened the very next moment.

About four people ran into the apartment, as they were catching a serial murderer. One of them handcuffed me and remained standing right next to me, while others were searching the bathroom, the private room, the kitchenette and the closet. Handcuffs painfully squeezed my wrists behind my back.

"Any more girls?" asked the one next to me, without stepping away, as he was preventing me from running.

"No," I said emotionlessly, waiting for them to take me to jail.

I felt drawn and depressed. It was only a matter of time how many months I would spend in jail before they would send me back to Russia. I thought that all I went through was for nothing. All predicaments, tortures, fight with life and my own self — everything was no bigger than a useless game.

Cops kept yelling, but I didn't understand anything any more. One of them put his heavy hand on my shoulder and shook it. I looked at him.

"Is Snezhana Gorbunova the owner of this place?" he yelled, looking strictly into my eyes.

I thought, they might have checked her mailbox. I didn't answer.

"Is Snezhana Gorbunova the owner of this place?" he asked me again, calmer this time.

"I don't know," I murmured emotionlessly.

I heard the landlord talking to another cop outside of the apartment. I couldn't understand words, just a charade of Chinese and American accents twisted together. Another cop who stood next to me removed handcuffs and cleared his throat.

"Look! We are not after you; we are after someone who handles the business," he explained in a friendly manner. "We'll let you go if you'll tell us who Snezhana Gorbunova is and whether it's her place."

I felt relieved with my hands removed from handcuffs, as if I took off very tight shoes I had spent all day in.

"I don't know who she is," I stated, not looking at him, massaging my wrists.

"The apartment is owned by Snezhana Gorbunova, the woman of 44. What is your relation to Snezhana Gorbunova?"

I didn't respond.

"Look, we won't hold you any longer if you'll tell us you worked for her. And she is the owner of this place."

"Put handcuffs back on her! Let's take her to the precinct!" another one shouted.

"Look at me," the friendly cop said, emphasizing the importance of the information they needed. "If you tell us who your madam is, we will let you go this very moment. If you'll remain silent, you'll have to go with us and there will be no way you'll be released."

"You understand what I'm saying?" he raised his voice.

I nodded.

I felt I would betray Snezhana if I would confirm she was the owner of the business, at the same time, I would betray myself if I wouldn't. It was my last chance to stay in the country. So far. I imagined her kind face for a moment, then I dropped that image. I heard her voice speaking in my mind, her laughter. I tried not to think of her. My heart was aching.

"It's her," I heard myself saying.

"Say it," someone commanded.

"It's her," I said louder, "Snezhana Gorbunova is her name. She is the owner of this place."

"Perfect," I heard.

Yet they didn't let me go as they promised. They made me text her and wait for her to return. I had no choice, besides sitting there and waiting for the one who trusted me the most. I wanted to wake up from this nightmare so badly.

"Is it her?" I suddenly saw her face almost in front of mine.

I instinctively wanted to cry, but I held it. Snezhana looked confused but courageous. Her brave eyes carried a mute question that I couldn't answer.

"Yes," I said and stared down.

CHAPTER 9

I spent about a week doing nothing. Snezhana's face was constantly in my mind. I had terrible remorse to the point of hating myself. In my mind, I was begging her for forgiveness, hoping that the situation was miraculously resolved without any bad consequences.

The police took my name, my address, and my phone number. They told me they might need me as a witness at Miss Gorbunova's trial. They warned me not to leave New York. They also warned me that if they caught me again doing this business, I would go to jail. At least they didn't know I was illegal.

I ate out and went to the movies with Rita. She finally told me that Besnik was married but promised to get divorced sometime soon. She also said that Natasha confessed she liked her, and Rita had to tell her these feelings were not mutual. She didn't want to hurt her friend, but there was no way of any continuation.

"I told her I like men," Rita stated. "But she continued insisting on trying something together, so I told her there is nothing going on, and there is no happy end whatsoever. I apologized for those drunk kisses; you know. I didn't know they would cause such trouble. I thought it was drunken fun for her as well. But apparently, not much fun."

"I told her several times, that I'm in a relationship with the man I love! And what she did! She left me an endless dramatic voicemail, saying that she's so much in love with me and seeing me hurts her, so we better stop all the communications at once," Rita added in a stupor.

"Oh my god, I missed so much! I hadn't realized something was going on!" I was shocked and felt somewhat guilty for introducing them.

"Nothing was or is going on!" Rita snapped angrily, then giggled and said, "You know, she left such a long voicemail, saying how badly she loves me and how great this feeling is on one hand, and how painful

— on the other, that she got shocked herself that it's even possible and blah-blah-blah and the voicemail's time finished before she finished."

"What did you do?" I asked, wondering why she found it so funny.

"Nothing," Rita answered. "There is nothing I can do. If she wants to stop communicating, it's all right with me. I like her as a friend, but I don't want to give her any hopes, especially after she made it clear — it's either yes or no."

I nodded. Our feelings are such a mess. How rare they are mutual. As it was said by someone, "one loves and another one only allows the first one to love". If that's the only choice, which position would I pick? I had no answer.

I was thinking about Snezhana a lot. She looked so confused, shocked and beautiful, and her eyes, her brave eyes, seemed to be in hurry to find answers to what was going on. Even when her hands got locked in handcuffs and she was about to get led away in an unknown direction, she didn't seem scared at all. I kept trying to convince myself that anybody would do the same, being in my shoes, with the choice I had. I could be departed from the country I loved, yet, Snezhana would only get a sentence or a fine. I didn't know what was happening and what she was about to get. I still couldn't let it go. I imagined her son, and a sharp pain squeezed my chest. What would happen to him? I kept thinking there could be some other way to solve the problem without victims, I kept wishing to turn back the time and do something different at that very moment when the police appeared at the door. But what?

"You are weird lately," Rita told me once, during the dinner in the sushi restaurant on Coney Island Avenue. "You look so stressed out, not doing anything."

It was warm May and the doors of the place were wide open, so we could feel the pleasant touch of fresh wind. We both drank Japanese beers.

Rita's small brown eyes were running over my face, examining every detail of it.

"Are you fired from your real estate company?" she finally came to a conclusion.

"I am," I breathed, admiring the best excuse she created for me.

"I knew that!" she yelled. "I figured you lied when you said it had a bad reputation and all that crap just to avoid taking me there."

I nodded, looking at my plate.

"Look," she said as she suddenly remembered, "Lina is kinda working somewhere else now. A few days a week. So, my boss is looking for a part-time bartender. I know, it's not what you need, but it's some money… and there is a possibility it can turn into full-time."

I took a few good sips of beer, carefully thinking about how to answer. She didn't know I had about $15,000 saved from the massage job. She didn't know I wasn't in a terrible need at in the end of February when I almost begged that boss to hire me. And she wasn't supposed to know.

"I'm planning to find some office job," I smiled. "Tired of all these running around positions. But thank you for the offer."

"How is Besnik?" I asked her. "Have you talked to him lately?"

She smiled and shook her head, then she looked away and murmured, "I want to cry so badly. He will never be with me. He only wants to have sex with me. Then he returns to his family, returns home. And I am all alone at the end of the day. Every day."

"Don't," she told me when I got up to comfort her. I sat back, not knowing what to say, as I knew there was nothing really to say.

"I know, it'll go away," she said. "Do you believe in mutual love?"

"I don't know. I haven't encountered any yet. I want to believe though," I sighed, then I laughed, "We have the rest of our lives to find out!"

Rita started laughing with tears in her eyes, raising her beer. "Cheers to that!"

Kostya called me the same night. He was worried about Natasha, wondering whether I knew what was happening with her. He said she kept telling him she would call him back later, but never did. He asked me if I knew whether she was involved with anyone. He asked if I knew, whether she fell out of love with him. He asked whether she was upset with him for some unknown reason. I told him I didn't know what was going on, at least she had never told me anything. Which was true, she had never told me anything. I felt bad for Kostya. I knew it was over.

I started applying for all office positions I could find. After attending a couple of interviews, my enthusiasm vanished. They only accepted legal residents, or people authorized to work in the country. Unfortunately, I didn't fit in either criterion. Getting depressed, slowly, but surely, I began playing with combinations of words and entered a new keyword "cash" in the job-search specification. And a few positions pumped up. Modelling was one of them. A jewelry company searched for new faces.

In the very first email I included my photos, and got replied to in five minutes. We exchanged a few more messages, after which I got on the phone with a pleasant-sounding woman, who wanted to see me in her studio in midtown Manhattan in two hours.

I picked the best black dress I had and a pair of sexy high heels, which were terribly uncomfortable, but incredibly beautiful. I spent a good amount of time on make-up and straightening my hair. Barely alive from the pain in my feet, I made it to the train stop. I arrived perfectly on time. The secretary sat me down in the waiting area and vanished.

I found myself nervous and grabbed a magazine to read, but the words wouldn't get to my mind. I only did real estate and left it, because I wanted to do something interesting, I repeated to myself. There is no way they could know about my police and massage experience. I had a slight fear that one of my former clients might work there. What if? And what if he discloses how we met? I decided to deny everything if anything. At the end of the day, no one had any proof. And why would they do it in the first place?

"Ma'am," said the secretary, pointing at the door. "She is ready for you."

"Thank you," I smiled.

I walked into a very spacious high-ceiling room with nothing inside, but a big white table and two white chairs. There was a woman sitting on one chair and a young, skinny, artistic-looking man with dark curly hair and thoughtful eyes standing beside her.

"Sooo, Ekaterina?" she exclaimed cheerfully.

"Yes," I answered.

The woman had beautiful long blond hair, fresh and toned skin, plump reddish lips, and very flirty eyes I was afraid to look at. It was hard not to notice her huge breasts and a cleavage which she intentionally emphasized. She seemed to be in her late forties, perfectly fit and very confident. She appeared to enjoy being in the center of attention and making people shy.

"Diane Sullivan," she pronounced slowly with a flirty smile.

"This is my assistant Mark," she added, pointing at the young guy.

"Hi!" I nodded to both.

"Tell us a little about yourself," said Diane without offering me a seat.

"Well… I'm originally from Russia. I live in Brooklyn. I have a master's in marketing…" I started nervously.

"Okay." Diane stopped me and got up from the chair.

She walked towards me in her huge heels and came so close that I noticed her eyes were exactly on the same level as mine.

"How tall are you, Ekaterina?" she asked.

"5'9," I answered promptly.

"What's your weight?"

"Mmm… Yesterday it was 125 pounds," I smiled, but no one else did.

"Good proportions. Don't you think, Mark?" she asked the guy, still looking at me.

"Very good," he stated seriously.

"What's going on with your arm?" Diane demanded an explanation.

I immediately turned red and murmured, "Hot water. It got damaged in my childhood." All of a sudden, I felt embarrassed about the truth.

"We can cover it, no big deal," she declared, turned around and walked towards the window. She did it slow and gracious on the huge, but elegant, red hills, like a movie star of an erotic thriller.

"Do you have any idea what it is to be a model?" she inquired, looking in the window.

"Honestly, I've never done modelling, but I do have an idea of what it is," I answered as clearly as I could before those eyes looked at me again and made me nervous.

"Okay," she said with the same flirty smile, then, all of a sudden, turned serious and sat back on the chair.

"What we do here is jewelry. I am the founder and the owner of the company. I design and sell products in stores, on my website, and at exhibitions in Manhattan. All you will have to do is to work with my product. We'll shoot you a few days a week and take you to jewelry shows a few times a month. I might need your assistance with paperwork as well."

"Sounds good to me!" I exclaimed.

"I like your attitude," Diane winked.

"I'm ready to start," I stated gaily.

She smiled with a warm and teasing smile and inquired, "Don't you have any questions, baby girl?"

"I don't think I do…"

I was wondering whether she hired me so fast and easy or if she played around like this with all candidates.

"That means you don't care how much you are going to make?" she giggled.

"Hm… good question." I tried to joke, feeling silly. "So how much…?"

She turned back to serious, "I'll pay you $25 cash per hour. As I said it's a part-time job. I will need you probably three times a week for four to six hours. Does it suit you?"

"Yes, it does," I answered, building a chain of calculations in my mind, coming up to $450 weekly in the best case.

"And yes, I'll pay you $200 per show," she added.

"Good…" I agreed. "Am I… hired?"

It was hard to believe I got the job so easily without any tests, additional questions, and most important, without any need for papers which I didn't have.

"Yes. I like you," she uttered, winked, and added seriously, "What I want you to do is to come to my apartment at 10 tomorrow morning. I have a few dresses I want you to try to model in."

"Okay," I nodded.

She wrote down the address on her business card and handed it to me, finalizing our dialogue with, "Don't be late."

The impression she had left was lasting for the rest of the day. I felt incredibly excited, and I couldn't explain why. Was it the result of getting the job, or people liking me to the point of hiring right away, or was it due to leaving the massage industry which I hated and feared at the same time — I couldn't say.

I had never done any modelling, and after all my shameful jobs, it seemed to be something I would be proud to do. It was a good beginning for an illegal immigrant. Even though I never aimed to be a model.

That afternoon I ignored Rita's invitation to GD to the "party of procrastination" as she called it. My party of procrastination had ended and I was ready for something productive. That night I took my time to do facial masks that I often neglected, I wanted to look excellent and feel great.

It was around 10 pm and I was about to go to bed when Natasha called me. She had disappeared from my horizons as she got entrapped into a conflict of feelings, the ones she didn't need, and others that were not needed.

"She said there's nothing's going on," Natasha breathed after telling me about her confession to Rita and about her feelings. She said she was planning on telling me about these feelings long time ago but was worried I would disapprove it.

"Hey," I stated. "You can tell me anything! It doesn't matter whether I'd approve or disapprove something. I will give you all needed support. I won't judge you."

"She said she likes men. Why did she, then, kiss me and flirt with me?"

"Well, I guess, she enjoyed it while she was partying, but she likes men. It doesn't have anything to do with you, she likes men in general." I tried to comfort her, feeling caught between two fires. "She has feelings towards the one, who doesn't care about her."

"I understand it," Natasha cried. "But why did she flirt with me? She told me she loved my kisses and even touched my breast while kissing! Didn't she think about men back then?"

"Ah, we don't always think about consequences, especially when drunk. We act on impulses. Perhaps, she did enjoy it, but didn't want any continuation."

"That's what she told me 'There is no happy end', imagine? 'There is no happy end whatsoever,' that is exactly what she said. This phrase keeps ringing in my ears since then. I can't stop thinking about it," she wept. "I left her a voicemail, describing my feelings to her with so much love and pain. And she never even called me back. She never talked to me about it. She just disappeared. Why is she so cruel?"

I didn't know what to say in order not to complicate the situation more.

"Maybe she just doesn't want to hurt you more?"

"But she could say something, at least?"

"Maybe you, guys, should meet sometime soon and talk about it?" I suggested. "So, you could get rid of many misconceptions and get back to being friends. Maybe you're not in love with her at all, but only got excited about this new experience and wanted to continue exploring your sexuality, but she rejected you. That affects feelings sometimes. I believe you develop strongest feelings for people once you discover they aren't mutual. What if you tried to explore it with some other girl?"

"Maybe you're right. Maybe we should talk. Would you suggest her to contact me? I don't want to burden her by calling her too often."

"Sure," I said.

We hung up our phones as she started sounding happier. I didn't mention anything about Kostya as I thought it would add more to her already hurt feelings. I instantly thought of Dmitry and decided it was the time to forget him. It had been too long that I savored the pain. It didn't get me anywhere, but to the loop, from which I couldn't see anything else, or meet anybody else — a tight gloomy loop. I forbade myself to think about him. I decided that every time I would catch myself thinking about him, I would switch to some other thoughts. There were a lot of things to think about.

Yet, I realized, almost everyone I knew was entrapped in feelings with no tomorrow. I thought about Kostya endlessly loving Natasha, who only cared about Rita, who, in turn, cared about the guy, that only used her for sex. This guy probably fancied someone else. Maybe someone secretly fancied Kostya. And Shawn. Who knows what was on his crush's mind. I hoped that, at least, this story would have a happy end. whatsoever.

I felt an urge to call Shawn, but it was too late.

I turned off the sound of my phone to provide myself some peace, and as I freed my mind from all analysis, I fell into a deep heavy sleep. I saw Snezhana's little boy I had never met before in the apartment I had never been to. Snezhana was pouring me tea from a small kettle and telling the story from years ago of her son bringing a big dead rat to her and another woman, she was chatting with, as they were sitting on a bench, watching their kids playing in a playground in Central Park, and asking, "Mama, what is it?" The boy was smiling. I was laughing.

I woke up laughing still, yet I immediately reminded myself of a recent accident, and police putting handcuffs on her, and her frustrated, but brave look. I destroyed two lives, I thought.

The same morning, five minutes to ten, I passed the dressed-up doormen of a fancy building on Fifth Ave in the very heart of Upper East

Side. One of well-mannered man announced that Mrs Sullivan was waiting for me. I took an elevator up to 35th floor.

"Hello, hello, my dear!" Diane greeted me, opening the door in the short pink silken robe. "Come over, I'm just finishing with breakfast."

She looked fresh and beautiful, with light make up on and smell of sweet tasty perfume.

"Good morning!" I emitted. "I hope I'm not too early…"

"You are right on time, sweetie!" she said, dragging me by hand towards the table. "Would you like some tea or coffee?"

"I'm fine with water," I answered nervously.

It was a huge beautiful apartment with white furniture and bright paintings on walls. Views were absolutely gorgeous, Central Park to the west, and the breath-taking skyline of midtown — to the south.

"My husband and I moved here from California five years ago, we fell in love with this apartment and signed the lease the same day we saw it. It's beautiful, isn't it?"

"It's gorgeous." I breathed. "How much is the monthly rent, if you don't mind me asking?"

"It's $18,000 for these two bedrooms," she smiled.

"Wow…" I vocalized.

She laughed.

"Okay, sweetheart," she grabbed my arm as if I were her old girlfriend, "Let's go to my bedroom, I want you to try the dresses I prepared for you."

We walked into a large white bedroom with a king size bed in the middle and about ten different dresses on the top of it.

"I'd like you to check this one first," she gave me a short black cocktail dress.

I looked around, "Where can I try it?"

"Right here," she answered. "Why?"

"Sure…" I pronounced shyly, and slowly started removing my clothes, not looking at her, yet I knew, her eyes were fixed on me.

I also knew she was smiling with her flirty smile. I didn't dare to make an eye contact.

"You are so shy," she concluded playfully. "You need to take off your bra too. You don't wear bras with these kinds of dresses."

"Okay," I agreed, feeling silly and somewhat entrapped.

She didn't move her eyes from me getting naked.

"You've got a nice body," she commented. "Very nice."

Diane was gently helping me to put the dresses on and take them off. Her soft arms and tasty perfume were making me dizzy. All of a sudden, I got a feeling that the woman wanted something more from me.

After we picked proper dresses, we went to the same studio I was interviewed in. Mark and his assistant were already there with jewelry, cameras, and umbrellas. The assistant did a quick makeup and Mrs Sullivan put the first pair of earrings on me.

We worked all afternoon. Earrings of different types and kinds switched one another, in lying, sitting, and standing positions, as were dresses, which this time I was changing in a bathroom. It took us four hours. I felt incredibly tired. I didn't know modelling took so much energy. I could make four times more for four hours of massages, although I was so much happier with $100 and a feeling of accomplishment.

"Okay, Ekaterina!" Diane said at the end of the shift. "Tomorrow at the same time in the same place!"

It was around 4 p.m. when I left the studio. I decided to take a short walk to Union Square. I didn't have a goal; I just went with the flow of my thoughts. A warm day of May comforted me with inspiration of approaching summer and new opportunities. I kept recalling Snezhana's face from my dream and from the reality, her last look at me, her eyes, her lips, her hands enclosed in handcuffs. I saw how she was leaving the apartment in an unknown direction. Maybe she found her way out, I thought. Maybe at this very moment she is pouring tea to her son at home. Maybe not.

I approached Union Square's chess players. With no intention to play, I came to the busiest game and stood nearby, gazing at the chessboard. All recent but forgotten memories of the end of February turned alive, as déjà vu, the taste of Snickers returned to my mouth and even a light chill of hopelessness passed through my body. I got a dose of shivers and then filled my lungs with oxygen. It was in the past. I would never let myself go back to that life again.

I arrived in Kensington, and even though it was too early for a nightlife, I walked home from a different street, further from GD, not wanting to be seen by anyone from there, as I needed to be in a good shape for the next day. It had become really easy to convince me to drink lately. Rita was getting ready for work. I suggested she talked with Natasha, clear the air and get back to being friends, only without kissing this time. She agreed, saying she wanted to do that, but as Natasha said it hurt her to see Rita, and she didn't want to cause her more pain.

"You know, now it's over-over-over between me and Besnik," she shouted all of a sudden. "And it's okay. I'll suffer for a while. I'll drink for a while. Then I'll be fine. I'll get over it. You know, as a child I always believed I had some special purpose in this life, I always knew that something marvelous would happen. I always believed in miracles and continue believing. And I know that something amazing is waiting for me! I'm so sure of it!"

I gave her a hug, saying that she is an amazing person and soon enough something great would definitely happen to her. She definitely deserved it. She smiled and left for work. I remained in a positive mood, thinking about Rita's attitude and her inner beauty. I was thankful to have her around. I thought I should learn it from her, this quality of being your true self.

The next day started in the same manner, besides Mrs Sullivan was wearing a red robe. I didn't see any breakfast on the table; she took me straight to her bedroom. It looked neater than the day before and there were no dresses on top of the bed.

"I really liked you yesterday," she said, sitting me on the bed, beside her. "You did a very good job."

"Oh, thank you, Diane, it was my pleasure," I responded.

I wanted to ask where the dresses were but decided not to. A little awkwardness filled up the room. She touched my shoulder, smiled and looked in my eyes. I smiled back.

"Are you shy in front of me?" she asked flirtily.

"No... maybe a little bit..." I murmured unsurely.

"You shouldn't..." she whispered right in my ear. "I couldn't stop looking at you at the shooting. You are gorgeous."

I got goosebumps all over my body from that whisper, and not knowing what to say, I stated, "You too."

She took my hand and put it on her breast. Then she moved slightly closer and kissed me. I moved back, nicely taking out my hand from her chest.

"What about your husband?" I dared to say.

"What about him?" she murmured.

"It's cheating," I pointed nervously.

"No, it's not, baby girl… you are so young, you will have to learn so much about life…" she verbalized quietly and flirtily. "He doesn't mind me having fun, as long as it's not with men."

"I couldn't sleep last night, thinking about you…" she added.

I got goosebumps again. She made another effort to pull me back to her and kiss. This time it worked. I slowly started to lose my mind and hadn't even realized how both of us got naked and sank deeper into each other on that wide white bed in the middle of a huge room. We kissed and bit each other's lips, neck, breasts, switching positions, twisting legs and arms and whispering tender sweet words of passion. Diane demandingly moved my head towards her favorite spot of the body, and I, terribly famished for the taste of her, kept making one beautiful discovery after another, causing her scream louder and louder. She didn't hesitate to do anything, without asking for silent permission, she did what she wanted, like a hungry animal, with moans of pleasure. Through the shyness and nervousness, I closed my eyes and let myself sink into the sweet ride of her tongue, which started becoming sweeter and sweeter and eventually blocked all my perception of that room, the time, and the entire world outside of those windows.

I felt high for the entire day of shooting afterwards as if I had taken an unknown drug, the effect of which was pleasurable and unexplainable at the same time. I tried to avoid eye contact with Diane and focus on the work itself, but all the recent scenes, whispers and emotions kept pumping up in my mind, making me smile and feel shy at the same time.

I needed to talk to someone. I was thinking to text Natasha or Rita, or Shawn and telling them everything. Absolutely everything in detail, in emotions; get drunk and let all my energy go, so I would be able to calm down.

Mrs Sullivan came to me at the very end of the session and commanded firmly, as a boss of mine, "Let's have dinner together, I need to discuss something with you."

Mark was silently packing his devices in a small black suitcase.

I couldn't reject it and gave up all my plans for the night. I didn't know she already made a reservation in one of the fanciest restaurants in New York, where all the waitstaff knew her by name.

We were seated at a cozy table for two, and Diane ordered a bottle of white wine right away. I moved left and right on my chair, trying to find a comfortable position and searched for a proper spot for my arms on the table, noticing how she held hers.

The ceiling was very high which made it look more like a church than a restaurant. Servers were only men, all about the same height, with excellent manners, dressed in black. Customers looked like they had just come from the red carpet. I briefly observed my dress and secretly hoped it didn't seem as cheap as it was.

"I hope you love Chardonnay?" she asked me.

"I do," I answered. "One of my favorites,"

Her eyes looked shiny and happy. She smiled at me without saying anything, and I felt so much warmth. I secretly wished that moment would never end.

"I like you, Ekaterina," she said. "I like the way you are, so sweet and intelligent, not a mean bone."

"Thank you," I responded shyly.

"Did you like what happened this morning?" she wondered so unexpectedly that I felt a bit embarrassed.

"I did," I murmured. Then added, "I liked it a lot. I loved it."

"I'm glad," Diane concluded.

"As I said, I really like you. I'd want to see you a few times a week outside of the business…" she said demandingly. "I don't know what this relationship will turn into, but for now, I'd like to enjoy each other for as long as we can. What do you think?"

I loved the offer. I liked Diane. I had never thought sexually of women before, but at the age of 23 I realized I did have some hidden passions, and I enjoyed that new little discovery.

"Do you do it with all your models?" I asked after the second glass of wine braved me up.

"No." she uttered firmly, "Just you."

I didn't believe it but decided not to bother her with it, and let time show what would happen.

The same night, after asking her spouse's permission, she got us a luxury room in a hotel and we spent the first night together. She left early in the morning to kiss her husband before he went to work, and I continued enjoying my slow awakening in the most luxurious place I had slept in so far. I had breakfast in the room and took dozens of breath-taking pictures of New York's panorama from the window.

We started meeting a few times a week. Sometimes at her place in the morning, sometimes in hotels after work and dinners. We would spend long sleepless nights under a light blanket in air-conditioned rooms. She would leave around five-six in the morning, and I would take my time eating breakfast in bed, watching sunrises from the top floors, and enjoying myself in the aroma-Jacuzzi.

Diane would buy me flowers and beautiful underwear; I would give her silken lingerie and her favorite milk chocolates. She would make me feel special, very special, exceptional. It was my reward after all the past predicaments I had to go through. I was constantly in a state of euphoria.

"So, you think, you are a lesbian?" Rita asked, pouring freshly made margarita into my glass once I had managed to tell her what was happening.

I smiled shyly. I couldn't talk about Diane without smiling. I couldn't think about her without smiling. I was constantly high.

"Well, I'm trying not to label myself. I'm just enjoying what's going on at this very moment," I confessed. "It's very new to me and it excites me so much. I'm only thinking about her. If you come to think about it, then I'm probably bisexual."

"You guys are going mad," she laughed. "First Natasha, then you. Does she know about it?"

"Not yet," I said, thinking about whether I should tell her. I didn't want to cause her more pain by describing my experience, since her desirable experience didn't happen and most likely wouldn't happen.

"Ah… would you ask her when she's available? You know, I don't want her to think that I want to go for it, by offering to meet. She might raise hopes. Not much fun. I'm available on Mondays and Tuesdays — pretty much any time, or during the day normally. But Mondays or Tuesdays will be the best," she declared sadly.

"I will," I uttered, digesting her sad and deep look. "Are you thinking about him a lot?"

"Sort of. Can't take him out of my head. I will get better, you know. I always get better eventually. I think, it's healthy to suffer time to time. Clears your mind," she laughed at the last sentence.

"Is there anything I can do for you?" I heard myself asking. "I don't know what I can possibly do. But let me know if something."

"Sure," she said, getting more alive. "Write about me."

I laughed, "Anything besides it? I have no idea, when I'll start writing and whether I'll start at all. But I'll do if I will."

Her eyes got sparkle.

"You know, the plot I told you about, the girl who got mistreated by life and abandoned by everyone, who suffers insomnias and drinks a lot and knows she needs to change something, but doesn't know what?"

"Yes."

"So, she figures what she needs to change. She needed real love!"

"But this is something most of us need," I interrupted her.

"I know, but she needs it more than anybody else, because she is dying from drinking and suffering, and she doesn't even care about any bad outcome. You know? Not much fun of a life. So, she gets in lots of trouble. Let's say even with the police! She writes beautiful poems, but no one to show them. It is a way of coping with this crap of life. So, she meets the love of her life and spends some happy time with this man. Then he leaves her. I don't know yet why, but definitely not betraying her. You know, something happened they both know he needs to leave. So, she is sad, she wants to die, but all of a sudden decides that life worth living, not leaving! Ha, good phrase, 'life worth living, not leaving'! You know, and she pulls herself and she feels like she needs to gather everyone she knows or ever knew for some unknown reason. She really wants it, but she lost touch with some people."

Rita made a few gulps of her drink and wiped her mouth with the back of her hand.

"Can you imagine gathering everyone you met in your life and see how they interact with each other and what they make you feel? You know, years later. You must feel nostalgic or something. So, she gathers everyone!"

"But how, if she lost touch with some people?"

"Well," Rita thought for a few seconds, "it doesn't matter. We don't always need to know everything, why, how, when, why? She just gathers them!"

I couldn't help laughing.

"So, they all came, some flew from different countries, met each other. Imagine, how interesting it will be for them to meet each other? Can you imagine how insane it is? And how cool? You know, everyone is so unique, and they all are trapped in one room. And she looks at all this and thinking that it's her life in front of her. It's her life in some shorter and smaller version. And while she is standing there, this familiar life is going on, you know? And it has an end — somewhere." Rita stopped and stared at me thoughtfully.

"And what happens then?" I tried hard not to laugh.

"Nothing…" Rita breathed. Her eyes were wet and shiny from alcohol.

"Nothing?" I wondered.

"Why something always necessarily has to happen?" she snapped. "Everybody expects something-something-something, like everybody's life is full of something. Bullshit! Human lives are mostly full of nothing. They just don't want to admit it."

"'Full of nothing' — I love how I said it! Ha!" Rita giggled. "So, this will be the most honest end. Just nothing!"

"So, what is the whole point of everything in this plot?" I asked, thinking whether it made sense to dig into her drunken imagination.

"Are you making fun of me?" my friend yelled with annoyance. "I've just told you! I explained everything to you."

Her face turned upset and she took a few more gulps of the drink. I got up and gave her a hug. She squeezed me harder.

"Of course, I'm not making fun of you." I murmured, "I think it's a very interesting plot. Thank you for sharing it."

I thought that she herself was much more interesting than this plot or anything else I had read lately. I didn't tell her. I thought I would tell her once she is sober. If I didn't forget about it, of course.

Diane went utterly insane with her new addiction, which was I. She started calling me a few times a day, sending me a lot of erotic texts and pictures, and once she got really hungry for spending more time together, she bought us tickets to California, to stay at her house in Silicon Valley for ten days.

I couldn't believe it all was happening to me. It seemed like a beautiful dream that I didn't want to end. Slowly, I started neglecting skyping my mother, who had no clue my life took a completely different turn. I minimized all communications with my friends in Russia; and for the first time in a long while I realized I didn't miss my homeland. I lived life to the fullest.

Diane's housekeeper picked us up from San Francisco airport in Sullivan's white Rolls Royce and drove to the Valley I had only read about in books. It felt so fresh and peaceful after New York.

Diane owned a huge seven-bedroom house on top of a hill. It was all white and elegant, every bedroom had a bathroom and an incredible view from the window. The hallway was wide and long, it contained a few colorful paintings just like in her apartment, but larger and brighter; it ended with the biggest bedroom in the house — her bedroom. There were two swimming pools and a Jacuzzi right outside of the house, all of which faced the rest of the beautiful Valley.

"Wow!" was all I could say after the tour around the house.

"I know, right?" Diane winked at me, dragging me to the biggest bedroom at the end of the hallway.

Those days everything went on around her bed. We would go to eat and return there, we would drive along the ocean and come back to the same spot, we would shop, or walk, and end up under the same blanket. She gave the housekeeper some time off, and we didn't have to separate at all.

We went to San Francisco, hung out in gay bars, drank shots of tequila and danced until almost morning. We drove to Cupertino, Palo Alto, and Santa Cruz, enjoying views and environment, landscape and the weather, but mostly each other.

"Are you illegal in this country?" Diane suddenly asked me.

"How do you know?" I wondered.

"I just guessed," she winked at me.

"But how? Seriously."

"A secret," she said.

"How did you guess, honestly?" I laughed. I was sure she had never seen any of my papers.

She left the question without an answer, but assured me, "Don't worry, we'll figure a way to make you legal."

"I researched that if I divorce Dan and marry you in the state, where it's legal, we still wouldn't be able to legalize you," she declared something I already knew.

Unfortunately, in 2010 same-sex marriages didn't work for legalization.

"But! If you'll be a good girl," she winked at me, continuing driving. "Dan will marry you."

I didn't respond.

"Of course, nothing sexual will be involved between you guys," she explained. "I'm too jealous!"

I smiled. It warmed up my heart. It was more than I could ask for. Every next day was bringing new surprises along with endorphins I could barely handle. I had a great feeling I was in a safe place in safe hands, and more than that, in a safe heart. I couldn't believe it was happening in reality.

I called Shawn one of those days once Diane went somewhere for work. I wanted to find out how his love was developing, if it was, and tell him about my new passion. He said that it was not really a phone talk and offered to meet me at the airport once I would get back to New York.

I thought thankfully about the massage job and admitted that if I hadn't gone through it, I would never meet Diane. I would never look for a job like that if not for the crisis and hunger. It's always too early to judge a situation as we don't know what it may bring with itself. It might take a few hours to see its influence on our lives, it might take long years. A black stripe can turn into a take-off strip. It was my runway. I felt I was finally taking off. Getting up in the air, where all the magic was happening.

We developed a habit of kissing each other in public, especially, once we would notice someone staring at us. It was funny to watch people's reaction of seeing two beautiful classy women making out. We would gently feed each other in restaurants, holding one another's chins with one hand while bringing fork to lips with another and silently watched surprised faces around us. People often thought Diane was my mother as she was about twice older than me, which made our erotic feeding even funnier. We would discuss it later, in the car, choking from laughter, "did you see how that old woman enlarged her eyes?", or "a man with a nasty smile, that got a smack from his wife!"

"You know," she told me at the end of the trip. "I don't want to go back to New York. I don't want to go back to Dan. I'm falling in love with you."

I didn't want to go back yet, too. I liked her terribly. I wanted to enjoy those sweet moments for as long as possible. But our plane arrived back very soon, and we went in different directions.

Diane couldn't kiss me any more, because her driver was waiting a few feet away from the airport's exit. She gave me a warm hug and got into the car. Shawn picked me up a minute later and we went to Brooklyn. He was perfectly shaved and dressed in stylish black pants and a tight grey shirt. I noticed he had gained muscles and his belly had turned flat. He had lost weight.

"You look amazing!" I exclaimed right after our prolonged hug and exchange of greetings.

He laughed and cleared his throat, "Thank you, dear. I started going to the gym every other day. Want to be fit for Laurine."

His face froze in a mesmerizing smile.

"Laurine! Beautiful name!"

"And my favorite," he murmured with so much love in his voice.

"So, how's everything going there?" I wondered. "Any progress?"

Shawn sighed.

"Not really. Sometimes I think she's flirting with me, sometimes she looks like she hates me. And sometimes she is so indifferent," he laughed. "I'm so dependent on her! I think of her all the freaking time. Can't focus on anything else. Sometimes I want to throw up from all these thoughts! Can I just go to the bathroom and throw up all my thoughts about her? Ah, if I only knew what's on her mind... I feel so shy to invite her anywhere because I don't know if she cares about me. I don't want to feel awkward. I don't know, Kate… I don't know."

I thought of Natasha and wondered whether she was going through something similar and whether it would be a good idea to suggest them to talk about this feeling.

"Remember, you told me about your love for Dmitry?" he smirked. "You wished me to experience this strong love one day. Can you unwish it?"

I laughed. I thought of love as an addiction. This drug could make you extremely high as much as badly sick. The unfortunate fact is that you don't have any control over it. The thought of thinking about Diane all the time scared me. I didn't want to get sick. I didn't know what to tell Shawn. I suggested taking one step at a time, to try to find out what she feels towards him first and then decide what to do.

We tend to love the unapproachable. Other people's feelings burden us because we're afraid of responsibilities. Unshared feelings are always the strongest in the long run. Shared passion doesn't last for too long — it dries out, and indifference takes over soon enough.

I told him about my affair with Diane. He was shocked and amazed by how things had turned, by how fast people replaced one another and now, instead of savoring pleasure of love with Dmitry, I was losing my mind for a woman of my mom's age.

Shawn had never been to GD before. I introduced him to Rita. She was completely wasted, but somehow, managed to make drinks and serve people. It wasn't busy, and the owner wasn't anywhere to be seen.

"Are you celebrating anything?" Shawn laughed.

Rita looked at us as something struck her, "Exactly! I'm celebrating!"

"Lina, I'm celebrating! Lina!" she shouted loudly. Lina lazily approached her and suggested to stop drinking. We agreed she had enough.

"Go fuck yourself, all of you!" Rita yelled. "I'll drink as much as I want to drink. Don't you understand, I'm celebrating my freedom?"

She walked towards the hard liquor section and took a few swigs right from the gin bottle, then put it back, turned to us and burped. I felt embarrassed and regretted bringing Shawn over.

Lina said she would manage the place alone since it was slow. Shawn and I carried Rita home. She turned completely legless. Her head was hanging down to her chest, her arms lost their grasp, her feet were drawing invisible lines with their toes somewhere behind us, and only random sounds, coming out of her mouth were indicating that she was alive.

"Don't write about this," she mumbled as we put her to bed.

"Or maybe write… or don't write? Ah, it's so confusing." she continued mumbling.

Shawn and I went to another bar for a couple more drinks. He said he was choked by this feeling for Laurine and the feeling itself wasn't making him happy any longer. He asked for my advice and I suggested writing her a letter with a confession. It's always easier to put things on paper, rather than to tell them in person.

"Can you help me with the letter?" Shawn wondered. "I don't know what to write and how to put my thoughts together."

"Sure," I said. "Once I'll be sober."

The first day of shooting after the California trip was way too long. I could barely wait for it to end. Time was crawling. My boss seemed pretty impatient, with a hint of lust in her look, she kept walking back and forth, fixing my dresses and jewelry, constantly checking her watch. She wore a cute pink dress that showed her beautiful legs, and of course, the cleavage. I tried not to look at her as often, and every time we made eye contact, I looked away, filling my lungs with oxygen and trying to think about something totally unrelated to her. I thought, our affair was obvious to others.

We went to a hotel right after and spent a beautiful night together. We couldn't wait to get close and started kissing each other right in the empty elevator. I don't know how we managed not to rip off each other's clothes as soon as we arrived in the room. I don't know how we managed to survive that insane night of love without heart attacks or bruises. It felt like we had reached a point of no return. It seemed like we were slowly becoming two inseparable halves of one substance.

"We need to live together," Diane told me in the morning in a bossy manner as if it was an order.

"What do you mean?"

"You need to move in with me and Dan. I texted him already. He doesn't mind." she stated and showed me her phone, "Here."

It scared me. I didn't look at her phone. I couldn't believe it.

"No," I uttered. "I don't think it's a good idea. I don't want to live with your husband."

She wrapped my hands with hers and murmured, "He won't touch you; I promise. He loves me and wants me to be happy, that's all. All I need for happiness is you. And him."

Nobody asked me, what I needed for happiness, I thought, but verbalized, "I'm not ready."

"When will you be ready?" she asked carefully, touching my hair.

"I don't know," I responded, thinking that most likely never.

She looked away and a little tear came out of her eye.

"Life is too short to waste it!" she concluded.

I didn't comment. My life was only beginning.

She finally burst out crying, trying to convince me. She was begging and sobbing all morning until we checked out. My affair took a totally different turn than I would never expect it to. I said "no," I went through unpleasant things with Dmitry, which cost me a lot, and now, I couldn't move in with someone I barely knew, especially with a couple. She made me promise to think for at least a couple of days, she didn't want to give up, she desperately wanted to take full control over me, not caring how I felt about it. Move-in. Or move out of my life completely.

Rita was terribly embarrassed the next day and a few more days after. She got embarrassed to the point of going back on the wagon.

"I can't look into anybody's eyes," she cried. "I can't believe I acted like that! Disaster! Shame is becoming my permanent feeling. My fucking satellite."

"You know, I wrote to Besnik! I kept sending him messages till he blocked me. I had no courage to reread those messages, so I deleted the whole conversation. I even called Natasha, but thank God, she didn't pick up the phone. She keeps calling me back though. I don't pick up, 'cause I don't know what to say. It's not much fun to drink," she sighed. "When did I go off the road and became this bad?"

"You're not bad," I told her. "You're going through a difficult period of your life. You're devastated, heartbroken, illegal. It will pass. One day you'll be sitting down in your beautiful apartment... let's say, on Park

Ave, enjoying the view, while your husband will be teaching your child to play chess. All these predicaments will seem so distant and funny to you. Life is worth living, not leaving, remember?"

She smiled, "You're giving me hope."

"Dear Laurine,

I'm sorry for bothering you, and I hope, reading this letter won't take much of your time. I hope it won't put much of a burden on you either. In fact, that's is the last thing I want to cause.

Due to being cowardly shy in your presence, I decided to write everything I have wanted to tell you for a long time. I'm deeply and hopelessly in love with you. I fell for your beautiful eyes and smile the first time I saw you. I never thought one could be so gorgeous. The image of you is always in my mind, as well as your voice, your smell, and your manners. I dream of you day and night, wondering where you are and what you're doing. I want to protect you from all life's disasters, I want to take care of you, I want to be next to you all the time… If you'd only allow me.

It's a wonderful feeling I want to scream about from all the rooftops. I had never been happier, and I had never been sadder. It makes me want to live and die at the same time. I love you, Laurine.

Always yours,

Shawn."

I shrugged my shoulders as I finished it and sent it to Shawn. I didn't know whether it was something he wanted, whether it was too full of love, or whether it would be better to simply invite her for a dinner. I would probably do the latter, but Shawn wanted beautiful words without any offers. He just wanted her to know.

I checked my phone right after I emailed Shawn the confession, but there was nothing from Diane. I hadn't heard from her since the morning we parted. I couldn't sleep all night. I was analyzing my life, from the beginning, I could remember to the very sleepless hour. It didn't look like the way up, it consisted purely of ups and downs, where I failed to determine my current position. I was thinking about my new passion and her husband, I thought how much I disliked the idea of all living together.

I treasured my freedom. At the same time, I did have feelings for her and didn't want to lose her.

"What would I do in this room I'm renting?" I asked myself out loud in order to get a clear answer. "What would I actually do with this freedom I have?"

I couldn't think too straight. I hadn't done anything productive since I separated from Dmitry, I didn't find a husband, I didn't work on anything important, and all the free time I had, went to waste. I wasted money and health, drinking in GD, I went there most of the evenings, some afternoons, and any time I had free time. I got plenty of drinking friends and buddies. Was it true freedom? Did this freedom make me happy? Did I need such freedom?

By early morning I admitted to myself, I was simply afraid of any changes, they didn't feel safe. I got very comfortable in my box and didn't want to get out. I thought that life had to be an adventure, a great journey, full of emotions and colors. What would I see in that box? Nothing. Where would it lead me? Not much further than GD. I had finally met someone who cared about me and offered help and support. Someone who had something to offer.

I gave up the idea of falling asleep when my room got filled with sunlight.

"I have changed my mind." I sent the message to Diane.

"Are you moving in with us?" she asked immediately, and I got a feeling she spent a sleepless night as well.

Mrs Sullivan left no room for any meaningful conversation or other topics, expecting only "yes" or "no".

"I am." I texted, disarmed, but determined.

"Great!" she replied.

"I'm talking to Dan right now... He is so happy... We are going for dinner... Tonight!" she texted.

A few minutes later she sent me the address of the restaurant and a lot of love messages, full of excitement and tenderness. I felt unprepared and nervous. Everything was happening too fast for me. It seemed to be a point of no return.

I found a moment to tell Rita honestly and openly about everything. While waiting for her approval, I silently blamed myself for putting her in the spot to look for a new roommate on such short notice. Amazingly, she said, "Wow! Sounds like a lot of fun!" and gave me a hug.

"I hope I'll be able to visit you sometimes," she smiled. "I was always wondering how these rich people live!"

"For sure," I told her. "Will you be looking for a new roommate or you're planning on staying alone?

"I would like to live alone for a while, I think," she answered.

"You need to promise me to take good care of yourself. Don't drink that much. You are so talented; you have a long life ahead of you. I'm sure, everything you want will come true. Just a matter of time. No need to damage yourself, cause of one stupid bastard, that's not worth it at all."

"You're right," she laughed, looking somewhere into emptiness. "Not much fun to drive oneself crazy for no reason. Or for reason that is not a reason. Reason, that is not a reason. Interesting, huh?"

"I shell write about it as well," I joked, giggling.

"For sure," she agreed.

Diane booked a table for three in a fancy Italian restaurant. So not ready, but obliged and determined to make it, I took a train towards midtown. I was becoming more and more nervous with each train stop. I arrived fifteen minutes prior to the dinner, and aiming to enter the restaurant right on time, I went for a short walk around the block, putting my thoughts together. I noticed a homeless person on the corner by a building with a husky dog sleeping nearby. I recalled my Snickers' diet and cold days of crisis and put two dollars into his box.

"God bless you," he murmured.

When time had come, I took a deep breath of a warm June air and walked in.

The couple was there. They got up as soon as they saw me.

"That's the gorgeous young lady she is talking about all the time!" the man exclaimed, giving me a warm hug.

"I'm Daniel Sullivan," he said, smiling and still holding my shoulders. "For you just Dan."

All my nervousness went away in a second.

"Ekaterina." I introduced myself. "For you, just Kate."

Diane was shining like a sun. There was a happy smile on her face, the one I hadn't seen even in California.

"I'm so glad you made this decision," she whispered, giving me a hug. "You can't even imagine how grateful I am now."

Dan was a very handsome and well-mannered man in his late fifties. He was blond, tall, and had light grey eyes on his childlike face. He appeared laid back and easygoing which automatically made me feel like I knew him forever.

"A toast!" he announced as soon as everybody got a glass full of wine. "For our new beautiful family!"

"For our new beautiful family!" said Diane, winking at me and touching my leg under the table.

Dan was living his life to the fullest. He seemed to be excited about everything, that dinner, the weather, his wife's young lover, and even waking up for work the next day. He was a great orator as much as a great listener, I found him a very interesting person. My "husband-in-law" was so careful with all statements and judgments he made, fully expressing himself, and giving a meaning to each phrase, no wonder why he was such a successful lawyer.

I hadn't noticed how during the conversation I told them the story of my life, my childhood and my single mother, even my electrocution — I revealed so many things I normally would avoid talking about. I was so surprised when the dinner came to an end, two and a half hours passed as fifteen minutes.

I felt happy. After we exchanged goodbye hugs, I walked a few blocks to the south, so euphoric, analyzing the recent conversation and wondering about the future. I was looking forward to becoming a part of the "new beautiful family".

I packed my stuff in hurry and moved in three days after that dinner. Shawn drove my two suitcases and me to the new fancy life and gave me a prolonged hug, saying he hoped not to lose me due to these changes. I promised it would never happen.

"Will you visit me as well?" Rita asked shyly when I was leaving the apartment. "Keep your key and come any time you want. I hope you guys will never fight, but if you'll need to spend some time on your own, you're always welcome back — for good, or for a while."

"Some time on my own? Is it possible with you?" I joked, hiding tears. People's kindness always touched me. And now, while I felt I was betraying her and leaving her alone at such an unmerciful time, I received so much understanding in return. We embraced each other, and I felt her rapid heartbeat.

"You know," I heard her saying behind my shoulder, and squeezing me harder as she wanted to hold on to me in order not to lose me. "I had never gotten attached to anyone in this country, like I got to you. You're just like my sister. You are my support. I always found it hard to open up to people, you know? I'm so grateful you're in my life."

"Of course, I am in your life, and will always be," I murmured. "And we aren't partying our ways. The fact that I don't live here any more won't reflect on our friendship. I'm always here for you!"

"I will miss you," she whispered with her voice cracking. I will miss you, too.

She apologized for not being able to help me carry suitcases down because her eyes were getting red and watery, and I knew she was too embarrassed to show her tears to anyone. I pulled my belongings out of the apartment and pressed an elevator button. She stood in her pajamas still in the late afternoon, biting her lower lip. I said, "Take care of yourself, please! Promise, you will. We'll see each other sooner than you think."

She smiled and nodded.

Dan prepared a great romantic dinner for three people the day I moved in. We were eating, sipping wine and talking about everything in the world. Diane was as happy as she could be. Dan reflected her happiness as a mirror.

I got a huge room with king-size bed right in the middle of it, and a private bathroom. My new views were absolutely gorgeous, Central Park on one side, south of Manhattan on the other, and 35 flights over the city. The room was part of the huge three-bedroom apartment with tremendous living room with a bar and a piano, fancy master bedroom, and a guest room with an office space for Diane. The couple moved here from the other apartment on the same floor, which was just a little smaller. Our new rent was $25,000 per month. I felt both awkward and guilty for not being able to contribute.

We made sleeping arrangements for the next few weeks. On Mondays, Wednesdays and Fridays, Diane was supposed to sleep in my room, for the rest of the week — in Dan's. These rules were making me feel awkward, although everyone else seemed to be comfortable with them.

Our family life started with genuine fun of going out and drinking, dancing, singing, and doing anything we could to get as much joy as possible. On the first Sunday morning in my new home, Dan organized a party in the living room. He made Bloody Marys instead of coffees, turned a loud music on, and prepared small sandwiches.

"No work today," he stated gaily. "Just fun!"

"Just fun!" Diane repeated.

She was dressed in a sexy and almost see-through pinkish lingerie. I tried to avoid looking at her, I felt incredibly shy in front of her husband. Dan opened the windows and let the summer freshness in. Both of us sat on the sofa while Diane was dancing in the middle of the room with a drink in her hand.

"Why won't we take some time off and go somewhere?" suggested my husband-in-law, finishing his first Bloody Mary. "Let's say, to Rome?"

"It sounds like fun." said my lover, continuing dancing.

"What do you think, Kate?" Dan looked at me. "I can book tickets and a hotel right now!"

I suddenly felt embarrassed about my situation. That very moment I realized why I didn't have even one American friend, I was so ashamed of being illegal, I was ashamed of letting people know I was illegal. It became my burden, everywhere I'd go, I'd take my status with me. And violating the rights of the country I entered, I felt I was violating the rights of every single American citizen living here.

"You guys go," I breathed sadly. "I can't really travel outside of the country."

"Oh, poor baby girl," Diane noted, sitting herself on my knees. "She is illegal. Dan, we must do something about it."

"Oh, right," he said understanding, "What is the procedure of you getting legal? Can Diane make you a working visa?"

"I wish," I vocalized. "It's too late for any types of visas. I've already overstayed mine. Now the only way to become legal is to get married or try a political refugee. But the refugee is such a long and painful procedure."

"I'm asking people." Diane smiled with her flirty smile. "I'll pay to whoever will marry my baby girl. I want to show her the world."

I laughed just to hold myself from crying. It touched my heart.

"Well," Dan concluded. "I suppose, if we won't find anybody, I can divorce Diane and marry you."

Diane winked at me as we just heard the proof of what she told me in California.

"Unless same-sex marriages will get on federal level," he added with a warm smile. "Let's see what's going to happen."

"Thank you," I murmured. "Thank you, guys, you know what it means to me."

"We know…" Diane whispered into my ear in a playful manner, moving right and left on my knees.

"Why wouldn't you guys go to the bedroom and I'll make some more Bloody Marys?" Dan offered.

Diane loved the idea, and the very next moment she was dragging me there, holding my waist with her soft arms.

I felt so happy, thankful, and high on feelings, excitement, and alcohol, that my brain was releasing ten times more dopamine than it should. I relaxed, letting my lover do anything she wanted. I didn't have control of myself any more. Through sounds of our moans, I heard that Dan had changed the music to the Beatles.

"Tell him to come here." she let out once we recovered from our orgasms. "His turn."

Still dizzy, I dressed myself and walked to the living room where the only man in the house was dancing with an imaginary guitar. His facial expression reflected the music and the entire dance was filled with the harmony of a rock lover of 70^s.

"She is waiting for you in the bedroom," I said after a few seconds of watching him.

"Oh yeah? All right!" he smiled enthusiastically and ran to the bedroom as a little child.

I grabbed my Bloody Mary and went to the balcony. A warm summer wind was playing with my hair and foretaste of something good filled up the air. I still couldn't believe I was the part of this crazy family. I couldn't recognize myself; I didn't want to know anything besides enjoying the great feeling of being alive.

Next couple of weeks we spent mixing work with pleasure. We dined out every night, we partied at home once or twice a week, and every Sunday started with Dan's cocktails and Diane's beautiful dancing.

In this chaos of endless sex, excitement, and mind-blowing life, Dan quietly turned 58. Unexpectedly for everyone, Diane decorated the apartment. She wanted to throw a party and insisted on inviting my friends as well. Dan supported the idea, furthermore, he was excited about mixing the young generation with friends of his and Diane's age. I was pleased with them wanting to meet my friends, even though I had to turn down this invitation. I was too embarrassed to invite people who hadn't gotten anywhere in life. Wonderful, smart, talented, warm-hearted, but illegal and poor, they shared small apartments in dismal neighborhoods of Brooklyn, they never wore branded clothing and never went to a fancy restaurant, their goal was to survive, rather than to enjoy life. I lied that all of them were busy at the time. We had a fine dinner party with a few of Dan's co-workers and a friend of Diane.

We were a happy and discreet family. My beloved kept searching for a husband for me. Her spouse, in the meanwhile, assured me he would do what he promised if no husband was found. I was modelling and helping our wife with tons of paperwork for her business and other matters, besides being a model, I became her personal assistant and secretary. All worked out great.

In about a month since I moved in, she went to Paris for two weeks to a jewelry exhibition. None of us could join her due to work or status.

Dan and I entertained one another as we could.

"It's hard not to love her," he said once, "isn't it?"

"It is!" I agreed.

"How could you manage to share her with me?" I asked the question that bothered me for a long time.

He smiled.

"Maybe you are too young to understand this… When you love somebody as much as I do, you want that person to be happy no matter what and with whom."

"And you are a very cute person to share my love with," he laughed.

I thought about Dmitry and the way I loved him. Would I ever share him with anybody? The answer was no. Didn't I love him enough then?

"Would you share Diane with a guy?" I asked Dan and put him into long seconds of thinking.

"I don't think so," he uttered and then corrected himself, "I don't know…"

I nodded.

Dan and I got to know each other better, exchanging stories from our childhood, first love, first depression, first genuine gratefulness. We as well skyped with Diane. She would give a private erotic session to each of us separately before wishing a good night. I couldn't wait for her to come back.

I got some time for myself while my girlfriend was away. I called my mom, without putting the video on Skype, pretending that I lived in the same Brooklyn apartment. She noticed I was "acting weird" and wondered why. I told her I was modelling for a small jewelry company and loved my job. She was happy for me, finally I had something good to share. There was nothing good I had shared with her ever since I arrived in this country.

"Your smile is the most treasurable occurrence in my life." she kept saying. "I only want this life to smile back to you, there is nothing else that would make me happy!"

However, it bothered me that I couldn't tell her the whole truth. I was living with the woman of her age and her husband. Besides being my boss, she happened to be my lover. Would I ever be able to tell her that?

I finally got a chance to visit my friends in Brooklyn.

I was planning to go to GD that night, but first, I met Natasha at the Mexican restaurant by Q train's stop. It was an empty afternoon. My friend was elated to see me, yet, she had a lot of sadness in her heart. After the rain of questions about living on 5th Ave and mesmerized looks with every answer and description of how rich people live, what and

195

where they eat, who they fancy, what they watch, what they read, which conversations they have during dinners and lunches, she confessed she always thinks about Rita. She stopped writing to our AA member, as she decided she was bothering her, yet she constantly thought about her. Anywhere she was, anything she would do, she wished Rita would be there with her. I knew this feeling very well. I suggested she move on and prohibit herself from thinking about something that will never happen. There is nothing pleasant in it, even though, all of us are addicted to suffering to some degree.

"I'm sorry for being so straight forward," I started hugging her as she began to cry. "I just don't want to give you fake hopes and support your desire to be with her. You'll feel better in a while. Don't be scared of the emptiness the absence of this feeling will create. Soon enough, it will be filled with new people, events, feelings. Soon you'll start experimenting more with girls and will find someone you'd fall for. Just give it some time."

Natasha silently nodded, and after a few seconds of thinking, said, "Do you think there is a chance I could talk to Rita still? I just want everything to be clear between us. I want her to know I want to remain her friend in the future, when my feelings will turn into something else, into warm friendly feelings. Do you think she'll want to talk to me?"

"Of course, she will. In fact, she does want to talk to you. She said Mondays or Tuesdays are the best for her to meet. Are you available either day?" I asked and realized it was Wednesday, almost a week prior to next Monday. "Actually, why wouldn't you go to GD with me? It's her shift. I'm sure she'll be happy to see you."

"Oh no," Natasha stated nervously. "I don't want to force my company on her."

"But you aren't forcing. Let's go, she wanted to talk to you anyways. It might be easier for you to get there in our presence. Shawn is going to be there soon."

She smiled, looking convinced, "But if she brushes me off, it will be your fault."

"Deal," I laughed.

We found Shawn sipping beer as we walked inside GD. We also found Lina, who told us that Rita got so wasted that she was sent and delivered home by the owner. And he was not very happy with her lately.

"She was so drunk, sooo drunk," Lina kept repeating. "She couldn't even walk!"

I sighed. I called her later that night, but she didn't pick up. We decided to let her sleep and check on her in a while. Natasha was disappointed.

"I don't think it's the right time for me to talk to her. Whatever is going on with her, I should let her get over it first," she concluded.

"She's healing her broken heart," I sighed.

Shawn smiled, clearing his throat. "We never appreciate what we have. Only appreciate what we don't have."

"Did you send her the letter?" I suddenly remembered.

"I did." he said.

It surprised me, that he never mentioned anything, "And?"

Shawn looked down and smiled, "I don't need your love."

"What?" Natasha and I both asked at once.

"I hesitated to send it for a few days. So, I knew she was going to be off for 3 days, and I had sent it right the night before the first day of her little vacation. She hadn't responded. To be honest, those were the longest 3 days of my life!" he laughed loudly. "She ignored me the entire shift when she returned to work. Then, after the day was over, she asked me to escort her to a train stop."

I noticed Natasha looking at him in a daze, with her mouth open. It was obvious to us, that things didn't work out.

"I was so happy you guys cannot even imagine! I had never walked with her outside of work. And it was a long block," Shawn giggled, taking a sip. "She said, 'I received your email. I don't need your love, but I don't mind your company.'"

Then silence began. Shawn was staring down at his beer bottle, peeling its label. Natasha was looking into nowhere, some space near him. I couldn't read their minds, but I assumed, Natasha thought about Rita, Shawn was hiding his tears, and I, in my turn, imagined how short of a block it seemed to him in the very beginning, and how long it appeared right after her cruel words. I. Don't. Need Your. Love. Only five of them, but how painfully they hurt. They can easily kill, and with the absence of the second one, they can easily revive.

"I'm so sorry, Shawn," I murmured, not knowing, what else to say. "I'm so, so, sorry…"

"It's okay," he tried to smile. "I still don't know what she meant about my company. Maybe she meant she wanted me to fight for her?"

"No," Natasha yelled. "Don't put yourself down. Now I see, how obvious everything becomes, when you look at it from the side. Fuck Rita. I don't want to talk to her any more. I hate her. That bitch wasn't brave enough to call me back. Why the hell I'm looking to get in contact with her? For what? To put myself down again? Hell, no! Not going to happen!"

She got up from the table, searching her purse, I assumed, for a wallet. Shawn's eyes grew bigger and he pulled her down, and hung her purse back on the chair, "Rita is not here. Sit down."

"I don't need your love. Fuck, yeah! I don't need it either, my stupid love for you. I wish I didn't have it. Not something that I want to possess." she almost shouted as she sat down. Other customers turned around to look at us.

"Stop, stop," I hugged her, glancing at Shawn. He only nodded.

That night we covered a lot of topics, drank a lot of beers with a lot of shots of tequila, and made a lot of plans of which Natasha and I remembered nothing in the morning. I texted Dan I would come home the next day before I got too drunk to type. We shared a lot of laughs, hugs, and gratitude for having one another. I didn't remember how we parted with Shawn, how we made it to Natasha's. I woke up with a horrible headache in the morning in the room that reminded me so much of my rape.

Natasha happened to remember the chronology of last night's events. She said Shawn left a couple of hours before we finished because he had to wake up early, and then Kostya stopped by being brought there by some unknown force. His presence made her completely furious. She screamed at him so loudly, that the owner told Lina to give us a check and asked us out of the bar. Kostya left, and then, after negotiation, the owner allowed us to stay there for a while. Then, Natasha said, there was a gap in her memory. In the next recollection, we were leaving the GD. Then we were leaving another bar, she didn't remember which one.

I instantly felt embarrassed about all the noisy drama we were making publicly that night. The worst thing was not to remember what you should be embarrassed of. We had breakfast with aspirin, bacon and eggs, and I made my way to the F train to get back to Manhattan.

Natasha thanked me for being supportive. I felt like we were partying for good. I gave her the warmest hug and wished her to take things easy.

Kostya called me when I was on the train, while it was still above the ground. I felt completely disarmed, as I didn't remember anything from the night before.

"What's going on with Natasha?" he cried. "Can somebody explain it to me? I don't eat, I don't sleep, I'm exhausted… I need to know!"

I pulled all my strength together and shot, "Kostya, I really don't want to hurt you, but I think, there is no way to avoid it. Forget about Natasha. She is confused in her own self. She is lost, and I don't know if she's ready for anything serious. I can't tell you anything, please, forgive me for that. All I can suggest you is to move on."

She doesn't need your love, I thought.

"But what is it?" he cried hopelessly. "What is it?"

"You are a great loving and caring person, you are the one that is not easy to find, so I'm sure you will find the girl of your dreams soon. Forget about Natasha. She doesn't want to be with you any more. I believe she loves you with some… hmm… different kind of love. Hello? Kostya?"

I didn't know where exactly we lost the connection, as the train went underground. I hoped he heard most of it. I checked my phone as I got off the subway, but there were no voicemails or messages from him.

I arrived home a bit after 2 p.m. Exhausted, I walked inside, hoping to take a short nap before I'd start doing Diane's paperwork, but a random sound in the apartment made me realize I wasn't alone there.

"Dan?" I called.

Light steps from the dining room brought him to the hallway. He wore a white bathrobe; his blond-grey hair was a mess.

"Where have you been?" he asked, looking irritated.

"I sent you a message," I stated quietly. "I met friends in Brooklyn and we stayed till late, so I decided to sleep there, at my friend's place."

"So, you are a little whore then?" he pointed sarcastically. His eyes were slightly red.

I was so shocked to hear that from him. I least expected this reaction.

"I stayed at my friend's. The best friend." I mumbled defensively. "What's wrong with that?"

"I don't think Diane would like it…" he smirked, walking towards me.

I made a step back instinctively.

"I don't think so…" I murmured.

"Oh, I know for sure. She can be a bitch." he laughed and added, "But we don't have to tell her anything, right, sweet little girl?"

He grabbed my shoulders and stroked his hands toward my elbows.

"I don't understand…" I let out.

"Yes, you do." he smiled and fixed his face next to mine. "You understand everything."

His lips touched mine and I screamed and jumped back.

"Unbelievable! Wild moody child!" he stepped closer to me. "You don't know what you're doing now. I'm giving you a chance to fix the situation."

I was so disappointed. I felt like a naïve child, who just found out that Santa Clause doesn't exist.

"I don't want to fix anything!" I cried, losing my last hope for a good life. "If that's the way, I don't want to be here!"

He started laughing out loud, looking somewhere in the air.

"If that's the way…" he repeated, continuing laughing. "If that's the way…"

"You know what?"

I kept looking at him without saying anything.

"You are just nasty and dirty illegal garbage!" he pointed angrily. "Not more than that!"

"Okay." I breathed.

Surprisingly, it didn't hurt me so much. Deep in my heart, I was prepared for a turn like this, even though I believed I had finally found a great human understanding and people who loved me for who I was. All

I knew was that I had to move out as soon as I could. Partially discouraged, I knew it would take me a while to start trusting people again.

"You thought you'd live on Fifth Avenue for free? Just like that, sleeping with my wife?" he smirked, making another attempt to kiss me.

I stepped back again.

"I can't believe you are so stupid," he uttered. "What does it cost you? We'll have fun once every week or so, and I'll be nice to you… and will let you live in our luxury facility."

He grabbed my arms again, using all his strength.

"Maybe you like being forced…" he hissed. "I can do that."

I was trying to free myself, but Dan was stronger. He held me against the wall in a position I couldn't move.

"You gotta pay for everything in life," he explained. "There is no free lunch…"

My arms kept pushing his chest further away, but he was getting closer and closer, squeezing my body. Without thinking for too long, I bent my right knee and hit him in between his legs as hard as I could.

The husband-in-law jumped and curved right away, howling like a wolf. He sat down on the floor and leaned against the wall, holding the injured part. He didn't seem to want sex any more.

I went to the room to pack all my belongings and locked the door.

"Little nasty illegal whore!" Dan was crying right outside my door. "I'll organize you a sweet life, bitch. I'll report that you have no papers."

"Then I'll report sexual harassment!" I yelled back.

He laughed loudly and hysterically. I couldn't say whether he was intoxicated or was going through some unknown manic state. Or whether it was just a normal part of him.

"Who's gonna believe you, filthy illegal immigrant?"

"You are so naïve. In this world, no one carries what dirty low-class people think, all appreciation and trust are for people like me."

I didn't respond. I was packing my stuff in a rush, somehow, just throwing one item after another into suitcases.

"You are not any better than the garbage that crosses the border to sneak around all their lives. You think your stupid master's degree makes any sense?" he yelled, giggling. "You are just like millions of other low-key illegals."

I knew that. I was thinking about it for months, since the first conversation with Shawn. I silently agreed, throwing my belongings in two suitcases, that I was not any better than others.

"I emailed Diane that you tried to seduce me." he uttered a few minutes later. "Don't you dare to explain anything to her. You know how dangerous it is in your circumstance. You'll be on the first plane to Russia, trust me."

"Okay." I murmured mostly to myself

It was very sad to lose someone dear so unfairly. I realized I would never see her again, I would never talk to her again, unless she would send me a bunch of angry text messages which would break my heart into smaller pieces. That thought made me even sadder. I knew she would hate me for the rest of her life. It's okay. No one owed me understanding.

"Life is so unfair." I kept repeating Vera's words in my mind. "Life is so unfair."

First time in a couple of months, I thought of Vera. There were no emails from her, not that I had noticed. I wanted to call her so badly, I promised myself I would.

Nothing could hurt me any more. I hung all my heavy bags around one shoulder and quickly adjusted suitcases' handles for a short ride downstairs. I wanted to say something deep and meaningful, passing through the door, but didn't find any proper words. Dan was standing right by the exit, looking at me with his eyes red, browsing my bags, as if I had stolen something. I gave him the last prolonged look and walked towards the elevator.

He didn't say anything.

The elevator took me down to the first floor. I felt used and thrown out. I wanted to cry out for this unfairness. I asked myself if this chain of endless trips from nowhere to nowhere would ever stop. If I would ever feel like a normal human being in the U.S.? If I would ever settle down somewhere with someone? Was there such an option for me? It felt like neither Russia nor America could offer me a home. I was a stranger, that got stuck in between two worlds.

I rolled my suitcases towards the F train, as I kept dialing Natasha's number. I forbade myself to think about what had just happened. I couldn't afford to think about Diane. I had no mental strength. I was trying to focus on GD, on drinking for the whole night; I wanted to get extremely drunk, I wanted to forget everything, including myself. I felt horrible calling a friend only when I needed one. I contacted Natasha right after the rape, and now I was calling her again to escape from another predicament. Where had I been when she needed support? Did I come over to her while she was crying over Rita? Rita, I thought, as Natasha didn't pick up. I started dialing Rita's number in hurry while approaching the train stop. My phone went off. I threw that useless black piece of metal in my purse with anger and hopelessness. I had a key to her apartment.

I kept holding tears all the way on the train. My moods were switching from sadness to anger, from frustration and confusion to the seductive pleasure of getting mad drunk the night ahead. I thought I would take Rita out if she would be feeling good enough after the previous day of drinking. I would invite Natasha. I was pretty sure, Shawn wouldn't make it, but I would invite him anyway. We'd be drinking till morning. I would, at least. I wanted to laugh hysterically, and I wanted to cry. I put all my efforts into detaching myself from all negative thinking. Everything will be all right.

I rang the bell when I got to Rita's. Nobody opened. After I rang it several times, I decided to enter, as I had her permission. I pulled my suitcases to the room I used to live in. I stood in the middle of it and browsed it for a while. It seemed hollow and hostile. A little more hostile then when I lived in it. Otherwise, nothing had changed, same, orange-colored walls, the same window facing nowhere, same noisy floor and memories of hunger, massages, and first dates with Diane. I sighed, prohibiting myself from thinking about it. Everything will be all right.

Rita's door was open. She was sleeping peacefully in her bed. She lay face-down in the outdoor outfit, I assumed, the same one she was drinking in the day before. I smiled and adored her, as she often fell asleep all dressed up, and in the morning kept spilling pickle juice all over her outfit, while drinking it carelessly. I closed the door and went to the kitchen to check if there was any alcohol, but to my big disappointment, found nothing. I poured myself a glass of soda. I didn't feel like unpacking suitcases, I didn't want to think about Diane. I went to buy a pack of beers and kill another half an hour by doing that. I checked on Rita again as I came back — there were no changes. I opened my first beer and put my phone to charge. I started getting worried as the day began moving towards the sunset.

"Rita!" I finally announced my arrival, standing at her door. "Wake up! I've brought a hangover remedy."

There was no reaction.

"Rita?" I repeated, coming closer to her bed and sitting myself down on its edge.

I touched her shoulder and got a weird sensation I had never had before. My hand crawled up to the back of her neck. It was cold.

"Ritaaaaaa!" I screamed. "Rita! Rita!"

I thought my screams would wake her up. I began shaking her by the shoulder.

"Rita, baby, wake up!" I heard my voice breaking up. "Rita, wake uuuuuup! It's time to get up, you've been sleeping for too long!"

"Wake up, God damn it! Wake up right now!" I shook her harder, because she had to wake up. Because there was a beautiful day outside, because there was a big deal of future ahead of her, a big deal of the world, a big deal of love, there was a big deal of life that was worth living.

I continued jerking her with both hands, losing my tears and mind, hoping to bring her back from where she went, because she belonged here, because she was one of the best people I had ever met. She had to wake up. It was getting late. Enough, Rita, enough.

I started sobbing. Louder and louder with every movement, I slipped down on the floor by her bed, and as my lips went to the level of her ears, I whispered, "Wake up, my beautiful friend, wake up, my sister, wake up, wake up..." I heard myself weeping, and sobbing, and whimpering, and all these noises sounded as they were not mine, as they were sounds of that room, of that apartment, of that building, of something else that wasn't present.

I pulled all my strength together and turned her over. Her eyes were peacefully closed, her face looked rested and sober. I stared at that face for a long time. It seemed like her lips were about to turn into a sudden smile and ask me, "Got scared, huh? Got scared?"

I hugged her motionless body, sitting myself back on the edge of the bed, holding her shoulders and head up in my arms, just like an infant. When I ran out of sobs, and my throat became too sore to make any noise, I whispered, "Why, baby… why?" "Why?" "Why?"

I heard myself calling 911, then I saw a lot of people running around the apartment, doing something, asking me questions. Then I saw Natasha and Lina and assumed I had called them. The place got filled with sounds of different kinds. I memorized Natasha's crying face. Then somebody was shaking me by shoulder. Then everything became bright, then it got back to normal. Then there was no Rita.

CHAPTER 9.5

There were no funerals. We had to call Rita's grandmother to report that her brightest light and meaning of everything, her only reason to wake up each morning — no longer existed. No more of this shiny beautiful smile, naïve eyes, and pure childish excitement. No more of this authentic and transparent human being. No continuation of her life's plot. Only pain. Enormous devastating pain, that wouldn't go away at any circumstance, at any meaning, at any point. Someone irreplaceable had gone. She had only one wish, it was Rita's body.

Grandma was waiting for her child patiently. She never lost hope, even when neighbors began saying that Rita won't come back and that she should stop waiting for that one phone call and begin enjoying the rest of her life and die peacefully. The old woman was waiting for Rita secretly, lighting candles in a church downtown for the loved one's health and wellbeing. She stopped counting years. She cried when she could. She waited by the phone and every phone call gave her a painful disappointment — it's not Rita. In her dreams, Rita always surprised her, just like this, she arrived without any announcement — and this was something you could expect from Rita. Grandma knew that day was approaching.

Rita always wanted her grandma to be proud of her. She wanted her one and only parent to know Rita was not a loser, Rita fought hard and won an award which she was bringing back home to make that old and wrinkled face smile sadly and kindly and her eyes to get sparkling wet that very first unforgettable minute grandma was anticipating a thousand times in her day and night dreams, and hug her child dearly, dripping dozens of warm tears on Rita's shoulder.

This day and this phone call happened very unexpectedly for Grandma. It was one of the hardest things in my life to tell the reason for the call. I could barely find words to talk and I still regretted not telling her how much Rita loved and missed her and why she couldn't call. Did she think that grandma truly cared about her triumphs? Did she really think that the poor old woman only wanted to see her successful and wealthy? What she truly wanted was to see her daughter healthy and happy. And it would cost so much less to achieve, a phone call once a week, a greeting card once a month, flowers for her birthday, and reminders, reminders, reminders of her child's love.

If Rita only knew that she, instead, would break the poor women's lonely heart into thousands of little pieces. And nothing, absolutely nothing in the world would be able to fix it.

We didn't know how grandma managed to survive it and we don't know if she did. The last time we spoke with her was after she buried our dear friend. She was sobbing and crying nonstop. We all were, back then. We decided to let her grieve. A month later nobody picked up the phone.

We cried helplessly, just like small kids, as we were saying goodbye to the last evidence of a beautiful human being we would never see again. It felt like all the lights in the world had gone off. No birds were singing, no wind was blowing, and no sun was rising above this cold and cruel Earth. Nothing appeared important any more. Nothing had any value. We felt lonely, all of us together and each of us separately.

My first few days after Rita's death passed in a drunken fog. I couldn't live in her apartment. I just couldn't. I temporarily moved to Natasha's room and cancelled the lease with the management.

Natasha's devastation had no beginning and no end. She regretted she never had a chance to talk to Rita, she blamed herself for bothering her with feelings and ruining their friendship. It was either Monday or Tuesday, but they both ended before they had started. I kept regretting not going to her apartment the night Lina told us she was sent home. Maybe we could prevent it, maybe we could save her, and we probably would. We probably would. Only Shawn was repeatedly saying we did what we did and nothing of it was our fault. We couldn't. We just couldn't. That was it.

All of us took something from Rita's stuff. Natasha took most of her clothing, she was hugging it while sleeping, she was hugging it while awake, and she wore some of it. They still smelled like Rita. I took her paintings and her unfinished pack of cigarettes with the lighter she valued because someone important gave it to her in Kazakhstan; she kept refilling it, and she took good care of it, now it was my reminder of someone very important I had failed to take care of.

I smoked some of those cigarettes in another drunken fog, I sniffed cocaine for the first time in my life with strangers I had no recollection of. And I dialled Rita's number, crying, waiting for a miracle, waiting for her to answer the call as I couldn't believe she would never pick up the phone again. I called Natasha after and told her to find that Albanian guy.

"We ought to beat the shit out of him! He is the reason she's dead!" I screamed. "Get ready and let's go!"

I called Kostya in order to get help from him and his mafia connections but didn't remember what he told me. Almost senseless and paranoid, I went to GD and began torturing Lina to give me Besnik's number or address.

"You're lying!" I screamed at her when she answered she didn't know anything about him, besides Rita loved him unconditionally. I continued screaming and crying until the owner came. He forced me out of the place and banned me from entering. Then I found myself screaming something in the middle of a street. Someone was about to call the police. I woke up at Natasha's.

I started hating Diane and her husband for keeping me away from my dear friend. I called her on one of my drunken nights and left a voicemail full of hate and blame. I knew it wasn't her fault. It was all me. It was me. I regretted not spending enough time with Rita. I regretted not giving her enough hugs, not telling her enough warm words during our very last conversation. If I only knew it was the last time I saw her standing by the apartment's door in her pajamas and fighting tears, I wouldn't go away. I wouldn't let her out of my arms. I would kiss her, I would tell her that I loved her, I would repeat it over and over till I'd lose my voice, because I never said it to her, I never said it to her. I never thought I wouldn't see her again. I would cry, I would cry and squeeze her in my arms. I would never go. I would never leave her.

I wrote about you, Rita, I wrote a lot, just like you wanted, remember? I'm sorry, I included some moments you asked me not to, but there was only a couple of them. Nothing more. And they were beautiful, just like your beautiful soul, regardless of anything you regretted and felt embarrassed for. There was nothing embarrassing in you, not even aggression or curse. I had never met someone as honest and kind, as marvelous, and as unique.

I wrote as much as I could, and I wish there was more to write. I wish you could give me more decades of learning you. I wish you could give me more of you. At least something. Another gaze, another smile, another plot, another story, another drop of pickle juice on your pajamas. I need more of you, Rita. Forgive me, there wasn't always enough of me.

I wrote about you, as you always wanted. You often asked me whether you're an interesting character, but I only laughed in return. And now, when it's too late, I'm telling you that you are the most interesting character I have ever met. You were the brightest of all living beings known by me. And no one in this world will ever take your place. No one I know is worth writing about more than you. And I wrote a lot. I wrote sincerely, warmly, hopelessly, with love I was always shy to show you, with gratefulness and appreciation of your existence, but no more, Rita. I cannot write any more. There is nothing left to say. No more stories, only random flashbacks. It is too painful to draw your name. It starts with R and ends way too early. And now, finishing this sad chapter, I promise to never-ever forget you. My heart will always have a special room for you, which I will visit time-to-time, just like the room I didn't enter on time, just like the room that got burnt into my memory forever. Goodbye, Rita.

BOOK II

CHAPTER 10

Exactly two years after, I was sipping wine on a rooftop of a Midtown East skyscraper with Snezhana. She was talking about her son, his school, school's teachers and a bunch of other things which didn't seem important to me. I wasn't listening, I was enjoying a light sweet buzz of white wine and warm July wind that gently tickled my face and neck. It was slow and calm there, all that my soul wanted, a good company and a great view.

"Are you listening?" she laughed, looking pretty tipsy.

"I am," I smiled and fixed my sunglasses.

I breathed in a dose of fresh summer evening and rested my eyes on a shiny silver pipe in the corner of the brick fence, while Snezhana continued her emotional trip to the recent past.

I was a semi-happy twenty-five-year-old creature in the middle of the universe of organic green century at the time of banning horse carriages and animal cruelty, the time of blossoming vegan restaurants and fresh-squeezed juices, recycle bins all around Manhattan; a time of care for health and the environment, after a long American hangover. Brand new middle-aged 2012.

I didn't raise too many hopes any more, my biggest dream was to visit Russia and see every single face I missed, hug every single body, just like I did it so many times in my dreams for about three and a half years. It wasn't easy to legalize, and with each sequent year, it seemed more and more of a miracle to find somebody reliable for money or love. I was searching through friends, Internet, speed-dating places, but had no luck.

I learned to wait. I tried to enjoy my youth and whatever it gave me. Snezhana got Real Estate license and we began working together, sharing all the income. Due to not being able to work legally, I pretended to be Snezhana's assistant and showed high-end apartments for rent in Upper

West Side. It paid rather well, enough to cover my living expenses and put something on a side.

Natasha got us a big and cheap two-bedroom apartment in Midtown West. In a project, Chinese people illegally sublet the governmental "gift", charging us only $1600 with all utilities included. It was a great deal for the area. I started appreciating it more when I learned to ignore the space between the apartment and building's entrance with its stinky elevators and dirty floors, a few violent tenants, and police raids every once in a while.

I enjoyed living in Manhattan after changing so many places in so many neighborhoods. In spite of all the building's dark sides, it was my favorite home so far. Natasha made a good roommate. For almost a year of living together, we never had a fight or disagreement. She got hired as a waitress in a fancy Italian restaurant and time-to-time would tell me about serving celebrities and bring some tasty freshly baked treats.

Kostya disappeared right after my last drunk conversation with him, from which I remembered nothing at all. Nobody saw him, nobody knew anything about him. His phone number got turned off, his apartment got occupied by someone else, who had never heard his name. Natasha said he was fine, he was a big boy, he found a way of dealing with his broken heart. I hoped so.

Shawn stopped volunteering for police and got back to his security jobs, trying to save money and open a business. He didn't know, what kind of business, he only knew he wanted to work for himself. Constantly elated, he often stopped by a familiar florist to buy a bouquet of pink roses for his beloved wife, Laurine. Yes, Laurine. They threw a small wedding a year after she told him she didn't need his love. Apparently, she was joking, apparently, she only wanted to tease him, and she fell for him right away as she saw him in their precinct, from which she was fired a few months before the wedding. Originally from Trinidad, same as Shawn, she had a working permit, and it was about to expire. They already filed all paperwork for her Green Card.

Natasha and Laurine made good friends, they began sharing secrets, meeting for coffee and shopping, and biking, and long walks. I didn't know what exactly they had in common, I was worried Natasha would fall in love with the love of Shawn's life, but she assured me, there was nothing going on. She was changing girlfriends faster than toothbrushes and seemed to enjoy her newly discovered sexuality.

Laurine was a tall woman with a voluptuous figure and dark curly hair. She had big brown eyes, thick cherry lips, and a flirty smile. She didn't talk much, she looked more of an observer, fully equipped with a knowledge of people's weaknesses, desires, and painful experiences. I didn't find her particularly attractive, but I could see, what Shawn fell for. It was the mysteriousness.

Dmitry seemed to disappear from my life for good. I hadn't heard from him or about him. Yet I missed him still, and sometimes I would wake up in the middle of the night, wondering how he was doing, where he lived and what he did, whether he had settled himself in America or gone back to Russia. Whether he had a girlfriend, or a wife, or maybe kids. I wondered if I would ever find out.

Diane Sullivan did send me a message of how badly she was disappointed with me and asked not to appear anywhere close to where they lived. I had neither desire, nor intention to appear anywhere they appeared, she got winded away from my head completely. My heart was sore for another woman I promised not to write about. Thoughts about Rita were just like injections of pain right into my chest from hundreds of different syringes. The lighter I always kept by my side, made me start smoking — lightly, rarely, precisely.

I buried myself into a dark non-escapable depression as I moved to Natasha's room in Brooklyn, exactly two years ago. Everything seemed so unfair and meaningless. I realized there was no point of life at all. There was no meaning. We are born, because we are a part of the mechanism of Nature, and all it does is gets rid of old lives in order to provide the environment with new ones, which, in their turn, will disappear soon enough in order to give a space for new continuations. Our cells, organs, flora, fauna, planets, stars, and universes are all parts of a huge mechanism where everything plays a role, perfectly complementing each other, and gets a different lifespan for that — it's an extremely beautiful and difficult project, besides it's totally meaningless. Once, it will be gone as well. In order to give a way to something new. But we won't know about it, none of us.

Every time searching the very bottom of life, I realized that life is bottomless. There is always a way to go lower, no matter how low you are. I was looking for my own bottom, sinking in the bottle of whatever would get into my hands. Every day was dissolved in alcohol and every morning would come with no remorse, crashing me with a heavier depression, and I continued dissolving myself.

I felt decades older than I was. I was watching arrows passing four, then six, then eight, then it was hard to remember which hour knocked me out. I got lost in nightmares that I often took for reality. Every day was a free fall down with no goals or intentions. Until Snezhana appeared. She stretched out a hand of help at the moment I had lost my human appearance. At the moment I didn't need it any more yet needed it more than anything else at the same time. Snezhana, the one who didn't punish me back for what I had done, who kept a good memory of me even after I betrayed her, a single mother, reached out to me and saved my life.

She came to Brooklyn to see how bad I was, sick, depressed, drunk, and totally broken — not dead, but not alive either. Natasha let her into the apartment in the hope to influence me to stop killing myself. I remembered a stranger in a perfectly fit suit sitting herself next to me, on the dirty floor, and telling me, "It's enough."

I heard her talking to Natasha. I didn't understand a word. The stranger gave me a pill to swallow. The same stranger forced me to drink a few glasses of water, and then the stranger hugged me and murmured, "It's enough. Stop hurting yourself. It's not your fault that Rita died. It's life. Forgive yourself."

I started crying in her arms. These arms smelled very familiar. She squeezed me harder and whispered, "Everything is going to be all right. You can do better than this drunken mess."

I embraced her and sobbed, "Snezhana! Forgive me... forgive..."

"Shshsh," she breathed, "I forgave you long time ago."

Snezhana left the massage business for good. Police released her after she helped them find a few similar places with the same businesses. She tried to contact me in a while after she got released, however it wasn't easy as the half-alive voice on the other side of cellular connection kept mumbling uncomprehensive moans over and over again. It kept happening until Natasha once picked up the phone. So, the stranger in a suit found her way to me.

Both Natasha and Snezhana helped me to sober up with detox pills. They fed me; they babysit me. They returned me back to life, and I decided to give it another chance. Snezhana became someone very important to me, someone who saved me, someone who truly cared about me, someone I would never betray again.

Later on, Snezhana said she would act exactly the same way I had acted when the police broke in. She said she understood everything and never blamed me for that. She also said, she told Natasha that we met in a department store. She said it was a stupid story, but she didn't have much time to come up with a better one once Natasha asked her. That's what we eventually told Shawn and everyone else who happened to wonder how we met each other.

I started living a new different life, I did let myself unwind on a way to freedom, I could almost feel myself as a normal human being, besides, I was illegally locked up in one country and constantly had to search for solutions.

"So, how are your dates going, hun?" Snezhana asked me, when she realized, I wasn't listening to her story.

I laughed, not too sure she wanted to know. The rooftop was getting busier.

"Not much fun," I said, "Apparently it's so hard to find love in such a big city."

"It's hard to find love anywhere," she corrected me, taking a bottle from an ice box and pouring us more wine, "Some people look for it all their lives and don't have any luck."

"Were you ever in love?" I asked, grabbing my newly refilled glass. She laughed, semi-sad.

"I thought I was…" she looked away. "I thought I was in love with the father of my son, but after he disappeared and left me with a little kid and no funds for life," she took a deep breath in, "I reconsidered my feelings."

"He has never contacted you, has he?" I wondered.

"He hasn't. I don't know anything about him. But you know what, if he will ever come back to check on the boy, I'll let him. I'm not mad at him any more. I went through my battle alone, and it made me strong. I am now thankful for what he had done."

"You're thankful that he left you?"

"Yep. Thanks to him, I became strong and independent. I really like the person I am now, and I wouldn't want to be any different."

I thought to myself, that forgiving is a prerogative of strong people, people with wide soul and a big heart. Poor-minded ones always collect all the hate and become rather vindictive. I couldn't stop admiring Snezhana.

"You are a really good person," I stated, a bit tipsy and touched, "I'm so proud to be your friend."

What I really meant was that I was happy to be forgiven, and the way I fitted into her philosophy showed me how weak and narrow-minded I was myself. She forgave me not because I was so good, but because she was so outstanding.

"Stop it," she tapped my shoulder. "Tell me how it's going with your dates."

I took a big sip of wine and smiled, looking at her eyes.

"Ah, not great. I met a few guys, but none of them was even close to what I'm looking for."

"What are you looking for?" she asked.

"I guess I have lowered my criteria to a reliable and educated guy my age. I also search for those who'll be willing to marry me for money. No luck in any searches."

"You can't look for both," Snezhana said, "You need to ask yourself what you need. Are you ready to meet a man to create a family with, or your purpose is strictly a Green Card? If it's the latter, you should put all your effort together to find someone reliable for that, if you want a real man, you should become The Love and be ready to give yourself to someone great. We don't find love, we create love."

She was looking at me.

"I so agree," I breathed these words, after digesting what she said. "I just haven't found anyone to give myself to."

I laughed, remembering the recent experience.

"I met one guy online. He seemed quite sane to me, worked as a sales representative in a medical company. Guess where he took me to eat? To some chip Irish bar. But it was only half of the disaster. The funniest thing was when his mother came to pick us up and drive us home. The same night I received a text that his mother approved me, so we can go on. But you know what? I'd rather not..."

Snezhana laughed loudly, repeating, "Oh My God! Really?"

"Another one emailed me the bill for the first date's dinner, after I refused to go on the second date. He counted everything in, all the wine we drank, food we ate, and the cab he paid for to send me home."

"Where do you even meet these people?" she asked, wiping tears from laughing with a black napkin.

"On dating web-sites," I said, "Wanna register there too?"

"I'm actually good for now, thank you," she smiled.

The time was passing by fast, but the extended day was still spoiling us with sunlight, and no signs of the night were approaching. We finished the second bottle of Sauvignon Blanc, and Snezhana looked at the time.

"I think we should slowly move out of here." she noted, and added, "Don't drink any more tonight."

"That's it?" I wondered, not wanting to stop enjoying the buzz.

"We have to do a lot of work tomorrow, honey. We can't smell too sour."

She got up, touching up her wrinkled skirt, and seeing me wanting a continuation, comforted, "We can always have more alcohol, but never less."

I took a deep breath of fresh rooftop air and got up, holding our purses tightly, while she was using the bathroom. I was looking at strangers, walking inside of the lounge, and going straight to the bar counter. There were young couples, and groups of people, all wearing casual and dark-colored New York-style outfits. They looked so carefree and laid back. I didn't want to go home, but I knew it was the right thing to do.

"How is it going?" I suddenly heard an accent from somewhere as if it was addressed to me.

I tried to focus on faces of that crowd to see if I knew anybody there.

"Hey!" shouted the same voice. It sounded very familiar.

"Katya!" It yelled. Then I saw a face I knew in a crowd of young guys sitting steps away from me. He got up and approached me, smiling.

It was Dmitry.

As he was walking toward me, I noticed that he had turned from a boy into a man, smooth masculine body with wide shoulders, a bigger chest, and a confident look. His white skin got some brown tan, which suited him very well. He let his blond curls grow down to the middle of his neck, and his blue eyes seemed even bluer — time was definitely on his side.

A quick hurricane went thought my heart and stomach and ended up somewhere in the belly. I couldn't believe it was real.

"What a coincidence!" he exclaimed.

"Yeah," I responded, not knowing what else to say.

I was wondering whether I would see him again for two and a half years, was picturing how it would go, how he would look, how he would act, was wondering what he had been doing all this time, and now, standing next to him at the rooftop, I had nothing to say.

"Wow!" he smiled again, showing his perfectly white teeth. "I can't believe we met here, on this roof! Wow!"

I looked back to see if Snezhana was coming but didn't see her.

"How have you been? What do you do?" Dmitry asked with true interest and excitement in his eyes.

"I'm good," I answered, feeling a little nervous, "I do real estate."

"Nice!" he concluded, "It must be really interesting."

"Not really," I smiled.

He laughed, feeling a bit awkward. Besides that, he acted as if nothing ever happened between us, as if we were old friends who just met after not seeing each other for a while.

"What do you do?" I asked and looked back again to see if Snezhana was coming.

"I am a model. May I treat you with a drink?"

"I'm fine," I answered. He did look like he took excellent care of himself. "What kind of modelling do you do?"

"Well… clothing, underwear, shoes. If you're interested, I'll give you links to look at me posing." he winked and pulled out his cell phone.

"I'd love to take you for a drink or coffee," he murmured. "Give me your number."

I was about to start dictating, but backed out, thinking whether it was a good idea. I recalled why exactly I ran away from him, and no matter how good he looked, he remained the same person inside.

"I don't think it's necessary," I declared.

Dmitry took my hand and brought it close to his face.

"Cold hands, as always," he laughed.

I smiled, trying to remove it.

"Please," he begged, looking into my eyes. "I won't bother you; I just want to keep in touch with you. We have so much history, and it would be too silly to destroy everything due to some negative emotions from the past."

I looked back and saw Snezhana waiting a few steps behind, playing with her cell phone.

"Okay," I said in order to finish the conversation. I didn't want to keep my friend waiting.

"Who is it?" she asked in the elevator with a flirty smile.

"Ah… sort of a friend of mine. We didn't see each other for a long time. Met accidently." I lied shyly, looking away at the floor count.

"He is very hot, I would say," she vocalized with admiration and tapped my back.

I shrugged my shoulders.

One of those days, Natasha returned home with very short hair. She said she wanted to look manly. She said girls like that sort of look. I didn't find her manly even with short hair, because her manners stayed the same, although I found it adorable and couldn't stop smiling, looking at her.

"What's the matter?" she would say, trying to sound tough.

There was really nothing to add. I only wished her the best.

She continued trying to call her mother once every three months, but the result was always the same. Having so much pity for my friend, I wrote a long email with explanations about why she stayed in the U.S., and how much she missed them, how much she needed them, how much she suffered without them — the mother and the sister. I sent it strictly to her mom and got a short response, "Please, don't write to us any more."

Natasha was talking about girls from a lesbian bar in West Village, they all were fat and masculine and she always wondered who could like them. She said it was so hard to meet a feminine lesbian in general. But the bar itself was fun and she kept insisting on taking me there.

"Come on! You've been with a woman. You know how things work over there." She would wink and smile.

I had no interest in further experiments with women at that time. My thoughts were with Dmitry. Two days passed since I happened to drink on that rooftop with Snezhana, and I couldn't rest my mind thinking about him. I was night and day dreaming about his blue eyes and blond curly hair, strong arms and warm body, I was imagining his sweet, and at the same time manly, voice whispering into my ear. Sometimes I felt like I was losing my mind, I hated myself for not being able to control my own thoughts and stop that childish nonsense. I needed a peace of mind and a reliable person by my side. I secretly hoped Dmitry would never contact me.

I didn't tell Natasha about our encounter. Just like everyone else, she would think I was stupid to give him my number or even talk to him. None of my friends, including my mother, ever liked Dmitry. Everyone said he was a user and a cheater and loved himself more than anything in the world. Vera could never stand him. She kept saying how fake he was and wondered, what I had found in him besides that cute face.

I kept my mind open, and regularly visited dating websites, without too many expectations. Time-to-time, I would find a good conversation holder who looked attractive 20 years or 50 pounds ago. Most of the people misstated their age, weight, life attitude, and ability to earn enough for living. I never understood why people lied. I assumed the point of it was to drag a woman to dates under any excuse and put all their efforts along with an "outstanding" sense of humor together to charm her and make her believe, that what she was looking for was not what she was looking for. That way I met enough "real estate investors," "Broadway producers," advanced "businessmen," and "famous actors" — I didn't even mind extending that list, yet my clock was ticking and the urge to legalize in America was growing.

Natasha loved listening to my stories about dates. She laughed as a child. She suggested visiting a lesbian bar, as she truly believed that the law allowing same-sex couples acquire residency through marriages will soon pass. She often helped me to get ready for dates, giving her opinion on my outfit, strengthening my hair in the back of my head, and telling how great I looked before I would leave the apartment. One of those dates stopped without starting. I saw a man in his 100^s, who was three times older than he said he was, and a few inches shorter, than he stated in his profile, at the corner of 56th and 8th, a few blocks away from the building I lived in. I just turned around and walked away. He held a sunflower with a long stem for me to recognize him, but unfortunately, so far, it was the only recognizable part. I felt disappointed and angry. I had spent about an hour getting ready, without making any other plans for the evening, and now, I had to turn around and mourn over wasted time and ruined Friday night. I wouldn't get that irritated if it were a single occasion. Unfortunately, I had a big collection of these inconclusive dates.

I wasn't interested in drinking tea with Snezhana. Tired of my own expectations and naivety, I went to a liquor store. I would never find anybody, I thought, walking home with two bottles of chardonnay. My mood went up from the thought, that I could at least get drunk with Natasha, who was off that night and had nothing planned so far.

"Hey, love, I'm all yours," I announced, walking into the apartment, and removing my uncomfortable pumps right away. "I've got some fuel. We can go anywhere right after we finish wine. I'd accompany you to your lesbian bar, if you want to."

I put the wine on the kitchen table. By the sound, coming from Natasha's bedroom, I knew she was at home. I walked straight in there and kicked the door open with my foot, as I always did, as we had no locks on either door, as I had no text warnings she was not alone, and I saw Laurine.

"We were choosing T-shirts online, you know, those ones with funny things written on them. They have sale. Wanna purchase one as well?" Natasha uttered anxiously, while two of them were standing with awkward smiles on their faces, fixing their clothing and looking somewhat nervous. Even a quiet and confident observer Laurine didn't seem comfortable.

"Guys," I said, losing my drinking enthusiasm. "I'm not stupid."

"What do you mean?" Natasha smirked in defence.

They both looked at each other and started laughing as they had no idea what I was talking about. I thought about Shawn and sparks in his eyes. I had never seen him so happy and inspired as he was on the day of their wedding, and when he learned Laurine was in love with him, and all the time right after that. My heart sank in deep emptiness.

"Stop it. Just stop it, guys. How long has it been going on?" I asked, feeling exhausted all of a sudden.

"For a while," Natasha looked down on the floor.

"Please, don't tell Shawn." Laurine shot at once, staring at me with begging eyes.

I turned around and walked back to the kitchen.

"Please, don't tell Shawn," She walked after me. "I love him, you know. So, it's not cheating. We meet only once in a while. There is nothing else going on between us, but sex. We'll stop as we'll get over each other."

"Laurine, can you, please, leave?" I asked emotionlessly, turning back to her. "I want to talk to Natasha."

She didn't mind. In fact, she quickly put her shoes on and showed Natasha her big eyes, bigger than usual. Then she left.

I slowly opened a bottle of wine and poured it into glasses.

"So?" I asked Natasha, handing her a glass. She looked like a misbehaved child that was waiting for punishment.

"All right." she said, "We started shortly after we met at their engagement party. I kissed her back then in a bathroom. Then we exchanged numbers and continued seeing each other."

"Are you in love with her?"

My friend looked away. I sighed. I didn't want to judge her. I didn't want to betray Shawn. I didn't know what to do.

All of a sudden, Natasha hugged me and started crying.

"I'm so sorry," she murmured. "I'm so sorry. I should have told you before. I was scared. I was worried you'd judge me. Everything happened so fast. I thought we'd soon get enough of each other and part our ways. I didn't know it would become so complicated. I'm sorry I didn't tell you."

She cried so bitterly and sincerely. I stepped back and pulled her chin up, looking into her wet eyes.

"I'm not a judge. It's not my place to say anything. I just feel really bad for Shawn. She doesn't love him, does she?"

She shook her head.

"That's what I thought. She married him for papers." I sighed.

Natasha nodded. I suddenly felt sick from that wine. I wanted something stronger.

"Get ready. Let's go to your lesbian bar, or whatever. We'll talk there." I heard myself commanding.

We kept silence all the way in the cab. I didn't know what Natasha was thinking about. I sank into a long-ago-memory, when Shawn told us Laurine didn't need his love. We both felt bad for him, we both told him to forget about her when he mentioned she didn't mind his company. How heartbroken he felt back then, and how elated he was now. And maybe it's not Natasha's fault she fell for Laurine, and maybe it's not Laurine's fault she fell for Natasha. We don't choose who we love. Unfortunately, we become either light or shadow in others' lives, lighting up their world, or staying hidden, out of their view, no matter what we do. The one who doesn't know how to replace the whole world for the other, is usually there, in the shadow, just like a ghost, always abandoned. I wanted to cry out of hopelessness, out of sadness. Life is unfair. Love is unfair. At the same time, there is no one to blame. At the same time, it's all fair. Nature didn't give us much choice — we don't control our feelings.

Laurine's affair with Natasha didn't change the situation much. Shawn's wife didn't love him. She only wanted a Green Card. She would leave him sooner or later anyways. If not Natasha, it would be someone else. There is always someone else if you need one. I had to do something to help my friend. I had to make him to look at Laurine in a different light. I wanted him to unlove her so badly. And nevertheless, I understood her need to obtain papers. I understood it better than anyone else.

"That's why I cut my hair. Laurine wanted me to look manlier," Natasha confessed in the bar.

It was a half-empty bar with a few drunk butches, an abandoned pool-table, and a jukebox in the corner. The place looked like it needed renovation. We paid $10 to get there, which I thought was too much, however I didn't verbalize it. A brutal tattooed bartender made us strong vodka-cranberries and winked at Natasha.

"Don't tell Shawn," Natasha looked at me as a guilty dog. "She was not in love with him before she met me. It's not my fault."

I nodded. I knew that. I only wanted him to be happy with a woman, who would truly care about him. Too bad, he didn't see anything around him, but Laurine. She was the entire world to him, and unfortunately, he was a stranger in that world, yet he didn't know it.

"She is a manipulator," I said. "Aren't you afraid to be left with a broken heart?"

"I don't want to look far ahead. I'm taking one day at a time."

Natasha and Laurine started seeing each other pretty much right after the engagement party. They rarely met outside of the bedroom, as she said, and there were only a few times they went out together. They didn't want to be caught, but mostly, as I understood, Laurine wasn't really interested in anything but sex with my friend. I thought, she would leave Natasha as soon as she'd have enough of her, and Natasha would end up mourning and healing her broken heart. Again. It saddened me a lot to look at her bright smile every time she spoke about Laurine. I recognized Shawn in that smile. I recognized myself in that smile every time I thought about Dmitry.

That night we spoke about a lot of things. I decided to take my time to think what to tell Shawn, how to exclude Natasha from this dilemma, and how to point out the absence of Laurine's feelings.

"Would you pretend to be my girlfriend if somebody would start bugging me?" I asked her after I had learned almost everything about this affair and Natasha's feelings, and notices some of the butches staring at me.

She put her arm around my waist and giggled manly, "Sure babe!"

We laughed and continued drinking. One vodka-cranberry switched another, and they seemed to become stronger and stronger. I lost the count, and it didn't matter anyway. We both wanted to get drunk and every tool was of help.

"Gosh! It's so hot out!" I heard a sudden man's voice near me, and automatically turned around. The dark-haired guy in the baseball cap on the back of his head, seemingly, in his late twenties, was sitting himself down the bar stool next to me.

"It is," I laughed. "And not much cooler here."

"I know, right," he smiled, taking off his cap and waving it by his neck.

Natasha pulled me closer to her and browsed the guy suspiciously.

"What's up?" she uttered.

"The coldest beer you have!" he ordered, as soon as the bartender approached him, then he turned to Natasha and responded, "Nothing much. How are you guys doing?"

He had a little beard on his chin and cheeks and smiling brown eyes. He seemed to be laid back and peaceful, dressed in sleeveless shirt, showing off his skinny arms; shorts and flip-flops, as he was going to the beach.

"Just chilling," Natasha stated, sipping her drink.

"Where are you guys from?" he turned his entire body to us with an ice-cold beer in his hand.

His face looked calm and satisfied.

"From Jamaica," I answered playfully.

"Oh okay," he giggled. "That's exactly how you guys look."

We all laughed, then he stretched out his hand.

"I'm James, by the way. You may call me Jim if you'd like."

"I like James better," I said.

"I'll call you Jimmy," Natasha declared, "May I?"

"Yes, you may!"

We clinked our glasses and introduced ourselves.

"I prefer to be called Tasha," said Natasha. "My full name sounds like a name of a prostitute from some low-budget Russian movie."

"No," I objected. "Such a nonsense! It's a beautiful name, much better than Tasha."

It was the first time I heard the Tasha version and wondered whether Laurine suggested it to her.

"So, you guys are from Russia?" James figured, opening his smiling eyes wide, looking at both of us.

"No," Natasha said. "We are honestly from China."

We all laughed again, and it seemed like the ice between Tasha and our new friend had melted.

James was a graphic designer and lived in West Village nearby the bar. He would stop by sometimes for a happy hour before he would meet his friends somewhere else, or after a long day at work to unwind before bedtime.

"Are you guys a couple?" he wondered, browsing Natasha's arm around my waist.

"No," I stated, and heard Natasha saying, "yes" at the very same time.

"Okay," he looked away, smiling.

"I thought you asked me to protect you," Natasha muttered madly into my ear in Russian.

"From these butches. He seems to be a nice guy," I responded.

Natasha took her hands off me and ordered more drinks.

"I hope I'm not disturbing you guys," James said.

"Don't worry, James," I responded.

That night Tasha met someone she knew and walked away with her to another lesbian bar. She was inviting me to join them, but I refused claiming I had to wake up early in the morning. I was partially relived when she left. I had a couple more drinks with James along with philosophical conversations about global warming and human life in the context of the universe, about love and death and many other things I couldn't remember in the morning. We exchanged numbers before he put me in a cab.

As I learned the next day, Tasha didn't even remember being jealous of James and leaving with a friend she met. She didn't drink nearly that much when I first met her. She was very sweet and homey, but after she broke up with Kostya she went wild, exploring herself and her capacity to drink. My drinking started worrying me as well.

"Did you like him?" she asked me, before I left for work.

"It's not about that, dear," I laughed. "He's just a cool guy."

We had a productive day at work, and Snezhana took me for dinner and drinks in Hell's Kitchen, and right after we were done, James called.

"Is it the same hot guy I saw on the rooftop?" she asked with big deal of curiosity.

For a second, I wondered why Dmitry hadn't called me yet and cursed myself for these thoughts immediately.

"It's a different guy," I said firmly.

"Citizen?" she asked playfully.

I squeezed her shoulders with my hands and demanded wryly, "Stop engaging me with everybody!"

"I'm just worried about you, hun, that's all," she noted, and kissed me goodbye before adding, "Don't drink too much. This morning you looked like a dying fish!"

I met James on a fancy rooftop he picked. It was a semi-dark and romantic place that faced busy Columbus Circle. The air was filled with jazz and cold smell of something sweet. I came fifteen minutes late, but he didn't seem to mind. That night he wore dressy shoes, black pants, and a purplish shirt with long sleeves. He had shaved his beard, which gave him a fresh and blossoming look. I felt a little awkward, being dressed in a light casual dress and every-day-flats.

"I didn't know it would be this fancy, James," I apologized. "I would dress properly."

"It's okay." he smiled and gave me a warm hug. "I'm glad you came here at all."

"Well, thank you for inviting," I said, browsing around.

We shared a bottle of wine, talking about history of New York, art, Russia, and politics. He loved Picasso and Dali, jazz and fortepiano, scientific books and documentaries about aviation.

He didn't have a real family. His parents divorced when he was a little child, and both moved to two different states, leaving him with a grandmother in Virginia. The old woman raised him in love and care, she became his guru and a best friend. He loved her endlessly. He visited her at least once a month after he relocated to New York to get his bachelor's degree. Three years ago, she died. He buried her in Virginia and never went back there again. It was so painful, he said, putting her in the ground, and it would be more painful to see the spot where he left his dearest person.

I got so touched, listening to his story, so I sat closer and embraced him. He responded with warmer hug and kissed me on my lips. I smiled and moved back. Too early.

We spent a great time together, talking till four in the morning. He got to know my sad story about dad, who I missed terribly my entire childhood, and mom, who had severe chronic pain. I told him about my aunt, her love and abuse. I disclosed my illegal status and all the pain from being bound to one place when my heart and mind were in another. They are far away on a different continent, with people that speak a different language and wait for you — day after day.

It seemed that we had so much in common. I had never opened up in front of a stranger. Yet, surprisingly, I didn't feel that James was a stranger. I felt like I had known him forever.

It was a beautiful night with a lot of lights and fresh wind that deluded summer's heat. James escorted me home. Neither of us was in rush. We were walking and talking about everything that would come to our minds, enjoying the leftover of the night.

"You are not a lesbian, are you?" he asked me all of a sudden.

I laughed.

"Seriously!" he stopped me and looked at me.

"No, I'm not." I smiled.

He breathed a sigh of relief and shouted, "Yes!" We continued walking.

"Don't tell me you live here!" he verbalized loudly, looking at my building, once we arrived there.

It did look like a typical project, dark brown, hostile and gloomy; a place you normally wouldn't want to be nearby.

"I do live here," I answered, and opened a purse to look for a key, feeling ashamed of my home for the first time.

He came closer to me.

"You don't even understand how fantastic you are."

I blushed. He kissed me on my lips again and this time I let it go for a little longer.

"Enough."

We met for lunch the next day and the day after that day. Then he took me out for dinner in a cozy Italian restaurant. I loved his company and personality. Time with him passed extremely fast, and glasses of wine switched one another rapidly. I tried hard to control my alcohol intake, and not to look like a "dying fish" every morning. The good and the bad thing about James was that he also liked to drink.

We started meeting almost every day, for lunches, dinners, and drinks. Sometimes James would pick me up from a real estate showing, or a dinner with Snezhana, or join us eating. Snezhana found him very gentle and educated and kept persuading me to hold on to him. I truly enjoyed James' company, and subconsciously, was making room for him every new day.

Then Dmitry called me. It was about two weeks after we saw each other.

He insisted on meeting, with a smile I could envision through the phone connection, and feeling weakness in my knees and ankles, I agreed without questioning whether it was right or wrong.

We met in a dive bar in West Village. Dmitry picked the divest place, it was dark and old, and totally quiet when I arrived. Around 8. He was 20 minutes late.

An old bartender slowly made us two vodka-cranberries and we moved to the table. Dmitry was dressed in shorts and sneakers, and smiled non-stop since he arrived, showing off his white teeth. He looked like that innocent boy I met at the airport almost three years ago, just like there was no conflict between us, no misunderstanding, no threatening, and no escape. I felt lost but tried not to show it.

"I missed you," he started the long night of drinking and soul-to-soul talking. "I had never stopped missing you."

He told me he was married to an older woman, who loved him more than anything. She used all her connections to make him a model. Even it was a tough business to get in, he couldn't make enough living, so the wife gave him a couple of thousands every month and on top of that, he got a green card through the marriage along with a membership in the most expensive gym and flights to Europe, first-class a few times per season with her. He had already seen half of the West and told me about his favorite countries, cities, parks, and other locations I only saw on maps. There were so many places to visit on his bucket list — everything besides Astrakhan. He just didn't want to go to Russia.

"I would give up anything to live in Emirates at least for a week," Dmitry breathed with his eyes shining, "I'm sure it's amazing there. But the cougar doesn't want to go there."

"I would give up anything to get to Astrakhan," I sighed. "At least for one day, at least for an hour…"

My eyes were getting wet every time I thought of possibility to see people I loved and the town I grew up in. It wasn't amazing, it wasn't beautiful, it wasn't even prettier than Worcester. It didn't have any significant places, but to me it was a center of the universe, absolute harmony of everything, my first love, my first happiness, success, dreams, plans, tears, first disappointments and life lessons. I remembered every street, every corner of the town, every building in my neighborhood with every tree, and I loved it with unconditional love that wouldn't change with years and circumstances — no matter what, it would always be my harbor.

"Astrakhan is a waste of time," he told me. "There are so many places in the world that are really worth seeing. You'll never move from the dead point if you'll keep coming back to the place that doesn't change!"

Dmitry confessed he regretted his behavior so many times after I left. He wanted to find me but didn't dare. He thought I hated him; he was afraid to scare me by intruding into my life. He knew I had left the job on Flatbush without even checking, he knew I had destroyed my old sim card without calling me. He asked Adil if he had heard anything about me, but Adil answered "No", which was partially true.

A couple of months later he moved in with the rich American woman he had met online. They got married right away and filed papers for his green card almost the next day. She owned a beautiful penthouse in Upper West Side, and my dear friend admitted he got spoiled by all that fancy living. They went through several big fights, but he didn't leave her, even though sometimes it was rather difficult to tolerate Miss Extravagant. There was not only the green card, but the life style, that spoiled him. He got addicted to it.

"I'm not going back to poverty," he stated. "I'd rather keep swearing to her that I love her, but I'm not going back to where I came from."

I looked into his scared eyes and saw a little child, hiding behind his mom's back. I wanted to embrace him but didn't. At that moment he seemed to be the only creature on the entire planet who understood me more than anybody else, because we had a long mutual history, because we needed each other, because he was from Astrakhan, although, he didn't miss it.

We spoke about all possible things, trying to catch up on whatever we had missed during these 2.5 years, and with each glass, it became easier and easier to go deeper into feelings, stories, and misadventures. I told him about Rita, about my affair with Diane and living on Fifth Avenue. I told him about the rape.

He comforted me with a warm hug, which carried so much compassion, so much care and love. I made an effort not to cry.

"It's my fault," he breathed. "I should have been there to watch out for you."

I rested my head on his shoulder, enjoying the peaceful feeling, which I had been missing for a long while.

Nobody knew Dmitry would come back to my life. He came back as a friend, as a soulmate, as a part of my home, as my new home. We began meeting secretly from everyone. I never mentioned anything to James. I started neglecting James. I started neglecting everybody and everything not related to Dmitry, including work.

Each of us was in a relationship, but we had no room for jealousy. There were no demands from either side, we enjoyed our togetherness and tried to make use of any free hour. I adored my soulmate and my new-old lover even more than the day he arrived in the U.S., even more than I did on our first dates in Astrakhan. I didn't want to separate from him, not even for a moment.

"You must be so in love with James," Natasha told me once, seeing me overly excited.

"Maybe. He is cute," I responded.

"He is okay," she spoke with a non-approving face.

Her affair with Laurine was getting more intense. Shawn's wife began convincing my friend to include a third person in their bedroom. Natasha didn't want to do it, although, she was willing to put up with anything to keep her lover. She admitted she was helpless and hopeless and fully dependent on the promiscuous woman. I began to hate Laurine. I knew I had to inform Shawn she didn't need his love, she never needed it, all she needed was a green card, all she wanted was attention, but not his attention.

James didn't seem to notice anything. We spent a good amount of time together while he was successfully falling in love with me. I didn't stop him from that, I knew I had to get married. I liked his personality and enjoyed our endless conversations, I loved the way he treated me and talked to me, the way he looked at me with his eyes full of love and admiration — it did flatter me.

Dmitry's wife would travel for business once or twice a month. We would borrow her car and drive upstate, to lakes and waterfalls. We would stop at cheap motels, enjoying ourselves and feeding each other's addiction, we would walk along rivers and lakes, we would bathe and hike, holding hands and kissing and doing everything we couldn't do in New York City.

"Seeing you is the best thing that ever happened to me," Dmitry told me once we were visiting Finger Lakes. "There was no one ever I had feelings for."

Deep inside I always knew that my feelings for him were stronger than his feelings for me. No matter what. But I never told him. I thought that everyone has different capacity for love, and it's nobody's fault that some people with small capacity do their best at running big. They might never be able to grow to your extent, but they might hit their highest bar, and for them, it would be the biggest achievement.

"You are the best thing that happened to me," I stated. But deep inside I didn't know whether it was necessarily a good thing.

We never took a single picture together, to protect our romance, he was saved as "Susan" on my cell phone, I was saved as "Harry" on his. We never sent a single love message to one another. We rarely went to restaurants or bars; we couldn't afford to walk around together, we adapted to this life in a span of two months of "dating". We patiently and passionately waited for Tuesdays and Thursdays, the days his wife would go to White Plains for business. She would leave early in the morning and return at 8 p.m. I would come over as soon as Dmitry would announce her departure and I'd leave exactly at 7 p.m., so he could have a room to prepare himself and the apartment for her arrival. They were my favorite days, my life was built around them, I dreamed about them, I thought about them, I even wrote about them. I felt devastated and elated, I could barely hide my excitement and love for life, for everything I could possibly think of. I couldn't understand myself, nor was I trying. Monday's nights seemed the longest. I loved and hated them at the same time. I often sat by the window with the view of Midtown and savored last hours of the day, as I would wake up in tomorrow and spend the day in the arms of someone I loved more than anything. Thursday nights were the hardest to survive. It seemed like five days in between were endless. No matter what I did, the time was crawling. And no interactions with him at all. Some days his Mrs would not leave, and "Susan" would find an excuse to escape to meet me by the river and we would take a long walk down to West Village or hide in Central Park. Eventually, we would go to a hotel. Travelling with Dmitry was my most favorite time, we had so much of each other, but never enough. It felt like a lifetime together wouldn't be enough.

I was barely holding my excitement about the upcoming Tuesday, sitting with James in an outdoor coffee shop, pretending to listen to him, on the warm Monday afternoon. Time was passing too slow. James was annoyingly happy. Coffee was bitter.

I didn't reveal any signs of shock when I got a phone call from Dmitry and automatically rejected it. He didn't seem to pay attention, until the phone rang for the third time. I turned off the sound and put the gadget in the pocket.

"Are you okay?" he asked, noticing my nervousness.

"Yeah," I forced a smile. "A client wants his deposit back. Not much fun."

"Oh…" he murmured, looking at me.

I smiled. He took my hand and held it with both palms. I was afraid he would feel my rapid heartbeat. He looked deep into my eyes and said, "I love you."

I didn't expect it. It was not the right moment, if there was any right moment for it. He stared at me, waiting for some sort of an answer, and I, feeling completely lost, smiled with a silly smile. I didn't want to lie, and at the same time, I didn't want to hurt his feelings. My cell phone vibrated in the pocket, and I knew I got a voicemail.

Dmitry never left me voicemails before. I couldn't wait to get to the bathroom and listen to what it said. I felt that urge in my stomach and bones, nothing on Earth seemed more important than it. Many guesses had entered my mind, a fear of unknown made me physically sick, I had to find out what had happened, I had to say something to James. I looked at him and let out, "I love you, too."

James moved his chair closer and embraced me. I embraced him back and felt his heartbeat. He squeezed me harder and his body started shaking rapidly, I figured he was crying.

"Forgive me, sweetheart," he breathed. "I'm just so happy."

I didn't know what to say and started caressing his back instead. I could feel the warmth of his body through the shirt, all his vibes and movements, every breath — it was so familiar, I did know how it was to be in love.

I pulled my phone out of the pocket as soon as I got into the bathroom; I could see a short voicemail on its screen. I played it right away.

"Ekaterina, Kate, or Henry" a female voice said. "Whoever you are, leave my husband alone. I'm not going to sit and watch how you're destroying my marriage. Stop calling, texting, and seeing Dmitry. Otherwise, you'll soon feel very sorry about it. I hope you are a smart girl and don't want any problems in your life. Enjoy the rest of your day."

My knees got weak, and I slewed down on the floor. I kept listening to the voicemail over and over again. Her voice was bossy and demanding. She sounded terrifying, as a woman who had something to lose. It didn't scare me. I was playing and replaying all our recent activities in my mind, to figure out where we made a mistake and how she found out about us. I had so many questions in my mind, how did she get my real name? How did she learn about everything? What is going to happen to Dmitry? I hoped she wasn't too hard on him. At the same time, I was sure she had forgiven him. Would she start controlling him more? Would she change their marriage conditions? How in the world could she find out?

There was only one person who could answer all these questions — Dmitry. I gave myself a command to calm down and wait. I was sure he would find a way to contact me and we would come up with a new strategy. Next time we would be extremely careful.

James was in seventh heaven. I hadn't seen him happier; he couldn't stop smiling, he couldn't stop talking about us and his feelings to me. He introduced me to all his friends and acquaintances. Snezhana adored him. She said she could see he was a nice guy, and the rest wasn't that important. The main thing in men, according to her, was the ability to take care of their family, and James had it.

I didn't look too far into the future; I was waiting for news from Dmitry. My heart was aching more and more with every day passing by without any signal from my beloved. I knew he would be able to find a way to contact me. I was checking all my old emails and messengers, answering all phone calls and even searching for notes by my building' or apartment' doors. I dialled his number from different phones and learned it was disconnected. I went to all bars we were hanging out at and asked bartenders and waiters if someone had left anything for me. I went to a couple of hotels we stayed a couple of times. I took long walks along Hudson River we happened to walk and visited Central Park's spots we hid a few times. I tried every possible herald out, but all my attempts seemed worthless.

When the second week of waiting came to an end, I fell into depression. I lost my appetite and enthusiasm, I was trying hard not to show it to people, I was trying to appear happy and life-loving, James-loving, every-day-loving. Every night, I would fall on my bed once I would come back from the outside, as I returned from war. There was the war, a brutal fight between reality, desires, expectations, and a need for solace I couldn't find anywhere.

The worst thing was that I didn't know what had happened to Dmitry. Maybe he got carried away to Emirates or somewhere else. Maybe Mrs Extravagant began controlling every step of his. Even if so, there is always a way to send a quick note. I could come up with plenty of strategies to contact someone without anyone else being aware of it, especially, when he knew my number by heart. Why didn't he ask a stranger on the street to call me or send me a message? Why didn't he dial me from a paid phone? One thought was too painful to admit, he simply gave up on me and preferred a quiet, worry-free relationship with his Mrs.

James kept coming up with ideas for trips around the U.S. such as driving across California or simply resting in Miami. I had a feeling he wanted to take me away from New York, from the only chance to reunite with Dmitry, and I insisted on staying, subconsciously counting how many days had passed without news. Two weeks. Or two and a half already. Does it work the same way with love, I wondered, if you survive without somebody for 21 days, do you become addiction free? If so, I was almost there. Yet to forget him, it would take me at least 21 years.

Overly excited, James booked a table in the restaurant on Pier 17 and waited for me being 20 minutes late. He was dressed up, and in spite of late September chills, wore a short sleeve pinkish shirt with a skinny navy-blue tie. He was perfectly shaved.

He took care of me as I was sitting down the table. His eyes were shiny.

"Please, no drinks tonight," he said when I opened a beverage menu. "I want us to be completely sober today."

I didn't like the idea but smiled and put the cocktail menu away. We both ordered salads, then I thought James winked at the waiter. For a second, I questioned my own sanity. I smiled again.

Through the crowd of people, I suddenly saw someone looking like Dmitry. He walked to a woman that was sitting on a bench by the water and hugged her. My heart shook painfully. I gulped half of the glass of water, swallowing ice cubes. There was not enough air to breathe. In a minute, the guy turned around and I realized it wasn't Dmitry. I was semi-relieved, and at the same time, I felt an urge to cry. A wave of emotions was coming up to my throat. I looked back at James, thinking that I was listening, he kept giggling and talking non-stop, yet I didn't understand a word as if he was speaking some other language that I had never heard before. I swallowed the pain and looked at the couple for the last time as they were leaving the pier.

"Didn't you want a salad?" James interrupted himself.

"I did," I answered, getting back to reality and grabbing a clean silver fork from a white napkin.

Having no appetite at all, I looked down at the plate and slowly started picking vegetables I liked. I felt that I hit something firmer than a plant with my fork and dug deeper in the salad to see what was there. All of a sudden, I needed another gulp of air and an alcoholic beverage, or better ten of them, with a decent time of solitude, there was a tiny pink velvet box.

I looked at James, not knowing what to say. My heart felt so heavy.

Fiancé went down to his knees, opened the box and pulled out a gold ring with a big diamond.

"Will you marry me?" he asked, smiling nervously.

For a moment I thought of Dmitry proposing to me on his knees. I wondered how he would do that, what he would say. My eyes got wet and I answered, "Yes."

James laughed in order not to cry and put the ring on my finger. I heard a tone of applauds from everywhere. Some loud slow music started to play. James squeezed me with his arms. I closed my eyes.

I thought, Snezhana would be very happy for me.

CHAPTER 11

We got married two weeks later.

James wanted to rather wait for a few months and organize a big celebration, inviting his friends, co-workers, ex-schoolmates, ex-groupmates, neighbors from Virginia and a bunch of other people I had only heard about, but knowing my urge to go to Russia, he gave up.

"I didn't get to spend enough time with my grandma before she died," he would tell me. "I don't want you to make the same mistake."

I truly appreciated all his efforts to make my wishes come true. He did everything to make me happy, and sometimes I thought he was aware of my broken heart and did all he could to heal it.

A day before the wedding, I bought a cheap white dress in the department store not too far from where I lived and borrowed a small milky clutch from Snezhana, who gladly agreed to be my witness as well. I didn't invite anybody else, just her and Natasha. James brought two friends, too.

He and I put brand new rings on each other's fingers, and our friends took a few merry pictures of us. I looked into his eyes, they were full of love and joy. I thought there was no price tag on happiness. It's there, it's free, and still, it's almost unachievable. I recalled Dmitry in that instant in my mind. Yes, we had many dreams about the future, including the trip to Marriage Bureau, honeymoon before and after the wedding and eyes full of love for the lifetime. However, I walked away from Marriage Bureau with another man.

It was a windy middle of October 2012.

Six of us went for lunch to a random restaurant in Chinatown. Barely speaking English, local waiters confused all the orders and prices, and brought us everything other than what we ordered. It didn't seem to upset anyone, especially James. He was the happiest I ever saw him, shouting and cheering with everybody, constantly getting up from his chair and hugging everyone he could reach. Even heartbroken Natasha was smiling. I thought of telling her the truth.

"Don't hire a lawyer for a green card," Snezhana murmured to my ear during the celebration. "It's a waste of money. I did everything myself, it's a pain in the ass because there are a lot of forms to fill out, photos and bank statements to collect, but other than that, there is nothing difficult."

"Thank you," I tried to put myself in the right mood. My American dream was finally coming true.

I thought of embarking on an airplane and flying to Russia. How would it feel? Will I lose my mind completely? How does it smell in the Astrakhan airport? Who will come to meet me along with my mother? My heart was beating faster as I thought about it.

"Do not send your green card petition right away, don't make it look like you married only to get a residence," Snezhana continued educating me. "Give it two-three months at least, I would even say six."

"No," I snapped. "I don't care! I'll do it right away!"

"I know, you must be very impatient!" she laughed.

I laughed too, looking at James. He was getting drunker and happier, his voice turned louder, and his mimics loosened up. It was the first time I truly imagined becoming legal in the Country of Dreams, legal just like a real American person, who wouldn't be threatened or discriminated, who wouldn't fear being reported to police, who wouldn't fear speaking up her mind. Absolutely legal and able to find a legal job with legal money, and pay legal taxes to the United States, legal enough to travel outside of the country. I felt extremely elated, thinking about my first mind-blowing trip to the Land of Childhood. I isolated my mind from that boring party and began dreaming about landing in Astrakhan.

I moved to James' in West Village. It was a small New York-style apartment with a queen-sized bedroom, living-dining room with a table for four people, and a tiny kitchen without much surface for cooking, but neither of us was really interested in cooking. The place was much smaller than the apartment in Hell's Kitchen, and it made me feel claustrophobic, besides it made me donate some of my clothing to Natasha, even though, she was much shorter than me. My friend was saddened by my departure. She said she wouldn't look for a roommate just yet, she could afford living there alone. She also said I was welcome back if things wouldn't work out, although, she sincerely wished me happiness. I had heard that before, around two years ago.

"Take care of yourself," I told her during our prolonged hug. "Don't let this bitch mistreat you. I don't want to lose you. I don't want you to lose yourself."

It wasn't difficult to learn to live together, my husband was an easy-going and open-minded person, and whatever had to be changed or adjusted was quickly changed or adjusted. We didn't have any arguments or fights. Everything was played by ear in a consistent order, groceries were done about twice a week, on Mondays and Fridays, drinks and friends — on weekends, laundry on Sundays, and cleaning occurred time-to-time when needed.

As chilling November came to its middle, a month after we got married, James insisted on going "at least to Florida" for a week.

"We have to have some sort of honeymoon, baby," he begged me. "I don't know what you guys do in Russia, but here it's a tradition."

He looked deeply into my eyes, as he was trying to get something out of them and figure out what was my secret or what else was there, behind my everyday calmness. I started to forget that my only reason to stay in New York was waiting for Dmitry to come back. It had been two months and I had heard nothing from him, and I even learned to live without him. I learned to stop myself from thinking about him and cut off the memories, as none of them ever happened. Just like I had done years ago. The side effect of that progress was a terrible emptiness that no James or Florida would be able to fill. I agreed to travel, and we embarked on our honeymoon trip.

It was my first time in Miami, a sunny land with an intense heartbeat. James booked us a room in a cheap hotel on Ocean Drive, which was right across the beach, in the middle of a chain of bars and restaurants that would open with serving breakfast and close with the last drunk client going to bed. A view of palm trees and tanned young people instantly relaxed my strained nerves and muscles.

South Beach bars offered a wide selection of beers and cocktails. Each drink was big enough for three people to share. Hostesses were dragging customers inside from pedestrian walkways by winking and waving at strangers, some of them would even cross the street to talk to tourists into entering the restaurant. We started off in a place like that and ordered two Grande mojitos. The music was everywhere.

Miami's parties seemed to never end. We didn't hesitate to enjoy them, hanging out till sunrise and waking up late afternoons, we would cure our hangovers in warm and refreshing ocean water. After a few hours of the cure, we would feel good and ready for new adventures.

"Happy honeymoon, Katyusha!" tipsy and happy James kept shouting. His stubbles grew a little over a few days and he started to look like the day we met. I felt endless warmth towards him, and little by little, I began realizing that this feeling was growing.

"Are you okay?" he asked me every time he found me gazing away. I would touch his arm and smile, and then watch his eyes filling up with love and tenderness. I loved his love.

One of the last nights of drinking, we witnessed two indecently dressed girls talking to significantly older men by a bar counter. They were flirting, laughing and winking at them until both men got up and left with the girls in an unknown direction.

"I would never go to a prostitute," James concluded.

"Not yet," I laughed. "You are still young and cute."

He looked at me rather agitated, taking off his hat and letting the wind from a ventilator in his hair.

"I will never ever do a prostitute," he verbalized slowly and clearly. "To me they are just so filthy."

"Okay," I responded, wondering why he started discussing it with me at that very moment, thinking, whether he knew anything about my past.

"So many men went through them," James continued. "Horny bitches charging money to enjoy sex."

He put the hat back and continued sipping his huge margarita.

"But I don't think they really enjoy what they do," I noted. "I don't think that's the reason they become prostitutes."

"Oh yeah?" he smirked. "Then why would they choose it among so many different professions?"

That very moment I felt a deep gap between us. James sounded as a close-minded kid. I sighed.

"You know, it's always hard to understand people who live a different life," I started. "You grew up in this country, in an educated family, you were able to finish school and college, you had all the right conditions for studying and finding a good job. Some people don't have any of it."

"Oh, I see," he interrupted me. "So, tell me, as a person who grew up in a different country, did you do prostitution when you came here? Life was hard, wasn't it?"

I felt like an electric impulse went through my chest and landed somewhere in my stomach. I looked down at his flip-flops, then took a big gulp of air and said "no".

"So, you see, everybody has a choice. There are always options!"

"We don't know anything about these people, we don't know how they grew up, how their families treated them, what do they need the money for!"

"Probably for drugs and slutty clothes!" James laughed loudly.

This bigotry started irritating me. Boosted by margarita, I wanted to yell at him, but forced myself not to.

"What if your son is dying from cancer and you have no money and no relatives to help?"

"God forbid, Kate!" he shouted, giving me a frustrated look.

"God forbid what? People are judgmental till a disaster knocks at their door. If something like that will happen, trust me, you will quit your job right away and will go somewhere you can earn the most. You'll go against your principles to afford an expensive surgery or medicine for your kid, you'll become a drug dealer, you'll turn into a drag queen, you'll sell your ass to male strangers — nothing would stop you!"

He didn't comment on it, continuing sipping his margarita.

"I know the story of a girl who came to the US from Russia to work for a summer after her mother got badly sick and needed a very expensive operation. She became a prostitute right away. Do you think she really wanted to do it? An educated person, she was getting PhD in one of the best universities in Russia. Do you think she enjoyed doing it? After four months, she returned home and took her mother to Germany for the surgery. And the mother recovered. She is alive now. How else could she make that much money in such a short amount of time?" I asked him, but he didn't respond. "Trust me, if the girl would think like you, her mother would be dead."

James shrugged his shoulders and looked away. I didn't add anything. I only recalled how judgmental I was before I went to do massages, and how much my values changed when I had nothing to eat. I embraced him. He embraced me back. It was not his fault he didn't know how bad of a lesson life can teach. I was glad he didn't. I wished I never knew it either.

We returned to New York tanned and rested, with endless supplies of energy for work and other big city duties. I started filling out immigration forms and preparing necessary papers.

We opened a mutual bank account as was required by USCIS and started collecting statements. I was making sure we kept taking as many pictures of us together as we could and saved all movie and airplane tickets, hotel reservations, utility bills, apartment lease with both names on them, and even restaurant checks paid with a card from our mutual account. The paperwork process required dozens of long hours of scrupulous work.

I could barely wait for the second month of our marriage to be over to send the package that was all prepared a couple of weeks ahead of time. I was trying to calm my mind down from the excitement I had about going to Russia, but it seemed to be stronger than me. I started having insomnia problems, and time-to-time I would remove myself from sleeping James' arms and come to the living room in the middle of the night, getting cozy on the sofa, to write emails to my friends in Astrakhan. I would tell them I would come in the beginning of summer, one of the best times in my hometown — it's a bit hot and dry, but mosquitos are not out there yet. We would rent a boat and ride it along the Volga River, we would throw a huge party with tents and guitars on one of its banks and stay there till we would run out of food and alcohol. We would go to see the lotus fields and take dozens of pictures. We would go clubbing, dancing, singing, and talking, endlessly. I dreamed about meeting my mother, holding her in my arms, and crying out of happiness. James would often find me sleeping with the laptop on the couch.

"What are you doing here?" he would ask suspiciously. "Are you chatting with someone?"

"With my friends in Astrakhan," I would smile.

"I'm jealous already!" he would jump on the sofa and start hugging and tickling me, biting my neck and squeezing my waist. "Maybe I shouldn't let you go there!"

"No way!" I would laugh, stopping him from tickling.

Somehow, time did run pretty fast. A month and a half after I had sent the package, I received an invitation to biometrics, a month after that, I got my work authorization card, and by the middle of April — notice for an interview scheduled for May 15th. I was overly excited and worried. The date became the most important mark in my calendar, my judgement day.

I began comparing prices for airplane tickets to Russia.

Natasha met me for lunch in a Thai restaurant in Hell's Kitchen. She looked completely devastated and poorly dressed. There were dark circles around her eyes.

"I was drinking for a few days in a row," she elaborated. "I even sniffed some cocaine."

"What are you thinking to do?" I asked, without clarifying what exactly happened. I knew it was Laurine.

"There is another guy now. She said she wanted us both. So, we did. I was disgusted, but she was so happy. I asked her to stay with me after everything had happened, but she left with the guy." Natasha was looking down as she was opening up, "I wanted to stop our romance, but couldn't do it. She wouldn't let me go. Every time I initiate a beak-up, she tells me how badly she loves me. She says she'll move-in with me once she gets her papers from Shawn. I'm powerless here."

I moved my chair closer to her, hugged her and kissed her on the forehead. Her body started shaking. I was afraid of losing her as I had lost Rita, someone very dear and irreplaceable.

"What can we do about it?" I murmured into her ear. "I'm here with you. I know how it feels to depend on somebody like that. Do you want us to come up with an escape plan?"

"Don't tell anything to Shawn," she mumbled. "I want Laurine to get legalized in this country."

"What the fuck, Natasha!" I yelled. "This bitch does whatever the hell she wants to you! I want to tell Shawn because I care about him as well. I care about you. And yet she uses both of you!"

"Please, don't tell Shawn." she cried.

I was holding her tightly, asking whether she wanted me to talk to Laurine, whether I could do at least anything to stop this nightmare. All answers were "no", but she did promise not to do drugs, not drink to excess, and create a profile on a dating website. As we spoke, Natasha got happier, and even started smiling. She confessed, that she wanted to break up with Laurine, and deep inside, she knew that this painful addiction would wear itself out one day, however she didn't know how many days would have to pass in order for this one day to arrive.

I had to find a way to tell Shawn. I couldn't think of any safe and gentle way.

James began predicting that my friend would turn into a junkie. He didn't like her since we met. He felt some inner jealousy coming from her and couldn't explain what the reason was; I thought, he was jealous as well. We would start arguing every time we would start talking about Natasha. I soon realized it was pointless to try proving anything to him. I began checking on her every day.

Big fight with the boss gave my husband a couple of unpaid days off, which he successfully drank away alone in the living room. Another argument with his employer moved his desk from a private office to a noisy advertising agent's area. I was afraid of further news.

"It hurts me to watch you suffering, honey," I told him once. "Would you consider looking for another company?"

"I'm totally fine, worry about your stuff, sweetheart," he insisted on leaving him alone with that issue.

I never knew his other side, the side of sorrow and irritation, in which he didn't let me in. Each sequent day became a new struggle for him, and unfortunately, I didn't know how to help. I was watching him lost and exhausted, not able to enjoy life any more, only looking forward to getting drunk after work.

One of the nights, he woke me up in agony. He started kissing and undressing me. Alcohol odor filled the whole bedroom.

"What are you doing, James?" I yelled.

He closed my mouth with his hand and continued removing my pajamas pants. I held it up, but he seemed to be very determined to finish what he had started.

"Let's make a baby," he muttered. "I want you to give me a baby."

"You are drunk!" I shouted after I bit his hand off my face.

"It's okay, the most important thing is, that you are sober."

"We can't have kids now!" I declared pushing him away.

He removed his hands from my body and sat back.

"Why?"

He looked completely worn out. His hair grew into a mess, his flannel shirt was all stained and wrongly buttoned. I inhaled some more polluted air and fixed my pants along with the top.

"Because we are financially unstable. Yet."

He laughed, looking up at the ceiling.

"Because you are only using me to legalize in the country."

"Where did this come from?" I wondered.

"It comes from what I feel…" he laughed again, holding his face with his hands. "You might wanna have a kid from your blondie boy. He is cute, he is cute. But I'm not ugly either."

"What?" I yelled loudly, getting up from the bed.

I felt like all my organs had turned upside down, and it became painful to swallow. My throat got dry. How did he know about Dmitry?

"Oh, don't make a fool of me, I saw how excited you were, getting messages from Susan, which doesn't even exist!" he smirked. "So, I followed you a couple of times, watching how you cheated on me."

I didn't know what to say. I didn't know whether I wanted to cry or laugh. I couldn't believe he knew everything and still married me. For what? It scared me.

"Yes, I had an affair," I confessed. "But I barely knew you. We were not committed to each other. There was nothing serious between you and me. I stopped seeing him a while before your proposal."

"And now he's waiting for you in Russia!" James concluded.

"No, he's not," I cried. "He disappeared from my life. I haven't heard from him since I stopped seeing him. That's it!"

I squeezed my head with both hands, something was hurting inside.

"I, honestly, used to have feelings for him, but it's all in the past," I breathed out and added, "Now I love you."

James moved to the other side of the bed and hugged his knees, breathing heavily. I moved closer. He didn't react.

"Why did you marry me, if everything was so bad?" I asked.

"I don't know," he started crying. "I thought I would get over it, but I failed. I hoped you were done with him, but then I saw you typing these endless emails in Russian, so excited about going there, and I figured, he must be waiting for you over there."

"You are stupid," I laughed, moving closer and embracing him. He embraced me back.

"Please, forgive me," I whispered. "It was my terrible mistake."

"I don't know where he is, but definitely not in Russia. He hates it there." I added.

I felt silly and embarrassed. It was a painful discovery for me to know James was reading my text messages from the beginning and watching that clumsy circus we played with Dmitry. I had no idea it was so obvious. At least I realized how his wife got to know about me.

"Then why don't you want to have kids with me?" he asked.

I pulled him towards the pillow.

"Let's sleep, honey. You're drunk. Let's talk tomorrow."

Tomorrow James got fired. I learned about it from the group message he sent to all his friends including me. It was an invitation to celebrate his freedom. By the time I saw it he was already in the dive bar in Soho.

To support him, I joined for a couple of drinks, even though he didn't look like someone who needed much support. He seemed happy and drunk, surrounded by a crowd of friends and strangers. He barely noticed my arrival, and only after one of his friends pointed at me, he moved closer and yelled, "That's my dear wife!"

I smiled at everybody.

He started to drink on daily basis. First, he went out and came back a little after twelve, then it started to last till four or five in the morning. I was getting more and more worried. Not knowing how to help my husband, I tried to surround him with love and understanding. But all my offers to spend quality time together were refused. He turned into a totally different person, a stranger to me. Perhaps, I didn't know him well enough, and the other side I got introduced to — scared me. I tried to recover the James I knew, but it was hard to catch him sober. I couldn't believe everything had changed so fast, in a span of a week or two, our life went upside down, and none of us had control of it.

He found drinking to be more pleasant than anything else. He didn't want to admit that something was wrong, every time I started this conversation, he would cut it short, saying he deserved some fun, that he wanted to celebrate his unexpected "vacations". He needed more space. And I gave him this freedom, hoping that something would get changed.

No improvements happened since then — it had been almost a month of "fun". The interview date was intensively approaching, and it didn't make me happy; in a way, it turned out to be very frightening and challenging. I became more of a roommate for him than a wife. Every day appeared to be the same as the previous, waking up to the terrible smell, then working, then lonely nights in a messy apartment. James grew very irritable. We didn't talk much any more; I was always looking forward to going to work and would work endlessly, refusing lunch breaks and staying for late showings. I would often stop by Snezhana's apartment and do homework with her kid, then watch movies with him and Snezhana. Some days heart-broken Tasha would join us, sharing her personal life's updates, which were not much of updates as Laurine held her tightly by coming over either once or twice a week with some other male, sometimes by herself only. It hurt me to see my friend suffering, so I decided not to complain about James. My home became the least desirable place to be in, I was afraid of discovering something I didn't want, my husband's life, unfortunately, had become a mystery to me. And one of those days, before I turned the key in the lock, I realized there were guests inside.

"Come over, Katyusha!" yelled James, who barely stood on his feet. "I'd like to introduce you to my friends!"

"Katyusha?" another unknown guy started giggling, smoking and throwing ashes right on the floor.

I walked into the nasty atmosphere of people I've never seen before. They looked like homeless, I assumed they had been drinking for a very long time by then. There were four men including my husband, and an older woman, all sitting at our table. The guys were in their mid-thirties, not shaved for days, dressed in size-less hoodies and constriction boots; the woman looked vulgar and somewhat scary. She wore pink blouse, that could barely hide her breasts. She was probably in her mid-sixties.

"That's how her relatives call her back home," James explained.

"Are you from Ukraine?" asked the guy, who sat next to the woman.

"From Russia," I answered in frustration.

"Same shit!" he stated. "Sit, have a drink with us! Jim, get a beer for your wife, you motherfucker! You don't want her to stare at as drinking all night, do you?"

Everyone at the table laughed. I wished I wasn't there. Deep in my mind, I cursed myself for returning home, but it was too late to change anything, and a drunk James was already approaching me with an opened bottle of beer in his hands. I didn't want to be rude and sat down.

"What part of Russia are you from?" asked the woman.

"South," I said.

"Is it far from Siberia? It must be cold even in the south!"

"Yeah!" the harsh-voiced smoker added. "Very cold! That's why everybody drinks vodka there, to warm up."

"That's why there are so many hot girls," vocalized the most silent one, and everybody burst out laughing again.

I tried to smile but found it extremely hard. James sat next to me and introduced everybody by name. I didn't memorize any, I only had one question in my mind, where did it all go? His life-style scared me. I returned home, which was full of strangers. I didn't feel safe there any more.

The "party" was getting more and more annoying. All new fellows went disgustingly drunk and started exchanging dirty jokes. The woman was constantly laughing; she did it so loud that I thought the neighbors might complain on us. James was jumping around trying to please everybody, serving more beers and pouring tequila shots. He pulled all the recent groceries from the fridge, everything eatable, and organized them into snacks in the middle of the table. A new mess started multiplying, the food got scattered everywhere in minutes — it got all over our already dirty apartment. The whole situation made me nauseas. I didn't want to see the continuation of it. I said I had to wake up early in the morning and needed to go to bed.

"Come on," agitated James yelled. "You haven't even finished the beer!"

"I have to wake up in the morning, too!" murmured one of the men, whose eyes were looking at each other.

"Me too," the woman claimed. "Everybody has to do something tomorrow! Let's enjoy life while we're all here!"

I was getting more and more anxious about our green card interview, which was just two days away. I reminded him a couple of times prior to the party of strangers and received "everything is under control" an answer, which didn't seem legitimate any more.

"Anyway, I'm going to bed," I declared, looking at James.

He was staring at me too. I received so much hate through this short, but intensive eye contact. I had never seen this side of him. I walked away in spite of all the awkwardness of the situation and closed the bedroom door.

I barely slept that night. The party lasted until midnight, and then they all left, including James. I didn't know whether I was happy that he had left with everybody or not. I was laying down in darkness, adjusting my ears to the newly grown silence. I went through the news on my smartphone and checked out a favorite immigration section. I learned that 1.6 million illegal immigrants were deported between 2009 and 2012. I thought about that number. It was Astrakhan three times. Three towns of broken hearts. Three towns of faded away dreams. I could live in one of them, I thought.

The green card interview was happening in a day, but no rehearsal was really done. I analyzed all possible ways of negotiating with James; it didn't seem easy putting him in my shoes and making him understand how it feels like to have no home for almost five years. All the questions I prepared to discuss along with my attempts to work on them were left without attention. I didn't want to push him, but time was ticking away, and every day was getting us closer and closer to the interview. I knew there wouldn't be another chance. I did all I could just to make this day happen, and then, when it was so close, I feared it more than anything.

James arrived around 7 in the morning. I woke up from the sound of his clumsy unstable steps. He walked around the living room, then went to the kitchen, then came back to the messy living room and fell on the sofa. I didn't get up until I was sure he fell asleep. Quietly, I started to clean the apartment. It was the day off I took precisely to prepare for the interview. My husband seemed to be deadly asleep. I took a second to look into his face. Handsome, with aristocratic features, but unshaved and swollen, he was sleeping like an innocent child. For a moment, I felt that nothing bad had happened, that there was no party yesterday, no terrible month of drinking, I imagined he never lost his job and remained the same lovely James I had met less than a year ago. A new pleasant feeling grew in my heart, I thought he would wake up in a good mood as it had been all the time before, and we would go out to brunch, coffee, or just a walk outside. It was such a beautiful day!

Shawn called me twice that morning. There was no voicemail. I knew I had to do something about his unfair marriage, but I first had to figure out how to fix mine. I decided to call him back later, after James and I would rehearse our interview. I also decided to be as nice as I could, ultimately, it's not my husband's fault he had to go through so much. We all are kids here, some of us are younger, some older; nobody taught us how to handle disasters, so we go through life, fragile and blind, trying to make something out of things we have no knowledge of.

The cleaning was done, and a light breakfast was prepared by the time he woke up, around noon. I sat next to him with the glass of water.

"Good morning, honey!"

He looked around, squeezing his head with both hands. Windows were wide open, but even spring's fresh air couldn't mask that terrible smell of hangover. He grabbed the glass of water as soon as he saw it.

"There is breakfast and coffee on the table, dear," I smiled kindly.

"What time is it?" he murmured looking around as he expected to see something.

"12…"

He put the glass down on the floor and switched to a sitting position, gave me a very unpleasant look and yelled, "Holy shit! You are a fucking liar! I hate you! And you know what? My friends didn't like you either!"

"What did I do to you baby?"

"You said you have to work today and it's 12 o'clock and you are still freaking at home! What was your urgency going to bed last night? Huh? You claim that you love me, but you can't wait to leave when we are together…"

"It's not true!" I started explaining.

"It's fucking true! I brought my friends home to introduce to you! And you disappeared as soon as you could. I saw your face...the way you met them like they are all trash! Do you think you are a queen here? Answer!"

"I'm sorry... I didn't mean to treat your friends like this. I was just very tired," I lied in order to stop the growing conflict. I was pretty sure he recently met all these people in some trashy bar and brought them home just to save money on drinking. "I respect your friends, honey. I was worried about our interview tomorrow.... That's why I took off today..."

"I don't give a shit about my wife's interview if she doesn't respect what I am! Go find some other idiot who will believe in your bullshit!" James blurted and went to the kitchen, "Where are all beers? Did you throw them?"

"I didn't touch anything..." I followed him to the kitchen. "There were no beers when I woke up."

"You are lying, fucking Russian whore! What did you do when we left? What did you do here?"

He put his hands on my shoulders and started shaking me, staring into my eyes with his mad animal look. I took off his hands and moved back, I couldn't believe in what was happening. I suddenly felt I had no control of my own life.

"James, sweetheart, let's stop this useless fight... It's not you, it's alcohol talking. We can take a walk and grab a few beers together. I just want to spend some time with you, discuss a few questions for tomorrow, maybe...? And then attend an interview in the morning — I'm sure we will be done by noon. Please... Don't be so cruel! I'm not going to bother you any more... if you don't want to..."

"All you care is the stupid interview," he shouted as loud as he could. "I should have figured before that all you needed from me is a damn green card!"

And he pushed me against the wall. The back of my head painfully hit the wall and it made my eyes teary. He left the kitchen. I couldn't move. Weak and fearful, I was losing the last hope to see my family. Everything seemed to be falling apart, and I didn't know what to do. I was trying hard not to cry; I took a big a deep breath and went back to the living room.

"James, dear, I married you because I loved you, and I still do. But besides love it's very important to me to get established in this country and be able to live a normal life, just like everybody else! I haven't seen my family and childhood friends in almost five years, I have two masters, but can't find a better job because I don't have papers, I can't travel at all... I'm begging you, James..." I fell down on my knees and took his hand. He was sitting on the sofa and staring at his cell phone. "Please, understand me, my dear! I swear to God, you can ask me anything you want after that..."

I couldn't hold myself any more and started to cry. I bent down and embraced his knees.

"I want you to leave me alone!" he snapped, after a useless attempt to stand up.

"Please, don't be so cruel!" I couldn't say anything any more, I tried to embrace him tighter. His pants got a few wet stains from my tears, but I wasn't able to stop. I ignored his efforts to get up until I felt a terrible pain in my stomach caused by his foot. I collapsed.

"I said leave me alone! Alone!" he cried, getting up. I tried to move, and he kicked me in my stomach again using all his strength. "I hate you, bitch! I wasted so much time with you building a relationship, but you only needed a stupid green card from me! It is unfair that whores like you are able to get someone to marry them, and other ones have to leave the country because they are not as tricky! Nobody should get green cards through marriages! I hope the next president will fix this up!"

He started kicking me as a soccer ball, as hard as he could. Then he stopped. I closed my face with palms and was waiting for what's going to happen. I didn't see anything but could feel him standing next to me.

"Fucking writer. Write letters to your mother, all right?" he smirked. "You think someone gives a shit about your writing? You can't even put two words together. Huh. Fucking writer."

He left in a couple of minutes and slammed the door.

I was lying on the cold floor for a few more minutes, not being able to believe in what had happened. I was afraid to make a move, afraid to open my eyes. I didn't know what to do on the entire planet. A dream that kept me alive for over six months had vanished as it had never existed, and I had to return to the same hopeless life with no tomorrow. Nothing seemed to be worth living at the moment, nothing at all.

My face was swollen. I recalled the night of the rape, I recalled bullying in the bathroom of my school and the desire to die on the cold tile floor. Was it worth surviving the electrocution? I asked myself. Then I stopped thinking, got up, and pulled out my suitcases.

I didn't want to bother Natasha at that very moment of her life, so I contacted Snezhana, who invited me over for as long as I needed. I decided not to think about James, as if he had never happened in my life along with a chance to visit my family and become a resident. I put on my light-blue jeans and a t-shirt, and shortly after, the two heavy suitcases were by the door.

After an hour of consoling, Snezhana put me to sleep. I heard her saying something about getting a driver's license in Chicago, as they don't check your legal status. I heard her saying there was an available studio in Harlem. I heard her saying something else I didn't understand. Then I passed out. I sank in a deep heavy dreamless sleep for long hours.

I woke up an hour after my unhappened interview. Forcing myself not to think about it, I slowly got up, took a brief look at my face as I passed the living area and walked to the kitchen. There were no signs of any presence of life in Snezhana's apartment, but a note on the kitchen table, saying that I was welcome to eat anything I'd find in the fridge. I smiled and made myself a cup of coffee. My head felt so heavy as it was me, who drank for a few days. I heard a knock on the door and dragged myself there. I knew the boy was in school, and the real estate day wasn't particularly busy, so Snezhana had probably decided to spend the day with me. I secretly hoped she brought something for breakfast.

"I know, there are no words to ask for forgiveness after what I've done," I heard a very familiar voice murmuring as I opened the door. "But trust me, I regret it more than anything in the world."

It took my exhausted brain a few seconds to figure out what was going on.

"I love you," I heard as my eyes were adjusting to the bright light of the building's hallway. "And will always love you, simply like that, unconditionally."

I instantly wanted to shut the door, but all of a sudden, a wave of anger passed through me. I looked at the innocent and shaved James's face above his clean and fresh t-shirt and wanted to stab a knife into it. The image of him with moving lips was standing right in front of me, but no words were heard, just like in a soundless movie, as if I had pressed mute on a remote controller. My fury was deafening.

I don't know where all the strength came from, and how I managed to break his nose, enormous rage took over, and I had no mercy for him. He stepped back, holding his bloody face. I felt both terrified by what I just did and proud of myself for being able to take revenge.

"I hate you! You ruined my future. You ruined everything I was living for!" I heard my loud voice that seemed to fill all hallways and staircases of the building. I didn't care about public disturbance or anything else, "Junkie!"

He burst out crying. I had no sympathy, but endless hate.

"Katya, baby," he began speaking in between crying outbreaks, trying to get as much air as possible. "Please, listen to me…"

"Get the fuck out of here!" my unfamiliar to me voice said. I was not in control of myself any more.

"Katen'ka…" he cried, "Please, forgive me. We can still fix everything. I know one lawyer…"

"Get out of my life," I shouted and pushed him in his chest as he started approaching me. "I was begging you on my knees to 'fix everything'. Now it's too late. Get out of my life!"

I heard him mumbling something else. I don't remember what else I heard and what else I said, I don't remember anything else, I only remembered him disappearing in a maze of staircases. I was terribly furious even after he was gone. I had so much strength. I wanted to smash Snezhana's apartment to pieces, I wanted to scream everything out of my lungs. I couldn't believe I had lost everything I had lived for.

I didn't tell anybody about what had happened that morning. I started planning my trip to Chicago, I checked out Harlem's studio and decided to rent it, I received text messages from Natasha, begging me to call her, I ignored new phone calls from Shawn, I felt like a robot, programmed to do things it needed to do.

I forbade myself to think about my failed interview.

CHAPTER 12

All wounded and hopeless, I moved to a new apartment in two days from James's visit. It was a small studio on 145th street in Harlem. Snezhana agreed to be my guarantor. We got approved in no time.

I had no furniture and no desire to spend money on it. I put two of my coats together on the floor by the only window in the apartment — that's how I made a bedroom. One suitcase made a fair table. It was enough to begin with.

I put Rita's paintings in the closet. They were all wrapped in paper, I didn't have the nerve to unwrap them. I carried them through all the apartments I lived in — wrapped and hidden.

A new summer was approaching along with unanswered James's phone calls, his unheard voicemails, and my semi-planned trip to Chicago. I booked a cheap hotel in the downtown area, a plane ticket for the very next day, and aimed to stay there for a week. I needed fresh emotions in a city that didn't know me, that never saw me, none of its buildings, parks or neighborhoods. I could start a life there from scratch, as if nothing bad had happened, as it was my first white sheet to begin the first sentence of a long novel. But I loved New York terribly; it was my favorite gift and punishment at the same time.

James unwillingly signed the divorce form. I filed it as soon as I could.

The only good news was Vera's decision to return to the US. She had sent me an email, asking to write her an invitation. I got it the same day I moved into the studio. I found a password-free wi-fi with poor signal, which still did the job. "Everybody should have another chance in life," her email was saying. True, I thought. I also thought that I had failed my chance.

Since I was illegal, I couldn't write an invitation, so I had to bother Snezhana again. She loved the fact that Vera decided to come, she had heard a lot about her, and she thought it would be much healthier if she would be living with me. She composed the invitation the very same day.

The very same day I remembered about missed calls from Shawn. I hadn't talked to him in a long while, mostly because I felt guilty for knowing what he didn't know and not being able to tell him anything. I had planned to figure out a painless way to inform him of his cheating wife, without unveiling Natasha's involvement, but I was constantly distracted by other issues. I took a deep breath and dialled his number.

"Did you know?" I heard an angry unfamiliar voice in my phone's speaker.

"Hey," I greeted him.

"Did you know, I'm asking?" the harsh voice repeated.

I instinctively wanted to pretend I had no idea what he was talking about but gave up on that pointless circus right away, "Yes."

"Why? Why didn't you tell me anything?" Shawn cried.

"Shawn, calm down. Please, calm down," I said in a calming manner. "I was thinking to find a way to tell you..."

"Yeah? How long have you been thinking for?"

"Can we meet and talk about it in person?"

"When did you find out?"

I sighed, "A while ago. Not from the very beginning. I wanted to find a way to let you know she was using you and cheating, which had nothing to do with Natasha. Natasha is a victim of the circumstances, just as you are. Laurine was cheating before and after Natasha. She was using you for a green card. I knew you wouldn't believe me if I said it with no proofs, you were so fond of her. I didn't want to mention Natasha, because it has nothing to do with Natasha..."

"It has!" he yelled at me, "You were covering up your cheating friend, who seduced my wife! You betrayed me. Have I ever done anything bad to you? I always moved your suitcases from place to place. I was always there when you needed a friend. I was always honest with you. I shared everything I had on my mind. And you... you..."

His voice started breaking. Then he hung up. I called back immediately. He hung up again. I left him a voicemail, begging to meet and talk about it. He didn't call me back. I sent a few text messages, but never got a response.

I felt devastated. I did betray him. And he was right, he had never done anything bad to me. He was always there. I was blaming myself for hurting a friend. I kicked my table-suitcase and sat down on the floor. I felt so sad. All of a sudden, I thought about Natasha with anger and disappointment. I wanted to yell at her. I called her right away.

"What had happened?" I asked.

She came over in two hours with a bottle of tequila, lemons, and big grey circles around her eyes. She wore sweat pants and a t-shirt. Her growing hair was a mess. She smelled like a hangover.

"I've decided to go back to Russia," she declared as we sat on top of my down coats, which we separated from one another and organized sort of a table of the floor between us. "I need my family. I really miss them. I forgot I have a family. I do have a family."

Something big and heavy got stuck in my throat. I swallowed it.

"Why did you decide to do it?" I murmured and gulped a shot of tequila without lemons or salt.

"I miss my family," she repeated.

"But wait, what had happened with Laurine? How did Shawn find out? How did you guys resolve this situation?"

Natasha drank her shot and sighed hopelessly, "I cried so much, I have no tears left any more. Shawn went to Philly for a day, so Laurine invited me over. You know, and he came back earlier or something. We were both naked. He started screaming and cursing and calling me names. Laurine screamed at me, she told me to get out and never come back there. She went to the bathroom, Shawn went there after her, and I heard her telling him she got lonely because he works so much, then I had a crush on her, so she went for me, so, basically, he pushed her into my arms. I got all dressed, and when I was leaving, Shawn stopped me by the door and hit me in my face."

I couldn't believe it was true. I didn't know what to make of it. I moved myself to Natasha's down coat and hugged her. She couldn't cry as she said. She looked very tired.

"Let's drink more," I proposed hopelessly. Everything seemed to be falling apart.

We had another couple of shots in silence.

"You sure you want to go back to Russia?" I asked her as if she would quickly change her mind.

She nodded, "I need my family right now."

We finished the bottle of tequila and went to a liquor store for another one. We also bought some food and snacks. We drank almost until the dawn — crying, laughing, hugging each other, crying, laughing. I thought Natasha would get over the idea of going home. Her home was here, in hatred and loved New York, among dirty streets and humid odor.

"Chicago is waiting!" the voice rang in my ears.

I squeezed my head as if I was holding it from splitting apart. A sensation of upcoming vomiting was in my stomach, throat, and even, somehow, in my head.

"Oh my god," I murmured, looking around. "I can't go to Chicago. I just can't"

"Come on, girl! You need a driver's license. You're staying in the country. Trust me, it will come in handy!" Natasha almost sang; she was still drunk.

She made me drink cold water from the sink, as we couldn't find my only mug, and forced me to a cold shower. Shortly after, I was on the way to JFK airport, holding my travel bag and not knowing what was packed inside of it. I had no strength to think about anything, I couldn't wait to board and get some more sleep. Trying not to faint or vomit, I finally made it to my seat by the window to get a cozy couple of hours of rest. I left the airplane feeling much better.

Snezhana provided me with contact of a Russian guy who worked in Chicago's licensing department and who was willing to lend his car and himself as an instructor to pass the driving test. He also provided a friend who allowed me to subscribe to a few magazines using his address, so I had proof of Chicago's residence. Of course, everything had its price.

I easily managed to figure out the subway system in Chicago and got to the California train stop on the blue line to meet the Russian man who was supposed to get $150 deposit from me and send me to my potential address to pick up letters and magazines with my name on them. I felt like a robot, programmed to do certain things, all my emotions were taken away by the previous night.

His building looked similar to the project where I used to live, just much smaller. I walked up to the third floor. A tall and chubby bald guy opened the door first with the chain on, but after scanning me for a second, he removed it.

"Are you Katya?" he asked loudly, standing in doors in sleeveless shirt.

He didn't invite me in. Obviously, he was getting ready for dinner, the smell of freshly cooked salty-savory food was everywhere in the air. I remembered I didn't eat all day.

"Yes," I responded.

He closed the door and disappeared for a minute. Then he returned with a piece of paper that he handed to me. There were two addresses.

"That's the guy who will give you envelopes. Try to get there tonight." he pointed at the first one. "And that's the place where I'll meet you tomorrow at 2 p.m. for the driving test."

I thanked him and gave him $150 cash as I was told before.

"It's for me and for the guy who gave you the address. Tomorrow, you'll give me another $150."

I picked up three letters from another man, who lived at the end of the same subway line and returned to my hotel on the South Side, not too far from The Loop. I felt exhausted and hungry. Not interested in any sightseeing, I unwrapped a sandwich I got in the Ukrainian Village as soon as I checked in to my room. It tasted better than the most delicious dinner I had for the past two months. I passed out right after I finished eating.

A new day started out sunny and promising. I had a coffee and a croissant in the café nearby and went to DMV in Chicago's Loop. I felt energized and ready for anything. That morning Chicago looked similar to New York, but slower, quieter, and friendlier. Subway trains were running right above ground level, unlike in Manhattan; people didn't seem to be in a rush, and there were not so many people at all. After New York, it appeared rather empty.

I successfully passed the theory along with the driving test and received my license card right away. Everything went unexpectedly smooth and fast. I gave another $150 to the Russian guy and we shook each other's hands goodbye.

Natasha, who still sounded drunk, checked on me the same night. It was the only good news; I finally had a driver's license. It was not a green card; it was, however, better than nothing. There were four full days to browse around and enjoy the new environment. I didn't have to work, stress out, think negatively, but celebrate my luck and be proud that at least something went right.

I spent three days walking around the city and got to see the Navy Pier, Willis Tower, museums and parks. I ate in restaurants and had a few drinks every night before going to bed. My budget was quickly decreasing — I had already agreed with myself that I would have to work hard once I'd return to New York.

I got bored wandering around the City of Winds alone and could barely wait to get back home. Nothing significant happened, day by day, sightseeing and aimless strolling among semi-rested-looking people were my only activities. On the last day of my stay, I decided to explore a wild nightlife of the city and went to The West Loop, checking out one bar after another. I was determined to get a better feeling of the town I might never revisit.

After a couple of ordinary pubs, I started googling lounges to brighten up the night, before I would return to the hotel and pack a few belongings for the flight. I had to have a story for Tasha, or at least a few more drinks. The third place I walked in was a Go-Go dancing bar. I found myself standing in a red summer dress and burgundy pumps, in the middle of the club, right after the security guy checked my new ID. The number of men in the place frightened me, and my first thought was to leave, but a moment later, realizing no one was even paying attention to me, I decided to stay for a drink and look around. It was a big lounge with a few small stages, each of them had a pole and a girl. Every stage was surrounded by men of different ages, they looked intoxicated and excited, and they were constantly shouting and putting money into girls' panties and bras which barely hid their breasts. Girls were showing all possible and impossible tricks on the poles, they were jumping on them, riding them, and licking them. I got myself a margarita and came to the stage with lesser people around. There was a blond skinny girl dancing there, she didn't seem very skillful, so I assumed she was new and hadn't made many fans yet. She bent down to collect the money after she finished the dance, and I, along with the men around the stage, put a dollar into her bright purple bra.

Another dancer with more curves came up to the same stage and the men began whistling and applauding. I applauded as well. She had tons of make-up and see-through underwear that was definitely getting her more cash. I ordered another margarita from a passing female bartender, and one of the strangers started a conversation with me.

"Is it your first time here?" he wondered. The man was dressed in an elegant suit and a skinny tie, just like people form Wall Street. He was not older than fifty.

"Yeah, I'm from New York," I answered, looking at him.

"And originally you're from Russia," he smiled.

"How do you know?" I asked, smiling back.

"How wouldn't I know?" his eyes laughed, "All Russian girls are extremely beautiful. Plus, your sweet accent."

I laughed and thanked him for the compliment.

We engaged in a light chat about nothing and ordered more drinks, cheering for Russia, for the U.S., and for peace between these two very different countries. We drank for peace in the entire world, for legalizing illegal immigrants in America, for beautiful girls, beautiful people, and beautiful minds. Then the friendly stranger bet $200 I wouldn't be able to get up and pole dance for a minute.

I took it as a disrespectful offer after such a nice conversation and my first reaction was to yell, "Who are you taking me for?" Yet my intoxicated brain turned excited and my energized body was craving adventures.

"What makes you think I wouldn't?"

"You look very shy," he winked at me.

I knew I would never do it in New York, but in the city of unknown people, where nobody would ever see me again, where everyone was a stranger just like my new fellow, where my footprints wouldn't stay longer than tomorrow's afternoon — it was absolutely fine.

"Sure, I can!" I asserted, thinking about making $200 for a minute of dancing.

My new friend clapped his hands and made a signal with his face movement to a dancing girl to leave the stage, then pointed at me. Everyone around there automatically looked at me clapping their hands as well. I assumed my stranger knew people in there and had some power over dancing decisions. Drunk and carefree, I got up on the stage, and projector's lights instantly blinded me. I couldn't see anybody or anything besides the pole. I had done nothing similar in my life, I had never learned, and I had never known how to perform seducing tricks, so I just grabbed the pole and started dancing with it, as if it was a person. I tried to move as sexy as I could. I had to do something for that minute.

"Take off your dress!" yelled somebody from the crowd.

I ignored the demand and continued moving around the silver stick, laughing inside at my own insanity and hoping that my stranger didn't run away with $200. When my eyes adjusted to the blinding light, I looked at the other girl dancing at the next stage, doing it so professionally and inspiringly, and tried to repeat a couple of her movements. She noticed that and smiled to me. I smiled back. Then all of a sudden, she jumped down. I heard some loud voices in the crowd but couldn't distinguish what they were saying. It was almost impossible to see anything below the podium. I continued to dance slowly until I sensed panic. I sat down on the stage to be able to get an idea of what was going on, and the first thing I recognized was a police officer. He stood right in front of me. The music went off.

"Let's go," he demanded, dragging me from the stage. "The show is over."

He walked me towards the exit. I couldn't realize what was happening and where he was taking me till we got out of the club, and I saw a few other girls locked in handcuffs and surrounded by police. My hands got locked behind my back the very same second. The feeling of cold raw iron around my wrists was unpleasant and familiar.

The arrested girls were being put into police minivan across the street. I was becoming anxious.

"Where are we going?" I asked the officer, but he didn't respond.

I didn't know whether it was immigration or regular police, and which was the worst. I had heard stories of places like that doing undercover prostitution and selling drugs; eventually they would get uncovered and face all logical consequences. I couldn't believe I was becoming a part of the consequences. Unfairly this time.

"I'm not even from here!" I protested, instinctively trying to remove my arms from the handcuffs. "I was just hanging out in the club. I'm from New York, I'm going back tomorrow!"

"You are not going back to New York any time soon," the officer announced, then threw me into the van and shut the door. I could see cops chatting outside in the crowd, and other men walking out of the club in anger. I realized I had left my purse inside.

There were about six girls in the van. All were dressed in shiny underwear which hid almost nothing and mega-high heels. Some of them looked calm, others, a bit nervous. It was hot and stuffy inside.

"Where are we going?" I asked them, looking from one face to another.

"To jail," said the calmest one, with huge breasts and tones of make-up. "They'll check your papers, and if you're clean, you'll pay a fine of $1000 for prostitution, then they'll let you go."

I felt so trapped and betrayed by my own self. I looked at all these women again, I couldn't believe I consciously brought myself there, to the final punishment, as if I screamed, "Look at me, I am an illegal immigrant!" Why didn't I leave after I had figured out what kind of club it was? Why didn't I think of a potential danger of being in the place where probably half of the girls were illegal? I couldn't believe I had gotten myself into such a problem out of boredom.

"I don't even work here! I only jumped on the stage out of stupidity!" I cried.

"I know you don't, sweetie," another one said. "Tell 'em!"

The van door opened, and I saw two more handcuffed girls right outside. I got up from my seat and started to scream, "Officer! Please! This is a mistake! I'm not working here, I'm just a visitor! I don't even live in Chicago!"

There were not enough seats to fit new girls in colored shiny underwear, and the officer called me with his index finger. It was pretty hard to move in the narrow space without using both hands, but I rushed out of the van and almost fell on the ground. He grabbed my arm to keep me up and walked me to a mid-sized police car. I got in. He locked the door and disappeared. Another police vehicle arrived and blocked my view, I couldn't see anything that was going on outside. I explored the inside and found it pretty similar to a cab, except there were metal bars, instead of glass, separating "passengers" from a driver. The officer returned and sat on the driver's seat. Nobody else got in.

"I don't work in this place," I started, moving closer to the bars. "I'm not a stripteaser. I came here as a visitor for the first time in my life!"

The cop turned around and looked at me. He had a wide and tired face with deep wrinkles on his forehead. I got an instant feeling he could barely wait to go back home, to his wife and small kids, and the warm food on the plate in a cozy eat-in kitchen but had to catch prostitutes all night long.

"Everybody says that," he answered quietly and slowly.

"But I'm not even from here. I'm from New York, I can show you my airplane ticket online, I'm supposed to fly back tomorrow."

"What are you doing in such place then, in another city?" he stared deeply into my eyes, but there was no straight answer.

The officer seemed to look older than he really was. Some people look younger, some people look older, but some people look like they look older. He had worn out emotions and faded eyes. I didn't think he was older than forty, but I felt as if he could be my father.

"I honestly came here to get a driver's license," I started rapidly. "I've never been here before. I don't have any friends here. I'm even staying at a hotel; I can show you the reservation! I decided to have some fun before I'd go back to New York. I didn't even know what kind of place it was before I walked in. I wish I walked away immediately!"

The car was still standing. I didn't know what we were waiting for.

"You came to get a driver's license from New York to Chicago?" he asked slowly and sharply, lifting his right eyebrow up.

That moment sobered me up immediately. I realized what a big mistake I had made, what a mindless creature I had turned into after all the ingested alcohol. I was looking into his eyes, tracking how he was silently figuring out my situation. I couldn't think straight any more. I wanted to lie that people say it's easier to pass the exam here, and I was not a good driver, then I came up with another reason, then another, then another. However, I didn't voice any of them. My eyes were starting to get wet, and a silent scream began coming out of my throat. I swallowed it.

"Okay! okay! I am illegal here!" I heard myself yelling with a voice I couldn't recognize, a voice I had never heard before. "But I wasn't always like that! I came here as a student, and I got a master's degree. I was working legally as long as I could, and I was paying taxes as all honest Americans do. I'm trying to legalize I'm really trying hard, but it's just not easy! I love this country and want to become its loving citizen! I want to be a writer! I want to write the book one day and give some of the collected money to charity. I want to help people here to find themselves and their ways in life, to find their meanings! I have never committed any crime, nor I was going to! All I need is the right of being myself in this country. But apparently, it's too much to ask. I know you guys will deport me, and all my years of struggle will go to waste."

He didn't say anything. He just turned on the engine and started to drive. I assumed he saw so many of "us," and all of us say the same thing. Nobody would describe oneself as a bad person, nobody would confess to committing a crime, and no one would tell the truth if they could use a beneficial lie. Why would he believe me?

I was watching him driving silently in an unknown direction, in a city where all directions were unknown to me. We were passing green lights of short blocks, one after another. Chicago was asleep. He was steering the wheel carefully, with both hands, looking straight at the street ahead of us, and time to time glimpsing at my reflection in the front mirror. The night was thick and heavy.

My heart trembled. I had no air to breathe. Dull fear and sick helplessness filled up my lungs. I thought about deportation — it seemed so real, too real, overly real, and I could do nothing to save myself.

"Dear police officer," I cried. "I would rather die than go back to Russia. I swear the God! I would rather die!"

He didn't react.

"I will do whatever you want as long as you won't send me back. I will literally do anything you'll tell me." I said as the last chance and closed my eyes. Tears started crawling down my cheeks and neck. I didn't sob, I was just listening to the silence, hoping, and at the same time, fearing to hear from him.

"I just want to live a normal life," I repeated quietly. "I want to have kids… a career… and a warm home… in America…I'd volunteer to feed the homeless… I'd do everything possible to make the United States a better country… I'd raise my kids as patriots and will give them the best education I can… I only want to live a normal honest life…"

The car stopped. I wiped out my tears and looked around the place, it seemed to be a quiet empty area without cops, people, or any presence of life. The officer slowly got out of his seat and walked around the car to open the back door for me.

"Get out of the car," he commanded.

I promptly removed myself from the vehicle and prepared for the worst. Standing next to him, looking into his small eyes, I was trying not to think about my upcoming torture. I took a gulp of air. Scared and lost, I didn't know where my own life was going any more. Every beat of my tired heart sent painful ripples throughout my body. My memory teleported me back to the snowy winter and the jiggling bus to Worcester. How comfortable the seats were, how exciting, and at the same time, frightening seemed the unknown. And now, the unknown had already turned into the known, and another chapter of my life was about to end sadly. I thought I would give anything to go back to that bus, to that comfortable seat, kiss Vera's forehead resting on my shoulder, and relive all these years differently.

Instead of giving me commands, the officer removed handcuffs from my wrists and stepped back, continuing to look at me. He was very tall and wide. I felt awkward and stared at the ground.

"What's your name?" he asked.

"Ekaterina," I said, continuing to look down. "Or Kate to be more Americanized."

"Her name was Svetlana," he said. "And she called herself Lana."

I dared to look at him, barely breathing.

"She was an illegal Russian immigrant, just like you. She even looked like you, she was about the same height, and she had long blond hair. We were dating. We were madly in love. I wanted to marry her and legalize her in this country, so we could have kids, a warm home, and all that stuff normal people have. She wanted to be a teacher, although her English was much worse than yours. She used to be a strip dancer, but after we met, she promised me she'd never do that again." he was speaking clearly and loudly, taking proper pauses between words.

"One day we fought," the officer uttered, and looked away in silence.

"She got drunk and went dancing in the club where she used to work. The police came to check it, but they didn't catch her, because a few guys from the club helped her out through the back door and drove her all the way outside of Chicago." He paused and took a deep shaky breath in. His face suddenly turned older than it already was.

"Then they raped her. Five men raped her all night long. After they were done, they left her there, in the middle of nowhere." he whispered the last sentence. I could see his eyes were getting wet in the darkness.

"Somehow she made it home," he continued, forcing every word out. "She took a shower, changed her clothes, and killed herself the same night, cutting her wrists with the razor."

Tears started to drop from my eyes. I felt that endless pain, I remembered it so clearly. It could be my story. I wanted to give him a warm hug but didn't dare to move.

"It was two years ago," he breathed with hoarseness in his voice. "Three of these animals were caught and claimed it wasn't a rape, but group sex. All they got is six years in prison. Just six years for a human life."

I thought about Svetlana's mother across the ocean. I thought about her fragile heart on the sixth, eighth, or tenth floor with windows facing a dull fake life, because the real life had ended two years ago, or maybe it had ended the day she gave Svetlana her final hug at an airport. And maybe that heart had never smiled, never shined, never felt anything but endless ache for the one who used to replace the whole world with herself since that day, which froze in her memory forever. And maybe this heart no longer existed, maybe it was crushed by the awareness of what it was aching for would never come back, not even for a moment.

"If I only could express how sorry I am, how much I feel your pain and your heart…" I murmured, swallowing my tears.

"I know you do," he said sadly.

"Do you have any money on you?" he asked promptly, changing the tone of his voice.

"I…" I began explaining how I lost my purse.

He stopped me, handing over a $50 bill. He put it in my hand and held it for a few moments.

"What you want to get in life," he stated, "it's all possible. You just need to give it a chance to happen. You are maybe at the beginning of your struggle, maybe at the end. Don't give up. Don't give up as Svetlana did."

I started crying openly, without loud noises, looking down at the darkness of the ground.

"You can get a cab right there," said the officer, pointing across the small field. "I have to leave you here, so no one will realize I let you go."

He walked away to the front of the car.

"Thank you! Thank you so much!" I mumbled, not being able to stop crying. "Thank you, dear officer!"

He looked at me and smiled sadly, then opened the door and got in.

"Go," he commanded. "I'll watch you."

I took a few steps towards the place and looked back at him. He nodded from the car. I took a few more steps and turned back.

"Thank you so very much!" I cried. My body was shaking hopelessly. "I wish you to have a great life, a beautiful cozy home and a loving family! You deserve it!"

He smiled again.

I wanted to say more and wish him much more than that, I wanted to come back and give him a hug and kiss his wrinkled forehead. I wanted to squeeze him in my arms and comfort him. I wanted him to be happy and healthy and have a warm home, a loving wife, and adoring kids waiting for him from work, a great career, and a wonderful life.

The last time I looked at him was after I crossed the field. I could see his car slowly starting to turn around. I ran into a taxi service's premises. I felt lost and miserable. I didn't say where I was going, I didn't utter a word. I saw my reflection in the huge mirror on the wall, it was an old woman with an exhausted face, lined with mascara along the cheeks and the chin, and dull faded eyes.

"Are you okay, ma'am?" I heard one of the employees asking. I looked around and found myself sitting on a cold chair, silently folding and unfolding the $50 bill.

"Yes," I murmured. "I need to get to my hotel."

CHAPTER 13

There was a huge cemetery in my soul, a cemetery that was made of broken promises, pain, hatred, disappointments and unfairness. There could be gardens of beautiful flowers and exotic trees, happiness and appreciation, love and hope. Yet, there was a cemetery, which was growing bigger and bigger with every obstacle, with every sorrow, month after month, day after day, and nothing seemed to be able to stop it.

I found my Illinois driver's license on the floor of my hotel room the morning I was leaving Chicago. I assumed, I had it in the pocket of my dress all the time and breathed a sigh of relief. At least, something had been accomplished.

Natasha met me at JFK airport. She looked much better than when I last saw her. Her face looked fresh and her clothing was perfectly ironed. I felt completely worn-out and hollow even after a decent number of hours of sleep. I had only one desire, to get home and rest on my uncomfortable bed.

"Hey," I stated, after we got into a yellow cab and my friend had learned about my recent adventures. "It's actually so easy to get a driver's license in Chicago. You should go! I have a contact of the guy who does it all."

"But I don't need it," she smiled sadly. "I'm going home, I told you."

I nodded in silence, biting my upper lip. I didn't think she was serious when she first mentioned it.

"I'm going home tomorrow night. I've bought tickets already," she murmured.

"Tomorrow?" a big lump crawled up to my throat.

She rested her head on my shoulder and breathed, "Yeah."

Disappointment and sadness filled my chest. I inhaled deeply and embraced her as if it would prevent her from going anywhere.

"I talked to Snezhana," she said after a short pause. "We decided to throw a good-bye party. Only three of us. At my place."

"Not a lot of us left anyways," I pronounced with irony.

"Come on," she uttered. "We are not parting our ways, we're still gonna be friends. We'll be in touch. We'll come visit each other, girl!"

"Yeah… yeah… You know how it happens. We'll be in touch for a couple of months, but in two years we won't recall each other's names."

Natasha gave me the look which made me correct myself, "Okay, we would probably still recall each other's names."

"We're meeting at 9 p.m. Promise not to drink before that." she declared when the cab stopped by my building.

I checked at my watch — it was only 3 in the afternoon. I wondered what I could possibly do for the next six hours, but nodded and said, "promise!"

I got to my place and locked the door behind. I was as empty as my apartment. I didn't want to do anything.

Don't. Don't. Don't, I repeated to myself in order not to slip into depression.

I lay down on the mattress and closed my eyes. Dismal thoughts were passing by, one after another, I tried to ignore them; however, there was nothing pleasant to think about. I couldn't believe Natasha was leaving. I started analyzing her recent past to find, what had pushed her to that decision, and my tired mind stopped me at the conflict between Shawn and her. I knew the conflict itself was not the initial reason, however, I decided to text Shawn. I wrote that Natasha was leaving, and she was deeply sorry for what had happened; however, he had no right to hit her. I asked him to apologize. Of course, it wouldn't make her change her mind, but at least it might soothe her pain.

After a couple of trials of falling asleep, I gave up and broke the promise given to Natasha. I filled quarter of a coffee mug with tequila I had left from previous session of drinking, and I gave myself a word to take a short nap around 6 p.m. in order to be fresh and sober by the party, and not to drink more than three quarters of a cup. My big rounded white clock by the only window showed 4 p.m.

The next time I looked at it, it was 5:45 p.m. I didn't feel like sleeping. I found myself crying on the floor, repeating that everybody abandons me. First, it was Rita, my dear Rita, who would always remain young and pure just as she was. I kept recalling her laugh, her voice, and the plot, she was consistently developing. I smiled, thinking about that weird party no one would ever throw, but Rita was so excited about the idea of turning the impossible into possible. Then I thought about her motionless body, doctors, police, and some other people I had no recollection of. I wiped my tears. Now Natasha was moving away. And her last sad party was approaching. The friend who went through so much with me was leaving. Life without her would be empty. We would be together tonight, but tomorrow we would come back to our routines and go to work, just like nothing had happened. In the of mourning the departure of my friend, I received "do not contact me any more" from Shawn and cried loudly, "Why does everybody abandon me? What have I done?"

It was around seven, when I decided to go to the store and get another bottle of tequila. All visible objects were duplicated and triplicated, so I had to keep one eye closed in order not to run into anything or anyone. Dazed giggling took over my tears, now life appeared funny, and every creature seemed to lead a pointless existence, but treat it as something important. I was laughing at it all the way down to the liquor store and back, then I found myself fighting with a neighbor next door. I don't remember what had happened, I only recalled taking solid swigs of alcohol right from the bottle and yelling, "Shut up! Don't give me orders!"

I was shouting about cruel life, walking around the hallways of my building. A couple of people tried to talk to me and calm me down. They suggested stopping drinking, and this suggestion made me furious. I began screaming that they were all dummies and morons and should go to hell. How couldn't they understand that alcohol was the only thing I had left? There was nothing in the entire world better and warmer than it.

Then I found myself on the floor of my apartment, holding the same bottle. Then police started banging on my door. I got up and instinctively went to the window, opened it and slipped to the fire escape stair. In my next memory, I was standing face to face with a cop down that stair.

"Give me my bottle back! This is a robbery! I'm gonna call the police on you!" I shouted when they took away my tequila and put cold iron handcuffs on me. "Again? You, suckers, again?"

I couldn't believe I was handcuffed second day in a row. My next recollection was me screaming out loud, "Fucking police every day! You kidding me? First in Chicago, then you... No! First one was at Snezhana's... but who cares...I'm so tired of it! Can you just kill me?"

Then I was in a vehicle of unknown origin — something between an ambulance and a minibus, threatening the police with suicide. I kept telling them I'd kill myself if they wouldn't let me go. I was telling them; they would go to prison for incitement to suicide and I hoped they would spend the rest of their lives there.

"I wonder, how you're going to do that." I heard a sarcastic note. That's where my memory ended.

I woke up from loud hysterical laughter. Through a terrible headache, I could distinguish other unfamiliar voices and sounds. I realized I wasn't at home. After a quick recollection of recent events, I opened my eyes. There was a light-blue curtain all around the bed I was lying on. A washed-out thin blanket covered me. I was dressed in an enormously large blue shirt and pants. I realized I was in a hospital.

I was drinking, I began to think. Staircase. Police. Fighting with them. That vehicle.

I tried to force my brain as hard as I could to remember what happened after, but it only gave me another dose of headache along with sickness in my stomach. The hysterical laughter was worsening my hangover.

"Good morning!" I heard a cheerful voice and saw a male nurse, who entered the space I was in. He opened the curtains and sat on the edge of my bed.

"I'm just going to take a teeny-weeny bit of your blood," he smiled, inserting a needle into my vein.

"Where am I?" I muttered.

"You are in Kings County Hospital. Emergency Department," said the man while drawing my blood.

His answer didn't tell me anything.

"When can I go home?" I murmured.

"A doctor will need to examine you first. He will make a decision." the nurse smiled.

"Wait, where can I get some water?" I asked right before he disappeared behind opened curtains.

"Right across the hall." I heard.

I managed to lift my body up and make it to the other side of my "room". I saw the water fountain right away. However, along with the fountain, I discovered a new unknown world of people talking to themselves, hitting their heads on walls, laughing, crying, screaming and doing all kinds of things I had only seen in movies. Electric impulses went throughout my body. Suddenly, the hangover stopped bothering me at all. I ran to the front desk and yelled, "Where am I?"

"Kings County Hospital. Psychiatric facility." said a female behind the desk. She was busy talking on the phone.

My heart started pounding.

"I'm sorry," I stated louder to attract the attention of the woman or other workers that were chatting with each other behind the same desk. "I need to go home. I'm here by mistake. I'm all normal."

"We can't do anything," one of them answered. "The doctor will make the final decision. Wait in your room. He should be there shortly."

"But I have to go," I cried helplessly, "I can't stay here, I have to go!"

I saw an exit door and started walking towards it, determined to leave regardless of anything.

"Go back to your room," I heard a demanding voice behind my back. "Otherwise, we'll handcuff you again!"

Someone in bluish uniform grabbed my arm, escorted me back to my bed and left. Fear and confusion froze my body in an uncomfortable position on the edge of the bed. I was staring at the floor, not knowing what to make out of the whole situation. It was absurd, yet it was real.

The laughter continued throughout my entire stay there. Random screams of someone else mingled with the laughter, and statements like "Jesus Christ sees everything" were coming from a third party. There were more voices, sounds, and conversations I couldn't distinguish. I didn't want to get comfortable on that bed. I didn't want to get comfortable in that place. I couldn't believe it was happening to me, and after everything I went through, I somehow ended up in the madhouse.

"Ekaterina?" a pleasant voice interrupted my thoughts.

I turned around and saw a handsome man in a colorless coat. He was tall, slim, with kind eyes and about half-inch short chocolate-brown hair.

"Yes," I uttered angrily.

"I'm doctor Holington," he smiled. "Let's move to a more comfortable place. I'd like to talk to you."

I decided to calm down and demonstrate my sanity as it seemed to be the only way to get out of there. We started walking in unknown direction. A nurse approached us with a paper bag and asked whether the belongings in it were mine. I saw my last night's outfit, my phone, an apartment key and breathed a sigh of relief, "Yes."

He didn't give it to me.

"When can I get my stuff back?" I asked the doctor.

"I'm sorry, you can't get it now." his eyes smiled at me. I instinctively smiled back.

"What about my phone?" I had to call somebody to let them know I was in trouble.

"You are not allowed to keep your phone, because you aren't allowed take pictures or record anything here."

It seemed like a bad dream. I wanted to both laugh and cry out at the ridiculousness of what was going on.

We went through a maze of doors and hallways, and an elevator took us up. We arrived at another section, which was much quieter and neater. Dr Holington took me to a room with a long table and a lot of colorful chairs around it. It looked like a typical kindergarten room, besides the table was taller and the chairs were bigger. We sat down, and he put a set of papers, he was holding all the time, onto the table.

"So, Ekaterina," I heard his calming voice. "What do you do for living?"

"I do real estate," I said.

"Do you like it?"

"It's all right."

"I've heard you were almost unconscious when police brought you here. What happened?"

The psychiatrist squinted his bright-blue eyes, looking at me as if he could read my mind. He took some notes. I wouldn't give him more than 40.

"Um," I paused, trying not to say anything, that wouldn't benefit me. "I got a little drunk and had an argument with a neighbor, so he called the police."

The doctor smiled, "What happened before that?"

"Nothing really…I had a few drinks, was getting ready for my friend's party, then went out to buy something to eat. On the way back…that… that neighbor started picking on me… pretty much for no reason…" I stammered, staring at the table. "Anyway, what am I doing in a psychiatric facility? I'm not, you know… not, um… like those people I saw."

The doctor was still taking notes when I looked at him. He had a very beautiful oval face with thick lips smooth button nose and abnormally bright eyes.

"Well, the police considered you suicidal," he gazed at me.

"What?" I tried to look shocked, which wasn't easy as I did remember screaming that I would kill myself. I suddenly felt embarrassed — lots of people had witnessed my shameful behavior. I thought I would need to move out of that apartment. If I'd ever get out of that hospital.

"You told the police you didn't want to live, and you told them, as well, to kill you," he stated, watching my reaction.

"Ah, I don't remember that!" I lied and wondered right away, "When can I go home?"

"We can't let you go today. We will detox you first. You shouldn't be worried; you'll be discharged as soon as we make sure you aren't in any danger."

I had no choice but to accept it. After asking a few biographical questions and marking something in his papers, the doctor walked me to another room of a smaller size. He told me to wait for a nurse and disappeared behind its doors. A slim, tall, young female was sitting on the red chair in the corner of that space. She nodded as she saw me. I nodded back and sat down on the further chair.

"You're beautiful," she said all of a sudden.

"Thank you," I forced a smile. "You're too."

275

"I'm Trinidadian, Jamaican, German, Polish, and Dominican, but I'm American because I was born here. I am a shark!" she stated loudly and looked at me with a hint of anger in her eyes.

I nodded in frustration. I still couldn't believe I was in a psychiatric facility. As a patient. I felt grateful when I heard my name from the outside of that room.

A short skinny nurse walked me to a spacious room with two beds, one of which was occupied by a very snoring person and another one was mine. The beds were attached to the floor, as well as nightstands and wardrobes. There was a bathroom by the entrance door. I looked around and saw no signs of time. It felt like the local life was frozen at no o'clock.

"It's Tracy," the nurse pointed at the snorer.

"This is your bed. I'll bring you a pillow and a blanket. Let me know if you need anything else," she said and left.

I lay down on the bed face up and took a deep breath to cure my growing anxiety. It didn't help. I was watching the ceiling and listening to Tracy's snores. Loud laughs were breaking out in between those snores. I tried not to focus on them. I felt insecure. I felt scared, like a little child, who got lost in a big cold world, where everything was a danger. I recalled my first day in Astrakhan's hospital, where I was admitted at the age of 7 right after the electrocution. As I got assigned to a bed in a room, I realized I didn't know the way back to the shredded old brown chairs in the lobby, where my mom was waiting for me. All of a sudden, I felt abandoned and fearful. Everything looked unfamiliar and hostile. After a failed trial of finding the path to that lobby, I ran back to the bed and buried my crying face in a pillow.

"What's the matter?" I heard a calming pleasant voice. "Wouldn't you rather sit with your mom, while the visiting hour is on?"

I jumped out of bed, wanting to dance and laugh. The nurse noticed my excitement and smiled. She took my hand and walked me to my mom. I felt so blissful when I saw her waiting for me. Her beautiful face brightened up, and I spent the rest of the visiting hour in her arms. It felt so warm and cozy.

I shook off the comforting memory. I wanted to talk to my mom more than anything at that moment.

"Ekaterina," someone called me from the corridor. "You have visitors."

It sounded very odd. It wouldn't enter my mind, that somebody could actually come there from the outside world to visit me. I didn't even know where exactly I was. It seemed like I was in a different dimension — completely unapproachable and absolutely impenetrable for ordinary people.

I saw Natasha and Snezhana as I reached the front desk. Tears of happiness wettened my eyes. I squeezed both the girls in my arms. I was not alone.

A nurse took us to the empty dining room. We had about half an hour. I finally saw a clock on the wall. No o'clock switched to 10:30 a.m.

"How ARE you?" they asked in one voice, staring at me, as soon as we sat down at the table.

I couldn't hold up any more and burst out crying. Seeing dear faces in that odd place made me overly sensitive.

"Hey, hey, it's okay," Snezhana said, moving her chair closer to me and embracing me. "It's okay to make mistakes. You aren't here forever."

I loved the smell of her perfume, it reminded me of my life routine, which I had already missed a lot. It felt like I had been there for weeks.

"I got so drunk, I can't remember anything," I confessed when I was able to stop crying. "How did you guys find out I was here?"

"Well," Natasha hesitated, while Snezhana was smiling with her comforting smile and looking around the dining area. "We waited for you all night and came to check on you in the morning."

"We decided it was not your style to disappear like that without letting know," Snezhana elaborated, stroking my back. "Apartment's door was broken. Neighbors told us you were taken away by the police. We went to a precinct. That's how we found out where you are, our troublemaker."

"Did you eat anything?" she asked. And without waiting for me to answer the question, she pulled out a sandwich from her bag. "We also brought your favorite ginger ale, but they don't allow any glass bottles in here."

"What about the door?" I wondered, chewing a sandwich, which appeared the tastiest I had ever eaten.

"Super had fixed it," Natasha breathed. I noticed her eyes were getting wet. "What are you doing to yourself?"

I shrugged my shoulders, "If I only knew it..."

"Wait," I exclaimed. "Aren't you supposed to be in the airport by now?"

"I was," she stated. "But how on earth can you travel anywhere when your best friend went missing?"

I felt warmth in my chest, she had never called me her best friend before. At the same time, I felt guilty.

"Did you cancel your flight?"

"I did, as soon as I learned you were taken to a psychiatric facility." she explained, then browsed my ashamed face, and added, "But it's okay. Maybe my decision was too rushed. Maybe I should stay here for a little longer."

I was delighted to hear that. No o'clock switched to 11. I didn't want to let my friends go. I kept holding both of them tight in my arms until the nurse said the visiting hour was over. They asked me what I needed and promised to come back soon.

I was laying down on my bed for the rest of the day, trying to fall asleep, but wasn't able to. Loud screams in the hallway kept me up, successfully reminding me where I was. Tracy wasn't in her bed, so I could have some peace of mind, which was far from peace.

"Ms Ivanova," I heard a male voice. "It's time for you to take medications."

I got up and agreeably walked towards the front desk, took place in a line of patients, and began observing the space around. It consisted of a long corridor with conference, dining, TV, and game areas in one part of it, and patients' rooms — in another. Reproductions of famous paintings were hung on the walls in-between doors, and a window with Manhattan's view finished the passage. Big shiny city seemed so far away.

"I'm Kate," I vocalized nervously after I had noticed Tracy right behind me. "Your new roommate."

"Tracy," she said emotionlessly.

She was tall, about my height, and chubby. She spoke slowly and quietly, so I had to listen carefully. She seemed neither friendly, nor hostile.

"How do you like it here?" I asked in order to ask something.

"It's not bad," she finally smiled, "the food is all right."

"Good," I stated, feeling better.

"Why are you here?" she wondered.

It was the first time I thought about the reason I was there. I must had had some diagnosis as all other patients.

"Miss Ivanova," I heard a hasty voice in the window of a front-desk and stepped closer to the woman, who handed me a small cup of water and another cup with two pills. I had no idea what those pills were and thinking about all disturbing movies I saw about normal people being medicated in madhouses to the point of losing their mind, hid them under the tongue and drank the water. I threw them away as soon as I stepped out.

"So, what are you doing here? What is your diagnosis?" my roommate repeated after taking her medications.

"I don't know, to be honest. I guess, alcoholism. And maybe I'm, um, somewhat, a bit suicidal."

Her curiosity seemed to be satisfied and she walked away. It was 8 p.m.

People kept coming to the front-desk to receive their dosages. One of them urinated in his pants while waiting, which immediately wet the floor under him and made other patients in line to relocate a few steps away. A short, bald, elderly woman was continuously murmuring something to herself, she didn't seem to notice the puddle and remained standing very close to the man. A young guy kept walking in a small circle right behind her. He wouldn't stop at all. I wondered, whether he ever got dizzy. Then an elderly woman in a wheelchair arrived. She stared at me. I tried to smile.

"You are fired!" she uttered loudly. I decided I had enough for the day and went back to my room.

I couldn't sleep all night. Tracy's snoring was so loud, that I thought the whole department could hear it. Time-to-time it broke into laughs and conversation with herself. Our room's door was being slammed every 15 minutes, non-stop, all night long. I couldn't wait till morning.

At no o'clock I stopped torturing myself with sleep and went outside of the room. It was quiet in the hallway. Extremely bright light was hurting my eyes till I adjusted to it. I reached the front desk. Out of having nothing to do, I began chatting with employees, who appeared very friendly, and learned a lot about the life behind the curtains of normality. Everybody was there for a different reason; those reasons weren't allowed to be disclosed. Some patients were living there, some — staying temporarily, others were hiding from the law. Everyone was on suicide watch, no matter how happy or sane one appeared. Therefore, our door was being slammed every quarter of an hour — medical personnel were repeatedly checking on us. I couldn't think of any possible method of suicide there, all furniture was attached to the floor, all containers, including trash ones, were made out of paper, shoelaces were removed from patients' footwear, and no plastic or glass objects were permitted within the facility.

There was no caffeine in coffee, even though one of two coffee containers said "regular". The dining area was under intense supervision as, pretty much, the whole department I stayed in.

Right after I had gotten my questions answered, I went to the only window with the view to watch empty streets waking up and getting filled with people rushing somewhere in a real world of that morning summer. I thought how beautiful it was. I had no time for that before. I was busy with anger, drinking, and running after unimportant tings. The most important thing was being alive and being able to adore everything the world had to offer. I laughed at myself, I had to go all the way to the madhouse in order to realize it.

"Ekaterina," said a melodious voice behind me.

I turned around and saw Dr Holington. His face looked fresh, his smile was warm and kind.

"Let's go," he offered calmly.

I couldn't help smiling, "sure."

We went to the conference room and sat at the table. He didn't wear a white coat this time. He was dressed in purplish shirt and black dressy pants.

"So, how was your first night here?" he asked.

"It was all right," I answered.

"Good," he grinned.

"Would you like to share why you drank so much the night before?" he gazed deep into my eyes as if he could read my mind. "Everything you tell me here, stays here, all right?"

I thought I had nothing to lose any more as I had already reached the bottom of life, and my honesty wouldn't do me any harm.

"Well, a good friend of mine told me she was leaving the USA and going to Russia for good."

"When is she leaving?"

"Um…" I faltered. "She was going to leave yesterday. But she cancelled her flight, because I got here."

"She must really care about you." the doctor said looking into my eyes. "She changed her life plans because of you."

"Yeah…" I murmured feeling warmth in my chest. I felt really grateful to have her as a friend.

"So why did you drink so much that night?" he repeated the question.

"Maybe because I've got in a habit of drinking." I breathed with sadness.

"Why did you get in a habit of drinking?"

This question did annoy me. "Because I love alcohol. It's the best thing ever happen to me."

"The best?" he squinted his eyes and smiled slightly.

"The best!" I blurted.

He smiled wider and asked, "What was the best thing ever happened to you? Besides alcohol."

I began thinking but couldn't come up with anything. Lately, there was nothing good. I told him that the last time I felt happy was when I planned my trip to Astrakhan. It didn't happen. And shortly after, I felt very unhappy. Before that, it was Dmitry. I felt amazing with him. Well, it ended very painfully as well. And as well, I was happy with Dmitry years before that, when he just came to New York. I went on and on all the way back through my college, and school, and childhood, and realized that the most distant memory of me being happy was with my father. I was the happiest next to him. I was the saddest when he left us. Every subsequent birthday, I blew the candles on my cake with only one wish — for my dad to come back to us.

Dr Holington was taking notes and giving me compassionate looks in-between.

As I realized there were not a lot of "best" moments in my life, I started telling him about the worst ones. I told him about my mom's incurable spine, my electric accident, bullying, harassment I kept receiving at most of my jobs. I told him about my shameful experience with "massages". I told him about Rita. I told him about the rape.

The session was over. I felt overwhelmed and relieved at the same time. The doctor's understanding gaze gave me a lot of support and his warm smile at the very end of my monologue made me feel very special.

"You went through a lot for someone your age, Ekaterina." he said with genuine sympathy. "We will get back to it tomorrow. In the meanwhile, try to rest and stay in the moment. Allow your life to wait for you outside of the hospital doors."

I nodded. He grinned, gazing at me. His bright blue eyes were sparkling. I couldn't hold myself from grinning back at those eyes.

"What about you?" I dared to ask.

"What about me?" he smiled with rather mischievous smile.

"Your story…" I vocalized nervously.

He gave a laugh, "I don't share my stories with my patients."

Breakfast time had started, and Dr Holington walked me to the dining area. He wished me Bon Appetit and left. I felt elated. I wanted to giggle out of excitement.

Tracy was sitting at the table alone, so I joined her. She complained the tea was cold.

"So, what's your diagnosis?" I asked her.

"Schizophrenia," she answered, chewing a nutritious bar.

"How long have you been here?" I wondered.

"For a month," she said and instantly asked. "How long are you going to stay here for?"

"I don't know," I confessed, "Dr Holington said, most likely for a couple of weeks."

She nodded, and I thought to myself that I wouldn't mind staying there longer. I had butterflies in my stomach. An elderly Spanish woman joined us. She confessed, she missed chocolate cakes and Coca-Cola, otherwise she was fine. She said she was there for legal reasons, for what exactly, I didn't dare to ask. She had been there for six months, and when I wondered how it was for her to be there, she answered, "Splendid!"

"Life outside is so harsh and monotonous. You're struggling for your whole life. You need to feed and educate your kids, you need to pay your rent, you need to work several jobs, and you have no time to live.

Once you become old, you take a look at your life as if from the outside, and you see, that all your struggle was for nothing. Your kids don't need you, your apartment is falling apart, and you have only a few years to live. Instead of the reward for all your hard work, you get oldness with all its aches and diseases. And loneliness. That's how the system outside works, so unfair."

"Here you feel better?" Tracy asked.

"Of course," she exclaimed. "I don't have to do nothing! I can play games, talk to people, sleep as much as I want, eat for free. What else could I wish for?"

I thought that my life outside wasn't much better. It was a struggle to nowhere. I also realized that it was much safer for me to be in that hospital than in my normal life as every day of that life was a danger for me to drink myself to death.

A very tall skinny man and 'The Shark' joined our table. The man listened to our conversation carefully, then said, "If not for my wife, I wouldn't want to be discharged from here either."

Tracy kept nodding thoughtfully. I was about to ask her whether she wanted to go back to freedom when the shark began shouting all of a sudden, "I'm Trinidadian, Jamaican, German, Polish, and Dominican, but I'm American, because I was born here."

Nobody at the table reacted to this. They were used to it.

"And I am a shark!"

Tracy taught me how to play her native game of cards. I successfully forgot where she was from, yet I memorized she was illegal. She had been married to an American man, who passed away a couple of years ago. When I asked, why she didn't apply for a green card during their marriage, she just smiled. I didn't know what it meant. We started playing this game on daily basis.

As Dr Holington had told me, I was given detox medications, I decided not to cheat any more and began taking them just like all other patients were taking theirs. The time I was called to take them was the same time The Shark took hers. We got to chat a lot and she became very friendly with me. She began sharing her objections and suggestions. She told me not to come close to the woman on the wheelchair as she could spit on me. She also complained that nurses kept giving her white pills regardless of her being black. She said it was discrimination, and I had to promise that I would tell it to authorities once I would be discharged. She constantly repeated her countries of origin, to the point that I memorized all of them and began listing them out loud with her.

That woman on a wheelchair was the "queen" of that hospital and she would often approach The Shark with one phrase I had already heard, "you're fired!"

"I'm a shark!" she yelled back one of those days.

"You're fired!" The Queen shouted with so much anger that she had to shut her eyes.

I burst out laughing unexpectedly to myself. The woman looked at me, and in fear of being spat on, I tried to stop laughing, but couldn't. All I could do was squeeze "I'm sorry" out of my lungs.

"And you are fired!" she stated and moved away.

I began having sessions with Dr Holington on daily basis. I was able to open up more and more and explore my emotions with his gentle help. I discovered guilt and regret I didn't know I had. I also felt more and more warmth towards him and didn't know what to do with this brand-new feeling.

"Rita's death is not your fault," he told me on the fourth session. "You've been caring this weight for years, it's time to let it go. She died, because she had a drinking problem, not because you didn't enter the room on time."

"I could have saved her. I knew she was in danger! But instead, I moved in with strangers and left her all alone."

"Kate," Dr Holington said thoughtfully. "Sometimes there is nothing we can do to help people. She was all alone. You were all alone, too. All alone, you went to live with those strangers, and living with them did hurt you. You were in danger of rape. Nobody saved you from going there.

You have a drinking problem. Your friends are well aware of it. However, none of them came to your apartment and prevented you from getting in trouble a few days ago. Does it mean they are bad friends? No. They just didn't know. Because it's impossible to know everything."

I nodded looking down. "I never told her that I loved her. Never said how great of a person she was. I never said she was an interesting character even though she asked me about it many times!"

I began crying silently. The doctor handed me a tissue. I felt very embarrassed and started apologizing. He said it was okay to cry. It was good to cry.

"Sometimes I hate her for leaving us!" I wept.

"Us?" he stared at me.

I didn't have enough oxygen, "Me! I hate her for leaving me! All I've got is her crazy paintings that I'm so scared of even looking at! She was supposed to tell me the continuation of her story, the party that I told you about. It's really stupid, but I often think about it, what was it all for and why did she tell me all of that? I feel like it's my duty to solve this."

"It isn't stupid, Kate," my doctor concluded. "You don't need to solve anything. Everything is already solved and is waiting for you. That's what Rita was trying to teach you, not to search for meaning in everything. Everything is as pointless as her paintings which you cannot unwrap, but you can get a lot of joy from looking at them. Same thing with this party, you can enjoy throwing it and being there. But once it's over, it's over. No continuation of it. Just like with our lives, we live, drink, eat, communicate, but once it ends, we no longer exist. What it was all for? Nothing. Did you enjoy it? That's the question."

He finished. I kept staring down. I recalled Rita's irritation when I asked for the meaning of her plot. It was so elementary for her. And I could never get there. I looked up at the doctor. He smiled warmly. I smiled back. I thought how unbelievably beautiful his eyes were.

"There were so many things in my life I didn't enjoy. Not because I didn't want to, but I couldn't. I was forced into certain circumstances which I had to survive." I said, "My recent disaster is losing my work authorization and screwing the green card interview. I told you. But I never mentioned that I didn't love James. I was never attracted to him as a man. I only wanted a green card. I had to tolerate him for so long, his love, his drinking, his friends. I had to have sex with him a few times a week and most of the time it felt like a voluntary rape. I was forcing myself and everyone else into believing that I had feelings for him, but I couldn't... The only thing that helped me to get through that horrible time was my desire to visit home. So, when I lost my potential green card, I realized that all that torture was for nothing. I felt devastated. I began drinking heavily."

"I'm awfully sorry to hear that," he murmured. "You learned your lessons…"

"Another instance was the rape. How can you enjoy life when all this trash happens to you?" I interrupted him with irritation. "It was the worst that ever happened to me. So cruel, so unfair! I still see it in my nightmares. I still smell the awful odor of that creep every time the recollection of that nasty event comes to my mind. I don't want to live when I think about it. I hate my body when I think about it. How to live with it?"

I started crying again. He gave me a tissue. I should learn to cry without feeling ashamed. I should learn many things that I wanted to know to outweigh many things I happened to know without wanting. I should learn to accept these things as a part of my past. This horrible knowledge of painful predicaments will always stay with me. All I can do is to learn to live with it.

Dr Holington gave me a warm compassionate look and it felt like a hug. He said I was a victim of the horrible circumstance and my body didn't need any more hate, it needed love. Only love could heal it. He said that continuing to hate myself is equal to continuing the rape. I abused myself enough, it was time to stop and break free. In fact, the rapist should hate his body. The rapist should be ashamed.

"I don't think these people ever feel ashamed," I smirked.

He touched the top of his head with his palm, then stroked it down to the back of his neck. "You know, some people do. It doesn't make this horrible crime less horrible, but some of these people truly regret what they had done. They wish they could reverse it. One of the former patients of this hospital jumped off the bridge a few days after he raped a woman. He didn't want to live with the knowledge of what he had done. It's not something that excuses him or makes him a better person. And definitely isn't something that should ease the victim's pain, but at least it would assure the victim that he is punished because he will live the rest of his life hating himself. And sometimes it's the worst punishment."

I shrugged my shoulders. He told me to start writing about my pain. Start writing about my hurt feelings, emotions, expectations. He told me to start writing if I wanted to become a writer.

"You don't write because of your fear of failure. You don't start in order not to lose. You have so much to say, but you're hiding behind alcohol and partners that abuse you. You keep punishing yourself for something you haven't done. What is it, Kate?"

"My mom," came out of my mouth. It shocked me. I stared at the doctor.

After the session was over, I went for lunch. Tracy and The Shark were sitting at the table. The Shark looked somewhat irritated and Tracy seemed somewhat absent-minded. I joined them. The nurses gave me my tray with food, but I had no appetite. I asked the girls if they wanted anything. My roommate took my main course and the irritated patient grabbed the salad. I heard a very loud spitting a couple of tables away from us. It was The Queen spitting in her own food.

"Ewww," Tracy commented. "It's disgusting."

"Does she actually spit in her own food and eat it afterwards?" I wondered.

"Yep," my roommate answered.

"Why would she do such thing?" I asked and looked at The Queen. There were two more people sitting at the same table eating lunch. I couldn't understand how come they still had an appetite. She kept spitting.

Tracy shrugged her shoulders indifferently and I began laughing at the absurdity of the situation. I rested my head on the table and continued laughing silently. I was laughing at the woman spitting in her own plate, at the people that didn't see anything wrong with it and continued enjoying their food. I was laughing at Tracy's absent-minded face and The Shark's irritation. I was laughing at my pain from the past, which seemed so present for a moment. I was laughing at the fact that I was one of these patients — patients of a psychiatric facility, and I could as well get used to it and begin taking all this absurdity as a normal thing. I laughed until my abdominals started hurting and a nurse approached me, "Are you all right?"

I found myself feeling happy there. I was elated. I couldn't remember when I was last laughing so much outside of the hospital walls. I couldn't remember my last genuine smile. Every morning started with a beautiful grin of the bright blue eyes and sweet but nervous tickling inside of my stomach and chest. It followed by discoveries of myself from all possible angles. I wanted to discover more of him, and sometimes, I would get a treat as an answer to one of my personal questions. He liked chess.

For the rest of the day, I would explore the life of unique people and try to communicate with them as much as I could. Snezhana and Natasha brought me a notebook and I began taking notes. One of the most interesting characters was the one who peed on the floor on my first night in Kings County Hospital. I called him Johnny Walker. Because he kept walking. He was walking back and forth in the corridor as a pendulum, from where it started to the window in the very end of the hallway, and back, without talking to anyone, without doing anything else, beginning early in the morning and finishing late at night. It was rather hypnotizing to watch him walking non-stop, although it was very amusing. He happened to be tall and skinny, had a beard and long legs — they were so long that bluish hospital pants would only reach his calves. Sometimes he urinated by the only water fountain in the whole department. Sometimes he urinated in the hallway or in the game room. Sometimes, in the middle of the line for medications. I learned to be very careful next to him.

I always wanted to ask The Queen why she spat on her food but had no courage to do so. I heard she spat on people as well, although I never witnessed such an occasion. I only saw her firing people. I wondered whether she ever hired anybody. Tracy kept saying how disgusting she was. I, in my turn, kept laughing myself to pain in the abdominals. There was always logic behind everything. Even the most illogical logic. She must have some explanation for her saliva discharge as if she was trying to moisturize her food. Or disinfect it. I asked a few other people, including the elderly lady who enjoyed staying there and the very tall man who missed his wife, but none of them had a clue.

One young man kept walking in circles. He was always whispering something to himself. He would make dozens of circles in one place and then move to another. He would do it in the game or TV room, by the front desk, and in the hallway. The latter would often interfere with the route of Johnny Walker. They would bump into each other, then Johnny would find his way towards the end of the corridor, while the other man would freeze for seconds whispering something to himself.

There was a man who consistently counted his fingers on both hands. He did it over and over again as if he was trying to make sure none of them got lost or stolen. He was somewhat adequate and could handle a simple conversation. The Queen liked watching him. She could watch him for a long time.

"How many?" she would ask eventually.

"Ten!" he would answer after finishing his math.

"You're fired ten times! Fired ten times!" she would shout with pride.

Dr Holington was surprised by how fast I had adjusted to the new environment. According to him, I was a different person than the one he met initially. He would stop by the game room where I'd be playing cards with Tracy and ask who was winning. He would join a conversation of me and a few more people for a minute or two and then would wish us a nice day and get back to work. A pleasant warmth would fill my chest every time I'd see him. I didn't want these times to end.

"Your mom was raising you alone. She always worked. She had several jobs. She never met another man. She didn't have a life," my doctor stated. "Right?"

"Yes."

"Was it all because of you?"

"Yes. And now I left her."

"And now you left her. After all she had done for you."

I nodded.

"Kate, a lot of children feel responsible for their parents' pain. It is normal for you to feel this way. However, you cannot continue your tradition of blaming self. None of it is your fault. She had back pain because she damaged her back before you were born. She raised you alone because your father left. She stayed alone because she chose to. She had several jobs because it was a very hard time in Russia and I bet many mothers or fathers had several jobs. It's okay to have several jobs. She is alone now because she doesn't want to meet anybody. Some people are asexual, others are just happy being alone.

And you didn't leave her. You will become a resident and visit her at the first opportunity. Many children live far away from parents. It's normal. There are families that live under the same roof but feel as if they are on different planets. You have the connection with your mom. Not everyone does."

Dr Holington waited until I nodded again and continued, "You became a people pleaser just because that's the way you grew up — pleasing your mom. You harm yourself in order to please others. You can't forgive yourself for not telling Rita's grandma how much she loved her, because you can't forgive yourself for not being able to help your mom when she was crying out of pain. So, you were actively drinking yourself to death. Kate, you wanted your mom to cry on your funerals. It was your best outcome, well-deserved, because you thought you were worthless. Your entire life was gambling with death. Absolutely everything, abusive partners, toxic people, dangerous neighborhoods, dangerous jobs, illegality which hurts you and scares you every single day, alcohol which is your best tool of self-murder. Stop it right here. Stop pleasing people right now. There's only one person you need to keep pleasing. It's you. Otherwise, why to live at all?"

In my mind I went to the early childhood and recalled praying for my mom to feel better, I recalled praying for my dad to come back, I recalled physical pain from the electrocution, then I recalled cruel bullying, my aunt, my abusive partners, my drinking, rape, my dirty job, everyday fear of being illegal, I recalled James and that morning he beat me up and took away my last hope, I thought about Chicago and Svetlana's mother, about Dmitry and endless pain, about Vera and her mom, about Rita's calm pale face. I wanted to cry and scream, and at the same time I wanted to fall asleep and sleep for days. Everything that had happened to me was a decades-long suicide attempt, and yet there was a lot of good in it, no matter how hard the realization of it was — it was my unique experience, and that experience was my ticket into tomorrow. I could build a beautiful life. Otherwise, why to live at all?

"You didn't ask to be born in the first place." The doctor continued, "You were the victim of circumstances. You were born into a hard time. You did the best you could. You keep asking yourself why your dad left and never even contacted you again. He left for one reason. He didn't know any better."

I gave a laugh. His face was serious. For the first time in my life, I had an answer. Now, at the age of twenty-six, sitting in the psychiatric facility and talking to a psychiatrist, I finally understood why he left us. He didn't know how to live with us. He didn't have a psychotherapist to help him figure out things. He had his instincts and nothing else.

Dr Holington also told me I was subconsciously choosing men that were going to leave me. I told him it was just one. One man. But who knows how many times he left me. And in my mind, he was still leaving me — over and over again. Just as with my dad, I asked myself a million times, why did he leave me? He left without saying goodbye. And I was wishing and wishing and wishing for him to come back. So why did Dmitry leave me? Simply because he didn't know how to be with me.

"I would like to return to the conversation about Rita. You said you regret not telling her that you loved her." my doctor said. "How can you fix it?"

"I don't think there is a way to fix it."

"There is a way. Start telling it to people now. Don't wait for tomorrow or the day after. Tomorrow might never come. Tell it today. Tell your friends that you love them. Tell your mom that you love her. Come to the mirror and look at this beautiful tall blond girl and tell her that you love her. And do mean it." he smiled and fixed his eyes on mine.

I smiled back and thanked him for the compliment.

"I really meant it." he vocalized with his melodious voice. Then he nodded and took a breath in. The session was over.

I was in the seventh heaven for the rest of the day. I finally thought about starting to live a new life with the new me. My heavy past was making my present heavy, and instead of helping myself to break free, I was consistently torturing myself and making it a complete nightmare. Now I knew, I didn't have to do this any more. I was determined to work out my way to freedom. I wanted to love that "beautiful tall blond girl" and make her life better, not worse. I also felt elated to hear it. These words coming from him were like an injection of a magic solution that made me overdosed on happiness, love, and excitement. I felt high.

That day I was more absent-minded than Tracy. I wanted to sing and dance and laugh. The Shark was in the room where I had first met her. She was sitting and playing music on the small radio. She got up when she saw me. I took her both hands in mine and we started jumping in the rhythm of that song. I was laughing out loud and she was yelling some random words I wasn't listening to.

"I love you, Sharky!" I shouted out of elation.

"I love you, too," she answered without any emotion. "I'm Trinidadian, Jamaican, German, Polish, and Dominican, but I'm American, because I was born here."

I realized I hadn't been so naturally happy and inspired for a very long time. I would never think I would ever get to a madhouse, and furthermore would love it there. I didn't want to leave. I wanted to be seeing Dr Holington for the rest of my life. I needed his bright beautiful eyes. I needed his warm smile. I was successfully falling in love with him. I didn't know what to do about it. I wanted to believe it was mutual. Sometimes it seemed like he flirted with me, and I dared to flirt back. Sometimes he was exceptionally serious. Sometimes he was more talkative than usual and willing to share certain personal things. He loved chess, off-Broadway shows, Jorge Borges, and dark chocolate. And I loved everything about him. Everything I knew of.

"Is he married?" asked Tracy with her quiet indifferent voice.

"Is he married?" asked Snezhana and Natasha during their visit.

"I haven't seen a ring," I smiled shyly. "So, I assume he isn't."

"I think he has a crush on me as well," I murmured, giggling.

"Wishful thinking," Snezhana winked at me.

"Who knows?" Natasha said. "Yes, he is a doctor, but he is an alive person as well."

"I think that doctors of his profession are not allowed to get involved with their patients," Snezhana stated.

"But I know for sure that stories like that happened!" Natasha insisted. "You'll get out of here; you are not his patient any more! So, you guys will be able to start dating!"

Snezhana shook her head and laughed. The thought of getting out of the hospital depressed me.

"You should tell him about your feelings. He is your therapist and needs to know, but don't count on mutuality." Snezhana touched my cheek with her palm. "I'm your friend and I don't want you to get hurt."

It didn't bother me. I thought, we could have a secret affair. I didn't mind anything. The girls both suggested to tell him. They also told me that Vera got her U.S visa and was coming to America soon. They also brought some make-up, which I sneaked into my wardrobe. I didn't care about hospital's rules, I only wanted to look good for him.

The make-up came in handy. I had noticed Mr Holington's extended gazes and more spark in his eyes. He started coming to my room and talking to me sitting on my bed. I was constantly nervous, and shy, but extremely happy. My heart was beating with enormous speed, and sometimes I thought I wouldn't be able to handle it. I played cards with Tracy every single night, I had a philosophical conversation with the old woman and the tall guy almost every day. I helped the staff to block 'The Queen's' wheelchair every time she got overly violent. I laughed a lot. I participated in all discussions at our dining table, I took long Johnny Walker's style walks with The Shark, listening about countries of her origin. Once she even revealed a secret of why she called herself a shark.

"Sharks don't give a shit!"

I dreamed a lot. Every night, before falling asleep I imagined my favorite doctor and me having dinner, walking out of a theatre and discussing a play. I imagined us renting a car and going on a road trip north to Maine, or West to Illinois, or south to Virginia. I imagined kissing him. I didn't allow myself to imagine further than that. I was dreaming of him all the time and everywhere, in my bed, in the game room, in the dining room, by the window, that was facing Manhattan, by the front-desk, and with every daydream it was becoming harder and harder to control my feelings, my elation, my love, and one daring evening, sitting in the conference room in front of him, I confessed.

"I'm in love with you."

His blue eyes focused on mine. They looked at me for a few long seconds. Then he calmly said, "Kate, do you understand I'm your doctor?"

"Yes," I interrupted him. "But it wouldn't matter if we went for a dinner. Or to off-off-off-Broadway show."

I giggled. He smiled. It was a warm beautiful smile. Then he grew serious, "Kate. It isn't going to happen. It's not even questionable."

"Not beautiful enough then…?" came out of my mouth.

His serious expression hadn't changed. He continued looking at me.

"I meant everything I said, although there were no romantic connotations in it. I am your doctor, I am your provider, and my job is to help you. You are very likable indeed, but for me you are a patient and will always remain one." he vocalized slowly, making proper pauses between words and sentences.

"Okay," I murmured, trying to look indifferent.

"I care about my patients and I do my best to help them. I love my job. I'm here to help. Nothing else is going on, Ekaterina."

I wanted to cry but didn't want to show my tears. It felt like the end of a beautiful dream, which became the reason I was waking up every morning. I fell down from the seventh heaven. I didn't know the rejection could be so painful. I didn't know one could turn so unhappy in a blink of an eye. I didn't know anything any more. I pretended I was fine. He smiled with his gorgeous smile. I wanted to die.

I wanted to scream, I wanted to sob, I hated my life again. The injection of the magic solution turned out to be artificial. I didn't know why to wake up any more, what to look forward to, what to be happy about. I buried myself under the thin hospital's blanket long before the sleeping time began. I slept for almost the whole day after that night had passed. I didn't want to be awake. I couldn't wait to leave that place. I wanted to get drunk.

I heard his steps and voice coming to my room but leaving after seeing me asleep. I didn't want to talk to him. I felt like there was nothing else to share, besides pain. I had a brand-new pain and it seemed it would never grow old.

Eventually, I had to face him. He stopped me on the way to the water fountain and took me to that hateful conference room.

"Kate," he said in his calming manner. "The feeling you have for me is not a romantic feeling. It's very common that patients develop feelings for their providers. You are confused and don't understand yourself. It's normal. We can work on it together. I will continue treating you after you'll get discharged."

"I won't be able to see you after I'll be discharged." I blurted.

"Why is that?" his melodious voice asked.

"I'll be busy drinking." I squeezed a painful laugh.

"Ekaterina," the doctor started.

"I told you it's the best thing ever happened to me," I stated, holding up from crying.

"Ekaterina," he vocalized and exhaled deeply.

"Ekaterina what?" I uttered with a sarcastic smile. "I live in a free country, I'm a free person. Nobody has a right to tell me anything. I can't wait to leave this place!"

"It's not funny," he said, giving me a prolonged concerned look. "You have a serious problem which brought you here. It nearly killed you. You are just being stubborn to admit it was far from the best thing. It's your murderer."

"I'll be drinking carefully this time to make sure I'll never get to a madhouse again." I blurted with anger, staring down at my hands that were grasping each other under the table.

"Kate, look at me," he murmured. "Please."

I looked at him against my will. His beautiful face with short brown hair and thick lips was so close to me that I could touch it. His bottomless eyes were gazing at me with their mesmerizing blueness. I wanted to cry. I couldn't bear that it was the closest we would ever get.

"I know, you are upset. It's okay. You have never been in therapy before. You don't know how to take your feelings. We will work on them and you will come to the realization that they are not romantic, but close to what you feel towards your mother."

I gave a laugh. He ignored it.

"As for now, the most important thing is to prevent you from drinking. We need to make a plan and stick to it. We will work on your addiction together."

"I'm fine," I stated. "My plan is to drink. I'll be careful this time."

"Kate," he exhaled with annoyance. "You are acting like a little child. We'll definitely be talking about it in the future. But right now, I want you to understand that there is no way anybody could practice careful drinking. The only way to drink carefully is not to drink at all. Alcohol is a drug, and the nature of any drug is to get you hooked and kill you. I used to work in rehab with lots of alcoholics and drug addicts. It was so scary and so sad to watch people die. Many young and talented people like you died in my hands."

He stretched his hands to me palms up, "In these very hands, Kate. In these very hands!"

"It's probably worth it to die in your hands," I smiled mischievously and sarcastically, "doctor."

He took a deep breath and stroke the back of his head. "You will be discharged tomorrow. Take good care of yourself," he said. Then he got up and walked away. I remained seated for minutes.

CHAPTER 14

Vera arrived at the very edge of my late youth.

I cleaned the apartment, the same apartment I had performed my pre-hospital circus in, unwrapped and hung the three paintings of Rita — two on one wall and one on another. It was easier than I had thought. I carried them with me for years, from place to place, from life to life, with enormous fear of opening them. And now, when I finally did, it was so strange to look at them. I couldn't capture my emotions, there was an endless pain with some odd satisfaction. I ate a sandwich and went to JFK airport with the red "Welcome to New York" balloon.

I was too embarrassed to talk to my neighbors. I tried to avoid making eye contact with anyone in the building. I tried to avoid interacting with the superintendent. The hardest was avoiding thinking about Dr Holington. He occupied my mind most of the time.

Dying in his arms didn't seem too bad of an option. In fact, it would be the most desirable death, a perfect end of life as I thought back then. At the same time, I deeply regretted verbalizing it. If I knew it would put an end to our relationship, I would never say it, I would never let any sarcasm pass through my lips, I would obediently do whatever he would tell me to do, feeling happy just sitting next to him, listening to his calming voice and looking at his mesmerizing eyes. I would come to therapy, keeping a tiny impossible hope in my heart, named "maybe", which, unfortunately, had already turned into a hope, named "forgive me". It wasn't his fault, that he became the main character of my thoughts and dreams.

I was leaving Kings County in pain. Natasha came to pick me up in the morning. Dr Holington was nowhere to be seen. I hugged The Queen, The Shark, Tracy, a couple of "philosophers", shook hands with the Asian guy, and left.

The early fall of 2013 was orange and warm. Worn-out golden leaves lay scattered on consistently wet ground. Black umbrellas kept closing and opening up next to half-available yellow cabs. The motion of the city seemed to be frozen as something magical was about to happen.

The airport hadn't changed since the last time I had been there, but unfortunately, Vera had. So small and shy, she walked out of the hidden space of customs, limping and dragging a familiar orange suitcase behind her.

"Vera!" I yelled, and she looked at me with an instant tired smile.

She didn't say anything but rushed to me and gave me the warmest hug as soon as we merged. It lasted for about a minute. I could read her mind through that hug. No words were needed. Endless unfulfilled desire for consolation.

All the way to Howard Beach station, she was talking about her long flight and a man who forgot to order a special meal and had to eat lentils just because there was nothing else on board. I was studying her face — wrinkle by wrinkle. She was only twenty-six but looked about seven years older, her skin had lost its bright color, her big green eyes seemed faded, and even her lips got pale.

Our trip home was exhausting. It felt as it was me who had just gotten off the airplane, drawn and absent-minded. Complaints about high prices and low salaries in Russia occupied my head and put me in a gloomy trance. Vera's life had become a hollow existence. She sold the apartment shortly after her mother died and moved to a small studio in a neighborhood polluted with empty vodka bottles and used syringes. All money from the sale was gone to psychiatrists, anti-depressants, and alcohol. It had been four years and eight months since that distant snowy day we arrived in the US.

"Shall we go and celebrate my arrival?" Vera asked as soon as I introduced her to my tiny studio with a queen-sized mattress in the middle of it, which I had bought a couple of days earlier. The kitchen cabinets were almost empty, there were two coffee mugs and two bowls. I planned to get a cooking pot sometime in the future. My suitcases, one on the top of the other, still served as a table, and only Rita's paintings made that hostile unit alive.

I hadn't had a drink for a little more than two weeks since the day police handcuffed me and took me to the hospital. I was amazed by how badly I wanted to get drunk the day I got rejected by the doctor, and how badly now I hated alcohol for the very same reason.

"Sure," I smiled. "I don't drink though, but I'd love to treat you with a few drinks."

Vera turned disappointed.

"Oh, I didn't know," she gave me a brief ironic look. "Since when?"

I suddenly felt guilty for not drinking and faltered, "It's a long story. There is a nice bar a couple of blocks away. Let's go there and I'll tell you everything."

She refused the food but ordered a glass of red wine as soon as we sat down at the unsteady wooden table. I had a virgin Mojito. Her tired dull green eyes were getting brighter with every sip, her cheeks were turning reddish, and her age — glass by glass as year by year — was moving back towards twenty-six. She was laughing at my experience in the psychiatric facility, she listened angrily to my story about police handcuffing me the night before I was admitted to the hospital, after which she got to learn about my feelings towards Dr Holington and the aftermath of my abrupt sense of humor. She was compassionately quiet. She hugged me after a few glasses and a few more stories, and both of us cried. I felt so close to her for the first time that evening.

I had to carry her home. I put her to bed, removed her shirt and pants, covered her with the light blanket, and looked at her calm and peaceful face for half of the night. In the morning I introduced her to Snezhana and Natasha in person. We went to a diner in Hell's Kitchen. That morning she was all sick and quiet. She only drank coffee, smiled, and nodded to almost everything my friends said. She knew most of the stories and people. She heard all the names. I kept her informed while she was preparing for her visa interview.

Natasha put her decision of returning to Russia on pause. She looked like a handsome boy with short and curly ginger hair and a man's bottom-up shirt. She lost touch with Laurine after Shawn witnessed their intercourse. She said, that the half-happy couple moved to Florida and she blocked the promiscuous girl on Facebook. I was amazed by how love may blind people. Does it actually blind us? Maybe it doesn't. And maybe there is nothing worse than to love someone, knowing of all low moral qualities, bad intentions, and indifference of the one, but continuing loving — hopelessly, powerlessly, not being able to do anything about it. I wondered, whether it was Shawn's case?

Snezhana announced she wanted to get into real estate sales and she did acquire some good connections in the meanwhile. She mentioned it to me in King's County, but I was too busy dreaming about Dr Holington. And now, I wanted to become too busy forgetting about him. I needed it more than anything in the world. Vera supported this decision of Snezhana and the decision by me. She said we could make a lot of money as long as we play it smart, and nobody would find out that I was illegal.

Vera thanked Snezhana for the invitation and Natasha for staying in touch with her while I was hospitalized. They didn't have a lot of time to get to know each other, Natasha had to run to work, Snezhana went to her son's school, and Vera and I — to Times Square. It's the number one destination one wants to visit and revisit in the beginning, and the number one district one avoids crossing at any cost in the end. Vera and I were on different sides of that spectrum. That day we got to see Central Park, Statue of Liberty from the pier, East and West Villages, Brooklyn Bridge. She was fascinated by the city where every single step made her recall famous artists, musicians, models, occasions, names of clubs, and restaurants in which many notable events registered themselves forever. Vera loved New York.

On the way home, we stopped by the same bar and ordered the same beverages.

"Don't you miss alcohol, at least a little bit?" Vera wondered. Her hangover was gone. She looked alive.

"A little bit," I said. "I didn't want it at all for two weeks I was in the hospital, but the five days since I left had been very challenging. Well, I'm not counting the day my doctor rejected me."

"So, you decided to stop for good?"

I thought about Dr Holington and wanted to cry. I took a deep breath and uttered, "We'll see. As for now, I need to take a break from drinking."

Vera nodded understandingly.

"So, you were in therapy in Astrakhan. How did it go?" I wondered as someone who got the bitter-sweet taste of it for the first time.

"Ah, I wouldn't call it therapy," she stated. "I first went to a psychotherapist a month after my mom died. It was a woman around 55. After she heard my story, she said, 'Your mom made you a gift, which is freedom. You can now do whatever you want. So many parents burden their children making them obligated to nurse them. It's a heavy burden. You can live your life with joy now.'"

"Wow!" came out of my mouth involuntarily.

"I started crying as she said it. I didn't want such joy. I didn't want such freedom. Seeing me crying, she said, 'If you will be crying a lot, none of the young men would want to date you, and your friends will eventually get tired of your mood. Nobody likes gloomy people.' I left her office, feeling worse than when I came. I wanted to die."

I took her hand and squeezed it slightly. She nodded with a sad smile which was her way of saying I didn't "have to" comfort her.

"Then my neighbor took me to another 'great specialist' and that specialist said that grief itself goes away within two weeks and what I had then, a month after mom's death, was just an excuse for not working. She said if I'd accept this fact and would find a job and become a part of a collective, I would feel much happier."

"Unbelievable!" I sighed. "These people shouldn't be doing psychotherapy. They can kill by their cruel words."

She nodded, and we sat in silence for a while. She drank about three glasses of wine and I was sipping my second virgin Mojito.

"You know, I often recall our bus ride to New York. There was something magical about it." I broke the silence.

"Oh yeah? What was magic about it?" she asked.

"I don't know. Our first adult trip so far away from home. It was like a bridge from childhood to adulthood. I felt like our childhood had ended there and we got off the bus completely grown-up people." I said and thought to myself, "And everyone was alive."

"I barely have a recollection of it," Vera giggled. "I overslept the end of our childhood, I guess."

We laughed. There were so many thoughts I wanted to share with her, so many things to catch up on. There were so many nights ahead of us. And I was excited about all of them. As for daytime, she planned to start looking for a job. Just like me, she had no right to work, although her English was much worse, and I couldn't use her help in real estate. We agreed that she would be trying out small restaurants for a waiting position.

Little by little, Vera began knocking on restaurant doors and talking to owners or managers. I was happy to see her go. I spent my last money on expensive suits and designer shoes to create an impression of a wealthy knowledgeable agent. I got business cards with a "licensed salesperson" printed right below my name.

Snezhana and I started off right away. My first middle-aged client was a millionaire, who happened to be on the cover of Forbes years ago and happened to tell every single soul about it. He contacted me regarding an apartment that didn't exist. I created it from pictures of beautifully furnished rooms I found in online magazines and attractive descriptions of the building's features. I did it because I had no listings of my own and didn't know anybody who would allow me to work on theirs. Later on, I learned that most agents practiced fabricating brand-new units to catch a client, but at that moment, I felt extremely guilty. However, I managed to switch the client's attention from the initial dwelling to truly existent ones.

Most of the apartments I showed him were located at luxurious Fifth, Madison, and Park Avenues. The majority of them were penthouses with great views of Central Park, Midtown, and Upper Manhattan. All buildings had doormen, who checked my authenticity of being a licensed real estate agent. Those were the most stressful moments. I just smiled and handed them my business card with the name of the real estate company on it, where nobody had ever heard about me. Doormen normally smiled back and would let me take the clients upstairs.

I often thought, what if someone from the same realty would be a seller's agent at a showing. What if they asked something regarding the company we both work for, in front of my client? These thoughts frightened me. I would easily lose the client, and if they did further investigation, Snezhana would get fired.

I never met anybody from the same realty, although my Forbes' client's unanswered questions regarding how certain coops and condos were taxed, and which condo insurance was better, made me feel very awkward. He disappeared after about 10th showing. I assumed he found someone more knowledgeable to work with. Later on, perhaps in a month, I googled his name, out of curiosity, and learned that he bought an apartment for five million dollars in Upper West.

"Don't take it personal," Snezhana commented on his disappearance, "people have different issues. Doesn't mean you did a bad job. He might have fallen in love with you and found another agent in order not to get his heart broken."

We laughed.

We gained a few more potential buyers after the first one left. I felt more confident. I didn't hesitate to talk to doormen or other agents any more. I could confess to clients I didn't know the answer to their questions, but I would definitely find out. And nobody ever had a suspicion that I was not a licensed real estate agent. Who would think I was an illegal immigrant without work authorization at all? Just because I was tall, blond, and white, nobody asked for my ID on the street, nobody refused any of the services I wanted, nobody discriminated against me, and yet I was no different from people who sneaked through the border and spent their lives washing dishes in steamy kitchens or selling their bodies to truck drivers. We had exactly the same rights and we needed exactly the same things. We all needed a chance. A chance to have a good life. A chance to get an education. A chance for legalization in the country we love.

I wanted to scream about it from all the rooftops when we made the first sale. An elderly couple kept thanking us for finding that beautiful two-bedroom condo, and we kept thanking them for buying it. They didn't know it was our first deal. They wrote an excellent review for each of us.

"It's not true that illegals are only housekeepers and prostitutes!" Snezhana laughed elatedly when we went to celebrate the success. "You gotta write a book about it one day! Really, think about it! An illegal girl without any permission to be in this country, a girl, who might be caught and departed any minute, sells apartments in Manhattan to people you see in magazines. Doesn't it sound any great to you?"

"Well, I can only write about it once I'm legalized." I hesitated.

"You will," she looked at me thoughtfully. "I have no doubts about it."

The money we earned was not big. After the transaction was over, each of us put $15,000 in our bank account. However, the happiness was everlasting, because it was my first serious deal, my first step in a new promising field.

I took a few days' break and went job hunting with Vera. It was almost the middle of a beautiful fall. It wasn't cold, and Vera and I wore light jackets. We stopped by a few restaurants with "waitress needed" signs to fill out applications. We walked into a few bars and stores to ask whether they were hiring. We tried to do as much as possible to fit her in the City That Never Sleeps. After tiring days of walking and inspiring nights of philosophical conversations, she was finally called for an interview in the Indian restaurant in East Village. And she got the job.

Along the way, I started having insomnia. Some nights I wasn't able to fall asleep till 5 in the morning, others till 7, tossing and turning, not able to switch off my busy mind. Some nights I stayed up all night, watching Vera's peaceful face, trying to guess, what she was dreaming about, and writing down random thoughts.

I couldn't stop thinking. I thought about Dr Holington. It was becoming harder and harder to recall his smile, but his calming voice was constantly sounding in my ears. I wanted to tell him so many things, starting with my insomnia and finishing with my sobriety. I stopped drinking because of him, in honor of my feelings for him, in honor of not dying, as there were no arms of his nearby. But I continued for myself, for this tall blond beautiful girl, who deserved to live. I was trying hard not to relapse.

One of those sleepless nights, as I turned sick of endless trials of falling asleep, I went outside to the fresh air of empty streets and called my mom. We hadn't spoken in ages. Natasha told her I went to the hospital and I emailed I was discharged once I arrived home. That was it. It was around noon in Astrakhan.

"You finally remembered about me?" she asked sadly. Her voice was so dear and soft.

I turned embarrassed for being so selfish.

"I was so busy. I hadn't even realized so much time passed," I confessed.

"I know, I know," she murmured. "I'm glad you found time."

The sound of her voice made me want to cry. I began squeezing my set of keys in the pocket.

"Why don't you sleep?" she asked.

"Ah…I slept… then woke up," I faltered. "I miss you,"

"I missed you too, my baby girl," I heard her smile. "How are you? Did they treat you good in the hospital? Did they feed you well?"

I started crying openly. I couldn't handle her kindness.

"Shhhhh," she said with a calming voice, and it made me feel like a little girl. "Don't cry, you'll get a headache. Just smile — and all the sadness will go away."

I felt like I would give anything just to hug her tightly for a minute.

"They treated me well, they fed me well," I answered and added in a few seconds, "I liked it there. It was an interesting experience. Will tell you more funny stories when I'll see you."

"I can't wait," she gave a laugh. I gave a laugh too.

"My dear daughter, Katyusha, baby," she vocalized with compassion. "You are a big girl, right? I hope you understand how damaging alcohol is to you. I hope you are aware of the fact that it can ruin your life. And you are such a nice, young, talented girl."

She broke in tears.

"I couldn't believe it when Natasha told me you were hospitalized. Can you imagine how hard it was for me to hear it? Can you imagine how it is for me to know that you are killing yourself on another continent and there is nothing I can do to help you?"

"I'm sorry…" I started. I imagined her crying all alone at home on the eighth floor with the view of dull sunsets. And her beautiful, fragile heart needed only one thing — to know that her daughter was safe. Nothing else in the world was important at that moment.

"You shouldn't be sorry," she interrupted me. "You should take good care of yourself. Darling, alcohol is not your friend, it will only kill you. You have your whole life ahead of you. The whole life ahead of you, my angel. And life has so many wonderful things to offer!"

"I know, mom," I breathed. "I'm done with drinking."

"I'm glad to hear it. I hope it will stay this way," she said. "Katen'ka, if you need to talk to someone, to take something off your chest, call me. You know, I'm always free for you. I'll always listen to you; I'll always console you. Don't look for consolation in alcohol, there is nothing in it. Only death."

It made me want to cry again. She was always there for me. She was willing to do everything for me. And what did I do for her? Did I ever do anything for her?

It was too sad, that her happiness depended only on me, someone who didn't know what she wanted from life, someone who didn't care about her own life. Someone, who would rather die in hands of a person her mother never heard of.

I still couldn't accept Dr Holington's teachings about my mom being responsible for herself and her own happiness. Piece by piece things made sense, I didn't ask to be born, I was a victim of so many circumstances, I was only responsible for my own happiness, and my mom chose to be alone. All these pieces would fit perfectly in one puzzle, but this puzzle would get crashed and all its meaning would disappear every time I'd hear a sad and kind voice of my mom. I wanted to make her happy regardless of whose job it was.

"I promise, I won't drink," I mumbled, not believing myself. "Thank you for your kindness, mama. Do you know, you are the best mom in the world?"

She gave a laugh. "And you, my darling, you are the best daughter!"

"How are you doing?" I asked. I didn't think I was the best daughter.

"I'm very good!" she lied.

"How is your back?"

"Almost doesn't hurt. I even forgot I used to have pain." she lied again, then added, "I'm worrying about you not sleeping. Anything happened?"

"Nothing, mom. I'm going to bed now," I lied.

"Good! Get a good night sleep. Say hi from me to Vera in the morning. But first rest, okay?"

We told each other that we love each other. We wished each other a good night and a good day. Then I returned home and spent another sleepless night there.

Vera didn't like the job in Indian restaurant, but it was something that paid her bills. Her English was too poor to find a better replacement. She understood it and obediently performed her new duties.

My insomnia worsened, and I began finding myself thinking about alcohol more and more often. It was over a month that I had stayed sober and I didn't want to ruin it. Real Estate success was very tempting, I hated to admit that my thoughts began sending me to a liquor store to celebrate a new listing or a new deal. I kept reminding myself of the reason I stopped drinking and this reason was to have a good healthy future, to love my life. I knew it would be impossible for me to love my life with alcohol in it. However, with enormous pleasure, I imagined buying a few bottles of Chardonnay and drinking them with Vera in the apartment all night long as we used to do before, across the ocean, dreaming of a bright future on its other side. I was ashamed to share these thoughts with anyone. All of a sudden, every day turned into a fight with cravings, and I didn't know where to hide from them any more.

One day on my way from work, I saw a sign "AA meetings" on the church in my neighborhood. I instantly thought about Rita. She didn't love it, and she said it didn't help her, but there were a lot of funny stories. I smiled when I thought about it. And yet I knew people which benefited from these meetings. I decided just to see what it was all about and went to one morning meeting.

"I am John and I'm an alcoholic," that's how it started.

"Hi John," the rest of the crowd greeted an elderly man.

There was a big square table with a pot of coffee and a jar of water on it, in the basement of an old church. Everyone drank coffee, constantly refilling their cups. I stuck to water.

John hadn't had a drop of alcohol in ten years. I wondered why he called himself an alcoholic. Wasn't it the reason he remained an alcoholic for so many years, just because he had programmed himself that there was no cure? He told his drinking story, which was more advanced, then mine. He lost his family, job, was arrested for drunk driving. He started crying by the end of his speech. Everyone stared at him with compassion. Monica had a similar story; besides she had never been arrested. A few more people shared their experiences. I thought, I would find it very tiring to attend all those meetings a few times a week and share all the same stories. I knew their philosophy from Rita. AA meetings were on one side of a medal, supported with endless desire to drink, but committed to sobriety, which was a heavy burden. In order to stay sober, they needed each other a few times a week, or even every day. It gave them a temporary relief, but not cure. It kept them hooked on alcohol, on its absence, on endless mourning. They programmed themselves on being alcoholics for the rest of their lives and they stuck to this belief, they kept reminding themselves they were alcoholics, not healthy non-drinkers. That's how they stayed in that prison. Once a junky — always a junky, they said. On the other side of the same medal were relapses and drinking to excess, supported by endless self-hatred and a desire to stop doing it, which wasn't easy at all. So, so-called alcoholics kept flipping the medal named "alcohol" for years and decades, instead of simply walking away from it. They complicated the escape, not knowing they had all the keys. It was something I understood right there, sitting at the big table on that very meeting, I was completely free.

"I see a new face," said a man, which, I assumed was a leader of that meeting. "Do you want to share your story?"

I didn't want to but thought it would be impolite to refuse.

"My name is Kate, and I'm not an alcoholic," I introduced myself as I got up, and after a short pause, I added, "I stopped by to see what's going on in here, but suddenly I realized I don't belong here."

The chairman nodded in confusion. I didn't want to be rude, but I didn't want to waste more time either, so I smiled and walked away. Fresh New York's air smelled good. I felt strong. I needed love more than anything in the world. I created a profile on a dating web-site as soon as I got home, but before I got there, right after I exited the church, I heard footsteps intensively approaching me. "Kate," they uttered.

I turned back and saw a tall bold skinny guy in baggy jeans. He looked shy, but excited, examining me with his big eyes, as he was trying to make sure I was the same Kate he knew.

A dose of the past got injected into my vein. Memories of Flatbush, Rita, Adil, rape and Brooklyn woke up in my mind. "Kostya!" I exclaimed and stepped towards him. We hugged.

"Wow," I laughed out of excitement. "It's been forever!"

"It's been," he laughed as well, stepping back to browse me. "You are as gorgeous as ever!"

"Thank you," I smiled. "You look great as well!"

He looked young and fresh. His eyes got sparkle I hadn't seen before. We stood on the corner of a block, and it felt like an eternity had passed, like he was someone I knew from my previous life.

"How have you been?" I asked impatiently. "You disappeared, and nobody knew what happened to you. We were only left to hope you were all right."

"Yeah," he looked away. "I had gotten busy with stuff."

"I understand," I nodded, knowing it wasn't true.

"What a weird place to meet years after, huh?" he exclaimed. "Do you want to grab a cup of coffee somewhere?"

"Sure! Aren't you already dehydrated after all this coffee at the meeting?"

Kostya giggled.

"You showed them a big deal of attitude," he stated. "Didn't you like it there?"

We went to a cozy coffee shop a few blocks away from the church. After we got accustomed to each other and the environment of the place, my past-life-friend shared that he had started drinking a lot right after he disappeared, and he disappeared for the very same reason he started to drink. It was Natasha. I listened to him compassionately, looking into his big brown eyes and feeling his pain. I learned, that he started binging for weeks, absolutely non-stop, he said he didn't leave his apartment, he didn't eat anything, but ordered endless supplies of vodka and kept falling asleep with the hope to never wake up. A friend forced him to detox, after which Kostya forced himself to start attending AA meetings. His goal was to get better and fight for Natasha. He was ready to do anything, he couldn't imagine his life without her. However, he met a woman at one of the meetings. First, she became his sponsor, then she became his lover. Now she was his fiancé. A semi-sad smile appeared between his skinny cheeks as he told me about their engagement.

"Are you still in touch with Natasha?" he wondered shyly.

"Ah… yeah," I faltered, not knowing what to add.

"How is she?" he asked with sadness and excitement at the same time.

"Do you really care, Kostya?"

We instinctively exchanged our phone numbers, hugged each other goodbye in doors of the cafeteria and went different directions.

"Oh yeah? AA?" was all Natasha said, as I mentioned meeting Kostya the same day I parted with him. "I didn't know he had a drinking problem."

"He developed it later on. That's how he disappeared." I didn't want to tell her that he developed it because she left him. Ultimately, it was not her fault. Just like it was not Rita's fault, that Natasha fell in love with her.

She didn't ask any questions about him. All of a sudden, as if she had read my mind, she uttered, "By the way, I was thinking a lot about Rita's boyfriend, Besnik. You never saw him. Lina never saw him. I never saw him. We all only heard about him. Right?"

"So far..." I mumbled.

"Exactly!" she exclaimed. "I think he didn't even exist! She invented him for me to leave her alone."

I grinned, "No, I don't think so. He already existed before she met you. And she was so badly in love with him back then. Why are you thinking about it?"

"I don't know," she let out sadly. "I was thinking about her a lot lately, the way she was. My feelings towards her. Then I thought about this creep she was so in love with. How come nobody had ever seen him? Maybe he just didn't exist."

"Why would she invent him?" I blurted.

"Maybe to have a reason for suffering and for drinking?"

"Natasha," I said rather irritated. "You are overthinking. He existed. He was using her for sex and fun and kept lying he would leave his wife. She kept waiting. Then she died, and I don't know if he ever found out. Is it so hard for you to admit she had an affair with someone else while she kissed you a couple of times?"

"Maybe," she shrugged her shoulders. "We kissed more than a couple of times. And once we even almost had sex in the closed kitchen. She probably didn't remember that."

"You never know," I said and hugged her. She squeezed me tighter. I thought of Dr Holington and let out, "I love you. I'm so happy I have you in my life."

Natasha stroked my back with both hands and whispered, "I love you, too."

I told Vera the whole story of Kostya and Natasha the day after. Kostya's sad eyes got registered in my mind as a reminder of the side of love no one wants to experience. Even this time when he was engaged, he didn't look happy at all. She only sighed and helped me to create a profile on a dating website. She came up with a short and meaningful message, which said, "A single soul is looking for a mate." I uploaded a picture of me that Mrs Sullivan took at one of her jewelry shows. I needed love more than anything.

My childhood friend needed it too. She had been unloved for a very long time. It was sad to watch her coming back from work she hated, bringing Indian treats and drinking by the window, smoking slim cigarettes and sharing her philosophical thoughts. I remembered her as an extremely shy and extremely smart girl, who read books by a window of our kindergarten, and accused kids that laughed at her love for literature, in ignorance. I remembered us sliding down snow hills with her mother watching us carefully in a distance. I remembered her exhilaration, when both of us got American visas and were packing to leave our homeland. Now she was sadly drinking by the window.

"You know," she once said. "I know there is something special there for me. A phone call, a visit from a stranger, a random gaze on the street. Someone will call me one beautiful day and ask, 'Is it you I'm looking for?'"

I examined her tipsy face and after a short pause verbalized it, "Then you can wait forever."

"Well, maybe I'm not planning to die at all," Vera stated.

I smiled, "Then this person better be as immortal as you are."

She gave a laugh and her big green eyes sparkled.

My insomnia was only worsening. I often gave up annoying attempts to fall asleep, and leaving my slumbered friend dreaming on her own, went out into a night full of stars, sounds and thoughts. I didn't crave alcohol as much as I did before I went to the AA meeting, although I still had the desire to drink. I knew, this desire would go away. It couldn't be genuine as alcohol is not essential. Love is essential, and it was something I wanted to fill my life with. I sat on benches, walked by the river, thinking about my perfect man. I was imagining the way he would look, the way he would speak. I wanted him to have Dr Holington's calming voice and his gorgeous eyes. I wanted my man to be a good listener. I wanted him to be. After those nights ended, I dragged myself around New York, showing apartments, meeting strangers, having short food and coffee breaks, and wishing to get home and have some rest the following night, but ended up repeating the same script. Insomnia did push me to spend more time on dating websites. I began understanding myself better and realized what I really wanted. I wanted to settle down. I wanted love; I wanted a family; I wanted to live in warmth and appreciation. I gave myself this chance. His name was Andrew.

He was 35 but looked like 40, conservative, nerdy, and very rational. He was coming from a rich Russian family. His mother died when he was a child. Shortly after her departure, his dad brought another woman home. The woman happened to dislike Andrew and did everything from picking on him to punishing him for nothing to make a little boy unhappy. Very often, he cried under his bed, kissing his mother's photo and praying to God to bring her back. This formed a tense sadness in his light-brown eyes, which seemed to be ready to smile at any moment, however, they rarely did. His forehead looked tired from overthinking, and three deep wrinkles on it showed all heaviness of his thoughts. He was a bit taller them me, big-boned, and tender-souled. His face was always perfectly shaved, his shirts usually smelled slightly sweet, his watch was minute-to-minute correct, and he was never late. He didn't say anything without thinking, his mind was constantly occupied with analysis. Sometimes it was too busy for talking.

He was vegan, but thankfully, he didn't try to influence me to go on a healthy diet. He was a teetotaler as well. I had no courage to tell him about my drunk predicaments and other adventures, however, after some time had passed, I gained my strength. He worked in finance. He was an American citizen, yet he was born and raised in St. Petersburg, to which he intended to come back. I thought he was only exaggerating his love for Russia. Besides his father's furniture factory and a memory of past days, he had nothing to return to.

We met in a small Indian restaurant, similar to the one Vera worked in. He brought two banal red roses and a serious face. I thought I would never go for another date with him as I was getting in a cab and waving goodbye, but he called me the same night and shared an amusing story about a date his friend went to. I didn't see any relation of that story to our dinner and that night in general, but the anecdote was so funny, that I couldn't stop laughing. Then I shared a story about a date I went to a long while before. Then we agreed to dine together again. Little by little the chain of dinners and roses had turned into our normal routine, and shortly after a few weeks, we turned into partners. Soon enough, my serious partner began joking about exchanging our apartment keys. Sometimes he had to explain his jokes to me. Sometimes I had to explain mine. Sometimes he hugged me, and it made me feel at home. Sometimes he put the laptop on my knees and said one world, "start."

"You'll get there," he kept stating with his rare and considerate-charming smile. "Just start writing. You know, Moscow wasn't built in a day."

"I want to write," I confessed, "but I have nothing to say."

I recalled Dr Holington telling me I needed to start writing if I wanted to be a writer. It sounded simple and logical, swimmers swim, cooks cook, writers write. But where do you get that first ingredient you want to start with?

"You have a lot to say. You don't even know, how much you have to say." he pointed with his analytic look, making the three wrinkles appear deeper. "The first ingredient is you."

He never wore jeans or sneakers. All his pants were classy. All his watches had roman numbers. His short greyish hair gave him a look of a wise man. I called him a sage. He only smiled when he heard it. It flattered him.

I managed to tell Andrew about my funny and sad adventures. I told him about my past, my childhood, my father, Rita. I told him about rape, about police and psychiatric facility, I skipped Dr Holington along with my broken heart. Then I confessed I was doing massages. I had never told anyone before, besides the doctor. Not even to Natasha. I didn't know why I opened up to him, I didn't know what I needed from that confession, I did expect a wave of judgements as a punishment for the past I hated. He hugged me tight, instead. He kissed my forehead. He gave me minutes of compassionate silence, then he whispered with his voice breaking, "I will always protect you. You are safe in these very arms."

My eyes turned wet. I didn't want to die in his arms, I wanted to spend the rest of my life there.

Andrew's father wasn't fond of his son, he never treated him well, furthermore, he kept accusing him of being as stupid as his departed mother, who devoted all her life to her family, and hence never worked. She was only 18 when she got married to a wealthy man quite older than herself. She was only 19 when she gave birth. She was only 25 when she died of cancer. The mother gave all her warmth and tenderness to Andrew. She raised him in love and care; she showed him the beauty of the world full of kindness and magic, which broke a young heart later when the boy learned of the other side of that world. The angry and greedy father didn't care about his son's happiness or personal life but wanted his brain to be fully functioning as he needed an heir for a furniture factory. Despite all conflicts with his dad, the sage planned to come back to Russia.

In less than three months, I found myself decorating his apartment in downtown Manhattan with my belongings. Part of his closet got filled with my suits and dresses. Some of his bathroom cabinets fitted my serums and creams. Half of his bed was mine. All of his love belonged to me. I learned to fall asleep in his strong, but tender arms. My insomnia was cured.

He made breakfast on weekends — vegan pancakes with jelly. We would often come back to bed right after satisfying our hunger for food. The smell of his body made me dizzy. There was something special in morning sex, there was less gentleness, there was more fervor and lust, more roughness, louder screams, frequent moans. Powerless, we would hug each other and talk about everything in the world. Then Andrew would give me a thoughtful look and say, "Why wouldn't we get some air? It's beautiful outside."

We loved taking long walks along the Hudson River. We would start at Pier 17 and finish around Upper West Side. There were a bunch of vegan restaurants he introduced me to — one by one. I, in my turn, introduced him to Vera, Natasha, and Snezhana, when they finally confronted me with hiding my boyfriend. Andrew invited them over for a dinner. He was an excellent chef, and regardless of being a teetotaler, knew a lot about wines. We created a beautiful table, full of appetizers with a choice of entrées, and red and white wines. I warned him my friends drank a lot. He only smiled.

"Well," my sage said, giving everyone at the table welcoming look. "I'm glad all of you were able to make it here today. I've heard a lot of things about each of you, now I finally got a chance to meet all of you in person!"

"What kind of things?" Natasha giggled. "Nothing is true!"

I realized I was proud of him, of his thoughtfulness and great manners, of his sanity and intelligence. It was the first time I enjoyed myself being sober while others drank. Only Andrew and I were in our clear minds. My cravings vanished in no time. I found it extremely interesting to watch people getting drunk and silly and think that I used to do exactly the same. Obviously intoxicated, Natasha told Andrew about her experience with Laurine, about the conflict with her mother, then she shared my psychiatric facility's experience, and eventually, in spite of Snezhana's pushes and pinches, she told him about my feelings towards the doctor, my desire to die in his arms.

I was staring at her with anger, wanting her to stop, yet, deep inside, I pitied her, thinking she would regret everything the next day. Embarrassed and guilty, she would call me with apologies.

"It's a nice apartment," Vera noticed in order to break the awkwardness. I silently thanked her for doing it.

"Thank you," Andrew smiled, looking at Vera. He didn't seem to be hurt by that information, unless he pretended. "I think it's time for Katya to give you the luxury of living alone."

"Like what...?" she murmured, and I assumed, she fully understood, what he intended to say.

Everyone at the table gazed at me.

"What do you mean?" I didn't find anything else to ask. I was enjoying our nights and weekends together but wasn't ready to give up my freedom completely.

"Oh, come one," Natasha laughed and mocked me, "What do you mean?"

Snezhana pushed her again, visibly stronger this time.

Andrew turned a bit nervous, looked at me, and swallowed loudly before speaking,

"Katya, marry me."

I didn't stay with him that night. I cried all night long as I came back home. I didn't want to talk to anyone and I wished I wouldn't have to. I buried my head in-between pillows. I felt lost and confused and didn't know what I wanted and whether I wanted anything.

"Hey," Vera was caressing my back. "He is a great guy. He seems to really love you. What is it, Katyusha?"

I wasn't answering. I thought, she would leave me alone after realizing I didn't want to talk.

"What do you want?" she nearly yelled at me. "What the hell do you want? Stop acting like a timeless princess! You wanted to get legalized in this country. There you go, here is a nice guy, who cares about you a big deal! What else do you want?"

"I don't know," I cried.

"Why are you dating him then? If you dislike him so badly?"

"I don't dislike him," I wept. "I really care about him. Maybe I'm even in love with him. I don't know."

"Then what is it?" she asked calmly "Is sex so bad? Or his absence of a sense of humor?"

I gave a laugh through tears and told her, "Sex is great. By the way"

"That's why you don't want to marry him, he's too good?" she giggled. "You need another jerk like Dmitry?"

"I don't want to marry him, because I don't know what I want."

"That's a good answer," she stated ironically.

"He is a great guy. I feel so good in his arms, but I don't know, I just don't know... I'm scared of letting him so close to me."

"You can always have your private space. Marriage doesn't mean becoming closer. It's up to you, which distance you want to maintain."

We spent the rest of the night drinking tea and talking about people, love, dreams, choices, and places. She confessed, that she loved the U.S. and didn't want to go back to Russia. She was so happy here, even not settled and afraid of everything that waited for her in the future.

"Sometimes I feel like homeless," she laughed, touching my hand with hers. "I don't really belong to Russia any more... and here I'm a nobody."

"Me too," I smiled, recognizing a very familiar feeling.

"Oh, God! After so many years you still feel homeless?" she exclaimed, searching for the answer in my eyes.

"I… do…" I nodded, silently asking myself, why?

"I still live in a small rental studio…" I said. "What makes you feel homeless?"

Vera thought for a second. She looked in the window, then closed her big green eyes and opened them back at me.

"I don't know," she verbalized. "I thought it's because I recently came and it's going to change over time… But you are saying it doesn't…"

"It does!" I giggled. "These are just different stages of homelessness!"

We burst into laughter. I hugged her warmly and whispered how happy I was to have such a wonderful friend. We talked until the very morning, then she went to work. I was sitting on the floor by the window, thinking to call Andrew and apologize. I said I had to think about the offer and left with the girls as we finished the dinner, pretending that nothing had happened. A very expected phone call interrupted my thoughts.

"Yes," I smiled, ready to accept apologies.

"I'm sorry," Natasha hoarsened. "I'm sorry, Katyusha."

"It's all right, girl," I said. "But for the future, please, don't share my stories with anyone… well, unless you've got my permission."

"Ah, right, I forgot," she mumbled. I could feel her heavy hangover through the phone. "I'm sorry for that too. There is something else."

A bit of silence passed. I couldn't possibly imagine, what else was there.

"Promise, you won't get mad," she begged.

"Hey," I uttered, getting anxious. "What is it?"

"Promise…"

"I can't promise as I don't know what had happened!" I almost yelled. "Natasha, what happened?"

She coughed, cleared her throat, then said, "Dmitry."

Another second of silence passed.

"Dmitry what?" I asked impatiently.

She sighed nervously, "As I came home last night, I found the guy sitting next to my door. He introduced himself as Dmitry. He said he knew you lived there and he came to talk to you. I was really drunk, I offered him to come for a glass of wine, but he refused. He said there was something crucial he needed to tell you and asked for your phone number. I was really drunk. You know. I didn't know what I was doing."

"Natasha, no, no, no, no, noooo," I cried.

"I'm so sorry, I'm so sorry, I have just realized I've done something wrong," she mumbled. "He was so well-spoken and polite, so I thought he had a good intention."

All the memories of him came back. Everything got mixed up in my head, our first kiss, our semi-happy time in Astrakhan, endless plans and empty ambitions, his lies and blackmailing, betrayal and vanishing from my life. I thought of the day James proposed to me with sad anger. I recalled his perfectly white teeth and blue eyes, his sweet smile and tender voice.

What did he want from me?

My heart sped up its movements. I turned dizzy. I asked myself if I missed him, and unfortunately, answered positively. I wanted to scream out of my own helplessness, "would I ever stop caring about him?" What a devilish addiction was it?

I called Andrew with a "yes" response and told him I was giving Vera the luxury of living alone. I could hear tears in his eyes through the distance of the wireless universe. I missed him, I said. I loved him, I stated. I apologized for acting the way I was acting. I packed in a hurry and moved downtown the same night.

I hadn't seen the sage that happy before. He looked intoxicated, he was laughing in elation, making plans for the future, constructing our house, creating our children. He said we could move to St. Petersburg eventually to rule his dad's furniture factory and I wouldn't have to work for the rest of my life. Our kids would attend best schools in the city. We would live a dream life. My guilt was growing proportionally to his excitement, ruining the last illusion of happiness. Sadly, there was some irritation along with that guilt. His excitement started bothering me and I thought I would tell him to shut up if I'd hear more joy in his voice. My phone rang the same night. After a dose of sore whispers into the cellular receiver on the bathroom floor, I accepted Dmitry's "invitation" to a conversation.

Andrew had been trying to seduce me for a while as we both got into bed. I had a headache, I said with an apologetic smile. I had no strength to talk to him, I had no strength to do anything with him. I took a sleeping pill in order to fall asleep. I heard him tossing and turning before I passed out. Tomorrow came earlier than usual.

"Did I do anything wrong, baby?" my fiancé asked in the morning.

"No…" I mumbled. "I was exhausted."

He enclosed me in his warm arms and kissed my forehead, "I thought you had gotten upset with me for something."

I couldn't wait for him to go to work. It took me so much emotional strength to stare into the computer monitor as there was something important, which couldn't stand any sort of interruption.

"I'll see you tonight, baby!" Andrew gave me a kind look before leaving.

"See you tonight," I faked a smile.

He unlocked the door, stood for a second, then walked to me and kissed me on the forehead and murmured, "I love you."

"I love you, too," I repeated.

He left. I felt like crying. I hated myself. I hated Dmitry. I couldn't believe I was betraying someone so great and pure. I was trying to convince myself I wasn't doing anything wrong by just going there. I was only trying to find out why he had contacted me. I waited impatiently till 3,30 p.m. I dressed up, put make-up on, I stood by the mirror for a few minutes, making sure my outfit was matching and my hair looked good. My hands were shaking as I tipped the cab driver, exiting in West Village.

Of course, it was a dive bar. I arrived a little before 5 and ordered a glass of seltzer. Dmitry was about fifteen minutes late. Sitting and waiting for him suddenly reminded me, that he was always late, every single time we met — it was sort of his business card to introduce himself to people. Or just to me.

Finally, he appeared, happy and refreshed, still tall and still skinny-athletic in light-blue jeans and white long-sleeve shirt under a down coat. He gave me a brief hug and sat next to me, by the bar counter. He looked deep into my eyes as if he was recalling something. I forced a smile.

"What are you drinking?" he asked warmly.

"Just a seltzer water," I answered.

"Why not alcohol?" he giggled. "Let's have beers, at least!"

"I don't feel like drinking tonight," I said, impatient to get to the point.

He ordered a beer and turned back to me on the round bar stool. His perfume smelled just like our Tuesdays and Thursdays, and for some reason, like that depressing day, when his woman called me. I suddenly found myself annoyed by the recollection of that love- story; a light headache started drilling into my head.

We relocated to the old wooden table right after he got his glass of beer. He seemed a bit shy, and it gave him certain cuteness.

"So, I'm done with Karon," he smiled with his naïve smile and paused to wait for my reaction.

"She dumped me; can you imagine?" he added.

"Why?" I asked.

"She figured I was using her. Whatever, old cougar! What did she want from a young guy like me, real love?"

He giggled.

I shrugged my shoulders.

"Guess what?" he winked, bending down over the table.

"What?"

"I'm all yours!"

Then he leaned back in his chair, smiling and looking at me. His eyes were bright and seemed loving and caring.

I browsed his childlike cute face, his perfectly white teeth, blond curls and blue eyes. He was so playful and flirty, caring and promising, serious and mischievous. It was hard not to like him; it was too easy to fall in love with that sweet handsome boy. And I had been. Mindlessly and powerlessly, I loved him more than I loved myself. He always needed attention, he needed to be admired, and I gave him all of that. Now I could clearly see why I got involved in that long devastating relationship.

It was difficult not to smile, looking at him. So, I did. He did too. Then he put his hands on the table, over mine.

"No," I said.

"No what?" he asked, keeping the smile.

"You are not mine."

"What do you mean?" corners of his lips started going down.

"I don't want this burden in my life," I stated, withdrawing my hands.

"Burden?" he pronounced, rather surprised, slowly raising up his voice, "I thought you loved me…"

"I did," I said calmly. "I loved you enough to bring to the U.S., enough to forgive for all your betrayals, to accept you after anything you would do. I waited for you after you were gone last year. I didn't want to live. I loved you as I never did before and maybe never will, but love can't be left out alone without any support for too long. Its battery dies."

He took a deep breath.

"You are unbelievable! I'll explain why I disappeared last year. For your information, Karon said…"

"It's okay," I interrupted him, "I really don't care what Karon said."

"But listen to me," he uttered, "so you can understand better."

"I really don't care," I said. "I needed to know last year. I was losing myself in search for you. But I do not have any interest any more. I have a great fiancé; we are getting married in a month. I love him and wouldn't let anybody to ruin my happiness."

He looked at me silently.

"I only came here, because you mentioned there was something very important. Though, there is nothing important at all. So, I shall go, I guess."

"Who is the motherfucker? Some rich citizen?" Dmitry smirked.

"It's honestly none of your business. I'd ask you not to contact me any more." I stated, getting up the chair.

His eyes turned red, yet he remained silent.

I got up and walked towards the exit. He ran after me and grabbed my arm so tightly that I thought he would leave bruises.

"I'm gonna call the police!" I uttered.

"Don't you love me any more? At all?" he cried. "I don't believe that no feelings left. Such a big love can't just go away with no signs!"

I tried to remove my arm, but he squeezed it even harder.

"No signs left. I hate you!" I yelled. "Leave me alone, otherwise I'll start screaming!"

"Please," he cried, "we can start from the beginning! I will marry you and we'll have kids and all that stuff. We belong together!"

"Remove your hand from my arm," I muttered angrily through my teeth.

He took it off, waiting for what's next.

"Get out of my life! I don't want to know you any more!" I threw all my anger in the last look and walked away from the crappy bar and a stranger by its doors.

"Okay, you, nasty whore!" he screamed so loudly, that people on the street started looking at me. "You gotta be happy, that I even put up with you and your ugly arm!"

"I was disgusted every time I looked at it," he yelled.

I walked faster.

"I wish you to get raped again!" he screamed louder. "I so wish you to get raped again, fucking whore!"

I wanted to come back and hit him, smack him, smash him, yet I walked further away instead. Random men stopped and turned around, but I didn't look at anyone, I walked faster and faster till I reached another block and made left. I jumped into the first cab I saw.

I didn't realize I instinctively told the driver my Harlem's address, and as the car began passing consistent green lights of Upper West Side, I decided, it was the right place to go. I was lost to the point that I didn't know what I felt. I was tired. I was drawn. I was relieved. Now I knew for sure, that horrible addiction was over, and I was free. Or had I always been free without knowing it?

The apartment smelled like heavy liquor. The light was on. Vera was asleep on the mattress. There were a few bottles of wine by the bed. I removed uncomfortable boots, dropped my purse on the floor, and hurried to open a window. A fresh breath of January filled the apartment. It started snowing. I sat on the window sill and sank in my thoughts, watching small snowflakes interacting with each other in their freefall. I finally felt free too. I finally felt strong and ready to build the future with Andrew. I had never known one could be so happy losing something the one could never imagine life without. I took a deep pleasant breath.

Vera looked like solitude. Wavy brown hair covered half of her face. The face showed neither satisfaction, nor disappointment. She was lying on her stomach with the head turned to the right. One of her legs was on the floor. She wore old sweatpants, warm socks, and a hoody. I suddenly jumped up and yelled, "Vera!"

My shout didn't change anything.

"Vera!" I shouted louder and ran to her. I fell on my knees and began shaking her shoulders.

She craned her neck and looked at me with irritation. Her eyes were red from the bright light and alcohol.

"What happened?" she moaned.

"Nothing, keep sleeping." I laughed. "I missed you."

I threw away all the bottles and put a glass of water by her side. I called Kostya as soon as I left the building. Vera needed a home, I thought, she was too homeless.

I didn't leave Andrew's arms for the whole subsequent night. It felt so safe and calm there.

"What happened, baby?" he asked me with his comforting and serious voice. "Did anyone let you down?"

His care made me feel valuable. For the first time in my life, I felt like I was a woman, a real woman, a female, a bride, a possible mother; I could fully rely on Andrew, without fearing being abandoned. I finally discovered what "man" meant. I had never had an example of an honorable man in my life. My father had left me and my mother to survive on our own, most of my friends' fathers did the same, others — were abusing their wives and children, and almost every male was an alcoholic during the tough Russian 90[s.] Then I encountered Dmitry, then James. I was raped. I was harassed. I was consistently harming myself mentally by doing erotic massages to strangers. I was handcuffed by men several times. I was rejected. Now I was in Andrew's arms and I couldn't think of a better place.

The date of our wedding was established. It was a happy and sad February 14th, 2014 which we would spend without our parents, but with love of each other and our dear friends. A lawyer told me about possible complications due to not showing for a previous interview, but my fiancé assured me that an officer would recognize our genuine union the very first minute. I believed him.

Kostya and I met in the same coffeeshop. It had been about three months since I saw him. He told me he broke off the engagement two months ago and was enjoying his freedom. I told him I knew it was going to happen.

"You looked very unhappy when you were talking about her," I explained. "Deep inside I even wished you to break up with her. I thought you would harm yourself more if you would marry her."

"You really did?" he asked and smiled.

"Of course! I didn't want to tell you back then because it was not my business." I noted.

His smile became wider, and his eyes got a sparkle.

"Did Natasha tell you to call me?" he wondered, giggling. "I mean, did she want to get together or just to find out how I was doing?"

I sadly admitted to myself that Natasha was the least interested person. Deep inside I thought Natasha might not even care whether he was dead or alive.

"No," I uttered. "Natasha didn't ask anything. She lives a new life, Kostya. You wouldn't even recognize her."

"W...why?" he faltered. "How does she look? What kind of life she lives?"

His smile was gone, and the sparkle got immediately dried up.

"It really doesn't matter. I would like to introduce you to a great, caring single girl of my age. She is looking for true love."

"Wait," Kostya mumbled hopelessly. "Why can't you tell me about Natasha?"

I let out a suppressed sigh. "Natasha is now exclusively dating girls. She cut her hair very short and wears men's clothing. She has no interest in men."

I gazed at his dry and disappointed eyes. "It has nothing to do with you. It's just the life she wants to live."

He took a deep breath and nodded. Then he said, "I knew she had something with Rita... But I didn't know it would go this far."

"Kostya," I said and waited for him to look at me. "It doesn't matter what she is. It is over. And there are plenty of single girls out there."

"I know, I know," he let out. "It's that I was so excited since the moment you called me to arrange to meet here today. I was sure Natasha wanted to reconnect."

"Sometimes there are people with which it's better to not reconnect. It's better to leave them in past as you remember them."

Kostya took another deep breath and forced a smile. "I gotta go. Here… the money for coffee… Should be enough."

I didn't stop him. I nodded and got up to give him a brief hug. Then he left, and I finished my coffee alone.

CHAPTER 15

Kostya called me back the same night and asked for the "great single girl's" phone number. I gave him the number and texted Vera that she was about to receive the phone call she had been waiting for years. At least, I hoped so.

Snezhana and Natasha were patiently helping me with the choice of a wedding dress. Three of us had completely different tastes and ideas of a perfect wedding, and yet we had managed to pick one all of us loved. After that, I took both friends for drinks to a nearby hotel lounge. Vera was supposed to join us later.

"Thank you for helping me, guys. You know, I really appreciate it." I said as we sat down at the table. "Andrew is thinking to cook a dinner and invite everybody sometime next week. What do you guys think?"

"As long as he will bake that vegan pumpkin pie, I'm in," Natasha joked.

"I'm in," uttered Snezhana. "Regardless of that pumpkin pie."

"He is a great chief," she added. "He doesn't allow you to help him with cooking, does he?"

"No, he doesn't. He likes preparing everything himself. He puts classical music on and the kitchen becomes his playground." I laughed. "And it's totally fine with me."

Our drinks arrived, and we clinked glasses.

"To our friendship!" I exclaimed.

"To our friendship!" the girls repeated.

"I've met someone," Natasha said all of a sudden after we put the glasses down.

"And?" Snezhana and I asked simultaneously.

She smiled shily. "We've been seeing each other for about three weeks."

"And you're just telling us now!" I exclaimed.

"Well, I didn't know how it was gonna go between us, so I didn't want to say anything, you know."

"It's understandable," Snezhana concluded. "So, who is this person?"

Natasha giggled, covered her happy face with both palms for a couple of seconds and declared, "A very beautiful girl from Jamaica."

"Jamaica, Queens or Jamaica, Jamaica?" I asked.

"Jamaica, Queens." she answered.

"Wow, it was my first neighborhood in New York."

"Everybody knows that," Snezhana smiled. "How old is she? What does she do?"

"What's her nationality?" I added.

"Well, she is Columbian, but grew up in Jamaica and still lives there. She is probably as tall as you guys. I feel so small next to all of you." she giggled shyly.

"Who cares about the height. It doesn't matter as long as you like each other." I exclaimed, and Snezhana nodded.

"She is 35 and..." Natasha gave me a prolonged gaze. "She is a psychotherapist!"

"Wow!" I uttered. "It's very sexy!"

"PhD?" Snezhana asked.

My thoughts went to Dr Holington and I wondered how he was doing.

"I believe she got a master's in counselling." Natasha vocalized. "She works most of the time. She loves her clients. They can literally call her at 10 p.m. and ask for an online video session, and she will do it for them!"

"Is she only practicing online?" I asked.

"No, it's for rare emergencies. She practices in Jamaica. She is thinking about renting an office in Manhattan, but worried that it would get harder for most of her clients to travel so far."

Vera ran in with apologies for being late, removing her brown coat and endlessly long green scarf on the way to us. She gave a brief hug to everyone, sat down, and asked what the girls drank.

"A quick question, before I forgot," Vera babbled as soon as she ordered a drink as if she was in enormous hurry. "Would it be okay for me to bring Kostya along to the dinner next week?"

She looked at me, then turned to Natasha and continued babbling, "I know, I know, you guys are not really on good terms. I mean, you don't want to see him, and I can understand that, but do you think you will be able to tolerate him for two hours? I mean, would you be fine, sitting at the same table with him?"

We all gazed at Natasha.

"I mean… sure!" she faltered. "Are you guys dating or something?"

"No," Vera laughed. "We met for coffee and I thought he was a nice young man. I told him about Katya, Andrew, you. He doesn't know Snezhana. So, he said he really wanted to meet everyone. I told him there might be a dinner party next week, but I didn't say anything for sure. I thought I would check with you guys first."

"You should bring your girlfriend along," I suggested to Natasha.

"I'll see if she's free," my friend let out thoughtfully. Then she turned to Vera and said, "But hey, you should bring him. I don't care. There is no undone business between us."

"Great!" she uttered happily. "Do bring your girlfriend! Snezhana, bring your match as well."

Till that moment I never imagined Snezhana in a relationship with anyone. It didn't look like she was interested in meeting anybody, didn't look like she had any sexual orientation as she always seemed so complete and happy alone.

"Trust me guys, you'll be the first to know once I'll get a match." she smiled.

Both Vera and Natasha began typing something in their phones. Snezhana and I clinked glasses with no toast. She wore a tight burgundy suit and a white sweater with a long neck. We had another round of drinks and left the lounge. Only after we parted, I realized we didn't ask Tasha what her girlfriend's name was.

Andrew continued praising St. Petersburg and describing its parkways, prospects, museums, old castles; in his mind, it didn't belong to Russia at all, it was a separate land of kind people, decadence, intellectual bums and inspiration. It is gorgeous and cold, something magic is always in the air. I enjoyed listening to his admiration for the city I had never been to; I adored Andrew getting so poetic. I knew his craving for homeland would go away and we would establish our own home in New York.

We picked an Italian restaurant for our wedding reception. We decided not to go for a honeymoon as we were living a honeymoon life already — day after day, night after night. I couldn't wait to become his legal wife. I wanted to treat it as my very first wedding. As my very first marriage.

Vera told me she met Kostya the very next day after he called her. They went to Russian restaurant in Midtown. They spent about three hours there and then Kostya put her in a cab and paid for it. She said that he was illegal. He was fixing computers for living. He told her about his broken-up engagement. He said, she was unbearably jealous and suspicious of everything. His former fiancée checked his email, his phone, his wallet on daily basis. Every new contact or a message from a stranger would cause a fight. Paranoid, he began deleting overly emotional messages from friends or grateful clients' emails. He never shared his number with any members of AA meetings. She went to most of the meetings with him. And she convinced him he would relapse without her support. Besides the fear of relapse, the last thing that bound him to her was the Green Card. He thought, at least, he would get legalized in this country. Then, all of a sudden, one cold and sunny day, he decided it was too much of a burden for him. It wasn't worth it any more. The Green Card lost its value next to the torture he would have to go through to get it. I listened with compassion and pity for him. I knew how it felt to go through torture like that, and I also knew there was no guarantee of the reward.

My childhood friend said that Kostya lived in Astoria, Queens. He was thinking about adopting a pet, but he didn't know what kind. She told him her sad story and his eyes turned wet as he was listening to it. This moment she felt connected to him. She also said she wasn't sure he was the guy of her dreams, but she kept in mind that dreams do change. Anyhow, she saw a great person in him and she thought they might at least become friends.

A couple of days after our gathering in the lounge, I met Natasha for a quick lunch and asked her whether she was truly okay with Kostya joining us, as I sensed some disapproval in her voice during that gathering. Her comfort and well-being were more important to me than Kostya's desire to come over. It didn't take her too long to disclose.

"You know, I talked to Daniella about it the same night we saw each other. And I realized I do feel hate for him. He hasn't done anything wrong. It's all me. I was always gay, since my birth. But you know how it is in Russia. You are not allowed to be yourself. So, I was growing up watching how "normal" people were supposed to live, and I knew that any "abnormal" stuff would be punished. I always liked girls, but I thought it was wrong. Sometimes I think that's why I came here. On a subconscious level, you know. I came here to hide from my family. I haven't been trying to contact them for a very long time, actually. I forgot when I did it the last time. I forgave my mother for abandoning me, and by the way, I decided not to come back to Russia."

She grinned. I grinned as well.

"I'm so happy you're staying here. You'll do much better here. Russia is a very homophobic country. And I know, you will get legalized here eventually."

"I will. I'll go to study once I'll get the Green Card. I want to study psychology."

"Wow! How come I missed so many changes in your mind? I'm glad to hear it. Is it Daniella's influence?" I exclaimed.

"I don't know…. But when I'm looking at her so excited about her job, when she explains to me the basics of psychoanalysis, I just know that this is what I want to do."

"That's amazing!" I uttered and was about to return our conversation to the initial question when she disclosed, "And regarding Kostya, I am upset with myself for giving my body to him, giving my body to a man in general. There was one more boyfriend in Russia… and him. And I hate them for they were granted access to my body and used it for their nasty needs!"

Tasha exhaled loudly through her nose and looked down.

"I know. I know how it feels, my dear." I let out. "I'm very sorry you're feeling this way. I had no idea. You can't change the past, but you can enjoy your present and future. I'm so happy that now a beautiful girl accesses your body and gives you joy."

She smiled.

"Do you think it would make you feel better if you told it all to Kostya?" I said and thought that it might ruin him.

"No, it's okay," she sighed. "Nothing's gonna make me feel better about it, just to switch my thoughts to something pleasant."

"But do you think it will be okay for you to see him? If not, I'll just tell him not to come. Not a big deal." I stated.

"No, don't do this. Let him come. I'm a little curious about what he looks like. And how he's gonna make me feel."

I looked at Natasha from a different angle that day. I had never known about her struggle, this particular struggle. From the side, it looked like her sexuality was a relatively easy and fluid thing, she liked men and she dated men, then she fell for one woman and she switched to women. And yet, it was all the top of an iceberg. Every single decision of hers had its roots in her childhood, in her family, in the country she no longer wanted to come back to. And I finally knew her girlfriend's name.

Andrew had been cooking for the whole day on the day of the dinner. He was chopping, peeling, cutting, steaming, frying, boiling, squeezing. The whole apartment smelled like a combination of sweet-sour-savory-spicy ingredients. I was not allowed into the kitchen, so I took my time to prepare the dining room and myself. The chef didn't want to invite his friends. He said he would rather make a separate dinner for them, but this time he wanted to have a better-quality conversation with people that were so dear to me.

"I hope your friends don't mind vegan food," he exclaimed, laughing. "I just can't cook any meat. The thought of holding it in my hands makes me feel sick."

"Well, our apartment, our rules," I supported him. I couldn't remember when I last had meat or fish and admitted to myself that I didn't have any desire to consume animal products.

Snezhana came the first with two bottles of white wine. She gave a brief hug to Andrew who was finishing something in the kitchen, then a prolonged squeeze to me. She kissed me on my cheek and immediately began erasing her lipstick from it.

"It smells so good!" she uttered. "Does Andrew need a second wife?"

Vera and Kostya arrived shortly after Snezhana. Kostya brought a big non-vegan cake. Vera brought Rita's paintings wrapped all together, and Bhagavad-Gita. She said she didn't believe in Samsara or any afterlife, but there were many useful points in the book, and Andrew and I could benefit from reading it. She also said she liked Rita's paintings, but thought they should stay with me. I introduced Kostya to Snezhana and Andrew, and the latter smiled to me when he saw the cake.

Natasha and Danielle arrived fifteen minutes late. They brought a beautiful bouquet of sunflowers and a bottle of Whiskey. Danielle was a tall rather feminine dark-haired brown-eyed young woman. Her small eyes were set quite apart from each other and her thick lips seemed to be in a constant smile, which gave her a lot of charm. Her curly hair was made in a ponytail. I found her very cute. She shook everybody's hand and introduced herself as "Dannie", then she congratulated Andrew and me on our engagement.

Andrew opened wine and whiskey and asked the guests what they preferred. Kostya, me, and my fiancé drank juices, Natasha and Dannie whiskey, and Vera with Snezhana wine.

Kostya nodded to Natasha once everyone got a drink. She nodded back, and he smiled. Then he stepped closer to her and said, "Good to see you. You look wonderful."

"Thank you," Natasha responded.

Kostya looked very nervous. It seemed like he wanted to say more but couldn't make another sound. So, he smiled, nodded and stepped back.

All guests and I sat at the table while Andrew decorated it with appetizers. When he was done, he stood next to me and raised the toast,

"Thank you for coming here, dear friends. As I already mentioned, Katya has wonderful friends, and I'm sure she is a wonderful friend to all of you. I'm so proud of you guys being together throughout the brightest and the hardest times of your lives. Life here and legalization was relatively easy for me, so I never had to fight for the right to live in this country. I cannot even imagine what you guys went through, all the misery of being mistreated and abused, all the fear of being deported. I have no idea how it feels, but I can envision how many of you still struggle through every single day. And it's not an easy struggle. I really hope all of you will get legalized very soon. You deserve it. This country needs you, your bright minds. And I truly hope that same-sex marriages will get on the federal level as well. It's such nonsense to evaluate love by genders. Cheers to all of it!"

Glasses clinked loudly. Natasha kissed Dannie, and Dannie whispered something to Natasha's ear. Andrew wrapped his arm around my shoulders and murmured, "I love you."

"I love you, too," I said.

Vera was sitting next to me. Kostya was sitting next to her. He and Snezhana were talking about something for almost the whole evening. Dannie and Natasha were between Snezhana and Andrew.

"I need to start thinking about how to legalize before my tourist visa is finished," Vera noted.

"I think you should go to a language school. They will make you a student visa." I suggested. "Do you know what you want to do in life? Like career-wise?"

She thought for a few seconds, then said, "I always wanted to be a doctor."

"Really?" I exclaimed loudly, and Snezhana with Dannie looked at us. "How come I never knew?"

She smiled shyly.

"I don't know... Just never thought I would become one. I first wanted to become a surgeon when this electric accident happened to you. I wished I could help you, but I couldn't. Then when my mom broke her hip years ago. And I always loved chemistry and biology. But when the time to decide on my future profession came, I was told that it wasn't worth it to study medicine. A doctor's salary in Russia is miserable. The work is very stressful and mostly unappreciated., and of course, the only medical school in Astrakhan is extremely corrupted."

"So, you went to study fine arts," I giggled.

"So, I went to study fine arts," she gave a laugh.

"I think, it's never too late," I told her. "You can go to a medical school and become who you want to be, no matter, how old you'll be by then."

Andrew was not letting me out of his arms. He kept holding my shoulders, or my waist, or just my hand under the table. His presence next to me gave me so much warmth. I felt drunk on him. I felt high and I didn't want to land.

"Kate, I've heard you lived in Jamaica!" Dannie interrupted my thoughts.

"I did," I exclaimed. "It was my first neighborhood in New York."

"Where exactly did you live?"

"By the last stop of F train. But on Jamaica avenue. Where do you live?"

"Wow, I used to live on Jamaica avenue by the previous stop," she stated, smiling with an adorable smile. "How did you like it there?"

"Well… it was okay. It's hard for me to say, because I worked at the bar and I hated the job, I couldn't tolerate harassment from my boss." I confessed. "So, it reflected on my perception of the neighborhood."

"Which bar is it?" she wondered.

"Ron's," I responded.

She gave a laugh. "You not gonna believe what's up with Ron!"

"Oh my god, you know him? So, what's up with him?"

"Of course," she uttered. "Everybody knows him! He won 50 million in lottery, sold his bar, and now driving his fancy convertible picking up young girls."

"Unbelievable!" all I could say out of the astonishment.

"How old is he now?" Andrew intervened.

"Probably one hundred," I blurted.

Dannie laughed. "He must be in his early seventies."

"It's just so unfair that nasty pedophiles like him are so lucky. Now he has all this money and this money enables him to do what he wants to do — harass young girls!"

"You don't know, Katyusha," Andrew stated. "This money might as well enable him to drink himself to death, or drunk-gamble all of it away."

"Or," Dannie articulated. "He could marry a poor young girl which would kill him and get all this money."

"Or," Vera added, "All this money enabled him to close the bar. If he wouldn't close it, he would harass many more poor, illegal girls there."

We laughed at so many reasons to be happy for the old man.

The dinner happened to be nostalgic, funny, informative, and very delicious. Natasha and Dannielle left first. Natasha gave hugs to everyone, and when it was Kostya's turn, she stretched her hand to him and he obediently shook it. Vera needed to go to work in the morning. She was slightly tipsy. She told Andrew how grateful she was that I had finally met a real man. Kostya was talking to Snezhana most of the night but got up as he saw Vera living. He thanked us and wished us a good night, then he smiled warmly to Snezhana.

"What were you guys talking about all night?" I asked Snezhana out of curiosity after everyone else had left.

"If I'll tell you, I'll have to kill you." she winked.

My second first marriage took place at the same Marriage Burau in downtown Manhattan. This time Vera was my witness. She said she always wanted to be the one and I would be her witness when the time would come. I wore a white dress with pinkish lace, it was covering my knees. My pumps were slightly pink. Andrew's suit was white with pink bowtie, and he wore pinkish shoes. Two of his old friends, which I got to meet before, came to the wedding. All of my friends were present as well. All, besides my mom. My memorable February 14th of 2014 excluded just one dear person, and at the same time it allowed me to get the base to fly over to this dear person one day. We became husband and wife exactly at 2 p.m.

I was crying out of happiness, Andrew was laughing, lifting me up in his arms and screaming how much he loved me.

"I promise! I promise! I promise!" I kept shouting with joy right after we exited the Marriage Bureau. "I promise, Andrew!"

There was no occasion I could recall I felt that happy. I wasn't trying to recall any. I just savored every second of us, every moment of that beauty and joy. It was priceless to leave the Bureau with the man I loved. Priceless to have the same person in your mind and in your arms. There was nothing better than to be married to the main character of your thoughts. Finally, I knew how it felt.

I also knew how it felt to be surrounded with great friends, the friends that became my family. I was very proud of them. I was watching them; I was trying to memorize them at that moment, the way they were, dressed up and smiley, excited and tipsy. Natasha was dressed in white pants and white vest; she was holding Dannie's hand all the time as if she was afraid to let her go. Their height difference was on their side and gave them more charm. Dannie wore flat shoes and a long grey dress. Kostya wore a black suit with a black skinny tie, and it was the first time I saw him in a suit. Vera had a black dress on, and Snezhana wore a tight white suit with a skirt down to her knees and a purple blouse under the top. I wanted to remember everyone, the way each of them was, the way each of them walked, talked, smiled. I wanted to remember every detail of them, from a little garment to the smell of their perfumes. I wanted to memorize that day and keep it as a sweet warmth in my chest, to make it a part of my present and future, a part of me.

The dinner was loud and animated. All nine of us sat at a big round table in a beautiful Italian restaurant and spent full eight hours of laughter, toasts, wishes, anecdotes, and anything that could possibly come to our minds. Danielle was talking a lot with one of Andrew's friends. Natasha laughed at something with Snezhana and talked to her partner time-to-time. Kostya was mostly listening to Vera's life story, and once Vera would begin talking to me, he would switch to Snezhana. Snezhana would stop by me every time she would get up to use the bathroom. She would hug me and tell me how happy she was for me. Natasha would do the same. I wrapped myself in Andrew's arms while his other friend was saying how much I meant for my husband.

"You are everything for him. Please, take a good care of him. Take a good care of each other. Love like yours is very hard to be find." he said, and then exclaimed, "Actually, toast! For love! For Kate's and Andrew's love! For their union to last forever!"

Glasses clinked. Shouts of joy filled the air. I felt intoxicated. My new definition of happiness was two high on each other people in the middle of the Universe with their lives put together for an unknown period of time, a period, the length of which was completely unimportant, because the beauty of the moment outweighed it because it was priceless. It was my moment, the most important person of my life sitting next to me, holding me gently in his strong arms, in which I felt as protected as I had never been before; all my friends, who became my family; my entire past and struggles, which was worth it — from the beginning till the very last minute. The moment I wanted to stay in forever.

Vera had too many glasses of wine and began falling asleep on the table. One of Andrew's friends was driving and agreed to deliver her home. We told Kostya there was no need to go with them, and as it appeared to me, he didn't even want to. His eyes were shiny, and his cheeks were pinkish, and his attention fully belonged to Snezhana. If I didn't know he quit drinking, I would say that he was drunk.

Natasha and Dannie were leaving shortly after Vera.

"You guys should come to Jamaica," Dannie suggested and winked at me. "We will give everyone a nice tour around the hood!"

I smiled. "We will one day."

Natasha looked elated. I hadn't seen this spark in her eyes since Rita died. She shook all men's hands and gave hugs to Snezhana and me.

"Are you guys into each other?" I asked Snezhana when Kostya went to the restroom.

The place was getting slower and slower. People were putting their winter coats on and leaving.

"Oh, come on," she giggled. "I'm almost 50 and he is only 35."

"So, what? Not that big of a difference. The woman I fell for, the jeweler, was twenty-something years older than me." I stated. "And to be honest, if not that predicament with her husband, I would stay with her."

"You mean, you could see yourself in a relationship with her?" Snezhana inquired.

"Absolutely!" I answered. "I even loved the fact that she was older. It gave her a certain charm."

Snezhana gave a laugh.

"Do you like Kostya?" I asked.

"I mean… he looks like a nice guy. And I love that he doesn't drink."

Then both of us looked back and saw Kostya approaching. He sat between us and disclosed to me, "I met Natasha waiting by the bathroom a couple of hours ago. I wanted to leave because I thought she didn't want to talk to me. But she stopped me and said, 'I'm sorry for disappearing on you like that back then'. I was so shocked she said it. I didn't know what to say back and I said, 'It's okay. I'm sorry for trying to get you back.' I felt so weird like nothing of that had happened in the past, and at the same time, like she was in my life forever in the role of this boy. My feelings for her are gone. I realized I loved an imaginary girl for all these years."

"I think, we always love imaginary people. And we blame real them for not having qualities we gave them; we start picking on them for being different from what we had imagined." Snezhana articulated.

"Let's not do that," Kostya said and looked at Snezhana. She grinned. And I could see it was a genuine grin.

"Let's not do that," Andrew mocked Kostya to my ear, embracing me from the back. I allowed him to embrace me tighter and rested my head on his shoulder.

My judgment day was five and a half years apart from that distant snowy night that took away my childhood and drove me into the big hostile world and its life I didn't know before. I got to abandon everything I used to know and cherish in my loving home and learn to live in the open space of maturity. I got to learn things I needed to learn, things I wanted to learn, and the things I never needed and never wanted to learn. My life was an open notebook without a single line in it and back then I didn't know how hard it would be to fill its pages. I didn't know how hard of a path I had chosen for myself. Back then I didn't know anything, I was just watching my first American night on the screen of a cold shaking window of the bus which was going right into the blizzard. I was frightened but full of hopes.

I was frightened and full of hopes on that very judgment day of my Green Card interview where my uneasy path took me after long years of struggle. Andrew and I arrived at Federal Plaza an hour before the time of our appointment but waited in the building's hall for another five. We were sitting close to the door from which officers came out to call petitioners inside. We were watching people. Some of them looked energized and excited, others anxious and dismal. Some smiled, some talked, some sat quietly. I saw people rehearsing questions and answers. I saw them disappearing behind that very door and returning in 15-20 minutes. They mostly looked happy. Some were obviously upset. Others seemed indifferent. I was wondering how I would look. All people were of different colors and nationalities. I heard some Russian speech as well. I was becoming more and more nervous. I wore a summer business dress and was freezing in that air-conditioned space.

After five hours of people watching, we were finally called by the officer. She escorted us to her office. It was a small room with a desk and two chairs next to it. She sat at the desk and we sat on the chairs. It was an Indian-looking American woman in her mid-fifties. Her face was very strict, and her eyes were cold and penetrating. She did look like a prison guard.

338

"Why did you overstay your visa?" she asked me shortly after we sat down.

I expected this question and did not hesitate to answer, "Because I didn't find any company to sponsor me for working visa. It was nearly impossible even with my master's. So, I decided to stay a little longer and earn some money to go back home with. I needed to return the money my mom had invested in my education. Especially, since the investment didn't work…"

"Why didn't you show up for your previous interview?" she interrupted me with her strict and demanding voice. "Why didn't you let us know you were not coming to the interview?"

"Why didn't you go back to Russia after you skipped the interview?"

I told her the truth. I told her everything about James and the fight on the day before our interview, and admitted I got lost and depressed right after it happened, so I didn't have the strength to contact the immigration service. I lied that I was planning to go back to Russia till I met Andrew. We fell in love and couldn't part ever since.

She kept silence for a while looking at our paperwork, mutual bank account's statements, and photographs in our scrapbook. Then, staring into my eyes, as she was trying to screen my mind, she asked the names of the people in pictures and the places where they were taken. Andrew held my hand, and squeezed it slightly, letting me know he was there with me. After each correct answer of mine, she looked at Andrew and he nodded.

Her cold look was making me very anxious. She asked me for my husband's full name and date of birth. Then she asked him for mine. Both answers were correct, and she told me to indicate our address.

I gave her my precise Harlem's address. Her cold eyes began to look bigger, but her poker face didn't change. I couldn't realize what was happening till Andrew whispered, "Katya!"

"I'm sorry," I faltered. "I'm… I'm just so nervous. No… we don't live there. We live in Downtown."

I began to shake. I had no idea how this address pumped up in my mind. My hands turned cold. I was trying to recall our street but couldn't. All numbers and letters got mixed up in my head and nothing was making any sense any more. The officer was writing something down, raising her eyes at me time-to-time. I felt dizzy. I was trying hard to recall our address but only made myself more anxious. My lips started trembling and I couldn't make any more sounds.

An instant picture of deportation intruded into my mind. I began blaming myself for failing the interview. I began thinking all those long years of struggle went nowhere. And I was done there.

"Katyusha," Andrew said with a smile. "No need to be so nervous. I forget it all the time!"

The officer switched her look to him and he told her solemnly, "There are so many numbers and letters to memorize. I tried to learn before but couldn't. At least she remembers her prior address. I don't remember any of my previous addresses. Some kind of homeless."

I gave a nervous laugh and regretted it immediately. I looked at the officer and saw a slight smile on her face.

"I hope you brought your copies of paperwork with you, so you know how get home." she joked.

I couldn't believe what was happening in that room. I only hoped she wasn't being sarcastic.

"We walked here," Andrew clarified. "Will walk back. My visual memory is good."

I didn't know his sense of humor was so daring. I was prepared for her to tell us to get out of the office, although she smiled instead and asked me how we met. I told her. She asked us a few more questions about hobbies, interests, and lifestyles. Then she marked my immigration applications and told us I would receive my temporary Green Card in three weeks via mail. We thanked her several times as we were leaving. I wanted to give her a hug, but I didn't. Her cold eyes turned smiley and she uttered, "Welcome to the United States."

"Thank you!" I uttered back. "Thank you! Thank you! Thank you!"

"Did I really get it? Did I understand her right?" I kept asking Andrew as we left the USCIS building.

"You did!" he shouted. "You did baby! You are a resident now! You ARE NOT illegal any more!"

"XX Duane Street, Apartment 21C, New York, NY, 10007!" I exclaimed. All of a sudden, my mind went back to clear and sharp.

"Good job baby. A little late though!" he commented, laughing.

I hugged him tightly and thanked for helping me out of my stupor. I had been waiting for this moment for long difficult years, imprisoned in my fears and prejudices. I didn't know whether it was going to happen or not, I carried on regardless. I was scared to give myself a hope, and at the same time it was just a hope that kept me going.

It was the most beautiful day of warm July of 2014. Andrew and I were walking home holding hands, and I wanted to memorize every moment of that walk. And each moment I memorized was worth all the struggle, unfairness, sacrifices, abuses, and other predicaments I went through.

"If only my mom was alive," Andrew murmured. "She would love you. She would absolutely adore you."

My temporary Green Card had never found me. It was lost on the way to our apartment. We spent hours on the phone, calling the immigration office and checking on its status. We filed the form for replacement of the unreceived card. Then there was silence for months. We called them to find out they never received the form. We sent another one and went to their center shortly after, and the friendly officer apologized for this inconvenience and told us there was some issue in the system, on which they were working.

In the endless race through that bureaucracy, the time to apply for the permanent Green Card came. The latter found us successfully. We were never called for the second interview, we were never asked for any additional papers, we just found it in the mail. I was crying and laughing the moment I held it in my hands for the first time. It had my name on it, my alien number, my picture. Just a small plastic card of a greenish color, as if I always had it, and yet years of mortal fights with myself and the world passed in order for me to walk this path till the end. Now it was over. I held my reward with tears. No more struggle. No more hopelessness. I was 29 years old and it was seven and a half years since I had arrived in this country.

By that time, Andrew and I became inseparable. We spent every weekend together, every morning and every night. We took a lot of vacations. We hiked and snowmobiled in Utah, we went on road trips to Main, Vermont, Niagara Falls, Michigan Lake. We walked along

Hudson River, holding hands, watching boats, ducks, swans, squirrels and people. He encouraged me to call my mom more often, he encouraged me to start writing a book. He kept saying I should just start and it will magically continue writing itself. He was right. He also encouraged me to move to St. Petersburg. Convincing me to do so became our everyday routine. He was raising this question more and more often, to the point that it became imminent.

"My father is dying, baby, and I need to take over the factory as soon as possible! It's my family business and it is the only thing that's left from my family. I can't sell it. And it makes so much money" he told me. He also told me, "St. Petersburg isn't like Astrakhan. It isn't like the rest of Russia. It's greater. It's sophisticated and fascinating. It's all about art and inspiration. You'll love it."

Since the moment we had met, he started talking about going back to Russia. He kept saying he had a Russian soul and felt like he belonged there. He never liked it in the U.S. He didn't hate it either. But he loved St. Petersburg. He always wanted to live there and raise his children there. And now, when I got my permanent residence, he insisted on going there immediately. We had no more time to lose, he said.

I wouldn't have to work, hence we could have as many kids as we want, we'd hire teachers and bilingual nannies, so we would be able to travel and enjoy our life inside and outside of the country. We would live in the most prestigious neighborhood in the city and drive comfortable cars. We would gain new friends and acquaintances. We would enjoy everything life has to offer and the most important, we would have each other. He always smiled, saying that. And this smile was lifting me up to the seventh heaven. I felt like I could go anywhere with him. Even to Russia.

This elation would go away as soon as my senses, along with logical reasoning, would return. I didn't want to live in Russia. I had enough of it. I achieved something I was only dreaming about, something that not everybody gets to achieve, something that now separated me from the unfortunate people who would have to live the rest of their lives in fear and hopelessness. I had never been to St. Petersburg before and it was on my list of places to visit, yet, only to visit, just like I wanted to see London, Paris, Berlin, Tokyo. There were so many places in the world I wanted to go to, but in-between and after this chain of trips, I wanted to come back to New York only. I didn't want to live in Russia. I loved America, it became my home, my shelter, my new homeland. I felt American, I felt I was my real self in the U.S.

Andrew began preparations for one of the most important steps in his life. He fled from his family, or whatever had left of it, almost two decades ago, and now, he was getting ready to come back and establish a new family there, a family of his own. I knew he would make a great father; I could totally imagine him playing with kids on weekends, helping them with homework during weekdays, being strict when needed. There was nothing in Andrew I didn't like.

One July's day, watching him putting some items for sale on the internet, I broke in tears and sat down on the floor next to the computer chair and cried, hugging his leg,

"Andrew, my love, my home, my everything, don't go!"

"Honey, aren't we going together?" he lifted me up and sat on his knees. "Try to look at the situation from outside of the box, you can be happy anywhere if you're happy within yourself. You only want to stay here, because you went through so much. But trust me, nobody will take away your Green Card, and we'll be coming back here once every half a year in order to keep it until you'll become a citizen."

I wanted to scream out of hopelessness. I hadn't been so lost in my entire life — for the first time I was standing on a junction of a crucial choice, and I didn't know what to do. I felt like a child lost in a big world, besides I was not a child and the big world was there, perfectly organized and comprehensive. My insomnia worsened again; I was waking up in the middle of the night in tears, that came from dreams of losing Andrew. I couldn't fall back asleep. Those moments I was waiting impatiently till mornings to tell him that I was going with him. Mornings would dry out my tears and turn my initial desires back on.

Why is that everything in my life gets ruined? I shouted silently. I thought I had finally found my happiness under the American sun. But that happiness was fleeing to the Russian sun as butterflies fly to the light. My unmerciful question was which light to choose.

"It's all up to you, Katyusha," said Andrew after weeks of negotiations and hopes that one of us would change the other's mind. He had a serious and considerate face. "I totally understand your concerns…"

We were standing in the middle of the kitchen that shiny Sunday morning, ignoring our breakfast and freshly boiled coffee. I wore a long sleeveless shirt that slightly covered my knees, my husband was in his navy-blue pajamas that smelled like soap and cotton.

"Who the fuck are you talking to? I'm not your employee to talk to me as a boss," I interrupted him with the shouts I didn't recognize. "You and your concerns should go back to where they came from! You simply don't love me!"

"Shh," Andrew uttered and came closer to me, trying to grab my hand.

"Don't touch me!" I yelled. "Why didn't you tell me in the very beginning, on the first date, that you're such a Russia-lover? I would find someone normal, not a weirdo-patriot like you. You are a traitor, you got it? A traitor!"

"Katyusha, listen to me," he started.

"I don't want to listen to you! I hate you!"

He tried to hug me, but I stepped back. He quit his attempts. I stood in the middle of that kitchen, crying, not knowing what to do, not knowing where to go and whether there was a point in going anywhere. Tears were all over my swollen face. I felt sick and destroyed. I only wanted that pain to end with any aftermath. Then short but heavy days began pressing me — one after another.

Andrew woke me up early in the morning. I opened my eyes to his kind smile.

"It's time to go," he said.

I unwillingly turned my head towards the electronic clock on our night stand. It was no o'clock. I couldn't eat anything but had a few sips of coffee. Yellow leaves got mixed with street trash. It was slightly chilling. We got in a cab and warm air brought light relief. Andrew embraced me; I did the same. I was holding back my tears.

New York looked different that early morning. Light fog covered all buildings, stores, not-yet-opened restaurants, homeless people and cars. The city was still sleeping.

"Which terminal?" asked an Indian accent.

"First." Andrew murmured.

He squeezed me stronger. I squeezed him back, and a puddle of tears started forming on his shoulder.

"I love you," I mumbled, not being able to speak louder.

"I love you too, baby," he almost whispered. "Everything is gonna be all right."

That ride to the airport was the fastest I had ever experienced. I laid my head on Andrew's wet shoulder and closed my eyes. It was too painful to keep them open. He was kissing my forehead and repeating, "Everything will be all right. Everything will be all right." The cab driver pulled out suitcases and wished us a good flight. We entered JFK airport.

Everything was so familiar and unfamiliar at the same time. People, rushing around, suitcases of different sizes and colors, scattered all over the airport; lines to customs, registers, and Andrew right by me, as a guru in the big and difficult world. We cradled each other, getting further in a long, but fast-moving line to a baggage check-in. My sage was stroking my hair, which calmed me down a bit. I took a big breath before we checked-in two suitcases.

We walked towards the lane that led to customs and froze by its entrance, next to the point of no return, that separated passengers from accompaniers. Andrew looked away into nowhere with his eyes full of ineffable sadness, and I thought, it was the very end of a beautiful journey. I suddenly felt so little in that huge airport with strangers all around. We took one step aside, to let other passengers pass, and merged into each other. I felt his heart pounding. My eyes were sore.

"Andrew, my love," I begged him, "maybe we don't have to do this!?"

"Shshshs," he let out and squeezed me harder, and kissed my forehead.

Then he looked at me, holding my chin up. His eyes were full of tears. I had never seen him crying before.

"Take a good care of yourself, promise?" he pronounced with his voice breaking.

"Andrew, I love you more than anything," I burst out of crying. "I'm sorry I called you a traitor. And I lied when I said I hated you! Forgive me for everything I said that morning, I didn't mean any of it, I didn't…"

"I know. I know," he murmured with his gentle voice. "I love you more than anything, too."

I was trying to calm down, but it seemed stronger than me. I took a few gulps of air.

"Please, promise to me, you are not going to drink no matter how bad you will feel." he said, looking deep into my eyes. "Promise you won't hurt yourself in any other way. I want you to live a healthy life in the country you always wanted to live. I want you to start writing. I want you to acknowledge that 29 is not a lot. You are at the beginning of your life and life is a very interesting journey in which you'll meet a lot of great people and will do a lot of amazing things. Just promise to take care of yourself in order for all this to happen."

I was feeling dizzy from all the crying. My eyes were hurting, I fixed them on his brown eyeballs and breathed, "I promise."

"I promise! I promise! I promise, Andrew." I repeated helplessly.

"It will be very empty when you'll return home, Katyusha." Andrew articulated calmly. "But I just want you to know, this feeling will go away. It might seem, it won't, but it will. Try not to stay alone. Call the girls. Go for a walk. Just don't imprison yourself in this sadness, okay?"

I nodded helplessly.

"Baby, don't listen to anybody who will accuse either you or me of some sort of wrongdoing. We loved each other. And I will still love you for a very long time, until this feeling will get worn out without your presence and will turn into a beautiful memory. We tried our best to be together, but it is impossible. I want to live in Russia and you won your reward here. This is where you belong. This is your home now. And it takes a lot of courage for me to admit it and to let you go.

I never wanted to let you go. Our marriage, our relationship was the most beautiful thing that ever happened to me. It made my life unbelievably beautiful. And I'll keep this beauty with me, I'll keep it in my heart for as long as I'll be able to."

I wiped my tears with fingers.

"Andrew, to be honest, I thought you will change your mind and will stay here." I emitted. I wanted to say how badly I wanted my mom to meet him. My mom, who would love him as her own son. My mom, who would be grateful for our union, and one day, would hold her grandchild with love and admiration. I wanted to tell him that I was so proud of him always being so sane and wise. I wanted to say I was so proud to be his wife. But I couldn't make a sound. I only hugged him, and feeling the warmth of his body, murmured, "Thank you for everything you have done for me."

The registration for the flight got closed. Most of the people had already passed through customs, and empty lanes were indicating it was time to go. He smiled through tears and I did the same, then he kissed me in the forehead, then he turned around and stepped over the line, showing his ticket to a chubby woman in a blue blouse, who was standing right next to it. He walked towards customs in his navy polo-shirt and black cotton pants. He never turned back. He handed his passport to an officer, then stored it in his pocket, then grabbed a blue bin and walked towards an x-ray machine. Then I could no longer see him.

I went towards the exit of the airport, but along the way, I found myself lightheaded. I sat on the first available bench, feeling lost and confused. My body didn't seem to belong to me any more, my feet were weak, my ears were clogged, I could barely see through my exhausted eyes. A random family took the rest of the bench. I couldn't move. I've heard children's laughter, loud conversation in a language I didn't understand.

You will learn to live without him, I said to myself. You will learn to live without him.

I bent down and put my elbows on my lap. I rested my forehead on my knees and recalled that distant and recent Sunday morning in the kitchen of now empty apartment and "I hate you!" shouted in my voice. I recalled Andrew trying helplessly to embrace me. I recalled myself sobbing in the middle of the kitchen, praying for all that to finish. A few seconds later I was hitting him in the chest, to remove myself from those strong arms I would never feel again. After seconds of that soundless fight, Andrew squeezed me so tight, that I couldn't breathe.

"It's all right, it's all right," he pronounced angrily, but calmly. "I know! I'm also in pain, trust me. I'm also in pain."

I stopped my attempts to break free.

"But we have to continue living, Katyusha! Life doesn't end. There are losses like this in life, but there are also good things, and those good things are truly worth living." he uttered. "Life is beautiful, and we need to enjoy every moment of it — together or separately. What's most important is that we met each other, we got to know what real love is. Most people die without ever experiencing this priceless knowledge."

"You will always have a special place in my heart," he breathed.

I kissed his neck and inhaled deeply — we had a couple of weeks of each other.

Now it was over. No more of each other, only endless emptiness in hearts. I don't remember how I made it home as if an invisible autopilot had delivered me there. I was afraid of entering our bedroom, I couldn't bear to see the kitchen, I went to the living room. My swollen face was hurting. I had no more strength to cry. It was too empty inside, and knowing it wasn't temporary, knowing he would never come back, gave me a strange feeling as if he had died. It was too empty to stay awake. I passed out as soon as my head touched the surface of the couch.

Andrew and I agreed not to communicate in order not to hurt each other more. Both of us wanted to settle down in one place and have a family there. Sadly, nothing could convince him to sell the factory, furthermore, to unlove St. Petersburg. Even me. I was first very upset that he cherished Russia more than he cherished me. Until I realized that the same way, nothing could convince me to move back to Russia. And it didn't mean that I loved America more than I loved him. These were two different loves. I put most of my youth fighting for the right to be American. I abandoned everything I knew and loved before in order to win this outrageous battle, and I wasn't ready to give away my reward. Even for him. None of us yielded. None of us could.

We filed for divorce a few weeks before our kitchen's conversation, and since we had no complications, we were granted it very fast. We only exchanged melancholic smiles and stored the decree away from our visual accessibility. Then our final countdown began.

CHAPTER 15.5

Dear Andrew,

Weeks have passed since we parted, but I don't miss you any less. I think about us every single day. There was no morning I woke up without recalling your kiss in my forehead. There was no night I didn't imagine being in your strong and gentle arms. Arms, in which I wanted to fall asleep every night. Arms, in which I wanted to live forever. Not a single dream had passed without you in it. These memories are following me everywhere, they make my morning coffee, they eat my lunch with me, the escort me to work, they put me to bed, they tell me to start writing. You are everywhere. I didn't know that feelings could hurt so much, I didn't know that one could be so wounded by mutual love. I never loved anyone mutually and I always thought of this kind of love as the best thing that could happen to anyone. It is. And it is not. I feel like a bird that fell from the sky and forgot how to fly. I no longer have a nest. And I thought about reaching out to you and making it to your nest across the ocean, but I couldn't, Andrew, I couldn't. My home is here, far from yours. We are not lovers, we are not friends, we are two people who got scattered over the continents and are now learning to live from the beginning in different time-zones, different nations, speaking completely different languages. We soon will acquire new friends and acquaintances, new habits and desires, tastes and preferences. We will eventually experience another infatuation, or maybe a real love; we will meet new people we might want to become partners with and produce brand-new lives together, and our feelings for each other will fade away. But before it happens, before we become strangers, I want to tell you that I'm letting you go with tenderness in heart, Andrew. It means that I'm sincerely blessing you to be happy in your new life. It means that I wish St. Petersburg will treat you well and love you back as much as you love it. It means that I want you to meet a wonderful woman who will give you adorable kids and who will have a beautiful kind heart — just like your mom's. I wish you to spend a lot of priceless time with this fragile and loving heart. I never told you that my mom would love you too. That she would treat you as her own son, and she wouldn't imagine any better person for her daughter. I never told you that I wanted my child to have your brown eyes and your serious smile. I never told you that our wedding day was the happiest occasion in my life and you were the best person I've ever been with. Please, forgive me for not saying it all on time. Forgive me for not accepting your love for Russia and for not respecting your decision to go back there. Forgive me for being selfish and for not giving you my blessing. Forgive me for contacting you regardless of our agreement and inviting you to this sudden and strange party (the invitation is attached). And I'm forgiving you in advance for not coming to it.

Dear friend!

You definitely remember a shy tall blond Russian girl who barely spoke English, frequently changed jobs and apartments, fighting for her place under this beautiful American Sun. In case if you were wondering what happened to her, I'm going to inform you, I finally made it. I became a permanent resident and wrote a book. It took me ages of constant struggle for survival and battle with everything, including my own self, in order for you to receive this invitation.

I'd love to see you before I depart to visit my homeland for the first time in long eight years, so please, join me for my Arrival-Departure Party at "EverythingIsPossible" restaurant at 12345 7th ave, at 6 pm on February 20, 2017.

Alcoholic and non-alcoholic beverages will be served all night long, along with vegan, vegetarian, pescatarian and everything-tarian dishes. So, please, come hungry and thirsty.

Feel free to bring your significant others, if you don't have any, just bring yourself.

See you soon!

Always yours,

Ekaterina Ivanova.

I won't tire you with details of how I managed to find everyone, and furthermore, convince them to come. It took me a lot of time, strength, and connections to find some characters, it took me no effort at all to find the others. There were a few who found me themselves. Most of the guests came from New York, some made it here from different states, and some arrived from other countries.

I had an irresistible desire to throw this party once I came to a realization that I was not that poor little illegal girl any more. I finally had my rights, and it was my basic right to gather everyone who participated in my eight-year-long way to this very moment. I wanted to see everyone who made my way the way it was and contributed into my today's character before my plane will take off and fly me to Russia for the first time. I wanted to thank every single person for being in my difficult immigrant's life as, without all of them and each in particular, this book wouldn't be written.

FEBRUARY 20TH. EVERYTHINGISPOSSIBLE RESTAURANT.

"Fired!"

A silence of uncertainty passed.

"I said, you are fired!"

"But he is… he no work here."

"I said, fired!" The Queen shouted with anger at James, then she turned to Adil and added calmly, "And you are fired, my dear."

Then she reclined in the wheelchair and closed her eyes. She froze in this position, and it appeared that she had fallen asleep. Adil and James browsed her with curiosity for a little while, then James took the last swig of his beer and asked the diplomat whether he needed anything from the bar. After the negative answer, he walked away from the confusing scene. He looked much skinnier than I remembered him. He wore blue jeans and a grey sweater. His beard had grown thick and curly, so did his brown hair. If he weren't so skinny, he would look like a bear.

Adil stood by The Queen for another minute, watching her face, her outfit. She wore a colorful blouse and reddish lipstick, long dark skirt, and sneakers without shoelaces. Seeing her dressed up felt unusual, but pleasant. I hoped she was enjoying it outside of the hospital. It looked like Adil was waiting for her to wake up, and as she did not show any signs of awakening, he gave up, smiled, shook his head, and left. He stopped by the bar and got a can of Coca-Cola. He told the bartender he didn't want a glass. His baldness was shining as it was polished. His navy suit was perfectly tailored and ironed. He wore a dark-red tie. It had been seven years since I had last seen him. The time didn't change him much, it only made him wider and heavier. His eyebrows had grown ticker. But his smile was the same. He reminded me of King's Highway, Dmitry, and the hateful job I had to do. The memory of our last encounter made me feel extremely embarrassed.

Shawn and Laurine passed by the bar and stopped by the window. There was a beautiful winter happening outside. It had gotten dark early, and a bright light of the streetlamps illuminated white sparkling snowflakes dancing in the air without order. I could see Shawn's wife was pregnant. Shawn looked happy. He was still tall and dark-haired. A short mustache appeared above his upper lip. He wore a black bottom-up shirt and black pants. Adil walked toward them once he recognized Shawn.

"Hello, my friend!" he exclaimed.

It took my friend a few moments to recall the diplomat, but as he did, he shook his hand warmly. Adil got introduced to Laurine, acknowledged her pregnancy, and then asked Shawn, "Are you work Queens still? You police?"

"No," Shawn answered, smiling. "We live in Florida. We have a small laundry business there."

"Oh," Adil commented. "I thought you determined police service."

Shawn gave a laugh then cleared his throat. "I was, but my wife got fired from our precinct, so I left shortly after. Lots of BS there. Cops have no respect for volunteers like me. And no respect for people in general... Not all, but most of New York cops."

"I see," Adil said thoughtfully. "You like laundry?"

Both Shawn and Laurine laughed. Adil smiled to their laughter. His English became worse.

"It's okay. It feeds us and pays our bills. And we know we will always have income."

"Yeah," Adil articulated loudly. "Everybody young first dream, they dream one job, rich, they all or nothing, no plan B. When older, they think what tomorrow bring. They know food, bills, apartment, children… they think for practical job and steady income. You good, very good business."

"But if you have a really big dream and a talent for it, you shouldn't give up at any cost," Laurine remarked. I thought she must have had a dream of her own.

Adil grinned at her and nodded. He looked at her face for a while. This look made her uncomfortable and she stepped closer to Shawn, who immediately wrapped his arm around her.

Dr Holington ran to The Queen as he spotted her left alone. She woke up, looked at him, and murmured, "You are my little baby girl". He grabbed the push handles and took her to the other side of the restaurant. It was quieter and emptier. The music wasn't loud. I could hear everything people said. The doctor had slightly grown his hair and brushed it back. It was still chocolate, and it was very shiny. He wore black pants and a black shirt. His eyes were still sparkling blue. He didn't look any older. It had been about 3,5 years since we parted in that quiet hospital room. Vera stopped by him as she was passing by. The doctor smiled at her and she smiled back. Then a very Russian "Hello" bumped into her from behind. She turned around and made eye contact with Dmitry.

"Hey," she mumbled without much enthusiasm.

"I didn't recognize you! I didn't know you're in the U.S," Dmitry uttered lively. He was dressed in dressy black pants and tight light-pink shirt. His teeth were still perfectly white and his hair perfectly blond.

Vera never liked him and now she didn't seem to enjoy the conversation with the smiley and flirty young man either. He asked her a lot of meaningless questions, after which he inquired what she was doing in the country. She said she was studying in a medical school for a cardiologist. Her dark hair grew long, and she made it curly for the party. She had gained some weight which gave her a very feminine look. Her big green eyes were examining Dmitry with annoyance and curiosity.

"Nice!" he exclaimed and answered Vera's unasked question. "And I am a model. I do underwear and nude. Kinda more erotic. All booked for the month."

I didn't know why he was telling her all that and I assumed, my friend didn't know it either. It looked like she did her best to break free from his company as soon as possible. I began to laugh as she made eye contact with me. She walked to me and squeezed me in her arms.

"I never understood what you found in him," she stated. "Full of himself!"

"Whatever it was," I said calmly, "it's over."

Everythingispossible restaurant consisted of a massive hall and a long glass wall through which one could see a beautiful snowy February with sparks in the air and yellow cabs on the ground from the inside, and dozens of people of different shapes, colors, and ages from the outside. If one would take a better look from the outside, then one would see an open bar on the right side of the massive hall, two long and one short tables by the glass wall on the other side of it. The first long table was full of cold and warm food, which, time-to-time, was being checked and replaced by waiters, the second one contained snacks, fruits and desserts, and the third was all about Rita, I decorated it with her paintings, all three of them, and a medium-sized photograph of her smiley animated face. This face looked more alive than dozens and dozens of others I got to know, it looked like it was going to wink, grin, and say, "you guys really thought you got rid of me, huh?" There were a few smaller round tables with chairs around them in between the end of the hall, the bar, and the glass wall which separated my guests from strangers on the dark winter street. These very guests were strangers at some point in my life too, and I couldn't say how much of "strangeness" still remained between us, I couldn't say whether it would change or go away, all I knew was they were entering the restaurant one after another, giving me instant recollections of my past with every movement of the door. I know, I told you I had never seen some of them again. Well, till now.

The crowd was slowly thickening. People were getting more and more engaged in interactions with alcohol, food and each other. Leisurely walking Ron accidentally hit Adil with his chubby arm and briefly apologized. His belly looked much bigger than when I last met him, his hair grew almost till the middle of his back; he seemed like he was enjoying himself. He wore a sleeveless leather shirt of red color and shiny black jeans. Unlike my expectations, he came to the party alone.

Adil stepped toward my ex-boss and asked, "You know... do you know where Kate... Ekaterina?"

Ron looked around, but didn't see me, and said, "I don't know. She always disappear. She come, it's she party."

It didn't take Ron too long to browse around and notice Sherry. She was holding a conversation with Bartek and Polly. My ex-boyfriend was entertaining women by telling something funny, gesticulating and making amusing faces. Sherry was laughing non-stop. I couldn't hide a smile. Queens of my life had happened to be a short period, but memorable, the first, the most challenging time in getting to know New York, and perhaps, the whole country of immigrants.

Snezhana and her son, Eduard, brought a huge bouquet of flowers. They immediately told something to one of the waiters, he nodded, carried away the flowers and returned with a big vase which barely fitted everything. They looked around, and not spotting me anywhere, went to the table with food. Snezhana was stylish as always. She cut her brown-burgundy hair shorter and now it ended on the level of her jaw. Her thin lips were dark brown, she wore another tight suit of cherry color. She was ageless. She always knew what to say, what to do. She was sane and consistent, and all these qualities looked beautiful on her. She and Eduard filled two plates with pasta and vegan sausages and sat at the available table. Eduard was mostly playing with his phone which was almost the size of a tablet.

"I'm a queen, and this is my kingdom," The Queen drove by them, making a brief eye-contact with Eduard, which somewhat puzzled him.

"You. Are. Fired!" she yelled at Snezhana.

Snezhana laughed, "Okay."

"Do you know her?" I heard startled Eduard inquiring as The Queen moved further away from them. He seemed a bit anxious.

"Long story." she smiled. "I'll tell you one day."

Snezhana's eyes got closed by someone's palms from behind.

"Guess!" Eduard yelled to help the "behinder"

Snezhana started to laugh, then tried to remove the palms. "Katya!"

"Failed!" Natasha uttered and gave five to Eduard.

"What's up dude?" he asked her.

"Nothing much," she hugged Snezhana, then sat at the same table. Then she got up and grabbed a plate and food, and sat back with friends. She wore a stylish fit black suit and a red bowtie, which matched her shoes. Her ginger hair was short and curly. Her smile was wide and genuine.

I saw Ted at the bar. He drank some dark liquid from a short glass and kept the corners of his lips up. I barely recognized him, the first person who met me in Worcester after my eternity-long and a blink-of-an-eye quick bus ride from the capital of the world, the very place which I didn't know would become my home and the very ride which took away my childhood and pushed me into the universe of unknown.

"Hi Ted," I approached him quietly.

He turned to me and smiled so warmly.

"Heeey, Ekaterina!" he said, hugging me. "How long has it been since I met you?"

"Literally 8 years and 1.5 months!" I uttered happily.

"Poor thing, you haven't been home at all for all these years?"

"Nope."

"I can imagine you must miss your family and your friends so much." he verbalized it with so much compassion.

"Very much," I answered. "I even miss every street. Every building. Every tree in my neighborhood. And I can't believe I'm finally going there."

"You look so different from that girl who I met at the station in Worcester. Your eyes have become very mature. Even when you smile, your eyes stay serious and alert. This is the sign that you became a strong fighter. You won all your battles and now you know how to fight to win. I'm very proud of you!" he disclosed with authentic compassion, and smiled, and raised his glass slightly.

"Thank you for your kind words. You are probably right. I'm too alert. I learned too much," I responded. "How are you doing? How are things in Clark?"

"Oh, I stopped working there about three years ago. I retired and moved to California. I've heard they closed the program that brought you here. Not a lot of students from Russia could afford to come here, so it became useless."

"I didn't know. Makes sense. Well, I don't mean to complain, but in my case the whole thing was useless. I never got any use of this degree neither professionally nor legally."

He gave a laugh. I gave a laugh as well. Then he nodded. I was sure he had heard similar stories. I let him enjoy himself and went to collect new moments, some of which I would want to keep in my memory forever.

"Ron," he declared with soft voice as he approached Bartek, Polly, and Sherry. "What a lovely couple and what a beautiful woman all alone!"

Sherry smiled awkwardly, while my Polish guest shook Ron's hand.

"Why she all alone? What she name?" my Trinidadian fellow got closer to my former landlady. I could see she didn't feel comfortable as he stepped too close to her, and somehow, his intention was too obvious. Then Shawn and Laurine approached them. I felt an immediate relief. Two Caribbean men gave each other a prolonged hug, then everyone got introduced to one another.

The crowd of guests was growing bigger and bigger, louder and louder. An elderly couple I babysit for walked in; they looked decades older. A worn-out pale boy was holding his mother's hand. I assumed; they couldn't afford a nanny. The boy ran to the table with food once he saw it, but the couple began looking around as they were carefully examining each part of the restaurant and people. Eventually they walked to the bar. Vera greeted them as she heard them speaking Russian. They exchange a few praises and smiles. Then my friend recognized Ted and they exchanged warm hugs. They started having a lively conversation. Then Chicago's police officer walked in. I jerked out of the excitement and ran to him at once.

"Hello officer!" I yelled, swimming through the crowd of other guests. He looked around for a few seconds as he was trying to distinguish where that voice was coming from.

"Officer!" I vocalized quieter as I approached him from the side. He looked at me and melted in smile. He hugged me tight and held for a while. His arms felt strong and safe.

"I was so pleased to learn that you finally got legalized in this country," he said firmly but kindly. His voice sounded so familiar — I heard it only once in reality but rehearsed it dozens of times in my mind.

I wanted to cry out of his warm-heartedness and compassion, out of his existence.

"Thanks to you, officer!" I uttered holding back tears.

"No, thanks to you," he declared stepping back as to take a better look at me, still holding my elbow in his big warm palms. "This country needs people like you, warm-hearted, talented, smart, and full of good intentions. America needs you. We need you."

I smiled. He smiled back, keeping his eyes fixed on mine. His pair of faded eyes was shining. And it was not due to tears or pain, there was something else which filled them with life.

"I was as well pleased to be invited to the party. It is so kind of you to think of me." he stated happily, "So welcome to this country! I hope it will love you as much as you love it. That's what struck me that night in the car when I was driving you to the precinct — the energy of your love and devotion to America. The energy of your good intentions. Not every immigrant has it. And not all those who have it, get what they want. Frankly speaking, this country is not completely fair to the immigrants. So that night in the car, listening to your speech, I realized how unfair it had happened to be to you and decided that the least I could do for you would be treating you fairly on behalf of my country and myself. Now, looking at you and all these people that care about you, I can say I made the right decision that night."

He smiled warmly, nodded, squeezed my arms and then removed his hands from them. He wrapped his arm around the tall pale-skinned blond woman next to him.

"This is my wife, Agnes," he said. His small eyes were sparkling like a Christmas tree. His wide forehead was rested, and the deep wrinkles didn't seem that extensive. He looked much younger than that frightening and kind night, even though 3,5 years had passed. His wife seemed happy. It must be great to be married to one of the most goodhearted men. I gave her a warm hug and thanked her for coming along.

I wanted to call everyone's attention to my savior, but he stopped me from doing that. He asked me to keep it a secret, he desperately didn't want to admit the fact my American dream came true partially because of him. He was firm and clear. Wide and tall.

"What is your name?" I finally asked him after long years of blaming myself for not knowing more about that kindest person, who gave me a second chance. Not once, I recalled the nameless police officer in the middle of the dark, deserted area, watching me walking away into freedom, jeopardizing his own career.

"Michael," he smiled. "Mike, to be more Americanized."

I laughed with both joy and sadness. I told the couple to enjoy themselves. I let them walk towards the bar, and I myself approached Kostya and Eduard. Eduard had just turned 14. His hair was less than half inch long, he wore baggy jeans and a black sweater. He was tall and skinny. He resembled bold Kostya and his usual outfit, although the latter wore a suit for the party. Eduard looked up to Kostya and copied him in many ways. Kostya became a good friend to the boy and remained him even after things didn't work out between him and Snezhana.

"Fired!" Eduard yelled at me as I approached them. Kostya and I gave a laugh.

Sherry joined us. It felt like time didn't change her at all. She looked no different than 7,5 years ago. Tall, slim, with short dark hair, big eyes and thick shiny lips. I felt like I had never left Jamaica. Just like yesterday, I was standing in front of her and explaining that I was broke, but I had a master's from Clark hence I'd find a job soon. Then I was telling her I would definitely be visiting her. And now she was telling me, "I was waiting for you to stop by, sweetie! You told me you would! I hope I was not a bad host?"

"Not at all! You were a great host."

"That's good to know. I called you a few months later, after you left, but the number was not in service. I was hoping you were all right, my dearest."

"I'm so sorry I disappeared like that," I explained. "I went through a really tough time. I had to change my number. Then other unpleasant things started happening one by one, so I got carried away with all that stuff. But I always remembered about you, Sherry. You were my first home in New York."

She smiled and stroked my arms tenderly. "I know, honey. Life in New York is tough. What I want to say is that you owe me lots of stories!"

We laughed. I surely have a lot of them. I thought of probably visiting her after my trip to Russia. She also said Ron was rather disturbing and she didn't wish to interact with him. I gave her my silent permission to show it off to him. She told me she lived in the same house and pretty much the same stewards rented rooms time to time, she started an affair with one of them, although he was in the air at the moment. She opened a small souvenir store on Jamaica Avenue. She would show it to me when I would visit her. It's only a ten-minute walk from her house.

Natasha and Danielle interacted with Shawn and Laurine. I was happy to see that my friend was in peace with them. The conflict was over. No hard feelings were left. Natasha and Dannie got married in a year after Andrew and I got married, and a few months later same-sex marriages went on the federal level, which enabled them to file a petition for Natasha's Green Card. I had never seen her crying out of happiness. I had never known her so grateful and so life-loving. She finally got so many rights. All of a sudden, she became a normal person, and she could love and be proud of who she loved. She informed her family but got no response back. She said she got used to the thought that she had no past, no family, no Russia.

"Ekaterina," I heard Adil's voice and automatically embraced him. He embraced me as well and stroked my back for a while. A wave of recollection of our last encounter made me feel embarrassed and I hoped he wouldn't bring it up.

"I'm glad you were able to make it from Turkey!" I exclaimed. "How have you been?"

"Very good! Retirement... sea... house... very nice!" Adil uttered, giggling.

"I'm glad you're enjoying yourself there!" I said.

"Ekaterina," Adil hesitated with the face expression as if something painful came to his mind. I strained at once.

"Please, forgive me... that day... I you met in that apartment."

I looked away in embarrassment.

"When I left, I come downstairs and was stand for long time. I was stand for maybe 30 minutes. I thought I must come back. Come back and take you from there. I almost come back, I walked one floor up and was stand there. Then I thought what will I say her? I said all I could. She just want to stay here. I felt upset because you beautiful smart girl but do this dirty job. But I left. I come Turkey but I feel so upset still. I blamed myself I let you stay there. I blame myself I let you go from our very nice Kings Highway apartment. I did not protect you. I'm so sorry, Ekaterina. I didn't mean left you. I didn't know... how bad you was."

It was an unexpected surprise that touched my heart. I had tremendous trauma from that dirty job and I will definitely work on it, but as for that moment, I felt better. Lighter.

"Thank you so much for your kind words, Adil!" I responded to his confession. "I felt very upset with myself that I had to do it. It was really bad. I had no money for food. I ate one Snickers a day and couldn't afford anything else. And I was really scared to think about what I was to do after I'd finish my last Snickers. I was so new to this country. I didn't know anything. I was afraid of homelessness. I was afraid of everything."

He bowed his head down and covered his eyes with one hand.

"Hey," I murmured, patting his shoulder. "I didn't mean to complain, I just wanted to tell you what pushed me there. I never thought life would force me to do such a thing. But I'm not there any more. I'm here, celebrating being legal and free with you and dozens of others."

He blew his nose in a handkerchief and nodded. "The bigger the dream, the harder the path."

"That's true."

"And I came over that your dirty job apartment only once. I don't come such place. Only once before Turkey, I don't know why. Just came to try. Saw you, never again, Ekaterina." he faltered. "Never again such place here or Turkey."

"You don't have to explain it to me, Adil. I won't judge you even if I'd know you go to these places."

"I don't go!" he uttered. "I think, poor girl who work there. No money, tough life, maybe one Snickers a day — the same, no-good diet. Will never go!"

I gave a sad laugh. He hugged me again. I stroked his back.

"Are you dating anyone?" I asked to change the topic.

"I retire, finish construction at home, then when it very nice, I go date so I can invite."

I grinned, he grinned back. I left him to socialize with people. I felt slightly upset after that conversation. And at the same time, somewhat forgiven and understood.

"I'm so sorry," I heard a shy fragile voice that spoke Russian. It was the old man I babysit for. I turned around with the strained smile. He looked very pale and very old. I was trying to assume his age, but gave up.

"I… when I told you… I meant for you to earn more money. Please, don't take me wrong." he murmured, smiling with polite altruistic smile. "And please, don't tell my wife. You know… I was thinking about your wellbeing… immigrant's life is hard, so I wanted to give you a chance. That's it."

His wife was browsing Rita's paintings, and the child was sitting quietly on a chair all alone.

I thanked him for that chance and said that, besides him, I had met a lot of other people which gave me such chances, which I had to refuse. These chances are very offensive and annoying. I told him that it would be helpful if before offering people chances, he would ask himself whether he would want his son to be given a chance like that If the answer is no, maybe it's better to keep such chances to himself.

The man stared at me in frustration. I nodded and walked away. There were so many people I wanted to communicate with. There was so much excitement, so much past and so much present. I had never been so present before. Not even with loved ones, I thought, as I heard a very familiar "Katyusha" from behind. I turned around and saw Dmitry. He looked all the same, besides, this time he held two faded away roses he probably quickly fetched at the pharmacy across the street. He smelled like spring, Astrakhan, and betrayal.

"I'm so sorry for the last time, I was…." he began with a modest, but shiny smile.

"It's okay," I interrupted, feeling annoyed. I grabbed his arm and walked him to Diane and Dan Sullivan who I had noticed a while before talking to Adil. They stood by the fruit part of the table, each holding a glass of champagne.

"Oh, darling," Diane exclaimed as she saw me approaching, "I missed you terribly. I wanted to contact you, but I thought you got mad at me. I just needed some time to accept the fact that you guys… you know."

She murmured the last sentence. And Dan looked away in awkwardness. She wore a short black dress with her breasts almost fully exposed. She looked older than I remembered her. Dan wore a black suit.

"Dmitry," I suggested, winking at her. "He is a model."

"And a very passionate lover," I added with a smile, wondering along the way whether it was nice of me to act this way. Then I thought that it was my party and I could do anything I want.

Diane and Dan stared at each other while Dmitry gave me a look of frustration. He kept holding the two worn-out flowers and it seemed like he didn't know what on earth he should do with them.

"You guys should get to know each other," I vocalized, holding back my laughter. Then I stepped back. Three pairs of eyes stared at me in confusion. I truly wanted them to get to know each other, my abandoned memories which have something in common. It's me, who created them and it's me who brought them together. A few moments later their lips started moving in each other's direction. First, shy smiles started appearing on their faces, then Dmitry nodded, told them he'd be right back, and came to me.

"You know. I know, you have the right to be so upset with me. But you're not the only one who was abandoned, I was abandoned too!" he stated firmly and continued uttering. "I had never told you that, because I didn't want our past to be on the way. But I did feel very hurt! That afternoon I ran to one pharmacy, they didn't have all items you needed, so I ran to another one to find the rest. After I stopped by three different pharmacies, I returned home, but you were gone. There were no suitcases, nothing. I fell into depression. I spent a few days in bed. I was picking up all calls, hoping it's you! I knew that the Turk knew something, and I was trying to get at least something out of him, but he played stupid, 'Ekaterina I don't' know, maybe go Russia'. I also realized he was into you. I realized it a long time ago. The way he was talking about you. Asking about you. I followed him a few times he went somewhere during evenings, but those were all bars where he sat alone and drank coke from the can. And I moved out."

"I didn't know that. I left because you started blackmailing me! Don't you remember?"

"I understand, but we could sit down and talk or something. I mean, I just want to tell you I was heartbroken and abandoned as well."

"That's why you left me later, to take revenge?"

"No, I'm not fifteen years old to take that kind of revenge. I left because Karon spotted us. And we had no future at that time anyways. So, I just hung in there. When we broke up, I found you the first thing. But you were about to get married. It made me upset. Sorry, I told you stuff, but I didn't mean any of it. I don't want you to get raped again."

I nodded.

"Are you married still?"

"No. I'm enjoying being single." I smiled. He wanted to say something else, yet I interrupted him and murmured, "Go back to them. She might find you lots of designers to model for. And he is very open-minded."

Dmitry smiled first, then uttered, "I'm not gay!"

"I'm saying he is open to sharing his wife with another person." I clarified. Dmitry kissed me on my cheek and said, "See you around!" And went back to the Sullivans.

Everything looked surreal. Years and chapters of my life were socializing with each other right there, all in the same spot, in front of me, as they were showing that everything was possible, and even impossible things do happen to prove it. I felt like a guest at my own party. Time froze in the moment which was absolutely mine. So many faces I thought I'd never see again. So many faces I did not want to see again. I saw James, chatting with Dr Holington and Sherry. I saw Shawn and Lauren discussing something with Vera and Kostya, they all looked happy. I was trying to recall whether Shawn and Kostya had met in the past before Natasha left him but couldn't. My mind was so overwhelmed. I saw Lina and waved at her. The woman with very kind eyes from the Russian brothel approached Lina. A slight worry that people would find out how I knew her went through my mind, then it vanished away. It's okay. I don't care any more. I did what I did, and I couldn't do otherwise. That was a big chapter of my life and it's already written. A few years after, Snezhana will tell Eduard everything about that business — he will understand and accept it, because her past is a part of who she is and maybe a part of who he is. Because everyone deserves love. Because life doesn't come with instructions.

Eduard is into skateboarding and music. He is growing into a good, strong, and kind man, a gentleman who since his early years never allowed his mom to carry a heavy bag, or to use a drill, or to hang a painting. He wants to become a rock singer. He has an electric guitar, he writes songs, he promised to give us a concert sometime in the future. He speaks mostly English but understands and tolerates Russian very well. Snezhana never speaks English with him, not a single word. She said he will thank her for it eventually. She also says she is happy he became such good friends with Kostya. Kostya is a good person to learn life from, he is well-mannered, respectful, considerate, and kind. Even too kind. It became the reason they broke up. She couldn't tolerate his willingness to help everyone in need. A few times in two years while they were dating, he went to his former girlfriend to help with her computer and with carrying her furniture around. He went to airports to meet friends, friends of friends, and even acquaintances of acquaintances. He helped others with painting walls, setting up dishwashers, replacing lightbulbs and other things one might need help with. Snezhana grew very irritated with him being available to everyone all the time. She kept saying that people were overusing his kindness and he kept promising to value his and her time more but continued staying "on call". He just couldn't say no. They had to cancel a few dinners, and evenings together, and she realized she had enough. She didn't want to date a wuss any more. Half year after the break-up, at the party, she said she might give him another chance if she'll see the changes in his behavior, and Kostya did look like someone who needed another chance.

The owner of the clothing store walked in and went straight to the food table, grabbing a glass of wine from the waiter on his way. It took me a while to recognize Ryan, his dark hair had grown almost down to his shoulders and he looked like a romantic singer from 80^s. He was chatting with Lina, who didn't change at all. I gave both of them a hug and learned that Ryan quit real estate and is working at diamond district on 47th street. I had no idea he always wanted to own a jewelry store. He said he was studying stones since his early years, and finally, he's doing something he's truly enjoying. Lina is still bartending, although she's working in a much better place, in Manhattan, in a very expensive restaurant. She shared that she doesn't know what she wants to do in life. She goes to different seminars by life coaches and other motivational speakers and communicates with other lost souls like herself. She will find it. One day it will strike her like a thunderstorm and she will wonder how come she never thought about it before.

"How are you doing, Kate?" the tranquil voice of Mr Holington startled me. I looked at him and melted in smile. He smiled back mischievously. My heart didn't jump out of my chest. It was calm.

"I'm so sorry for what I said…" I started in embarrassment, ignoring his question.

"You shouldn't be sorry. You said what you felt at that moment. I was waiting for you to return and talk more about it." he articulated, looking at me with compassion.

"I thought you didn't want to see me any more." I blurted sadly.

"I never said that. I felt really bad for you killing yourself and not taking it seriously, and I felt really upset that I couldn't help you. I left as it was the end of the session, and there was nothing more to discuss with you being very stubborn and trying to punish me for your feelings toward me."

"Ah… I mean… I've been regretting my behavior for so long!" I mumbled.

"I didn't know that. I'm sorry I didn't make it clear that it was just the end of the session, not the whole treatment. I wanted to continue our therapy and I thought we were going in the right direction. I was waiting for you to contact me."

"I'm glad to hear that, even post-factum." I grinned. "By the way, I don't drink at all since then!"

"I know," his melodious voice stated.

"How do you know?"

He began nodding, smiling at me. Then said, "I knew it as you realized that alcohol was not the best thing that happened to you."

I grinned.

"And I'm glad you eventually decided to throw this party. You were thinking for too long whether there was a point in throwing it."

"No, I wasn't thinking to throw anything. I was just telling you Rita's plot. I was looking for the meaning of it."

"Did you find the meaning?"

"Not yet."

"No, you did," he stated, smiling mischievously. "You have already thrown the party, and all of us are already here. You transcended the question. Your very question has become your best answer."

All of a sudden, he turned around and ran to The Queen who was telling something to the amorphous, pale about ten years old boy and his mother. I was not sure they understood English. I was left thinking about my best answer. So many thoughts were bumping into my mind. I felt the motion of time in that restaurant space. I realized that the party had never begun. It was always on, before we came over before we were born.

I was watching Dr Holington for a few seconds. He bent down, telling something to The Queen. I thought about his arms. I thought they were different kind of arms, the ones to die in, to live in, to be close to or not to be any close to. There are always things to live for, no matter whether you're aware of them or not. And there are always moments of confusion which monopolize your brain as drugs, changing your chemistry and behavior, turning you into a zombie, and fooling you into the belief of dependency. They aren't permanent, their effect will wear off, and the hangover will go away in a while. You'll see people or situations in their actual light — neutral. The moments of confusion always go away, and the moments to live for are always there, around the corner, they probably laugh hysterically making you question your own sanity or giving you a chance to embrace everyone who'd been crawling from chapter-to-chapter of your life up to this very moment which you thought might never happen. There are always things to live for. There are always reasons to attend the party.

"Hey beauty!" a harsh throat-clearing voice interrupted my thoughts. A shot of nostalgia and guilt startled me. I turned around and hugged Shawn. I wanted to cry out of happiness of being forgiven. His arms felt so kind and familiar, he smelled like home.

I gave a brief kiss to Laurine. She was very close to the end of pregnancy.

"A boy or a girl?" I asked.

"We don't know. We decided to keep it a surprise." Shawn elaborated and embraced his wife's waist. "Are you thinking about having kids?"

He did smell like home, yet there was a distance between us, miles of his unrequited love and my guilt. Laurine looked older than I remembered her. She gained some weight and wrinkles. She wore tight jeans and a brown sweater. Her hair was made in a ponytail. She was holding a glass of orange juice and smiling. I wanted to talk to Shawn, to ask so many things, to share so many stories, to laugh and whine just like in old good times, but instead I murmured, semi-joking, "I first need to find the father for these kids."

"Natasha told us you got married, but then you guys had to break up. I'm sorry about that." Shawn sighed. "If I were you, I would probably do the same, I'd chose to stay here. Hey, you were fighting for it for so many years, it's your home now."

I nodded; America indeed became my home. I truly hoped he found a home within Laurine, and this home was warm and welcoming. Very soon there will be another human being, and I don't think I will get to know it.

"I heard you are now in the laundry business," I said in my turn.

Shawn and Laurine looked at each other with smiles.

"Yeah," Shawn admitted unwillingly. "This is something that feeds us. kay for now. But for the future, we'll open some other business. We don't know what yet. We know for sure we don't want to work for anybody."

"That's good. I'm sure you guys will figure something out." I commented, letting them into the crowd of known and unknown people. I was happy to acknowledge that Natasha made peace with both of them, and everyone forgave and is forgiven. I told Natasha how happy I was, and she confessed that she felt there was some unresolved business between her and Laurine, but she didn't want to go there and talk about it. There was no point in resolving it, she said. She grabbed my arm and leaned her head on my shoulder and we silently looked at three paintings of Rita, and the photograph of her right in the middle of the table. I could hear her voice in the air, I could smell her perfume. She was so alive.

There were illustrations of funerals with smiling people around the grave, dead creatures with exposed colorful organs, bleeding kids, playing in coffins decorated with shiny silver snowflakes and stars. I recalled that gloomy and rainy afternoon I moved in with her, that presence of alcohol in her room, and her lively smile. That day she introduced me to her paintings and I decided she was insane. I never questioned that decision afterwards. I simply fell in love with her insanity. I thought about her drunk brown eyes, pure soul, and beautiful personality. I was in the middle of her plot, or at the very end of it, its harsh critic and the main character at the same time. Maybe it was supposed to be her party? Yet she left it before attending. Or maybe she never left. Or maybe it's just a party that is happening on its own without being anyone's plan. And all you can do is to enjoy it while it lasts.

A dark-haired bearded middle-aged man shyly walked to the table and stopped by its corner. He wore black pants and a blue shirt under a cotton vest. He was about my height. He fixed his eyes on Rita's photograph and he stared at it for a long time as if he was recalling something dear to him. There was a lot of sadness in that look. I asked Natasha whether she knew him, and after she answered in the negative, I approached him and wondered politely, "Excuse me, sir, may I help you?"

"Ah... I'm looking for Ekaterina," he pronounced shyly with an accent I couldn't recognize. A light smile followed his words. Oddly, it gave his face even more sadness. He quickly browsed me, then Natasha, who stood by my right shoulder.

"This is me," I stated.

"Oh, it's good to meet you. I hope it is okay with you that I came here, even though you did not invite me," he hesitated. "I won't stay long, I promise."

Natasha and I waited silently for him to continue. He had very dark brown eyes, thin roman nose. His lips were hidden in the black curly beard and it felt like the words were coming from some invisible speaker.

"You probably don't know me, but I do know you. We have a common friend. Well, we had."

I knew who he was before he introduced himself.

"My name is Besnik. Rita and I used to have a relationship."

"Oh my God..." Natasha murmured.

Opposite feelings started fighting in me. I wanted to tell him that he made her so unhappy and drove her to this fatal drinking, and I wanted to thank him for coming to my party after almost seven years since Rita's death.

"I wanted to see her friends I never got a chance to meet, so once I heard about your party, I thought it might be the only chance to do so and to say a proper goodbye to her," he spoke quietly and calmly with pauses between phrases and clauses. "I never got to say goodbye to her."

"We heard about you," I said. "As I remember Rita, she was always waiting for you."

He nodded sadly. "I loved Rita."

"Bullshit," Natasha muttered to me and I pushed her slightly with my elbow.

Besnik gave her a brief look, then stared back at Rita's photo and continued, "I had a wife and two children, and a grocery store in Queens with several employees. I was working 14 hours a day and was always tired in the end. I once drove to our date in Brooklyn after the long day and got in a car accident. Police and ambulance came, but I refused to go to the hospital. And of course, didn't tell her. There were times I just passed out in my store and woke up too late. And she was waiting…"

He took a deep breath.

"I wanted to leave my wife and be with Rita but found out that my wife got pregnant. After that, it was not questionable and I had to stay with her."

"How did she get pregnant if you loved Rita so much and had a relationship with her? It's cheating." Natasha interrupted him.

"Well, some things are impossible to explain. My wife needed intimacy with a man and it was the least I could give her. I felt very guilty for not loving her and planning to leave her. Then I began planning to tell Rita that I couldn't leave my wife. I knew she would get devastated. Maybe I did start avoiding her to postpone that unpleasant conversation. And shortly before I collected the right words to present the truth to her, Lina told me that Rita…was no longer alive."

Lina successfully kept secretly in touch with Besnik. In a way, it made me respect her more. She didn't reveal his information to us, drunk and angry. I recalled myself asking her where to find this guy who had "killed" our friend. That's what he told me next.

"I know you were looking for me. And I understand why. I wanted to meet you and talk to you earlier, but I didn't have the nerve, then it was never a good time. So, I found you and came here seven years later. Today must be the best day to meet her best friend. She was very fond of you. And I was very fond of her. I couldn't believe it when it all happened. I was devastated..." he looked down and took a deep breath. "Thank you for keeping this beautiful memory of her."

"These paintings," he smiled slightly. "I loved these paintings. She said they mean 'life is pointless, but beautiful'. You paint them, you enjoy the process, you look at them, you enjoy colors, but they themselves are just indifferent pieces of fabric and wood. Eventually they will perish. Just like all of us. Just like this party. Rita really wanted to throw this party. She also really wanted to get legalized in this country."

We all nodded sadly.

"Thank you for listening to me. I must go now." Besnik calmly interrupted the silence.

"Stay for a bit. Have a drink. Lina is here," I uttered.

"I don't drink," he smiled. "I already said hi to Lina. I need to close my store."

"Wait," I said. "Take a painting with you. I'm sure, Rita would want you to have one. You were a very important person in her life. The most important."

His eyes got watery. He looked away.

"Your family shouldn't be able to guess where it's from. You will make up a story. I'm sure you'll come up with something," I suggested.

He gave a laugh and said, "It's very kind of you. I'll take the funeral one."

He nodded silently, thought about something, then said, "Thank you. Thank you so very much for welcoming me and accepting me. I feel relieved."

Natasha shook his hand, and I gave him a prolonged hug. For a very strange reason, I didn't want to let him go. As if it was Rita standing with us, another side of her — diplomatic, sober, and shy. I wanted to tell more kind words to him but didn't know which ones. All I knew was when he's gone, Rita will be gone, too. I will let her go the very moment

I'll let Besnik out of my arms. It is my goodbye to her as well. The last piece of the puzzle came along, and the game was over. The Albanian man was taking away this puzzle from my head along with the painting — into the snowy American night. Everything at once got dissolved in that night, my childhood, my home, my Rita.

"She didn't even consider herself a painter," I heard myself murmuring once Besnik had left. "She only wanted to be a good wife and a good mother."

Natasha nodded in sadness, then said, "Speaking about wives and children, Dannie and I are planning to adopt a girl."

"Really?" I exclaimed.

"Yeah!" she uttered, smiling. "We really want to have a child but producing a brand-new kid while there are so many children in need of homes is unfair and pointless."

"It's a good point," I added. "Whose decision was it?"

"Dannie offered, and I supported it. Dannie's parents are very supportive of this idea. They said they would babysit the kid. You know, they treat me with so much love and appreciation. It makes me both happy and sad. My own family doesn't want me for who I am, but my wife's family loves me more than my family ever loved me."

I stroked her back. I could only imagine how painful it was for her to be forsaken, how awful it must be to realize the people you love, don't need you. That's it, you don't know them any more. They will never see the beautiful little girl growing in the loving family, they will never know Natasha as a lawyer, a handsome and honorable professional willing and able to solve any complicated situation.

"I've decided it's good we already have a psychologist in our family, now we do need a lawyer to feel completely secured. I have my Russian bachelor in Geography. Ha, ha! I always thought it was a useless degree, but now it's big deal of help. I had to request my Russian University to translate it in English and send both copies to the Law School center here. You know what? It took them four times to get it right! Finally, it got accepted. The admission test is so difficult. But I'll make it. I know."

She'll make it. She'll become a great lawyer — fair and compassionate.

"You're fired! Fired! Fired!" The Queen yelled at Ron who now switched to the kind-eyed woman from the Russian brothel. The woman didn't look neither annoyed nor happy communicating with him. She started laughing when her majesty began firing.

"I don't even work here!" my ex-boss cried in despair. "I told you!"

"FIRED!" she screamed so loud that most of the guests turned around and looked at them. Dr Holington promptly ran to her, whispered something to her ear and took her away from the scene with an apologetic smile. The brothel woman continued laughing even harder, which made me giggle. Ron stepped back and gave her the look of a scared child. I had never seen him so lost before.

He stared at me when I burst out laughing. He smiled, shook his head, and walked toward me.

"Where on earth you found she?" he uttered, giving me a brief hug.

"It's a long story," I answered, giggling. "I heard of your good luck!"

"Well, I don't know luck or no luck. I have nothing to do. Every day all alone or with strangers. I became very lonely. I drive my car everywhere. Sometimes I don't know where to go and I go upstate or long island — just to kill the day. I come home tired, sleep, new day starts. See? When I was working in the bar, I had something to look forward to. I was running the bar; I was socializing a lot; my customers were my family. Nice girls came to work for me…"

Then he looked at me from head to toe. "You are gorgeous! Even better then I remember you. So many years passed."

"Thank you," I smiled. "Maybe you should get some hobbies or invest into new projects…."

"How you got legalized? Through the marriage?" he interrupted me.

"Yes," I answered.

"To a girl?"

"No, to a guy. Why?" I wondered, quite surprised.

"I thought you were a lesbian."

"Why?"

"I tried to pick you up a few times, but you had no interest in men."

I started laughing. "Wait, I never said I had no interest in men, I had no interest in you."

"Isn't it the same thing? I am a man!" Ron stated with a flirty smile. I envied his self-esteem.

I wished him to enjoy the party and watched him joining Sherry and Dannie. Dannie shook his hand, then gazed at me and gave a laugh. I did the same.

A pair of kind eyes of the woman looked at me and nodded. I nodded back. Then doors of the restaurant got wide open and a huge man stepped in. He was pushing a wheelchair with someone else in it. A sudden shot of pain entered my vein and something cold and heavy flew from my chest through stomach to my toes, then back to my heart, it was Dad with my rapist in the chair. I wanted to cry and scream at the same time. How on earth did they get here?

They were the only people I never wanted to see again. They were the only people I wanted out of there immediately. I thought about finding Kostya and letting him know they had come, I thought about talking to a waiter to escort them out, and I thought about calling 911 and reporting the rape. I thought Shawn was big enough to beat them up, then I began searching for Natasha in the crowd of people. I wanted to stab a knife in the rapist's chest. I didn't know what to do. I just wanted to disappear. I made the first step towards them and approached them.

Tears of anger, pain, and hopelessness blurred my vision. I had nothing to say, yet I needed to say something. I needed to say something because I needed to hear something back. And I heard it.

"Please, give us just a minute," said Dad, "just a minute of your time and kindness. Then do whatever you want. You can call cops if you want. Anything."

He said it quietly and calmly in a loud voice. Every word was clear, and it felt like it had its shape and borders. My throat instantly turned dry; I couldn't say anything.

"I came here to apologize," the rapist murmured looking down. "No, I came to beg your forgiveness."

He had a huge scar on his cheek and a part of his ear was missing. Dad stood still.

"All my life, I lived getting everything I wanted one way or another. A jerk. I thought I was a fucking God…"

"Please, leave the restaurant before I call the police." I heard myself mumbling. My body was shaking.

"Okay," Ralf sighed. "I just wanted to let you know how sorry…"

"He tried to kill himself," Dad stated.

"Dude…" the rapist muttered.

"He jumped off the Brooklyn bridge the night you guys…"

"Dude…"

"How sorry can one be to do that?"

My perception of light had changed. Everything went pale. I needed more air.

"What the fuck is going on here?" Kostya's sharp yell intruded into the unknown.

"Wait," I breathed.

"I'll break your fucking skull," my friend snapped, then turned to me and asked whether I was all right.

I wasn't. In my mind, I went to the night of rape, revenge, to the very moment of the party and regretted organizing this gathering at all. I couldn't say much. I answered, "Yes".

In the very next scene; I found myself listening about the continuation of that night, of which I didn't get to know much, of which I thought I would never know. I learned, that after we left, he spent decades of minutes lying on the ground. He got up and got a cab. He went straight to the Brooklyn Bridge and jumped into the water. Then he was rescued. He cut his veins later on, after he was discharged from the hospital, yet again, no luck. He was put on suicide watch in Kings County, in the same department I stayed, under the supervision of the same psychiatrist who saved me from self-harming and possibly death, who put him on the highest dosage of antidepressant and two different mood stabilizers. My doctor suggested Ralf to write down everything that ate him. So, he wrote letters to all the sex-victims he found, to sex victims who revealed themselves on social networks to forgive "them", rapists, he wrote on behalf of all abusers, he wrote a lot, and he cried and cried and cried. It was around the time Rita had died. He wanted to be dead, too. He didn't deserve to live, he said. He didn't deserve to be well. His spine got permanently damaged from the jump, neither one of his legs could move. His dreams turned into constant nightmares. He abandoned and got abandoned by everyone, yet the only friend of his remained faithful in this cruel routine, the one who also felt guilty for not being able to prevent neither causes nor consequences.

"I had no remorse, never had any remorse in my life until the moment I saw your kind eyes, ma'am. They begged your friends to let me go. You looked at me and told them it was enough... but yourself begged me to let you go when I hurt you so unfairly...and I didn't. You... you saved my life... so unfairly to you, ma'am. So unfairly! That very moment I... you know... started wanting to die. That very moment I stopped feeling physical pain. Nothing bothered me any more. You were so kind and so compassionate. I saw you as the most beautiful human being in the world. I knew I didn't deserve it. And I knew you didn't deserve what I did. If only there was a way to undo it, I would give anything to make it happen. And the only way to make it happen became obvious to me. Before you guys left, I knew I was to jump off the bridge."

He couldn't speak any more. He broke into tears. Silently, he covered his face with his palms, his body started to shake. He tried to say something, but he couldn't. It felt like everyone else at the party stopped existing. I was looking at him silently, not knowing what to think. A mix of contradictory feelings occupied my mind like a whirlpool, I still had hate towards him and at the same time strange motherly feelings were filling my heart. I pitied him. I bent down and murmured, "I'm forgiving you and I'm forgiving myself for forgiving you."

He began to sob. His sobs were turning louder and louder. He was mumbling something non-understandable. I stepped back and let people surround us. These sobs soon filled every square foot of the space. They were everywhere. They eventually merged with other people's voices. They were wondering what was going on. I didn't know anything any more. I didn't understand any words. All I knew was, that they were alive, words and people, events and feelings, and it was life that held us together. Inside and outside of the party.

"Kate!" Dr Holington's voice intervened with the life. Ralf and I were two patients of his but on completely different sides of one spectrum. He treated my abuser before he treated me. Did he know that the jumper was my rapist when he told me that story? Did it even matter any more? I looked at him and saw so much warmth and understanding in his beautiful eyes. So much sympathy. I hadn't realized how it happened, but the very next moment I was enclosed in his gentle arms. We squeezed each other for a few seconds, stroking each other's back. It felt wonderful and maybe that was exactly what I needed from him, exactly what I was waiting for all these years. I knew for sure I didn't want to die in these arms, but I was grateful for their existence — the arms of compassion and understanding. They felt like home, yet a temporary home, a place you could always rest and find support before a long trip. That's exactly what he was telling me 3.5 years ago, I loved him as a parent. It was a parent's home. And I'm always forgiven, yet I'm only learning to forgive. And every time is like the first time.

Dr Holington and I smiled when The Queen parked her chair next to Ralf and fired him. Then she said, "I'm The Queen and you're all fucked up here."

"I know," he answered. I nodded to him. He nodded back. I walked away from the scene, leaving my doctor with the curious crowd. The air was full of assumptions. Life doesn't come with instructions, unfortunately.

Forgiven for not showing up, Andrew arrived in the fall of the party. He looked so fresh, and well-shaven and was dressed in a dark grey suit and navy-purplish shirt. He held a huge bouquet of purple roses. His face melted in a smile. He only came for one night and his plane would take him home next morning, very early. Unfortunately, there are no straight flights to St. Petersburg from New York.

"You are as beautiful as I remembered you," he told me after I accepted the flowers.

"You know, it took me a long time to get over you. I was mad at you in the beginning. I was hoping that you'll change your mind and come to St. Petersburg. We could live there and come here twice a year to keep your Green Card on. There were so many ways to play around this, but you were so stubborn! You didn't even want to consider any other option. You wanted to live only in the US — all the time! I was really hurt by that. Back then, to me it meant only one thing — you didn't love me.

As time passed by, I realized that you did love me. And you gave me all of you. It's just that you loved America, too. You got my love fast and easy, but it took you years to earn the love of this country. As I realized it, I became very happy that my love helped you to get the other love, the love you always wanted, the love you truly deserved."

"Thank you for your beautiful words, dear," I breathed and hugged him. His body was so warm. It felt like home, yet not mine. I'm sure, one day he will become a great husband and a dream father. I knew he will provide his family with everything they will need and want, including his soft, warm, and almost unconditional love.

Vera ran to Andrew and embraced him in her tight arms. She always liked him and thought he was perfect. Kostya and Eduard shook his hand with wide smiles. I felt eternal warmth towards him, I wanted him to meet many people at the party. I wanted him to meet Dr Holington and Mike, I wanted to tell him about Besnik, I wanted him to know about Natasha's and Dannie's decision, I wanted to share the rapist's story and my answer to it. I wanted him to catch up with all that he had missed, including me. I was so grateful he made it to the party, and yet I didn't need more of him any longer. It took me a while to get over my sorrow and adjust my mind to the new life, and now I was completely free. I knew he would leave the next day and that would be it — our final goodbye and our first and last sane and painless contact. The music stopped, and a tall skinny waiter handed me the microphone. I gave him a nervous smile. Andrew lifted his glass of water and clinked it with a spoon. One, two, three, four, five, six, seven, eight, I counted the number of clinks.

"Dear guests, Ekaterina has something to say to all of you." Andrew uttered it so loud that he didn't need a microphone.

I began shaking and hoping that nobody noticed it. Dr Holington grinned, looking at me, and I grinned back. His eyes were shining. Vera's eyes were shining as well. So many eyes were looking at me — so many months and years of my life. It's my country. It's my thrill.

"Dear guests," I said and tried to make eye contact with everyone who was looking at me. "Each of you played a significant role in my existence since January 2009 when a very young, naïve girl got off the plane in New York and got onto the bus on her very first trip into life. That girl will turn 30 in two months. She is no longer very young and naïve, she travelled a journey of eight harsh years towards this very moment, and I would like to thank each one of you for participating in her trip, if not for your presence in her life one way or another, this party would not happen.

I gathered all of you here to celebrate me being a lawful resident of the United States. Being an immigrant is a very hard duty. Being an illegal immigrant is a pure torture. Every day is full of fear, pain, unfairness, every night you want to give up this uneven battle, but every morning you give yourself another chance. I gave myself hundreds of chances, and on 2017 I succeeded. But the price of this success was very high. I had to learn this life from scratch. I learned things I wanted to learn, things I needed to learn, and things I neither wanted nor needed to learn. And all this knowledge I gained, brought me here today to this very restaurant. It brought you here as well, as you became reasons or consequences of my learning. You planted the seeds a number of years ago and today they grew into my skills, appreciations, happiness, sadness, strengths, weaknesses, and traumas. And regardless of the nature of your seed, my tree has grown strong enough and tall enough and reached its biggest dream and became absolutely licit on the ground it was planted. I gathered all of you here to say thank you, even though some of these "thank yous" are very hard to say and nearly impossible, yet, each time I manage to do it, it makes me stronger. And now, it's my time to cut off this tree and go back to where I came from to take it to my family, friends, my streets and neighborhoods, and my childhood. In a way, I'm taking all of you there. And in a way, I'm leaving all of you here. In a way, this party has never started, and in a way, it will never end. Each of you will leave at a different time and eventually this bright light will go off and the restaurant's doors will get locked, but the party will go on. So, all of you, enjoy the party even after you leave, and let nobody ever tell you that it ended.

My party, my story, and my life are very typical and common. And I am a composite character of the history of this country. There are so many people who threw this party or really wanted to throw it, people who fought and won, who fought and lost, who are still fighting. I'm only a tiny part of this harsh process, an example of the fact that everything is possible. Thank you for coming to my party."

All hands began clapping at once. The clapping was becoming louder and louder, and I started laughing. Andrew, who stood next to me, grinned. I saw Natasha's wet eyes and Vera's sad smile in the crowd. All of these emotional looks were mine. I felt the worth of these eight years in my bones. Two snowy nights of the beginning and the end merged together for my event, the first one took away my childhood and the second was celebrating my reunion with it. Nothing else mattered.

Dr Holington approached me before leaving to deliver The Queen back to the hospital.

"I'm very happy to see you finally achieved what you wanted. You gave an excellent speech, Kate. Thank you for inviting me over, I'll take this party with me and won't believe anyone who'll say it ended." he said, smiling.

I gave a laugh.

"I also want to share with you that the only arms you should wish to die in are the arms of your declining years. The very end of them. That would be the only fair death." he articulated with a calm compassionate smile.

I thanked him but didn't dare to hug him again. We nodded to each other. The Queen fell asleep in her wheelchair. It was about no o'clock.

All of a sudden, I thought that I might never see him again and uttered loudly as he began pushing his patient towards the door, "Dr Holington, thank you so much for all you've done for me! I will always remember you as a brilliant doctor and a wonderful person!"

He turned around and gave me the most beautiful grin of his. His sky-blue eyes were sparkling, and for a bit, it appeared to me they were wet. He stood like that for a few seconds, then nodded again and walked away into the night of snowy 7th avenue.

Dan, Diane, and Dmitry left early as well, without saying goodbye. They tried to make it look as if Dmitry had departed on his own, a minute later, however it only made the scene awkward, I saw them getting all in the same cab across the street. I smiled. I expected Dmitry to say something before he left. And at the same time, I knew "goodbye" was not his favorite thing. I left him once, too. It's very possible he might appear in my life again.

Shawn and Laurine rushed out shortly after. They invited me to visit them in Florida once I'm back from Russia. I thanked them and hugged them, and thought that I wouldn't go to Florida, and deep inside I knew they said it only out of politeness. My beautiful friendship with Shawn was over, and I thanked him for being in my life in my distant speech. I truly hoped Laurine appreciates his love, and there was nothing else I hoped for.

I gave warm hugs to both Mike and Agnes. I told Mike that the big deal of thanking in my monologue was dedicated to him for saving my future and possibly my life. He only waved away modestly and repeated he was proud of me. They gestured goodbye to me again at the exit. I gestured back. Then Mike nodded just like on that scary night in Chicago when I was walking towards the car service — so lost, worn out, and so illegal. Everything is going to be all right, that nod said to me. I know, everything was going to be all right. Thank you, officer. I nodded back.

I saw Steve in the thinning crowd. A stick from a lollipop was sticking out of his mouth. He pulled it out and waved it to me as we made eye contact. I smiled and nodded. He didn't change at all. I felt like it was yesterday he yelled at me for being late, and I kept looking down, nodding, and agreeing with everything he was saying. Pockets of his baggy jeans were fully packed and looked heavy. I assumed there were lollipops in there as well. He didn't remember how I left his company, there were so many girls working for him. He said they switched one another so often that it became hard to keep track. He said he still did the same work in the same warehouse, then congratulated me on becoming a resident, and offered me a lollypop. I thanked him, grabbed the lollypop, and began walking towards Ted and the nameless woman but was stopped by a tipsy James.

"I'm so sorry for being a jerk..." he uttered right away.

"Thank you for being a jerk," I interrupted him. If he wasn't a jerk, I would never meet Mike with his kind heart and sad story, Dr Holington and the whole kingdom of the most interesting people I've ever known. I would never meet Andrew and learn what the perfect man and a perfect relationship meant. I smiled with pleasure thinking about all that. "You are a wonderful jerk. Back then I was really pissed at you, because back then I didn't know what a marvelous turn my journey was about to take."

He was looking at me in stupor. Then he told me he was still single and had a job he liked. Happy with my forgiveness, he became very talkative, but in my plans was to finally reach Ted with the kind-eyed woman. And I did it.

"I never got a chance to talk to you," I said, giving her a hug. "What's your name?"

"Guess," she uttered with a smile. Her eyes were still very kind. Her black hair was long. I recalled that night of despair and fear.

"How can I guess?" I gave a laugh.

"Ekaterina," she pronounced slowly and quietly.

"Oh, wow!" I uttered. "So, welcome here, Ekaterina!"

"I thought you knew all people at the party?" Ted wondered.

"Everybody always forgets my name," Ekaterina stated before I began searching my brain for a possible explanation. I laughed. She laughed, too. Ted was smiling. After he left, we spoke about that business, and the torture we had to go through. She told me she quit it a year ago, she saved enough money to buy a house in Brooklyn where she and her two children resided. She worked as a secretary in a law firm and loved it very much. She said she graduated from a law school in Russia. I was rather saddened to hear that. An immigrant's life is too unfair. We do things that nearly kill us regardless of our degrees and brilliant minds. I'll introduce her to Natasha and Dannie and they will make friends. Katya will become a member of our small community. Eventually all our friends will get to know how we met and what we did, and surprisingly to me, they will accept it with sympathy and understanding.

Ron tried his last semi-hopeless moves on Lina, who was seeking to get more of Ryan's attention. Then he grew tired and sat on the chair right by Rita's paintings.

Vera came to me and hugged me tight and soft. She said she wouldn't change anything if she could. She also said, I shouldn't regret anything I had done, regardless of whether I wanted to do it or not, whether I achieved the desirable or I didn't; she said everything I had to do, I did it because I had no other choice. If something becomes the only option, it's not an option any more. I told her that we needed to start thinking about what she was going to do after the language school, so she had better options than I did. Snezhana hugged us both from the back. It felt so warm and cozy.

"We are really-really strong people," she verbalized. "We survived all that dirty ugly torture. Now we sure can go through anything in the world, and yet, let's choose our future carefully. Let's love our lives and treat ourselves with good things. I'm thinking to give Kostya another chance. Vera, you have to plan your profession now. Katya, you've got to publish this book."

Natasha and Dannie were fully absorbed by the conversation with Sherry and Ekaterina. They will definitely become great parents. They will soon adopt a beautiful girl and raise her with love and support. They will do their best to understand the girl's needs, they will never abandon her for carrying out a mission different from theirs, and they will not punish her for living against their expectations. They will not repeat Natasha's parent's mistakes. It took her a long time of endless conversations with Dannie and other professionals to realize it was not her fault that her family forsook her. It will take her about the same time to accept it and forgive them for being themselves.

My memory sent me back to Rita and her dream to have a family here, in this country. I thought she would make a great caring mother. I wished she could be present at this party, however she remained in the past forever — always young and always illegal.

I stared at the older Russian couple, buttoning up the cardigan on their son. As I counted, he was supposed to be around 10. He was still pale, still quiet. Steve gave him a lollipop. I gave my lollypop to Vera. The owner of Flatbush store was telling something to Kostya and Adil. I missed the moment Ralf and Dad departed. Molly was sitting on the chair by the table with Rita's paintings next to Ron, caressing her belly as if she had overeaten. Bartek squatted next to her, he was saying something that was keeping her smile on. They lived in Atlanta still and didn't want children. Friendly waiters began removing food from the tables.

This party won't end. The waiters will remove all signs of presence from the tables, the guests will leave, the light will go off, and the doors will get locked, but the party will go on. It will move into the next, and then the next day, carrying most of us along. It never started, it was always going on, switching the places and visitors, minutes and years, snowflakes of Massachusetts' blizzard and the warmth of the bus seats. And we are all in it, performing different roles and chasing different dreams. All living beings, all legal here, at the party. Andrew will stay with me till the very last guest leaves and will help me carry flowers, symbolic gifts, and the rest of Rita's paintings home. He will leave early in the morning while I'll be asleep. He will send me a text message when he'll get to St. Petersburg. I will wake up in a brand-new day. This chapter will be completely over. A sunny morning will greet me through the window. I'll start packing right after breakfast, and I will need to buy a new suitcase, the other two are way too battered.

CPSIA information can be obtained
at www.ICGtesting.com
Printed in the USA
LVHW010902160723
752256LV00006B/255